THE PARIS AFFAIR

Also by Teresa Grant

Vienna Waltz

Imperial Scandal

His Spanish Bride

THE PARIS AFFAIR

TERESA GRANT

KENSINGTON BOOKS
www.kensingtonbooks.com

KENSINGTON BOOKS are published by

Kensington Publishing Corp.
119 West 40th Street
New York, NY 10018

ISBN-13: 978-0-7582-8393-1
ISBN-10: 0-7582-8393-8

First Kensington Trade Paperback Printing: April 2013
10 9 8 7 6 5 4 3 2 1

Printed in the United States of America

For Mélanie Cordelia,
who arrived during the writing of
this book and made life infinitely more fun.
Welcome to the world and a lifetime of reading.

ACKNOWLEDGMENTS

Fervent thanks to my editor, Audrey LaFehr, and my agent, Nancy Yost, for their wonderful support of Malcolm and Suzanne and of me. From e-mails to lunches your advice, input, and friendship mean the world to me.

Thanks as well to Sarah Younger of Nancy Yost Literary Agency and Martin Biro of Kensington Books for answering questions, sending out ARCs and coverflats, and generally helping make a writer's life easier. To Paula Reedy for shepherding the book through copyedits and galleys with exquisite care and good humor. To Barbara Wild for the careful copyediting. To Alexandra Nicolajsen for the superlative social media support. To Kristine Mills Noble and Jon Paul for a beautiful cover that evokes the mood of the book and looks like Suzanne. And to Karen Auerbach, Adeola Saul, everyone at Kensington Books, and Adrienne Rosado, Natanya Wheeler, and everyone at the Nancy Yost Literary Agency for their support throughout the publication process.

Thank you to the readers who share Suzanne's and Malcolm's adventures with me on my Web site and Facebook and Twitter. Thank you to Gregory Paris and jim saliba for creating my Web site and updating it so quickly and with such style. To Raphael Coffey for juggling cats and baby to take the best author photos a writer could have. To Jayne Davis for quickly, cheerfully, and brilliantly answering grammar questions. And to the staff at Peet's Coffee & Tea at The Village in Corte Madera for fabulous lattes and cups of tea and an always warm welcome to Mélanie and me while I wrote and Mélanie took in the world.

Writers work in isolation, but writer friends make the process infinitely easier and more fun. Thank you to Lauren Willig for series strategizing over lattes in New York. To Penelope Williamson for support and understanding and endless hours analyzing everything from *Measure for Measure* to *Mad Men*. To Veronica Wolff for wonderful writing dates during which my word count seemed to magically increase. To Catherine Duthie for sharing her thoughts on Malcolm and Suzanne's world and introducing them to new readers. To Deborah Crombie for supporting Malcolm and Suzanne from the beginning. To Tasha Alexander and Andrew Grant for their wit and wisdom. To Deanna Raybourn, to whom I totally owe a pony. And to my other writer friends near and far for brainstorming, strategizing, and commiserating—Jami Alden, Bella Andre, Isobel Carr, Catherine Coulter, Cara Elliott, Barbara Freethy, Carol Grace, C. S. Harris, Candice Hern, Anne Mallory, Monica McCarty, and the fabulous History Hoydens.

Finally, thank you to Raphael Coffey, Bonnie Glaser, David Dickson and Patrick Wilken, and Elaine and Wayne Hamlin for making it possible for me to be a writer and a mother. And to my daughter, Mélanie, who was born during the writing of this book and was wonderfully cooperative about letting me finish it.

DRAMATIS PERSONAE

*indicates real historical figures

British Diplomats and Soldiers and Their Connections

* Arthur Wellesley, Duke of Wellington
* Sir Charles Stuart
* Robert Stewart, Viscount Castlereagh
* Emily, Viscountess Castlereagh, his wife
* Lord Stewart, his half-brother

Malcolm Rannoch, British attaché
Suzanne Rannoch, his wife
Colin Rannoch, their son
Blanca, Suzanne's companion
Addison, Malcolm's valet

Colonel Harry Davenport
Lady Cordelia Davenport, his wife
Livia Davenport, their daughter

* Lord Fitzroy Somerset, Wellington's military secretary
* Emily Harriet Somerset, his wife

Earl Dewhurst, British diplomat
Rupert, Viscount Caruthers, his son
Gabrielle, Viscountess Caruthers, his wife
Stephen, their son
Gui Laclos, Gabrielle's brother
Christian Laclos, Gabrielle's cousin

French and Their Connections

* Prince Talleyrand, prime minister of France
* Edmond de Talleyrand-Périgord, his nephew

*Dorothée de Talleyrand-Périgord, Edmond's wife
* Wilhelmine, Duchess of Sagan, her sister
* Count Karl Clam-Martinitz, Dorothée's lover

* Joseph Fouché, Duc d'Otrante, minister of police

Antoine, Comte de Rivère

Manon Caret, actress at the Comédie-Française
Roxane, her daughter
Clarisse, her daughter
Berthe, her dresser

Emile Sevigny, painter
Louise Sevigny, his wife
Jules Sevigny, their son
Jean Carnot, Louise's son

Paul St. Gilles, painter
Juliette Dubretton, writer, his wife
Pierre St. Gilles, their son
Marguerite St. Gilles, their daughter
Rose St. Gilles, their daughter

Christine Leroux, opera singer

British Expatriates and Visitors to Paris

David Mallinson, Viscount Worsley
Simon Tanner, playwright, his lover
Aline Blackwell, Malcolm's cousin
Dr. Geoffrey Blackwell, her husband
* Lady Frances Wedderburn-Webster
* Captain James Wedderburn-Webster, her husband
* Granville Leveson-Gower
* Harriet Granville, his wife
* Lady Caroline Lamb, her cousin
* William Lamb, Caroline's husband

Doubt thou the stars are fire,
Doubt that the sun doth move,
Doubt truth to be a liar,
But never doubt I love.

—Shakespeare, *Hamlet,* Act II, scene ii

CHAPTER 1

The hanging oil lamps swayed and gusted at the opening of the door. The wind brought in the stench from the Seine. A man and woman stepped into the Trois Amis tavern and stopped just beyond the door. The man was lean and dark haired and perhaps taller than he looked. He slouched with a casual ease that took off several inches. A greatcoat was flung carelessly over his shoulders. Beneath, his black coat was unbuttoned to reveal a striped crimson waistcoat. A spotted handkerchief was knotted loosely round his neck in place of a cravat.

The woman, who leaned within the circle of his arm, wore a scarlet cloak with the hood pushed back to reveal a cascade of bright red curls, brilliant even in the murky light of the tavern. Glittering earrings swung beside her face, though surely they must be paste rather than diamonds. Her rouged lips curved in a smile as her gaze drifted round the common room with indolent unconcern.

The other occupants of the tavern glanced at the new arrivals. It was an eclectic crowd, a mix of sailors, dockworkers, merchants, women who plied their wares along the docks, a few young aristocrats in sporting dress. And soldiers, in the uniforms of Russia, Prussia, Austria, Bavaria, England. These days, less than two months after Napoleon Bonaparte's defeat at Waterloo, one couldn't go anywhere in Paris without seeing soldiers.

After a moment, the crowd returned to their dice, drinks, and flirtation. The accordion player seated in the center of the room, who had paused briefly, launched into another lively air.

The couple moved to the bar, where the gentleman procured two glasses of red wine. While he was engaged with the barkeep, several men ran appreciative gazes over the lady. One went so far as to put a hand on her back. "How much?" he asked, his head close enough to her own that his brandy-laced breath brushed her skin.

The lady ran her gaze over him. Her eyes were an unusual color between green and blue. She brushed her fingers against his face and then put a gloved hand on his chest. She gave a dazzling smile. "More than you can possibly afford."

The man regarded her for a moment, then shrugged and grinned. "Can't blame a man for trying," he said, and moved towards a fair-haired girl by the fireplace.

The gentleman turned from the bar and put one of the glasses of red wine into the lady's hand. If he had noticed the man making her an offer, he gave no sign of it. He touched his glass to hers, and they threaded their way through the crowd to a table neither too obviously in the center of the room nor too deep in the shadows. Experience had taught them that the easiest way to hide was often to remain in plain sight.

The lady tugged at the cords on her cloak and let it slither about her to reveal a low-cut gown of spangled white sarcenet. The gentleman shrugged out of his greatcoat, slouched in his chair, and ran an eye round the room.

"I don't see anyone matching the description," the lady said in unaccented French.

"Nor do I," the gentleman agreed in French that was almost as flawless.

"We're a bit early."

"So we are. But I'd give even odds on whether he actually puts in an appearance. He's never been our most reliable asset."

The lady tossed back a sip of wine. "Oh, well. At least we've had a night out."

The gentleman grinned at her. "I can think of places I'd rather take you."

"But this one has a certain piquancy, *chéri*. An evening without diplomatic small talk. Bliss."

The gentleman slid his hand behind her neck, then went still, his fingers taut against her skin.

The lady had seen it, too.

The man they had come to meet stood by the door, a short, compact figure enveloped in a dark greatcoat. He removed his hat to reveal hair that was several shades darker than its natural color. A good attempt at disguise, but nervousness still radiated off him.

"Well," the gentleman murmured to the lady. "People can surprise you."

The lady touched his arm. "I'll take care of it, Malcolm."

Malcolm Rannoch caught his wife's wrist. "Be careful."

Suzanne Rannoch turned to look at her husband. "Really, *mon amour,* you'd think you didn't know me."

"Sometimes I wonder." Malcolm pulled her hand to his lips, the gesture flirtatious to anyone watching, but his grip unexpectedly strong. "Remember, we're in alien territory."

She squeezed his fingers. "When are we not?"

Suzanne moved into the room, her spangled skirts stirring about her, and bent over the accordion player. He gave her a quick smile. A moment later, he launched into a lilting rendition of *La ci darem la mano*. Suzanne began to sing, her voice slightly huskier than usual. She moved towards the nearest table and brushed her fingers against the face of the portly man who sat there, then bent over a young Russian lieutenant at the next table, her burnished ringlets spilling over his shoulder.

The buzz of conversation stilled. The dice ceased to rattle.

Malcolm allowed himself a moment to appreciate his wife's skill, then picked up his greatcoat and glass of wine and strolled across the room to the corner deep in the shadows of the oak-beamed ceiling where the man he was to meet had taken up his position.

"My compliments, Rivère." Malcolm dropped into a chair across from him. "I gave even odds on whether or not you'd actually put in an appearance."

Antoine, Comte de Rivère, cast a quick glance about. "For God's sake, Rannoch, what do you mean coming up to me openly?"

"You were thinking we'd pass coded messages back and forth instead of having a conversation?"

"If we're noticed—"

"My wife has things in hand."

"Your—" Rivère stared at Suzanne, who was now perched on the edge of a table, leaning back, her weight resting on her hands, her skirt pulled up to reveal the pink clocks embroidered on her silk stockings. "Good God."

"I don't think you've seen Suzanne in action before. We're both more accustomed to disguise than you are."

Rivère looked from Suzanne to Malcolm. "The way you're dressed you can't help but attract attention."

"But the man and woman people will remember seeing tonight will seem nothing like Malcolm Rannoch, attaché at the British embassy, and his charming wife." Malcolm pushed his glass of wine across the table to Rivère. "You look as though you need it more than I do."

Rivère took a sip of wine. His fingers tightened round the stem of the glass. "I pass messages. I don't—"

"Indulge in this cloak-and-dagger business. Quite."

"It's all very well for you British." Rivère twisted the glass on the scarred wood of the table. The yellow light from the oil lamps glowed in the red wine. "You're protected by embassy walls and diplomatic passports. It's getting more and more dangerous for the rest of us. The Ultra Royalists have been out for blood ever since the news from Waterloo. I sometimes think they won't rest until they've rid the country of every last taint of Bonapartism. I'm not sure even Talleyrand and Fouché can hold them in check." He grimaced. "*Mon Dieu.* That I'd ever be calling Fouché the voice of moderation."

"If nothing else he's a survivor," Malcolm said. "As is Talleyrand." Prince Talleyrand, who had once been Napoleon Bonaparte's foreign minister, and Fouché, who had been his minister of police, had both managed to survive in the restored Royalist government.

"Even they can't hold back the tide," Rivère said. "Look how Ultra Royalists are going after men like la Bédoyère—"

"La Bédoyère was the first officer to go over to Bonaparte when he escaped from Elba. You aren't on the proscribed list."

"Yet." Rivère cast a glance about and leaned forwards, shoulders hunched, voice lowered. "Fouché receives more denunciations every day. You've heard Royalists in the Chamber of Deputies clamoring for blood. Cleansing, they call it. It's the Terror all over again."

Malcolm cast an involuntary protective glance towards Suzanne, who was tugging playfully at the cravat of a Prussian major. He looked harmless enough, but these days Malcolm's every sense was keyed to danger. There was no denying France in the wake of Napoleon's defeat was a dangerous place. Frenchmen clashed in the street daily with soldiers from the occupying armies of Prussia, Russia, Austria, Bavaria. And, Malcolm could not deny, England as well. Royalist gangs had ravaged Marseilles and Toulon and other cities. "It's dangerous," Malcolm conceded. "But that doesn't mean you—"

"My cousin's in the Chamber, and he wants me dead. My father got the title when his father was guillotined in the Terror. He wants it back."

"There are legal avenues he could pursue."

"But getting rid of me would be quicker. And it would be vengeance for his father. He's worked his way into the Comte d'Artois's set. It's only a matter of time before I'm arrested."

The Comte d'Artois, younger brother of the restored Bourbon king, Louis XVIII, was known for his zeal in exacting retribution on those who had supported Napoleon Bonaparte. It had been easier when Napoleon was exiled the first time. After his escape from Elba and his second defeat, at Waterloo, the Ultra Royalists wanted blood.

Malcolm studied Rivère's usually cool blue eyes. "The irony being that while you served Bonaparte you passed messages to the British."

"But there's no way I can prove it, damn it."

"We could help. But being a British spy isn't likely to gain you favor with the French, even the Royalists."

"Precisely. I'm damned either way."

"You're not generally one to talk in such melodramatic terms."

"I don't generally fear for my life." Rivère cast another glance round the tavern. Suzanne was now standing on one of the tables, arms stretched in a way that pulled the bodice of her gown taut across her breasts. A whistle cut the air.

Malcolm reclaimed his glass and took another sip of wine. "What do you want, Rivère?"

"Safe passage out of France."

"I can talk to the embassy—"

"Not through official channels. That will take too long. Get me out of Paris and across the Channel within the week. Once in England I want a pension, a house in the country, and rooms in London."

"You don't set your sights low, do you?"

"Do you have any idea how much I'm giving up leaving France?"

For a moment, Malcolm could smell the salt air at Dunmykel, his family home in Scotland, and hear the sound of the waves breaking on the granite cliffs. It wasn't easy to be an exile. Even if one had chosen the exile oneself, as he had done. "We don't turn our back on our own, Rivère."

"No?" Rivère gave a short laugh. "What about Valmay and St. Cyr and—"

"*I* don't turn my back," Malcolm said. Far be it from him to defend the sins of British intelligence. "But I can't make you guarantees of that nature on my own authority."

"Take it to Wellington or Castlereagh or whomever you damn well have to. But I want an answer within twenty-four hours."

"You seem very confident."

"I am." Rivère reached for the glass and took a long drink of wine.

A whoosh sounded through the tavern. Suzanne had jumped off the table and landed in the lap of a red-faced gentleman in a blue coat.

Rivère set the glass down but retained hold of the stem. "Tell your masters that if they don't meet my demands, the information I reveal will shake the British delegation to its core."

Malcolm leaned back and crossed his arms over his chest. It was not the first time he'd heard such a claim. "It's not as though the British delegation has never weathered scandal. And the behavior of most delegations at the Congress of Vienna rather changed the definition of scandal."

"This goes beyond personal scandal."

Malcolm pulled the glass from Rivère's fingers and tossed down a swallow. "Enlighten me."

"Oh no, Rannoch. I'm not giving up my bargaining chip. But mention the Laclos affair to Wellington and I think you'll find the hero of Waterloo is all too ready to accede to my demands."

Malcolm's fingers went taut round the glass. "What the devil does Bertrand Laclos have to do with this?"

Rivère's brows lifted. "That's right. I forgot you were involved in the Laclos affair. I think I've said enough for now. Just take my message to Wellington and Castlereagh. I doubt either of them wants to see England and France at war again."

Malcolm kept his gaze steady on Rivère, trying to discern how much was bluff, how much was real.

"I may only be a clerk," Rivère said, "but clerks are privy to a number of secrets. I didn't just ask you to meet me because you're Wellington's best agent. I asked you because what I know about you should guarantee you'll help me."

"Oh, for God's sake—"

"For the sake of your family."

"A bit extreme, surely," Malcolm said in a light voice that sounded forced to his own ears. "My family are a long way from Paris."

Rivère leaned back, holding Malcolm's gaze with his own. "Given her varied career, it never occurred to you that she might have had a child?"

Oh, God. Rivère knew—

"Your sister," Rivère said.

For a moment, the blood seemed to freeze in Malcolm's veins.

His acknowledged sister, Gisèle, was seventeen and safely in England with their aunt, where she had made her home since their mother's death. Even given Aunt Frances's penchant for scandal and his own absence, he couldn't believe Gelly had had a child without his knowledge. So Rivère must mean—

"Yes." Rivère reached for the glass and tossed down the last of the wine. "Tatiana Kirsanova."

The blood roared in Malcolm's head.

So that it took a split second for him to register the gunshot that had ripped through the tavern.

CHAPTER 2

Malcolm sprang to his feet and reached into the pocket of his great-coat for his own pistol. A Prussian sergeant stood across the room, his arm still extended holding a smoking pistol. No one appeared to be hurt, but the shot was the signal for chaos. A Russian corporal sprang at the Prussian, knocking him to the ground. The gun went flying. Another Prussian made a dive for it. A man in civilian dress jumped on top of him, knocked his head into the floorboards, and grabbed the pistol.

Suzanne, perched on top of a chair, was sensibly standing still. She had her own pistol tucked into her corset, but Malcolm knew she wouldn't use it except as a last resort. As he moved forwards, a table crashed to the floor and a wine bottle smashed into the wall. A girl screamed and ducked under a chair. Another sprang onto a table. A third hurled a tankard at one of the men.

Malcolm dodged past an English soldier and a Bavarian who had begun pummeling each other, took a glancing blow to the shoulder, jumped over the wreckage of a chair, ducked as a tankard sailed overhead.

Metal clanged against metal. The Prussian and the Russian had pulled out their sabres and were dueling in the middle of the room. Two men with their hands locked round each other's throats lurched towards Suzanne. Suzanne snatched up a wine bottle and hit the nearest man on top of the head, sending them both crashing to the ground.

Malcolm skidded over the wine-soaked floorboards to his wife's side.

"I was doing very well," she said as he lifted her from the chair.

"Just trying to keep it that way."

A hand closed on Malcolm's arm and spun him round. "Bloody frogs," a British dragoon said in a slurred voice. "Taking all the girls." He landed Malcolm a blow to the jaw.

This was no time to try to explain about nationalities. Malcolm dealt his offensive countryman an answering blow that sent the dragoon reeling to the floor.

Suzanne screamed. Malcolm whirled round to see his wife clutching her arm. Blood spurted between her fingers. "Sabre cut," she said as he caught her in his arms. Her voice was level, but she swayed against him. "He didn't mean to get me."

A Bavarian and an Austrian had also drawn their swords. Malcolm pulled Suzanne beneath the shelter of the nearest upright table, tugged off the handkerchief round his neck, and bound it round her arm. "Can you walk?"

"Don't be silly."

He crawled to the side of the table where the tangle of feet seemed least dense and pulled her up.

A pistol shot ricocheted off one of the hanging lamps and buried itself in the wall. Malcolm wrapped his arm round Suzanne and edged towards the back wall. Not unlike making one's way through the press at a diplomatic reception. Save that at a diplomatic reception one didn't encounter stray blows, broken glass, and random pistol shots. A stream of ale hit the back of his neck. Several blows glanced off his shoulders. Broken glass sliced through his coat. But he and Suzanne reached the back wall and were able to inch along the edge of the room.

A Prussian captain leaped atop one of the still-upright tables, jumped to catch hold of the hanging wrought-iron chandelier, and swung forwards to spring onto two of the sword fighters. The three of them thudded to the floor in a tangle of boots and swords.

Malcolm pulled Suzanne to the table where he'd left Rivère. No sign of Rivère. Not surprising he'd fled. No, there he was. He'd taken refuge under the table. Malcolm could see his boots. "Rivère!" he yelled.

No response. The roar from the mêlée was deafening. Malcolm pushed Suzanne into a chair and knelt beside Rivère. "Rivère. Let's get out of here." He reached out to tug on Rivère's shoulder and felt no response. He ducked beneath the table to see Rivère's staring eyes. A knife protruded from his chest.

Suzanne felt more than saw the tension that shot through her husband. He got to his feet with an appearance of casual ease, picked up his greatcoat and threw it round her shoulders, wrapped his arm round her, and pulled her to the door. Behind them glass shattered and sabres clanged.

A gust of wind and the stench of the river greeted them. Yellow lamplight pierced the gloom. Malcolm paused for a moment, and she knew his senses were keyed to pursuit. Then he drew her down the street, past two Prussian soldiers arguing over which tavern to visit next, past three Frenchmen defiantly singing the *Marseillaise,* round the corner, past an alley where a couple were making love urgently against a wall, through the crowds round the doors of two more taverns, and down a side street, where he pushed her into the doorway of a shuttered shop.

"Is Rivère dead?" Suzanne asked.

Malcolm nodded. "Stabbed. By a professional by the look of it."

"So the fight was started as a diversion."

"Probably. If— But no sense in refining on that now."

Suzanne studied her husband's face in the moonlight and the glow of the lamp across the street. His eyes were dark, his features set in harsh lines. "Am I going to get the lecture?"

"Lecture?" He pushed back the folds of the greatcoat and undid the spotted handkerchief he'd tied round the wound in her arm.

"Where you turn into a combination of Brutus and Hotspur and say you're a bad husband for letting your wife go into danger."

"Brutus and Hotspur didn't let their wives go into danger.

Though Portia ended up dead anyway." He reached into a pocket of the greatcoat, pulled out a flask, and splashed brandy onto her arm.

She suppressed a wince. The cut wasn't deep, but the brandy stung against her skin. "As I was saying. Portia might have done better if she hadn't been left behind."

A faint smile flashed through his eyes. "Never let it be said I've learned nothing in the past year. I have my protective instincts well under control." He tugged a clean handkerchief from another pocket and bound it round her arm. "Will you be all right until we've talked to Wellington and Castlereagh?"

"Is that a rhetorical question?"

"It might as well have been." He knotted the makeshift bandage. "Just remember pushing the stoicism until you collapse isn't brave, it's foolhardy."

"I know my limits."

He gave her a quick, hard kiss. "My darling, I don't think you've ever reached them."

She looked up at him. There were ghosts in his eyes that went beyond the fight and Rivère's death. "Malcolm? What did Rivère say to you?"

"He made some vague threats to shake the British delegation to its core if we didn't help him." Malcolm paused for a fraction of a second. She heard the catch in his breath. "And—"

"And?"

His fingers trembled where they still gripped her shoulder. "He said that Tatiana had had a child."

Suzanne went very still, her gaze fastened on her husband's face. "Oh, darling."

"He could have been lying of course," Malcolm said in a quick, level voice. "But—"

"We have to learn the truth. And find the child if there is one. Naturally."

He released his breath and looked down at her for a moment. "You're remarkable, Suzette."

"Yes, well, I'd like to think I'd have said it in any case, but it's much easier to deal with Princess Tatiana and your obligations to her now I know she was your sister rather than your mistress."

"I've put you through an intolerable amount, sweetheart."

She forced a smile to her face, swallowing the instinctive bite of guilt. For in the scales of guilt in their marriage, her own unacknowledged sins weighed far more heavily than he could imagine. "Don't be silly, darling. But I'm glad I know the truth."

He drew the folds of the greatcoat about her with gentle fingers. "Say nothing of this to Wellington and Castlereagh. I don't want Tania's child becoming a pawn. Even of my own government. Perhaps especially of them." He paused for a moment, his fingers still on the folds of the coat. "If Tania had a child, the father could be—"

"Tsar Alexander or Prince Metternich."

"Quite. Or Napoleon Bonaparte."

Suzanne shivered, considering the implications of Tatiana Kirsanova's illustrious lovers.

"Or someone else far less well known," Malcolm added. "We have no way of knowing how old the child is. If there even is a child."

Suzanne studied her husband's face, haunted by unanswered questions. "But you think there is."

He drew an uneven breath. "Yes."

Lord Castlereagh, Britain's foreign secretary, advanced into a salon in what had once been the villa of Napoleon's sister, Pauline Borghese, and was now the British embassy. He was immaculate in cream-colored knee breeches and a dark coat, his fair hair gleaming in the candlelight. He moved with his customary control but stopped short as he looked from Malcolm to Suzanne, Malcolm in his unbuttoned coat, striped crimson waistcoat, and no neckcloth, Suzanne in her spangled gown and red wig. "Good lord," he said on a rare note of surprise.

"Your pardon, sir. Your Grace. Sir." Malcolm nodded at the Duke of Wellington and Sir Charles Stuart, who had followed Castlereagh into the salon. "But I didn't think this should wait for us to leave off our disguise."

"Disguise?" Wellington said. He too wore evening dress, the civilian dress he often favored, though there was no denying his military bearing. "Oh, that's right, you were going to meet Rivère, weren't you?" His sharp gaze moved to Suzanne. "My dear girl, are you—"

"I'm fine."

"Spoken like a soldier who's just been hit by grapeshot." Wellington studied her for a moment, with that gaze she had learned frequently saw more than one wanted, then glanced at Malcolm. "What the devil happened?"

Malcolm pressed her into a giltwood chair. His hand taut on her shoulder, he recounted the night's events in clipped tones. Save that he made no mention of Rivère's claims about Princess Tatiana's child.

Wellington surveyed Malcolm from beneath drawn brows. "You going off to meet agents and the agents ending dead is becoming something of a pattern, Malcolm."

"Unfortunately, I'm afraid tonight's events hold more than a glancing similarity to Julia Ashton's death in Brussels."

"I knew things had been too quiet." Stuart leaned against the wall, ankles crossed, arms folded across his cream brocade waistcoat. He was a decade younger than Wellington and Castlereagh and less inclined to formality in dress or speech.

Wellington took a quick turn about the white-and-gold room as though it were a field he was surveying, hands clasped behind his back. "You think Rivère was deliberately targeted?"

"That knife was wielded by someone who knew what they were doing," Malcolm said. "And Rivère was away from the main fight. It's hard not to draw conclusions. Especially given what he told me just before he was killed."

"Which is?" Wellington studied Malcolm across the crystal and gilt of the salon.

"He said if we didn't help him he'd reveal information that could shake the British delegation to its core. Then he told me to mention the Laclos affair to you and Lord Castlereagh."

Wellington's gaze shot to Castlereagh and then to Stuart.

Suzanne watched her husband glance between the men. Malcolm had served all of them for years, in the Peninsula during the war, in Vienna at the Congress, in Brussels at the time of Waterloo. He respected them, Suzanne knew. That didn't mean he trusted everything they said. "What don't I know about the Laclos affair?" Malcolm asked.

"Whatever it is, we don't know it, either," Castlereagh said in a clipped voice.

"For God's sake, sir, I have a right to the truth. I was part of it."

"Have I mentioned your lamentable tendency to assume there are secrets lurking everywhere, Malcolm?" Wellington inquired.

Malcolm met the military commander's gaze. "Perhaps because all too often those secrets are there, sir."

Suzanne looked from her husband to the duke to Castlereagh to Stuart. She could practically see the lines of tension in the air. "Once again I feel as though I've stumbled into a play in the middle. What's the Laclos affair?"

Wellington and Castlereagh exchanged glances. Stuart drew a breath.

"If you want us to investigate," Malcolm said, "we're going to need to know."

"He's right, you know," Stuart said.

Castlereagh shot a glance at him. "It's not your decision."

Stuart returned his gaze. It was no secret that he wanted to be British ambassador to Paris when Castlereagh and Wellington returned to England, but he was not afraid to confront the foreign secretary. "Perhaps not. But Malcolm isn't an easy man to keep things from."

"No." Wellington turned his gaze to Malcolm. "He isn't."

"Arthur," Castlereagh said.

"It's nothing Malcolm doesn't know," Wellington said. "Nothing he can't tell Suzanne. And Malcolm is irritatingly right as usual. We need their help."

Castlereagh's mouth tightened, but he turned to Malcolm and Suzanne. "The Comte de Laclos and his family emigrated to England during the Terror. In '07, their son, Bertrand Laclos, returned to France to fight in the French army under Bonaparte. Quite a coup for the French to have one of their own back. As you can imagine, they made much of it for propaganda purposes."

"Save that Laclos had in fact offered his services to British intelligence." Wellington paced to the white marble fireplace and stood staring down into the cold grate. "He returned to France as our agent."

"For four years he provided us with excellent information," Castlereagh said. "Our best asset. It was a very advantageous situation."

"Too good to be true," Stuart murmured.

"He was a double?" Suzanne asked.

Wellington gave her a bleak smile. "As usual, my dear Suzanne, you're two steps ahead of us. Yes. In 1811 we discovered that Laclos was giving us just enough accurate information to ensure our trust while passing along false information to us. And giving information on our activities to the French."

"What happened?" Suzanne asked. The air in the room had turned as heavy as if it held the promise of a thunderstorm.

Wellington's gaze met Castlereagh's again. "He knew too much," Castlereagh said. "Names of British agents. Codes. He was too dangerous a liability."

"So you got rid of him."

"He died in a tavern brawl," Castlereagh said in an even voice.

Suzanne glanced at her husband. She'd heard the guilt in his voice when he first mentioned Laclos. "Darling? You said you had something to do with it?"

"I was the one who discovered Bertrand Laclos was a double." Malcolm's voice was controlled, but his hand tightened on her shoulder. "I intercepted communications he'd sent to a courier. I took the information to—"

Malcolm bit back his words. Castlereagh met his gaze. "My brother."

"Lord Stewart was my adjutant general at the time," Wellington said.

Suzanne began to see the dangers. Lord Stewart, Castlereagh's half-brother, was a hotheaded man given to impulsive behavior and bursts of temper. Suzanne could well imagine him leaping to the conclusion that Laclos must be got rid of.

Sir Charles Stuart, who saw Lord Stewart as a potential rival for the ambassadorship, kept his gaze fixed on his shoe buckles.

"The evidence seemed conclusive," Malcolm said. He looked from Castlereagh to Wellington to Stuart. "Sir," he said, in a voice taut with strain, the word addressed to all three of them. "Could we have been wrong?"

"Nonsense," Castlereagh said. "There's nothing to suggest—"

"Rivère said what he knew about the Laclos affair could shake the British delegation to its core."

"That doesn't—"

"And he implied it could bring about renewed hostilities between us and France."

"A preposterous suggestion—"

"Laclos's father is a crony of the Comte d'Artois," Malcolm persisted. "If he learned the foreign secretary's brother gave the order for the death of his son, who was in fact working for us—"

"It's a theory, Malcolm." Wellington advanced into the center of the room, as though laying claim to the Aubusson carpet. "But Rivère was a desperate man. Desperate men will say anything."

"But this desperate man was murdered just after he said it."

Wellington's gaze flickered to Castlereagh again.

"The intelligence was good," Castlereagh said. "We had no reason to doubt it."

"But that doesn't mean we haven't wondered," Stuart said.

Wellington grimaced. He was not a man to shirk harsh truths. "We didn't misread the intelligence. It would have to have been faked. Which would mean Laclos was set up."

Silence hung over the room for a moment, as the implications reverberated off the gilded moldings and damask wall hangings.

"If the French had learned Laclos was our agent—," Malcolm said.

"Why not simply kill him themselves?" Castlereagh said. "Or feed us false information through him."

Stuart moved away from the wall. "If it wasn't the French it would have to have been one of our people."

Castlereagh drew a sharp breath.

"Only stating the obvious," Stuart said.

Wellington gave a curt nod. "One way or another we have to

know. What happened to Laclos. What Rivère knew. And who killed him." He looked from Malcolm to Suzanne. "It looks as though you needn't fear being bored in Paris."

"Malcolm," Suzanne said to her husband when at last they were in the privacy of the robin's egg blue walls and white moldings of the bedchamber in their lodgings in the Rue du Faubourg Saint-Honoré. "Even if you were wrong about Laclos, it's not your fault. All you did was pass along information."

"If the information was wrong, I should have seen it." Malcolm cut off a length of linen with a sharp snip of the scissors.

Suzanne looked up at him from her perch on the dressing table bench. She knew that set mouth and those hooded eyes. She knew the weight of guilt it meant he was trying to hold at bay. "I hate to break it to you, darling, but you aren't superhuman."

"I should be able to recognize faulty intelligence." Malcolm placed a pad of lint over the wound in her arm, then secured the dressing with a strip of linen. "A man's dead, Suzette."

"Which is tragic. But not your fault."

He knotted off the ends of the bandage. "You're stubborn, sweetheart."

"I'm practical." She pulled her dressing gown up about her shoulders. "Tell me what else you know about Bertrand Laclos."

Malcolm snapped closed the lid on her medical supply box, which seemed to get as much use in peacetime as it had during the Peninsular War and the Waterloo campaign. "He was a couple of years older than me. He went to Eton, so as a Harrovian I didn't see a great deal of him until we both got to Oxford. He tended to keep himself to himself. He was serious, but he had a quick wit. He was a decent man. I liked him." He put the medical supply box on the chest of drawers.

Suzanne drew her legs up on the rose-flowered white silk of the dressing table bench and hooked her arms round her knees. "And after he went to work for the French? And supposedly really for the British?"

"I didn't have any contact with him in the Peninsula. He must have reported to someone in military intelligence. I'll see what

Davenport knows." Malcolm pushed aside the silk bed-curtains and leaned against the white-painted bedpost. "Bertrand Laclos made a rather interesting friend in the French cavalry before he was sent to the Peninsula. Edmond Talleyrand."

Suzanne frowned. "You said he had a quick wit. Edmond Talleyrand can't talk about anything but horses and gambling. And women."

"Yes, well, Laclos was playing a part."

Suzanne rested her chin on her updrawn knees. "Did Edmond's uncle have anything to do with the two of them becoming friends?"

Edmond's uncle, Prince Talleyrand, who had survived Napoleon's downfall to now head the government under the restored Louis XVIII, was a master manipulator. He was also an old friend of Malcolm's family. "You mean did Talleyrand put Edmond up to it because he guessed Bertrand Laclos was a British agent? Or because he knew Laclos was in fact working for the French?" Malcolm shook his head. "I wouldn't put it past him. But I've no proof."

"I'll talk to Doro. Though she's not exactly on terms of intimacy with Edmond even if she is his wife." Dorothée de Talleyrand-Périgord had served as hostess for her husband's uncle, Prince Talleyrand, at the Congress of Vienna. When she returned to Paris, she had taken up residence with Talleyrand, rather than with Edmond himself.

Malcolm nodded. "I'll talk to Talleyrand, though as usual I have precious little hope of getting much out of him. But I also need to ask him about—"

"Tatiana."

Malcolm's mouth tightened. "Yes."

Malcolm rarely mentioned Tatiana, but Suzanne knew he carried the guilt of his sister's death like a talisman. Sometimes she would catch him staring off into the distance and know he was replaying some moment of his time with Tatiana, especially those last weeks, wondering what might have been different. "In Vienna Tatiana supposedly said becoming pregnant was one mistake she'd never made."

"So she did. But then Tania wasn't above lying. Especially about something like that. Quite the reverse in fact."

"And even a clever woman can make a mistake," Suzanne said. Her chest tightened as she framed the word, but Malcolm, so quick to see so much, didn't seem to notice anything amiss.

"As I've said before, I'd like to think she'd have told me if she'd had a child," Malcolm said. "But I can imagine any number of reasons she'd have kept it secret."

"Including to protect you. If the father was someone powerful enough."

Malcolm shot her a surprised look.

"I understand Tatiana rather better now than I did at the start of things in Vienna," Suzanne said. "She had her own sort of honor. And she cared about you. A great deal more, perhaps, than even you realized."

Malcolm swallowed. "Sometimes I argue with myself until it seems blindingly obvious that there was a right course of action I could have taken. That would have ensured she was here now. Much good it does. Except to cause sleepless nights and endless questions."

Suzanne stared at him, startled not by what he had admitted but by the fact that he had admitted it at all. A year, even six months, ago, he would not have spoken so to her, nor would have he let her see his face as raw and cut with torment as it was now. She too knew what it was to carry guilt, too keenly to try to argue his away. She got to her feet, went to his side, and took his face between her hands. "All we can do is do the best we can within the moment, dearest. You do that better than anyone I know."

He gave a bleak smile. " 'Render me worthy of this noble wife.' "

She returned the smile, her own deliberately playful. "You promised not to turn into Brutus."

"Brutus appreciated his wife's strength. I can at least do that. While not making the mistake of not confiding in her."

She slid her hands behind his neck and kissed him, the tang of guilt on her lips. Because when it came to confiding in one's spouse, she had her own sins on her conscience.

CHAPTER 3

"How should I have the least idea what Edmond may or may not know?" Dorothée de Talleyrand-Périgord flung herself down on the rose and gold silk chaise-longue in a stir of blue-sprigged muslin. "I'm the last person in Paris he'd confide in. You should have seen the way he was looking at Karl and me at the opera the night before last."

"I did see. It argues something other than lack of interest." Suzanne took a sip from the gilt-rimmed coffee cup Dorothée had given her.

Dorothée grabbed a cushion from the chaise-longue and plucked at the fringe. "Edmond isn't any more interested in me than he ever was. His pride is piqued. Stupid honor."

"I couldn't agree with you more there."

Dorothée flung the pillow aside. "I'm sorry, Suzanne, I'm not usually so pettish. It's being back in Paris. Having Edmond here even if I see next to nothing of him. Facing down the gossip. Worrying about Karl."

"And then there's the strain Monsieur Talleyrand is under," Suzanne said.

"That too." Dorothée reached for her own cup of coffee and took a careful sip. In Vienna, she had fallen in love with the handsome Austrian Count Karl Clam-Martinitz, who was still her lover. But her relationship with her husband's uncle, Prince Talleyrand, had also deepened in ways she would not admit even to a close friend like Suzanne. Perhaps not even to herself. "Who is this man who was a friend of Edmond's?"

"Bertrand Laclos. He came to France in 1807 and died in the Peninsula in 1811."

Dorothée frowned a moment, then shook her head, her glossy brown ringlets stirring about her fine-boned face. "I didn't marry Edmond until 1809. Paris bewildered me, and I tended to want to sink into the shadows. His friends were all a blur."

"What are you looking so serious about?" Dorothée's eldest sister, Wilhelmine, Duchess of Sagan, swept into the room with a rustle of Pomona green sarcenet and a waft of custom-blended scent. She dropped down in a chair and began to strip off her gloves. "Do pour me out a cup of coffee. I drank too much champagne at the Russian embassy last night."

"Do you remember a Bertrand Laclos?" Dorothée asked, reaching for the silver coffeepot. "A friend of Edmond's."

"I make it a point to avoid Edmond's friends." Wilhelmine accepted a cup from her sister and took a grateful sip of coffee. She lowered the cup and looked at Suzanne over the gilt rim. "Is this to do with the Comte de Rivère being killed last night?"

"That's quick even for you," Suzanne said. "How did you guess?"

Wilhelmine tugged at the ribbons on her cottage bonnet and lifted the straw and satin from her burnished gold curls. "Someone dies under mysterious circumstances, and you and Malcolm start asking questions. I've learned to put two and two together."

Dorothée regarded her sister. "Besides, I suspect Lord Stewart told you."

"Possibly." Wilhelmine took another sip of coffee, then shrugged her shoulders, fluttering her gauze scarf. "Oh, very well. I was there when he got the message from Castlereagh this morning."

"I don't know what you see in him, Willie." Dorothée made a moue of distaste. "When I remember how he pinched me at the Metternichs' masquerade—"

"I admit Stewart isn't always subtle—"

"That's an understatement if I ever heard one. I think Talleyrand would have struck him at the masquerade if I hadn't intervened."

Wilhelmine took another sip of coffee. "Yes, well, we know how protective Talleyrand is when it comes to you."

Dorothée flushed. "Don't make this about me, Willie. I liked Alfred—"

"Alfred, if you'll recall, left me." Wilhelmine rubbed at the lip rouge smeared on her cup.

Dorothée bit her lip. "I'm sorry, Willie—"

"Don't be. Every love affair has to end with someone leaving." Wilhelmine's mouth curved with customary cynicism. Yet in Vienna last autumn, Suzanne had seen how deep Wilhelmine's feelings for Alfred von Windischgrätz ran.

"Then there was Fred Lamb," Dorothée said. "I liked him as well."

Wilhelmine leaned forwards to pour more coffee into her cup. "Agreeable. But not serious."

"And now Alfred's in Paris and seems very—"

Wilhelmine clunked the coffeepot down on the silver tray. "Are you saying you think I should come running the moment he crooks his finger?"

"No, course not. But if you love him—"

"I don't believe in love. Or at least I don't trust it." Wilhelmine tugged out her handkerchief and wiped at the coffee that had spattered on the tray and the porcelain tiles of the table. "Whatever Alfred may think he feels, within a few years he'll be married to a nice, respectable girl. It was never going to last—"

"And you think—" Dorothée stared at her sister. "Willie, are you considering *marrying* Stewart?"

Wilhelmine lifted her cup, full to the brim, and took a careful sip. "You say that as if marriage was some new form of sin."

"You've sworn you're never going to marry again."

Wilhelmine, twice divorced, gave her sister a careless smile. "You've known me all your life, Doro. Surely you realize I'm changeable."

Dorothée shook her head. "I can't believe you love him."

"My dear child. You're almost two-and-twenty. You can't still think love has anything to do with marriage."

"It does for some people." Dorothée flicked a glance at Suzanne.

"There are always exceptions." Wilhelmine's face relaxed into a smile. Then she studied Suzanne. "Though I don't know that even Suzanne would claim her marriage began with love."

"It began with necessity," Suzanne said. Which was the truth. Though, as with so much else to do with her marriage, a twisted truth.

Wilhelmine's gaze held perhaps more understanding than Suzanne would have liked. "There are all sorts of reasons one marries. Necessity. Security. Position."

Dorothée stared at her sister, as though she were a puzzle with unexpected angles. "And you think Stewart will give you—"

"His brother is the foreign secretary of England. It might be amusing."

"It sounds beastly." Dorothée reached for her lace shawl and pulled it tight round her shoulders. "Take it from me, there's nothing worse than being tied to a man one can't respect."

"But then I'm not a romantic, Doro. That makes it easier." Wilhelmine turned her gaze back to Suzanne. "I don't know anything about this Bertrand Laclos, but if you want to learn about Rivère, you should talk to Lady Caruthers."

Suzanne was used to making quick leaps of thought, but this was too much even for her. Gabrielle Caruthers was a French émigrée now married to a British officer. "Why?" she asked. "What does she have to do with Rivère?"

Wilhelmine settled back in her chair. "She was his mistress."

"Gabrielle Caruthers?" Dorothée said. "That's a bit of gossip I hadn't heard." Her eyes narrowed. "I suppose Stewart told you."

"No, Annina did. Maids always hear gossip first."

"Lady Caruthers seems so demure."

"They're often the most scandalous ones."

Dorothée shot her a sisterly look. "You've never been the least bit demure, Willie."

"There are always exceptions." Wilhelmine settled back against the cushions, cradling her coffee cup in one hand. "It's odd you were just asking about Bertrand Laclos. Gabrielle Caruthers is his cousin."

"I hadn't realized," Suzanne said. She still found the family trees of Malcolm's friends difficult to sort out. That Bertrand Laclos's cousin had been Antoine Rivère's mistress strained coincidence.

"She went to England with her uncle and aunt as a child during the Terror," Wilhelmine said. "I think her parents were both killed."

Dorothée shivered. "The Laclos family have been through a great deal."

"Like many French families. And like many émigrés, I imagine they're now hoping to have their estates restored." Wilhelmine took a sip of coffee. "I expect you want to talk to Lady Caruthers. I understand she's in the habit of taking coffee in the late morning in the Café Luxembourg. Quite like a Frenchwoman. Which of course she is. Though she hasn't lived here for years."

"Much like me," Suzanne said. Which was a truth, caught in the myriad lies she told about her past, even to her closest friends.

"Is that why you're looking into Rivère's death?" Dorothée asked. "Because you suspect Lord Caruthers was involved?"

Suzanne took a sip of coffee. "Until two minutes ago I hadn't the least idea Lady Caruthers was involved with Rivère."

"According to Annina, Rivère and Lady Caruthers had become quite reckless," Wilhelmine said. "Though Lord Caruthers doesn't particularly seem the jealous sort. He strikes me as decidedly—" Wilhelmine's delicate brows drew together as she searched for the right word.

"Temperate?" Suzanne suggested. She pictured Lord Caruthers, well-cut features, an agreeable smile. The sort of man to get a lady lemonade at a military review or return to the carriage for her parasol. And it was all done with sincerity rather than an attempt at flirtation.

"Yes, that's it precisely." Wilhelmine nodded. "Too well-bred to fight a duel."

"That's all very well," Dorothée said, "but betrayal can take people the oddest ways."

Suzanne reached for her coffee, a dozen thoughts tumbling through her brain, not all to do with Antoine de Rivère and the Carutherses. Her fingers closed hard round the delicate porcelain handle. "So it can."

"Malcolm." Colonel Harry Davenport looked up from his paperwork with a grin. The grin held the familiar ironic mockery but considerably less cynicism than it had before the battle of Waterloo. Two months could change a lot. Two months and reconciling with an estranged wife against all the odds.

Malcolm pushed aside a stack of papers and perched on the edge of the desk where Davenport was working in the attachés' sitting room at Wellington's Headquarters. "Do you remember the Bertrand Laclos affair?"

Davenport grimaced. "Difficult to forget. It was a bad business."

"I was the one who uncovered the information that led to his being exposed." A dozen uncomfortable questions circled through Malcolm's brain. "I knew him a bit in England as a boy. But I didn't work with him in the Peninsula."

"Nor did I." Davenport leaned back in his chair, flexing his bad arm, a legacy of the Peninsular War. "I didn't even know about him except by his code name until after he was exposed. He had very special handling. He only reported to Caruthers."

"Rupert Caruthers?" Malcolm asked in surprise.

"You know him?"

"Off and on growing up. He's a couple of years my senior, and he went to Eton. I know his father better." Earl Dewhurst, Rupert Caruthers's father, was a senior British diplomat who had been sent to the Peninsula on several special missions and was currently attached to the British delegation in Paris.

"I remember when Dewhurst came out to Lisbon," Davenport said. "Caruthers retreated, metaphorically, and literally when he could. Not an easy father to live up to, I imagine. I often thought

Caruthers went into the army to differentiate himself from his parent."

Malcolm grinned at the image of Lord Dewhurst's imperious face. Just a lift of his eyebrows could dampen all pretensions. "I didn't realize Caruthers was so involved in intelligence."

"I think the Laclos affair gave him a distaste for it. He asked to be transferred to Clinton's staff not long after."

Malcolm stared down at a bronze paperweight atop what looked like a pile of coded documents. "I remember when I gave Stewart the information about Bertrand Laclos. I've never heard such invective." He drew a breath. "I tried to convince Stewart not to act precipitously. But it seemed conclusive."

" 'Seemed'?" Davenport scanned his face. "You're questioning what you learned? Does this have to do with Antoine Rivère?"

"My God." Malcolm lifted his gaze to his friend. "I forget how quick you are. How did you guess?"

"I can still do simple arithmetic." Davenport twisted the handle of the coffee cup beside the papers on his desk. "Were you there last night when he was killed?"

"With Suzanne."

"I might have known it." Davenport regarded him for a moment. "What's the connection to Bertrand Laclos?"

"I'm not sure yet." Malcolm told Harry what they'd learned, omitting Rivère's claims about Tatiana's child. He trusted Harry Davenport implicitly after their time at Waterloo, but Tania's secrets at once were too dangerous and too intimate to share.

Davenport frowned. "Difficult to sort truth out from bluff in Rivère's claims."

"There was enough truth that he thought his threats would work."

"Have you searched his rooms?"

"Not yet."

Davenport picked up a jade-handled penknife. "There's nothing like being confined to a desk with a wound to give one a longing for adventure."

"You only had to ask," Malcolm said. "I'd love the company."

* * *

Gabrielle Caruthers sat at one of the outdoor tables at Café Luxembourg with a relaxed ease that most Englishwomen did not possess, the folds of her embroidered muslin gown falling loosely about her. Her thick dark gold hair was gathered into a loose knot, tendrils escaping round her face beneath the brim of a chip straw hat tied with blue ribbons the color of her eyes. She was bent over a sketch pad, a cup of coffee at her elbow, but at Suzanne's approach she looked up and greeted her with a smile.

"Mrs. Rannoch." Her voice had the faintest lilt of an accent, for all she had spent most of her life in England. "So agreeable to be in a country where ladies can sit in cafés, don't you find?"

"Very much so." Suzanne returned the smile. She and Gabrielle Caruthers were hardly confidantes, but they saw each other frequently in British expatriate circles and they had young sons who were of an age, which helped forge a bond deeper than that of casual acquaintances. "Do you mind if I join you?"

"I'd be delighted." Lady Caruthers signaled to a waiter to bring another cup of coffee as Suzanne dropped into a chair across from her. "It's odd," she said. "I can't even remember Paris and yet I feel so much at home here. Do you feel the same?"

Suzanne glanced round the tables crowded beneath the green-and-white-striped awning. Two British cavalrymen were lounging at the nearest table, a Prussian and an Austrian tossed dice at the table beyond, and a trio of Dutch-Belgians had just come through the doors of the café. Would her throat ever cease to close at the sight? "I'll never forget this time in Paris," she said truthfully.

The waiter brought her coffee. She stirred in milk.

Lady Caruthers closed her sketch pad, which held a study of the Prussian and Austrian officers, quick and impressionistic, with vivid life in the strokes of pencil.

"I didn't mean to interrupt you," Suzanne said.

"It's no matter. I'm glad of the company." Lady Caruthers paused a moment, her gaze moving over Suzanne's face. "Though somehow I think you didn't just happen by the café." It was a statement that held a question.

"No, as it happens." Suzanne set down the coffee spoon and

took a careful sip. "I wanted to offer my condolences, Lady Caruthers."

Lady Caruthers put up a hand to adjust the brim of her hat. "For heaven's sake why?"

Suzanne settled her coffee cup in its saucer. "On Antoine Rivère's death."

For a moment Gabrielle Caruthers's eyes held naked shock. Then she drew a quick breath, defenses slamming into place. "I can't imagine—"

"Lady Caruthers." Suzanne leaned forwards, her voice lowered. "I have no wish to cause you scandal or to disrupt your marriage. But you must wish to learn the truth of Monsieur Rivère's death as much as my husband and I do."

"I can't imagine—"

"I know. I can prove it, if you like, but I don't imagine you want me prying any more than I have to."

Gabrielle Caruthers pushed back her chair and sprang to her feet, spattering coffee from her cup onto the table. "I have no need to listen to this impertinence." She snatched up her gloves and reticule with shaking fingers and reached for her sketch pad.

"Lady Caruthers." Suzanne gripped the other woman's wrist. "It's beastly. I hate prying into people's private affairs. But Antoine Rivère's death is unfortunately a political matter as well as a personal one."

Lady Caruthers jerked her hand from Suzanne's grasp. "Antoine— Monsieur Rivère died in a tavern brawl. I hardly see anything political in that."

"It may have been more complicated. My husband and I were there—"

"You were at the tavern?" Shock shot through Lady Caruthers's eyes, momentarily overwhelming her anger.

"Malcolm had a meeting with Monsieur Rivère. I was assisting him. We found his body. His death did not appear to have been part of the brawl. Lady Caruthers, I believe you'd prefer to answer questions from me rather than my husband. Or Wellington or Castlereagh."

Lady Caruthers's gaze slid to the side. The buzz of conversation,

the rattle of dice, the clip-clop of horse hooves from the street created good cover, but the conversation had quieted when she sprang
to her feet. She dropped back into her chair, picked up her coffee
cup, and took a sip, as though playing for time.

"It must be dreadful," Suzanne said in a quiet voice, once the
buzz of conversation had resumed round them. "Grieving for
someone and not being able to talk about it."

Lady Caruthers put her hand to her mouth and gave a strangled
sob. "It's been hell. I couldn't even admit—" She swallowed and
stared at the coffee spattered on the marble tabletop. "You must
think me a dreadful person."

"No, I assure you."

"You're kind."

"I hope I'm understanding. One never knows what goes on inside anyone else's marriage."

Lady Caruthers tugged a lace-edged handkerchief from her
sleeve and blotted the spilled coffee. "I've always been . . . fond of
Rupert. I've known him since we were children. He was good
friends with my cousin Bertrand."

"Bertrand Laclos."

"Yes. I came to England with the Lacloses—my uncle and
aunt—when I was four. My parents were dead, and at the time I
thought my brother was as well. But I had Bertrand and Étienne."

"Bertrand's brother?" Suzanne hadn't realized there was another Laclos son.

"Yes." A shadow crossed Gabrielle Caruthers's face that had
nothing to do with the brim of her hat. "Bertrand was seven when
we came to England. Étienne was ten." She smoothed out the
handkerchief and stared at the coffee-stained linen. "It's hard,
being a foreigner among the English ton."

"I was much older before I came to England, but I know precisely what you mean. One can never really be one of them." It was
something, Suzanne knew, that Malcolm would never quite understand. *Of course you belong,* he'd told her once with a quick smile.
You're my wife. Not that I can quite imagine wanting to belong here.
That was the irony. Malcolm might have little use for the British
beau monde, yet he'd be one of them his entire life, like it or not.

"Lord Dewhurst—Rupert's father—and my uncle were old friends. Lord Dewhurst had been sent to the University of Paris, in the days when one could still travel easily between the two countries. He met my uncle there. Because of Lord Dewhurst, we were more fortunate than most émigrés. He brought us into his world. And Rupert's friendship with Bertrand helped even more. I think I was half in love with Rupert at the age of eight just for that. I had friends, I was invited to parties. Even though I never quite forgot that my clothes weren't new or fashionable enough. Clothes matter so much when one's that age."

"In this world clothes always matter."

Lady Caruthers smoothed the cuff of her blue sarcenet spencer, trimmed with lace and twists of satin. "How very true. When I was fourteen, my brother Gui was discovered alive, hidden away with a farm family in Provence, and smuggled to England. Rupert and Bertrand took him under their wing. I was good friends with Rupert's sisters by then. Henrietta and I made our débuts together, which saved my uncle and aunt no end of expense. Rupert danced the first dance with me at our come-out ball." She traced her fingers over her initials embroidered in the handkerchief. "There was no dearth of young men to dance with me that season. But I quickly discovered that it's one thing to be an acceptable partner for the *boulanger* or the *écossaise* and quite another to be an acceptable wife with no dowry."

"It does come back to money so often."

"Quite, as my husband would say." Gabrielle's fingers tensed on the handkerchief. "When Étienne left university, he went to work as Lord Dewhurst's secretary. Lord Dewhurst is in the diplomatic service. But of course you know that. You know him."

Suzanne nodded. She had met the earl on a number of occasions. A courtly man with a powerful presence and a keen gaze. She'd always been wary of him.

Lady Caruthers took a sip of coffee. "Lord Dewhurst has always been kind to me. But I've never quite forgiven him for pulling Étienne into it."

" 'It'?" Suzanne asked. She hadn't realized any of the Laclos family tragedy revolved round Bertrand's elder brother. Had Éti-enne somehow been responsible for Bertrand's defection?

Gabrielle grimaced. "Étienne's head was stuffed with a lot of noble ideals. And Dewhurst fed them. He's one of those English-men who thought the clock could be turned back to before the Revolution. Of course I suppose one could say now it has been." Lady Caruthers cast a glance round the café. "But one can never really go back, can one?"

Suzanne glanced round the café as well. The British cavalrymen were flirting with two Parisian girls in flower-trimmed bonnets. Two Frenchmen in civilian dress stepped beneath the awning and stared from the cavalrymen to the Prussian and Austrian to the Dutch-Belgians, tension running through their shoulders. One took a quick step forwards. His companion gripped his arm. Suzanne swallowed, a lump in her throat. "No."

Though what Paris was turning into was anyone's guess.

Gabrielle Caruthers glanced at the Frenchmen as they moved to a table defiantly close to the English cavalry officers. One stopped to sweep a sardonic bow to the Parisian girls. "Étienne was enraged by the Duc d'Enghien's execution. He went to Paris in secret with English gold, embroiled in one of those half-baked Royalist plots that were so common then. Something to do with killing Bonaparte with a bomb at Malmaison and replacing him with one of the royal dukes. It was discovered before it ever really amounted to any-thing. Étienne was arrested and executed. Lord Dewhurst came to tell us. Rupert and Bertrand were at Oxford, but they both came to see us as soon as they could. At the time I thought it was the worst tragedy that could befall our family. Then Bertrand left England and went to France to fight for Bonaparte. Étienne had romantic ideals. Bertrand went in the opposite direction. Suddenly I was a traitor's cousin."

Gabrielle Caruthers obviously hadn't known her cousin was supposedly a British agent. "Hardly a traitor. Your cousin was French."

"Yes, I suppose that's one way of looking at it. To own the truth, I've never cared much for countries. But to nearly everyone we knew Bertrand was a traitor. My uncle wouldn't speak about him at all. Rupert was kind. He told me Bertrand was still my cousin and it was impossible to know why someone did a certain thing. That there were things I didn't understand. Then he left for the Peninsula as well."

"You must have been lonely."

Lady Caruthers shrugged her slender shoulders. "I still had plenty of dancing partners. I'd received one or two offers of something more serious, though it didn't entail marriage." She cast a quick look at Suzanne. "I didn't—"

"It's different when one's an unmarried girl," Suzanne said, though for her it hadn't been precisely. But then to call her childhood and young adulthood eccentric would be a laughable understatement.

Gabrielle Caruthers nodded. "I was a bridesmaid when Henrietta married Lord Sherringford the spring after we came out. And then two years later when her younger sister Clarissa made her début and married in the same season. I was getting to be positively on the shelf. My brother Gui had gaming debts." She frowned at the handkerchief. "I even considered hiring myself out as a governess, but my uncle wouldn't stand for it, and in truth I doubt I'd the temperament."

"A woman has few options to make money."

"Yes." Lady Caruthers folded the handkerchief carefully into squares. "Then we got news that Bertrand had been killed. My uncle suffered a stroke. My aunt's health already wasn't good. I'm not much of a caretaker, but there was only me. I did what I could."

"Thank goodness they had you."

Gabrielle gave a bleak smile. "I owed them everything. The roof over my head. The food I ate. My life. This was little enough to do in recompense."

A burst of laughter came from the Parisian girls and the British cavalry officers. "And your brother?" Suzanne asked.

Lady Caruthers smoothed a finger over the handkerchief. "Gui tried. He was having enough trouble sorting out his own life at the time."

"So all the burden fell to you."

Lady Caruthers shrugged. "As I said, it was the least I owed them. But I don't pretend to have been very good at it. And the gossip only got worse of course. Either people dropped us from their invitation lists, or they called on us, avid for information, like the latest installment of a lending library novel. Henrietta and Clarissa tried to help, but they were both busy with their own families by that time. Clarissa had just had a baby and Henrietta was about to be confined. Then Rupert returned to England on leave."

Suzanne noted the way Gabrielle's eyes softened. "It must have been a great relief to see him."

"A massive understatement." Lady Caruthers tucked the handkerchief into her reticule. "I still remember the day I came down the stairs, after soothing my aunt's hysterics, to find him standing in the hall. I fairly ran down the last of the stairs and flung my arms round him, in a way that would have scandalized my aunt. He was so kind. I can't tell you what it meant, having his support. Just little things like the way he could talk to my uncle and aunt and sometimes even get them to smile. And Gui always listened to him. Under Rupert's influence, Gui stopped gaming and drinking quite so much. Also— Rupert missed Bertrand as well, and remembered the good times." Lady Caruthers put a hand to her face, tucking a strand of dark gold hair beneath her bonnet. "We spent more time together than we ever had. And then he asked me to marry him."

"Was that a relief as well?"

"It answered so many problems. I went from a social pariah wondering how to buy sugar to the wife of a future earl." Gabrielle Caruthers stared down at her hands. She touched the plain gold circle of her wedding band. "You must think I'm dreadful, betraying a man who gave me so much."

The word "betrayal" echoed in Suzanne's head as it always did. Malcolm too had given her an unimaginable amount. Even before he'd given her any portion of his heart. "That depends upon the terms of the marriage. I'd never claim to understand what goes on between any two people in such a private relationship."

"Though a relationship played out on the public stage." Lady Caruthers twisted the ring round her finger. "I'd been half in love with Rupert for years. His coming to my rescue like that was enough to tip me over the edge. For a few weeks I was deliriously happy. It wasn't the most romantic of proposals. Rupert didn't go down on one knee or clasp me to his breast. He took my hand and said he thought we could be happy together. But I thought his restraint was just typical British reticence. It wasn't until after we were married, after the wedding journey, after we were settled in London— Rupert is . . ." Lady Caruthers hesitated, her gaze moving restlessly over the café tables and the street as she searched for the right word. "He's kind to me." The way she said the word "kind" held the pain of a dagger thrust. "I think he's fond of me. I know he loves our son. But there's a wall I'll never break through."

Suzanne forced her breath to stay even. It was so like a description of her own marriage to Malcolm that she felt as though she'd been punched in the stomach. "British men don't show their affections easily. As you said."

"No, but I can read the difference." Gabrielle looked directly into her eyes. "One learns to read one's husband, don't you find?"

"Yes." Suzanne's fingers curled round her coffee cup. Malcolm loved her. He'd said the words and miraculously she believed them. His eyes showed it when they rested upon her in an unguarded moment as did the touch of his hand when he pulled her to him in the dark. But there were different kinds of love. The wall, as Gabrielle had said, was still there. She was quite sure it always would be.

"I thought I could live with it," Gabrielle said. "I told myself I had more than I'd ever thought to have. That Rupert had never promised me more." She took a sip of coffee and grimaced as though it was bitter. "It was easier when he was in the Peninsula. I didn't see him every day, and I could pretend—" She shook her head. "Now, living together, seeing each other every day, facing each other over the breakfast dishes, going to entertainments on his arm—I can't avoid it. And I've discovered I need—" She frowned into her coffee cup.

"Passion?" Suzanne asked. It was often a surprisingly difficult need to admit to, despite being so basic.

Gabrielle frowned. "That too. But I was thinking of intimacy."

"Most people need that as well," Suzanne said in as steady a voice as she could muster.

Gabrielle picked up the silver spoon and stirred her cooling coffee. "Antoine wasn't— It's not that I thought he was the love of my life. But he understood me. And I didn't have to pretend with him." She set down the spoon. "I could be myself with him. I don't think I've ever been so much myself with anyone. I miss that. I miss him."

Sometimes, Suzanne felt she'd forgot what it was like to be herself. Or forgot who that person was. She reached out and laid her hand over Gabrielle's own. "Did Antoine Rivère indicate to you that he had any enemies?"

"His cousin. He wanted the title and estates. Antoine was sure he was lobbying to have him proscribed."

"Did he tell you he was trying to get out of France?"

"How could he not be?"

"Did he tell you what he was doing to get out of France?"

Gabrielle's gaze shot over her face. "He threatened Mr. Rannoch, didn't he?"

"Was Monsieur Rivère in the habit of threatening people?"

"No, but—" Gabrielle pulled her hand from Suzanne's grip. "Antoine knew things." She rubbed her arms. "He acquired information in his work. It could be useful."

"Did he tell you whom he had this information about?"

Gabrielle hesitated, frowning. She chewed on her lower lip. "He didn't tell me precisely. Not in so many words."

"But . . . ?" Suzanne leaned forwards. "Lady Caruthers, any information you have may help us find the man behind Monsieur Rivère's death."

To Suzanne's surprise, Gabrielle gave a laugh, sharp with irony. "I'm not sure you want the information I have, Mrs. Rannoch. Your husband will find it decidedly awkward."

"Then perhaps there's all the more reason we should know."

Gabrielle snatched up her cup and took a sip of coffee. "Antoine and I exchanged a few words at the Austrian embassy reception last week. He said it was amazing how some of the most powerful people could be bent to his will." She lifted her gaze to Suzanne's face. "He was looking at the Duke of Wellington when he said it."

CHAPTER 4

Harry stared up at the wrought-iron work and elaborate plaster moldings of the building before them. "Rivère was living well for a clerk in the foreign ministry."

"Evidence perhaps that he'd been putting the information he gathered to use well before his death," Malcolm said.

The concierge directed them to the second floor, where Rivère had occupied a spacious suite of rooms overlooking the Palais Royale. The door was unlocked. Faint thuds sounded down the entryway. They entered the central sitting room to find a dark-haired man in his shirtsleeves kneeling on the floor surrounded by boxes, in the act of filling an open box with books.

"May I help you, gentlemen?"

"Forgive the intrusion," Malcolm said. "My name is Rannoch, Malcolm Rannoch. I'm an attaché at the British embassy. And this is Colonel Davenport. Antoine Rivère was a friend of ours." A stretch of the truth, but the word "friend" could cover a multitude of relationships.

"I'm Duvall. I am—I was—his valet."

Malcolm cast a glance round the room. Bare picture hooks and tabletops of marble and ormolu and polished mahogany swept free of ornaments. "You're packing up his things already?"

"His cousin was here this morning and asked me to do so. I need to be quick about it so I can search for a new situation." Duvall looked from Malcolm to Harry. "If either of you gentlemen knows of anyone in search of a valet—"

"I'll put out inquiries," Malcolm said. "However, at the moment what we do need is information."

Wariness and calculation flickered in Duvall's gaze. "About?"

"What may have led to Monsieur Rivère's death."

Calculation gave way to surprise. "He died in a tavern brawl."

"But his death may not have been accidental."

Duvall's gaze widened further.

"We would of course compensate you for any information," Malcolm said. "We understand the trouble you'd be taking."

Duvall pushed himself to his feet. "I don't know that I know a great deal."

"I'm sure you underrate yourself." Harry spoke up. "A good valet always knows his master's doings."

Duvall straightened his neckcloth. "I never pried. But of course one can't help but notice—"

"Of course," Malcolm said. "Just what did you notice?"

"Monsieur Rivère ran risks. Surprisingly so for a government clerk."

"I see a decanter of brandy," Harry said. "I'm sure your late master wouldn't object to your having a glass. And perhaps sharing one with his friends."

Duvall's posture relaxed slightly as he poured three glasses. The aroma of good cognac wafted through the room.

Malcolm accepted a glass and took a small sip to put the witness at his ease. "Had Rivère said anything to indicate he was afraid of anyone?"

Duvall tossed down a large swallow of brandy. "Isn't everyone in Paris with a connection to the Bonaparte régime afraid right now?"

Harry turned his own brandy glass in his hand. "You must have been concerned about your employer perhaps being thrown in jail."

"I—" Duvall took another sip of brandy.

"Or did you have reason to think Rivère wouldn't be arrested?" Malcolm asked.

"Why should I think that?"

"Perhaps you knew Rivère had leverage?"

"Monsieur Rivère made a habit of knowing a great deal."

"Who else was Rivère close to?" Harry asked.

"Monsieur Rivère was discreet."

"Meaning he had a mistress, but you don't know her name?"

"In a word. This particular lady never came here."

"But other ladies did?" Harry asked.

Duvall shifted his weight from one foot to the other.

"Any information could be of use," Malcolm said. "We can certainly make it worth your while, as I said."

Duvall hesitated a moment longer. "There was a lady who visited him here on occasion. Dark haired. Petite. I didn't know her name."

"What did Monsieur Rivère call her?" Malcolm asked.

"Christine."

"How old was she?" Harry asked.

Another moment of hesitation, though this time Duvall seemed to be considering. "Young, but not in the first blush of youth. About five-and-twenty perhaps. She was— I use the word 'lady' loosely."

"Who else visited Rivère?" Malcolm asked.

"Colleagues from the foreign ministry occasionally. Monsieur Rivère's cousin once. They weren't on the best of terms."

"And—?"

Duvall splashed some more brandy into his glass. "Monsieur Rivère had a visitor late two nights before—two nights before the brawl. He let the visitor in himself, but I heard raised voices."

"What did they say?" Harry asked.

"I couldn't make out all of it."

"But I'm sure you did your best."

"I heard the visitor tell Monsieur Rivère he 'wouldn't get away with it.' And Monsieur Rivère respond that the other gentleman wasn't 'in a position to make threats.' "

"And then?" Malcolm asked.

"I heard the door slam. I stepped out into the passage. I was—"

"Curious. Naturally. Did you catch a glimpse of him? Can you give us a description?"

Duvall drew a breath, as though not sure how his words would be received. "Tall. A sharp profile. I believe he would be known to both you gentlemen." Duvall took a swallow of brandy. "It was the Duke of Wellington."

Malcolm bit back a curse and kept his gaze level on Duvall. "Interesting."

Duvall looked a bit dashed that his words had not produced the intended effect. Malcolm presented him with a purse and suggested he might like to retire to a nearby café for an hour or so. Duvall hesitated, glanced at the purse again, and nodded.

Harry stared after him as the door closed and his footsteps retreated down the stairs. "Wellington gave you no clue?"

"None."

"Interesting man, our duke. Do you think Rivère approached him about the Laclos affair himself?"

"Then why Rivère's dramatic approach to me last night?"

"Cover?"

"They wouldn't need the cover for the Laclos affair, since Rivère brought it up to me. But if he approached Wellington about something else—"

Harry met Malcolm's gaze for a moment. "Wellington can be ruthless." It was a flat statement about the man they had both served for years and risked their lives for. "We considered in Brussels that he might be capable of murder."

"But in the end he wasn't behind Julia Ashton's death."

"Which doesn't mean he isn't behind Rivère's death. Julia was an English lady. Rivère was a French double agent who was trying to blackmail the British." Harry kept his gaze on Malcolm. Uncompromising, yet oddly compassionate. "War isn't played by gentlemen's rules. You know that."

"Neither are politics or diplomacy."

"Go carefully, Malcolm. Wellington can be dangerous."

"At least I know him."

"That's precisely what makes him dangerous." Harry cast a glance round the room. "You take the boxes on the left. I'll take the right."

The boxes contained bills, innocuous correspondence with an elderly aunt, tradesmen, a school friend who was an advocate in Provence. And books—an eclectic collection of Montaigne, Voltaire, and Rousseau, bawdy novels, and some bawdier love poetry, and a few volumes of military history. But all free of notes in the margin or papers tucked between the pages or sewn into the binding.

"Here's something." Harry was kneeling beside the swept-clean writing desk, the empty drawers pulled from their slots and stacked on the floor beside him. He was pulling a small drawer from the top of the desk and reaching behind it. He withdrew a crumpled paper. "Something whoever swept the room clean missed."

Malcolm crossed the room as Harry smoothed out the paper on the desktop. It was a letter. A partial draft later rewritten or abandoned and never sent.

> *Ma chère Christine,*
> *You can't seriously have thought I meant to end things. I won't say you should have more faith in my constancy, but surely you have faith in my common sense. How could I let something as rare and valuable as you slip through my fingers? I'll admit to having been preoccupied of late, but not because of another woman. We've both always been able to juggle more than one of that sort of interest. No matter who else was in my bed, it couldn't lessen my desire for you. No, my mind has been preoccupied by something rather more urgent. The prospect of riches.*
> *You'll appreciate I can't put more in writing. But should we meet tomorrow night—*

The writing broke off, with a stroke of black ink across the bottom of the page. "We need to find this Christine," Malcolm said. "She seems to have been one of the few people Rivère confided in."

"I'll work on it." Harry picked up the letter and tucked it into his coat. "I have contacts in the Paris demimonde. Purely professional."

"No need to explain yourself."

"I'm not. I'm confessing that even at the worst of our estrangement I was too obsessed with my wife to have much thought for anyone else. I'll handle this. I suspect you have other things to keep you busy."

Malcolm cast a sharp glance at his friend. Harry's answering look was bland as butter. "After all," Harry said, "you're a busy man, Rannoch."

Suzanne slipped into the high-backed bench at the back of the café. A typical sort of Parisian café, with newspapers rustling, games of chess in progress, glasses of wine and cups of café au lait circulating. The sort of café frequented by midlevel clerks and middling tradesmen. As innocuous and unremarkable as the red wine being poured or the prints of the French countryside that hung on the blue-papered walls.

Enough women were present—talking with friends, flirting with gentlemen, with children in tow, with shopping parcels beside them—that she didn't stand out like a sore thumb. It was blessedly easier to move about on the Continent than in Britain.

She ordered a bottle of red wine and two glasses. Coffee would have been safer, but she needed the fortification. She'd sent her message on short notice, but she knew he wouldn't fail her if he could help it. She sipped from the glass of wine the waiter poured her and waited.

He came five minutes after the appointed time, wearing a plain dark coat. Though he made no obvious effort at concealment, somehow he blended effortlessly into the crowd, so that it was a moment before even she noticed him. He approached her table without haste and at last met her gaze.

Since the day she'd told him she would no longer work as his agent in the service of Napoleon Bonaparte, she and Raoul O'Roarke had met at least a dozen times. They'd exchanged greetings at receptions in Brussels and Paris, ridden past each other in the Bois de Boulogne, sat in adjacent boxes at the theatre. He'd tipped his hat to her and Colin by the fountain in the Jardin des Tuileries and admired Colin's dexterity with his toy boat. At Tsar Alexander's military review last month Raoul had stopped by Malcolm's and her carriage for a few minutes. But they hadn't met in private. It made all the difference. Memories thickened in the air like drops of condensation.

"Thank you for coming," she said. Her throat was surprisingly dry.

"Did you doubt that I would?" Raoul asked, with the lift of a brow.

"No. But I'm sorry—I didn't mean to—"

He regarded her for a moment, then dropped onto the bench across from her in one economical motion. "I don't recall either of us imposing a rule that we could no longer meet in private. I'll even go so far as to say I was glad to hear from you. Save that I confess I fear your running the risk means something's wrong. Given that you're the one with more to lose."

"Am I? If you were discovered—"

He leaned back against the bench. "I've been a few days from the guillotine before."

A chill cut through the sarcenet of her spencer and the muslin of her gown. "It's not funny."

"No. It's a fact of our life now."

She tugged at one of her gloves. "A foreign ministry clerk named Rivère was knifed in a dockside tavern last night."

Raoul reached for the bottle and filled the second glass. "Yes, I heard. Were you and Malcolm there?"

Her fingers froze on the threadnet glove. "Don't tell me you were following us."

"When have I ever had you followed?"

"I don't work for you anymore." She set the glove down with care. As well as she knew Raoul, she'd never know his limits. "The rules have changed."

"My dear girl. Some things are off-limits. Besides, I trained you well enough to know following you would be a waste of time." He took a sip of wine. "Rivère was a British agent. I assumed he was in that tavern to meet with someone from the British delegation."

She scanned his face, alert to clues. "How long had you known?"

"That he was reporting to the British?" Raoul draped one arm along the back of the bench, the wineglass held between two fingers of his other hand. "Since before Waterloo. I used him to pass along false information more than once. I assume he wanted Malcolm's help to get out of France. His cousin's been making things difficult for him."

"He threatened to reveal information if the British didn't help him. Information that could bring about renewed hostilities with France."

"Regarding?" Raoul watched her for a moment. "Or would you rather not say?"

"I need to. I need information." She took a sip of wine to swallow a curse of frustration. "Regarding Bertrand Laclos."

"I see." Raoul tilted his head back, his eyes narrowed. "That could cause complications."

She scanned his face, seeking clues in the familiar lines and hollows, the hooded gray eyes. "You knew Laclos?"

"Rather well." Raoul took another sip of wine. "And yet I never tumbled to the fact that he was working for the British. One of my most egregious failures."

"When did you find out?"

"Not until after he died. The circumstances of his death were suspicious. And we'd intercepted a communication that suggested the British might have been behind it. I searched his rooms. I found evidence he'd been working with the British—well concealed, but there was one coded letter locked away that I decoded."

"The British thought—"

"That he'd been a double working for us all along. Extraordinary."

"He wasn't?" Suzanne studied his face, trying to peel away layers of defense and pretense. She could almost always tell when Raoul was speaking the truth. Almost. But not invariably.

"No." Raoul's voice was flat.

"Can you be sure? You didn't run the only network in the Peninsula."

"But I knew the others who did. I made inquiries after Laclos's death. I'm as sure as I can be. Someone wanted him out of the way."

"Not the French?"

"We didn't know he was a double," Raoul pointed out. "Besides, we wouldn't have used such convoluted methods. I'd say someone British wanted him dead. British and highly placed."

"Did you find anything in his rooms to suggest who?"

"A love letter to an R. Seemingly a longtime lover in an affair that went beyond the trifling. But there were impediments to their being together."

"So if R. had a jealous husband—"

"It's one possibility."

Suzanne turned the stem of her wineglass between her fingers. "Malcolm intercepted the documents that incriminated Laclos."

Raoul's mouth tightened. "Malcolm will take that hard. He still thinks one can be a spy and maintain one's integrity."

She jerked her chin up and met Raoul's gaze. "He manages far better than most agents."

"Yes. I should think it's a large part of why you love him."

She felt herself flush. "Rivère had other information. This was just the first thing he tried as leverage." She tightened her fingers round her glass, willing them to be steady. "Malcolm and Harry Davenport are searching his rooms."

Raoul's gaze moved over her face, at once sharp and gentle. "You're asking me if he knew about you?"

She swallowed. "Could he have?"

Raoul reached across the table and touched her hand. "I very much doubt it."

"But you can't be sure. Of course." She forced a sip of wine down her throat. "Malcolm will talk to Fouché about Bertrand Laclos."

"You shouldn't have anything to fear from Fouché." Raoul's mouth lifted in a faint smile. "Which may be the first time I've ever said that about him."

The wine lingered bitter in her throat. "You can't be sure—"

"I never used your name with Fouché. And I never told him one of my agents had married a British diplomat."

She looked into the familiar gray eyes that always seemed to hold surprises. "Why not?"

"No need to share information when not necessary. Particularly not with a man like Fouché. Besides, I thought that eventually—"

"Eventually what?"

He picked up the bottle and refilled her nearly full glass. "I thought that one way or another you'd want to preserve your marriage. The fewer people who knew the truth of your past the better."

The rattle of dice, the rustle of newspaper, and the slosh of wine being poured echoed in the stillness. She could see Raoul's cool, dispassionate gaze in a Lisbon plaza the day they'd discussed Malcolm's proposal of marriage to her. "You thought—I went into my marriage to spy on the British through Malcolm. How could you possibly guess I'd want to preserve it?"

Raoul reached for his own glass. "What were you planning? To walk away one day when you'd got all the information you could from your husband? And take your son with you?"

"No. Yes. That is—" Her throat tightened. "The truth is I scarcely thought of the future at all." Shame washed over her like a bucketful of icy water.

He gave a faint smile. "Understandable. We were trying to win a war. The present objective seems all that matters. But I'm rather older than you. I knew the war would end eventually, one way or another, interminable as it seemed."

"And you thought I'd want to stay with Malcolm." She held his gaze with her own, trying to pin down some core of truth within its depths.

"I thought it likely."

"It was only a year ago that I realized I loved him."

His gaze remained on her own, steady and unusually open. "It was perhaps obvious to an outside observer rather sooner."

Her mouth curled. Raoul, committed to his cause, was the last to focus on personal relationships. Unless of course he thought he could gain by them. "Next you'll be saying you foresaw a happy ending."

"Is that so extraordinary? Though of course the story's still unfolding."

"I'm not the happily ever after sort." She ran her finger over a wine stain in the tablecloth. "I knew it would be hard. Seeing foreign soldiers overrun Paris. I didn't realize quite how hard it would be."

His hand slid partway across the table, then stilled. "You aren't alone, *querida*. However it may seem."

"Aren't agents always alone?"

"We aren't agents in everything we do."

She studied his face. There were new lines round his eyes and mouth since Waterloo, but the real scars of the battle showed when she looked into his eyes. "I keep hearing about more names on the proscribed list," she said. "It's difficult to take in."

"Yes." He snatched up his glass and took a long swallow of wine.

"Raoul?" She watched him closely. "That's what you've been doing, isn't it? Helping friends get out of Paris."

His gaze fastened on the vase of bloodred geraniums on the table. "Difficult as it may be to maintain integrity in the espionage business, I've always felt a certain loyalty to my people. Losing a battle—even a war—doesn't change that." He reached for his glass again. "Forgive me. It's been a difficult day."

She stared at him. She used to be quicker. She'd been too absorbed by her own concerns. Now she saw the strain in the set of his mouth and the worry at the back of his eyes. "Who?"

"Who what?" He took another swallow of wine.

"You're worried about someone new. Someone who's been proscribed? Or is about to be. I should have seen it."

"*Querida*—"

She sat back against the bench, hit by the reality of how much things had changed. "You don't trust me." It was as though a well-worn cloak had been lifted from her shoulders on a cold day. "Can you honestly think I would betray one of our comrades—"

"I trust you with my life," he said in a low, rough voice. "I'm trying to keep you from the intolerable burden of divided loyalties, my darling idiot."

"It's a bit late for that. You let me marry Malcolm. Not that I'm sorry you did."

He kept his gaze on her face. "And I'm trying to avoid doing more damage to your marriage."

"Since when have you been so driven by personal concerns?"

"Perhaps since personal concerns became all that are left to us. Or perhaps you had a somewhat exaggerated view of my ruthlessness."

"You've quite neatly managed to change the subject." She leaned forwards. "I won't let you wrap me in cotton wool any more than I'll let Malcolm do so." That had become doubly important to her since she had left the work that had been the focus of her life for so long. "Who are you worried about now?"

Raoul released his breath in a harsh sigh. "Manon Caret."

Suzanne drew a sharp breath. "But she's—"

"No longer untouchable. She may still reign over Paris from the Comédie-Française, but that won't hold much weight with Fouché."

Suzanne swallowed. "Fouché knows Manon was a Bonapartist agent?"

"More to the point, others do and have denounced her. He'll look soft if he doesn't move against her. With the Ultra Royalists claiming he's too moderate—God help us—he can't afford any hint of softness. And I suspect he's worried about what she knows."

Suzanne shook her head at the idea of Manon Caret, the celebrated actress who had kept Raoul apprised of the doings of Royalists for years, facing arrest. "She's on the proscribed list?"

"No, and I doubt she ever will be. Too many embarrassing questions. I doubt there'll even be a trial. But Fouché's planning to take her into custody. She'll quietly disappear, probably never to be seen again."

Suzanne nodded. Spies were rarely dealt with through official channels. "When?"

"According to my sources we have a week at most."

Suzanne stared at the candlelight flickering in the depths of her wineglass. They had drunk Bordeaux the night she first met Manon Caret. Suzanne had been sixteen, raw from the dubious results of her first mission. Raoul had taken her along when he went to meet with Manon at the theatre late one evening. They'd watched the last act of *The Marriage of Figaro,* joined the throng of Manon's admirers after the performance, then lingered on in her dressing room. Suzanne still recalled Manon going behind a gilt-edged dressing screen and emerging in a froth of sapphire silk and Valençiennes lace, despite the frivolous garment somehow transformed from charming, imperious actress to hardheaded agent. Hardheaded agent who had been remarkably kind to a sixteen-year-old girl still feeling her way in the espionage business, far more uncertain than she would admit to anyone, even herself.

She had drunk in the talk of the seasoned spies that night, as they sat round a branch of candles and a bottle of wine, surrounded by costumes and feathered masks and the smell of powder and greasepaint. She had met Manon a handful of times in the next two years, though Suzanne's work had been on the Peninsula. And then, in 1811, Suzanne had been called upon to assist Hortense Bonaparte, the Empress Josephine's daughter and Napoleon's brother's wife, who found herself with child by her lover. Suzanne had thought they were safe when Hortense delivered the baby safely in Switzerland and gave it into the care of her lover's mother. But returned to Paris, Suzanne had learned that evidence about the child had fallen into the hands of agents in the ministry of police, still loyal to Fouché, though he was out of power at the time. Fouché had long been an enemy of Josephine and despite—or because of—the fact that Napoleon had divorced her and Fouché himself had been forced from the ministry of police, Fouché wouldn't have hesitated to use the information about the child against Hortense or her mother. Suzanne had stolen the papers from the ministry of police before the agents could send them to Fouché. But she had had difficulty slipping out of the ministry. With a knife wound in her side and one of the agents on her trail, she had sought refuge at the Comédie-Française with Manon. If she'd been caught with the stolen papers in her possession, she'd have faced prison and very likely execution as a spy, no matter that she was working for the French. Manon had dressed her wound between scenes, bundled her into a costume, and hidden her in plain sight onstage as one of Phèdre's ladies-in-waiting. All at considerable risk to herself.

Suzanne snatched up her glass and took a sip of wine. "Manon probably saved my life. I've never forgot it."

"Nor have I." Raoul's mouth turned grim.

One would almost think he blamed himself for her predicament that night, save that that was so very unlike Raoul. Suzanne pushed aside the thought. "What are you planning?"

"Suzanne—"

"You must have a plan."

He hesitated a moment. "I've made contact with the Kestrel."

"The who? One of your former agents?" It wasn't like Raoul to go in for fanciful code names.

He shook his head. "Not one of mine. Or anyone's. He works for himself. For some years he wreaked havoc by rescuing Royalists from our prisons or from certain arrest."

"And now he's rescuing Bonapartists?"

"He claims to deplore wanton killing."

"And you believe him?"

"I don't have many other options. He was behind the rescue of Combre and Lefèvre's escape."

She leaned forwards. "I can help you."

"No." His voice cut across the table with quiet force.

"Since when have you been one to refuse aid? I assure you, I haven't let myself grow rusty."

Raoul's gaze darkened. "For God's sake, Suzanne. You have a husband, a son, a life. To be protected, for all the reasons you so cogently explained when you told me you were stopping your work."

"This is different. Stopping my work doesn't mean turning my back on my comrades."

"The risk is still there."

She gave a laugh, rough in her throat. "We live with risk."

"You don't have to anymore."

She stared at him across the geraniums. "This isn't like you."

"Perhaps Waterloo changed me. Or perhaps I've always been less Machiavellian than you were inclined to believe."

She pulled her wineglass closer. She'd loved Raoul, but she'd always known she couldn't trust herself to him. Had her judgment of him been a form of defense, a way of protecting herself from disappointment? "I need to help. I need to do this."

"*Querida*—" His gaze turned soft, in that way that always disconcerted her. "You don't owe anyone anything. Least of all me. And Manon would tell you she knew the risks."

Suzanne drew a harsh breath. For a moment, the table and the wineglass, the bottle and the vase of geraniums swam before her eyes. She saw Manon's daughters, asleep on the sofa in the room that adjoined her dressing room. Then she saw Colin, eating a boiled egg with concentration when she had breakfast with him before she left the Rue du Faubourg Saint-Honoré this morning. "I have to help, Raoul. Or I'll go mad."

"Why—"

"Because I'm safe. Or safer than most of us. Because I live in luxury, with the man I love and my child. Because I dine and dance with the victors and even count some of them as friends. Because for hours together I forget who I am and what I fought for. I forget that we lost."

"All the more reason—"

"I wanted to stop betraying my husband. I didn't want to lose myself."

"You'd never—"

"You told me when you first recruited me that it was my decision, my choice what risks to run." She saw them in the cramped, gaudy room in the brothel in Léon where he'd found her, surrounded by gilt and crimson draperies. "You always let me make up my own mind." She swallowed, holding his gaze with her own. "It was one of the reasons I loved you."

He returned her gaze for a long moment, his own steady and unreadable, then sat against the bench. "The Kestrel has a plan to get Manon out of Paris. Getting her out of France will be more difficult."

Suzanne released her breath. "You'll need travel documents. If I get you Castlereagh's seal can you forge the rest?"

"*Querida—*"

"It's far less dangerous than half the things I did in Lisbon or Vienna. Castlereagh's fond of me. I help smooth the waters with Malcolm."

He took a drink of wine, as though still deciding. Then he gave a crisp nod, transformed back into the enigmatic spymaster. "I'll be at the ball at the British embassy tonight."

She nodded. "If you bring me the papers, I can add the seal, then return them to you. It will be simple—"

A faint smile crossed his face. "Don't say it, *querida*. It's like wishing an actor good luck."

"Malcolm." Wellington looked up from the papers strewn across his desk. "I knew you'd have information to report before the day was out."

Malcolm advanced into the room. "I went to see Rivère's rooms and spoke with his valet. From the style in which Rivère lived and the testimony of his valet, I suspect Rivère was blackmailing people well before his threats about the Laclos affair."

"Not entirely surprising." Wellington leaned back in his chair. "Do you know whom he was blackmailing?"

Malcolm stopped a few feet from the desk, his gaze fixed on the duke's sharp-boned face. "We heard about one person he quarreled with two nights before he died. A gentleman who called on Rivère and told Rivère he 'wouldn't get away with it.' Rivère countered that the other man wasn't 'in a position to make threats.' "

Wellington had gone white about the mouth, but he said nothing.

Malcolm kept his gaze steady on the duke. "What did you and Rivère quarrel about, sir?"

"It's immaterial."

"You admit you called on Rivère?"

Wellington pushed his chair back, scraping the legs over the carpet. "I'd be a damned fool to deny it, wouldn't I?"

"Rivère tried to blackmail you."

Wellington pushed himself to his feet. "What Rivère and I discussed is none of your affair."

"We're in the midst of a murder investigation, sir."

"And my quarrel with Rivère has nothing to do with it." Wellington strode to the windows. "My word on it."

"Sir—You can't know that."

Wellington spun round to face Malcolm, the light at his back. "Are you saying you think I'm behind Rivère's death, Malcolm?"

"I'm saying you can't know how pieces of evidence may be connected. Withhold any one piece of information and you're concealing part of the puzzle."

"This isn't part of the puzzle. I'm saving you from wasting time on it." Wellington strode back to the desk and slammed his hand down on it, sending papers fluttering to the floor. "If my word isn't enough, my authority will have to suffice."

CHAPTER 5

Suzanne felt a smile break across her face at the sight of her husband approaching down the street, the angular set of his shoulders, the quick, intent gait unmistakable. When her life seemed the most complicated, the sight of him could always steady her. For all the elusive texture of their marriage, the shape and substance of what was between them was enough to sustain her through her worst moments. She might not believe in happily ever after, as she had told Raoul, but she knew enough to grab on to what she had in the moment.

Malcolm's brows were drawn, but he looked up and met her gaze and grinned. "You look as though you've had a successful morning."

"So do you."

His grin changed to a grimace. "I'd say productive rather than successful." He held out his arm. "You first."

She curled her fingers round his elbow, absurdly reassured by the warmth of his flesh beneath the threadnet of her glove and the superfine of his coat. "Wilhelmine told me Antoine Rivère was having an affair with Gabrielle Caruthers. Lady Caruthers just confirmed it."

Malcolm swung his head round to look down at her. "Good

God. Not that anyone's infidelity is so surprising, especially after Vienna. But I wouldn't have thought Rivère—"

"He evidently had unexpected depths. Or hidden talents. What was your sense of the Carutherses' marriage?"

"They always seemed happy enough. Rupert's not overly demonstrative, but then he's a British gentleman to the core."

Suzanne tightened her fingers round her husband's arm and grinned, though Gabrielle's description of her husband's remoteness, so like Malcolm in so many ways, lingered in her memory. "Yes, I know a bit about that. It can be deceptive."

The smile he gave her was one of his rare ones that were as intimate as a kiss. "I've never heard any suggestion that Rupert had a mistress. But then I never heard a suggestion that Gabrielle had a lover, either."

"It sounds as though in Gabrielle's case she found it difficult to get beneath her husband's gentlemanly veneer."

A shadow crossed Malcolm's gaze. "Some men don't share easily."

"Or perhaps Lord Caruthers's feelings weren't engaged. Gabrielle says she loved him when they married, but she thinks he proposed to her out of pity." As soon as the words were out she regretted the choice of them. "An unequal marriage can be difficult."

She saw the flinch in his eyes, but they remained steady on her face. "There are all sorts of inequality."

Sometimes once an uncomfortable issue was raised it was best to confront it head-on. "There's the emotional inequality and then Gabrielle feels indebted to Lord Caruthers. He came to her rescue when she was a penniless social outcast. She feels she owes him everything. That can be a difficult debt to carry." Suzanne tightened her fingers round her husband's arm. "Unless of course one's saved one's husband's life on numerous occasions. That has a way of balancing the scales."

A smile lightened Malcolm's eyes. "I'd say it could tip them clean in the opposite direction."

"Unless the husband has done his own share of lifesaving."

He tucked her arm tighter against his own. "I'm sure the husband would have the sense to realize he'd got by far the better end of the bargain."

Suzanne turned her head so her cheek brushed against his shoulder, tears prickling behind her eyelids. "Gabrielle also said Lord Caruthers and her cousin Bertrand Laclos were friends."

Malcolm nodded. "And Harry says Rupert Caruthers was Laclos's contact in Spain." His frown deepened, and she knew he was once again replaying the events of the Laclos affair.

"Do you suppose Rivère got his information about Bertrand Laclos from Gabrielle?" she asked.

"That would mean Gabrielle Caruthers knew her cousin had been framed. In which case one would think she'd have gone to the authorities."

"She might not have thought she'd be believed. She clearly felt like an outsider in England, and her family suffered a great deal when Laclos left, just because people thought he'd gone to fight for Bonaparte. Lord Caruthers must have known the truth. At least the truth that Laclos had supposedly been working for the British."

"And then as Laclos's contact, he was probably told Laclos had been a double," Malcolm said. "I need to talk to Rupert."

"There's more, darling. I asked Gabrielle if Rivère had enemies. She said he found it useful to keep information." Suzanne hesitated a moment. "And she thought he had information on Wellington."

"He did." Malcolm grimaced. "Though damned if I know what it was. He apparently quarreled with Wellington two nights before he died." He recounted his and Harry Davenport's visit to Rivère's rooms and their conversation with Rivère's valet and then the scene he had just had with Wellington himself.

"You think Rivère was threatening Wellington with more than the Laclos affair?"

"I do. Rivère thought the Laclos affair was something new when he brought it up last night. This was something that affected Wellington personally. If it was the Laclos affair, there'd have been no reason for him to refuse to discuss it with me."

Suzanne looked up at her husband, seeing Wellington ruffling Colin's hair in the British embassy drawing room two nights before. "Darling, you don't seriously think that Wellington—"

His mouth tightened. "I've learned not to make assumptions about anyone. Even those closest to me."

She should know that better than anyone. It wasn't like her to offer blind trust. She was slipping shockingly.

Malcolm pulled his watch from his pocket. "Nearly three. Still plenty of time until we have to get ready for the embassy ball tonight."

"I need to collect Blanca and Colin. We're meeting Cordelia and Livia in the Jardin des Tuileries. Unless—"

"No, don't disappoint Colin. We do enough of that as it is. I need to see Rupert Caruthers. And then what I need to do next is best done alone."

Suzanne looked at him in inquiry.

His gaze shifted over the street ahead. "I've asked Annina to meet me. If anyone will know if Tania really did have a child, it's her former maid."

"Malcolm." Rupert Caruthers got to his feet and crossed the sitting room at Allied army Headquarters with one of his easy smiles, hand extended. He looked much as he always had, tawny hair, fine-boned features, the easy self-assurance of one who had never doubted his position in the world. "It's good to see you. Here we are in Paris with a lot of old friends, and it seems we spend so much time at state functions we never get to talk."

Malcolm shook his university friend's hand. "I understand you're working with your father."

Rupert grimaced. "Father has permission from Fouché to interrogate some of the Bonapartists who've been proscribed. Those we think might have information of value to England. I've been seconded to him. And to think I joined the army to get away from my father. It would be enough to make me long for battle if I didn't remember the hell Waterloo was."

"You seem quite recovered from your wounds."

"Oh yes. Just a scratch really. I didn't suffer nearly as much at Waterloo as some did. Damnable to have lost so many friends."

For a moment, Malcolm felt the weight of Alexander Gordon in his arms and saw the life bleed from Colonel Canning's eyes. "Quite."

"Though Fitzroy's making remarkable progress learning to write with his left hand. You carried him from the field, didn't you?"

Malcolm nodded. "I was there when he was hit." Lord Fitzroy Somerset, Wellington's military secretary, had lost his right arm at Waterloo. But at least he would recover, unlike many of their friends.

"And Davenport's getting about splendidly. I hear the two of you got quite friendly."

"We worked together in Brussels. And yes, he became a good friend."

"Damned edge to his tongue, but a good man. And more agreeable lately, now he and Lady Cordelia have reconciled. Suzanne's well?"

"Being Suzanne, she came through Waterloo with her practicality only enhanced. Gabrielle?"

"Enjoying being in Paris," Caruthers said with an affectionate smile. If he had the least suspicion his wife had been another man's mistress, he was an excellent actor. "She hasn't seen it since her family fled when she was four years old. She has few memories, but so much is familiar from her aunt and uncle's stories. Odd if you think about it, both of us marrying Frenchwomen. How does Suzanne find being back in France?"

His wife, Malcolm realized, had made no comment on being back in France one way or another. Though from the look he caught in her eyes at unguarded moments, he suspected it stirred some uncomfortable memories. Even now there were things Suzanne didn't discuss with him. "Suzette left France when she was a baby. She has no family left to seek out. But I suppose it can't help but serve as a reminder of the life she lost."

"Quite." Rupert nodded, gaze darkened by memories of the past. Then he brightened. "Young Colin must be getting on for two now."

"He turned two on June fourteenth, as it happens. With Brussels on the brink of war. But I think he managed to enjoy his birth-day. Children are blessedly resilient."

"So they are. And I should have remembered he's two. Stephen was four months old when you wrote to me about Colin's birth."

"How is Stephen?"

"Shooting up. Chattering away. It's nice to have one thing in one's life to view with wholehearted pride."

"Just so," Malcolm said. It was similar to his view of his own son, but he was surprised to hear such words from Rupert. Rupert had always seemed comfortable with his position in the world and confident of the rightness of his work as a soldier for king and country.

Rupert scanned Malcolm's face. "But I don't suppose you came here merely to talk about friends."

"No, unfortunately."

Rupert waved him to the leather-covered sofa by the window. "Wellington has you looking into something?"

"Yes. And it becomes more complicated. Tell me what you re-member about Bertrand Laclos."

Rupert went still. His gaze darted over Malcolm's face. "What have you learned?"

"I'm not quite sure yet. I'd rather hear what you have to say first. Unbiased."

Rupert stared at the heavy gold signet ring on his left hand for a moment. "Bertrand was my friend for as long as I can remember. One of my earliest memories is visiting the Lacloses in France be-fore they emigrated. Before the Terror. My father helped them es-cape to England, and they stayed with us for some months." He grinned. "One of the happiest times of my life. I'm three years older than my eldest sister. Suddenly it was as though I had two brothers in Bertrand and Étienne. And my father was distracted and less exacting than usually." He ran a hand over his hair. "Later Bertrand and I went off to Eton together. You know what value a friend can have when one's first packed off to boarding school."

Malcolm recalled the labyrinth that had been Harrow, how very tall and mocking and self-assured the older boys had seemed, his relief when he met David Mallinson, who was his best friend to this day. "Quite."

"The Lacloses used to come down to Dewhurst Hall frequently and sometimes just Bertrand would come home with me for holidays. The Lacloses didn't have their own country place, of course. They got out of France with almost nothing, like so many others. It was hard for them. You remember the way people used to talk about émigrés. The sympathy at first, but then being kind hosts began to pall, and they were treated like guests who'd outstayed their welcome."

Malcolm nodded. He had vivid memories of some unpleasant remarks he'd overheard growing up. "As I recall you were friends with Bertrand's brother Étienne as well?"

"Yes, though he was older and always seemed twice as self-confident. And Gaby. Gaby lived with the Lacloses, since they were the ones who got her out of France. Her parents both died in the Terror, and no one knew what had become of her brother for a long time."

"He was smuggled out of France later, wasn't he?" Malcolm said. "I remember it made quite a stir."

Rupert nodded. "He'd been saved when his and Gaby's parents were killed, and hidden away. If it was difficult for Bertrand and Étienne, you can imagine what it was like for Gui, coming to England at fifteen after living on a farm in Provence. I've always thought that's why he went a bit wild."

Malcolm had images of Gabrielle Caruthers's brother drunk at an Oxford tavern, being sick into a potted palm at a London ball, hunched over the green baize of a card table. "So Gui didn't become as good a friend as Bertrand and Étienne?"

"Gui thought Bertrand and Étienne and me sadly staid. But Bertrand and Étienne tried to keep an eye on him." Rupert's eyes darkened. "It was easier when Étienne was still alive. Both Bertrand and Gui looked up to him."

"A sad business. I remember how distressed Wellington was when he spoke about what happened to Étienne."

Rupert shot him a look. "If I know Wellington, 'distressed' isn't quite the word. I imagine he had some pithy comments about incompetence."

"You know Hookey."

Rupert's mouth twisted. "Étienne became my father's secretary when he came down from Oxford. Father was behind orchestrating the failed plot against Bonaparte. I've often thought—" He shook his head. "Not the first time I've disagreed with my father's actions."

"Bertrand must have taken his brother's death hard. As I remember they were close."

Rupert nodded, brows drawn together. "Étienne had all the burden of being head of the family. After he died Bertrand took it on."

"I remember how David changed when his father inherited the earldom and David realized he'd be Earl Carfax someday."

"I think that was when it started. My father offered Bertrand Étienne's old position, but Bertrand wanted something more." Rupert pushed himself to his feet and crossed to a drinks trolley by the window. "We were just down from Oxford, trying to decide what to do with ourselves. I'd made up my mind to join the army. Father said it was no place for an eldest son, but I—"

"Was determined to do something different from your father?"

Rupert shot him a smile. "Quite." His gaze hardened. He turned back to the trolley and poured out two glasses of brandy. The heavy cut glass of the decanter sparkled in the light from the windows. "I assumed Bertrand would join me in the army. We'd talked about it. Not having yet served in the army, I thought it would be a grand adventure. A sort of continuation of cricket matches and playing knights at Dewhurst Hall. But then Bertrand said we had to talk." Rupert set down the decanter. The rattle of the crystal echoed across the room. "That was when he told me he was going to return to France as a British agent."

"You must have been surprised."

"To own the truth, at first I had a hard time taking it seriously. It sounded like something out of a novel." Rupert crossed back to the sofa and gave Malcolm one of the glasses of brandy. "Bertrand got quite sharp with me. He said this was serious, we were grown-up now, and he knew what he owed to his family and his country. He didn't say so in so many words, but I assumed it was because he felt he owed something to Étienne's memory. When I said so, Bertrand said this was bigger than any one person. But he didn't deny Étienne's death was part of it. He explained he'd already spoken with Lord Carfax—" Rupert shot a look at Malcolm.

"No, Carfax didn't say anything about it to me," Malcolm said. "But it sounds just like one of his plans." Lord Carfax, David's father, was the chief of British intelligence.

"Then Bertrand told me he wanted me to be his contact." Rupert took a sip of brandy. "I confess I was flattered. I hadn't thought of myself doing anything so daring. Or so serious." He twisted the glass in his hand. "In an odd way, I think that's the moment I grew up. Though I did protest that perhaps someone with more experience would be better. But Bertrand said he needed someone he trusted absolutely. And also that if we ever were caught communicating, people would only think our friendship had survived his return to France."

"That was when you moved into intelligence?"

Rupert nodded. "Bertrand and I met with Carfax. We established codes and systems of communication. Then he left." Rupert took a drink of brandy. "I got so caught up in the preparations, I somehow wasn't prepared for him to leave."

"And you had to play the part of the betrayed friend."

"Yes. It seems I'm better at playacting than I credited, for all I wasn't in theatricals as you were."

"Did you ever suspect—"

"No." The single word had the force of a blow. "Bertrand sent me coded information. Once he was sent to the Peninsula and I was established there as well we met occasionally. He'd give me information. I'd pass it along through the appropriate channels. It always seemed sound. Bertrand always seemed committed."

"When did you first realize?"

"After he was killed. Stewart told me." Rupert's fingers curled round his glass. "He didn't come right out and say we were behind Bertrand's death, but the implication was obvious."

"The Bonaparte government could restore his family's estates to him. It would have been a powerful motive."

"Not to Bertrand." Rupert shook his head. "He was a Royalist to the core. If you'd heard him talk about the loss of his family—"

"Perhaps he saw the Bonaparte government as different from the Revolutionaries."

Rupert shook his head again. "He had nothing but contempt for Bonaparte. I knew him, Malcolm. From boyhood. He couldn't have been pretending all that time."

Malcolm's mind shot back to Vienna. "Even one's friends can surprise one."

"This was less than a year after Étienne died. To think that Bertrand turned round and went to work for the same people behind his brother's death—"

"Perhaps Étienne's death convinced Bertrand of the futility of trying to bring down the Bonaparte régime. Perhaps he decided joining them was the only way to recover the family estates."

"You can't expect me to believe my friend was so lost to honor."

"Honor has a way of meaning different things to different people."

Rupert scowled into his brandy. "I was on leave in Lisbon when it happened. I keep thinking if I'd been there—"

"You doubted the information?" Malcolm asked.

Rupert's gaze shot to his face. "All my instincts as a friend told me it couldn't be true. But I had no evidence—Why are you asking me all this, Malcolm?"

Malcolm drew a breath and took a swallow of his own brandy. It burned his throat. Or perhaps that was the bite of regret. "Some new information's come to light—"

Rupert stared at him. A mixture of hope, rage, and grief shot across his face. "Bertrand was innocent."

Malcolm returned his friend's gaze without flinching. "We have reason to reconsider whether the information against him may have been faulty."

Rupert pushed himself to his feet. "I knew it. If only—" He rounded on Malcolm. "How the hell could they have made such a mistake?"

"It was more than a mistake." Malcolm got to his feet. "Rupert, you may not know this, but I was the one who intercepted the incriminating information about Bertrand."

For a moment, Malcolm thought Rupert meant to strike him. "And you passed it along to Stewart."

"I had no choice. It appeared to reveal a dangerous betrayal."

Rupert drew a shuddering breath. "It was your duty. I assume you had reason to believe it."

"Every reason. It looked incontrovertibly damning. I'd have questioned it myself otherwise."

Rupert's brows drew together. "So if you're now questioning it—"

"If Bertrand was innocent, someone went to great lengths to set him up."

Rupert swallowed, stalked back to the drinks trolley, and refilled his brandy glass. "Why?"

"That's what I'm endeavoring to discover. Who were Bertrand's enemies?"

Rupert tossed down a swallow of brandy. "No one that I knew of. He was a likable fellow."

"Who stood to lay claim to the title?"

"Gui, I suppose. His cousin. But—Good God, Malcolm, he's my wife's brother."

"Which wouldn't preclude him from turning on your friend."

Rupert dug his fingers into his hair. "This is mad—"

"When did Gui come to England?"

"In '02. He was fifteen. My father learned he might be alive and tracked him down in Provence. Father went to France quite frequently in those days and worked with the Royalists. He smuggled Gui out. The Lacloses took him in, as they had Gaby."

"Were he and Bertrand friendly?"

"They had the usual rivalry between all-but brothers, but yes, more or less. As I said, Gui was always a bit more . . . wild . . . than Bertrand."

"Gambling?"

"And women. The usual thing."

"What about Bertrand?"

"I told you, he and Gui—"

"What about Bertrand and women? Was there anyone in particular?"

Rupert frowned. "Honestly, Malcolm, a gentleman doesn't discuss—"

"I'm trying to determine who may have had a motive to want to get rid of your friend."

Rupert dug his fingers into his hair again. "He always had a cluster of girls round him. For a time I thought he might make an offer for Emily Carrington, but then he went off to France, and it came to nothing. We were young. I didn't marry Gaby until years later."

"And in Spain? Was there anyone he talked about?"

"We weren't meeting to gossip."

"You were friends. You must have talked."

Rupert paced across the room. "There was a girl named Inez, I think. The daughter of a local family."

"So it's possible they disapproved."

"Perhaps. But you can't think—"

"If Laclos was innocent, someone framed him."

Rupert met Malcolm's gaze, his own gone uncharacteristically hard. "Someone on our side would have been more likely to have the resources, wouldn't they?"

Malcolm returned his friend's gaze. "So they would. Did Bertrand have enemies among our own people?"

Rupert frowned, as though seeing into the past. "Bertrand was well liked. But he was French. That made him an outsider. Which was enough for other fellows not to get so drunk with him they'd confide their most intimate secrets. To think twice before they introduced him to their sisters. But to set him up for a traitor—" He shook his head. "It doesn't make any sense."

"Does it make any more sense that Bertrand actually was a traitor?"

Rupert's gaze hardened. "No. It doesn't. Find who did this, Malcolm."

CHAPTER 6

Suzanne fixed her gaze on Colin, her two-year-old son, leaning over the edge of the fountain in the Jardin des Tuileries to throw a piece of bread to the swans. Her companion, Blanca, kneeling beside him, had a light hand on his shoulder. Blanca's other arm was wrapped round four-year-old Livia Davenport, who was stretching her arms out over the water, on tiptoes on her black-kid-slippered feet.

"You'd never guess they were in a house full of wounded soldiers two months ago," Cordelia Davenport said. "Children are wonderfully resilient."

For a moment Suzanne saw the black-and-white marble tiles of their house in the Rue Ducale in Brussels, covered with wounded men on pallets, Cordelia bending over her injured husband, Malcolm dripping blood onto the floor. "I find it hard to remember myself. And yet in many ways the conflict isn't over."

The gravel crunched as a pair of British soldiers strolled by. They tipped their hats to the ladies. Suzanne returned the nod, though she flinched inwardly as she always did when she saw the foreign occupying troops on French soil.

Cordelia's gaze lingered on Suzanne. For a disconcerting moment Suzanne was afraid her friend had seen through her. But instead, Cordelia said, "You and Malcolm had something to do with the Rivère business last night, didn't you?"

Suzanne smiled. "Our friends know us too well."

"I merely have to look for the most dangerous events to know where to find you. Another investigation?"

"Just a few questions for now. Did you know a Bertrand Laclos in England?"

"Of course. All the girls were mad for him. He had dark hair and broody eyes and that wonderful accent and all the romance of an émigré. He was bookish and not inclined to flirtation, but that only added to the romance. And he had an unexpected sense of humor." Cordelia's brows drew together beneath the satin straw of her hat. "It was quite a shock when he ran off to France to fight for Bonaparte. Especially then. The world seems more complex now."

Suzanne's gaze fixed on Colin, now tossing bread to the swans while Blanca gripped his waist. Her English son. Last summer in England, he'd wanted one of the white Royalist cockades that the vendors in Hyde Park were selling.

"Is Bertrand Laclos mixed up in this?" Cordelia asked.

"Possibly. We're not sure how. I've been trying to find people who knew him more recently. Apparently he was friendly with Edmond Talleyrand after he came to France, but Doro claims to scarcely remember him. And she's not precisely in a position to talk to Edmond about it."

"How odd," Cordelia said. "Bertrand Laclos and Edmond were the last sort of men I'd have thought would become friends. And Edmond never mentioned Bertrand to me."

Suzanne cast a sharp glance at her friend.

Cordelia gave a wry smile. "Edmond Talleyrand and I were—Rather close for a time. In Paris a year ago. After Bonaparte was exiled the first time." Cordelia's gaze focused on her daughter as Livia set a toy boat to sail on the smooth water of the fountain. "Edmond was—Amusing in a certain crude way." She turned her gaze to Suzanne. As usual Cordy didn't flinch from an uncomfortable truth. "I'm sorry. I know how close you are to Dorothée."

"Doro would be the first to say her marriage was over long before you met Edmond. Or that it never really began. I'm only surprised—"

"That I sank so low?" Cordelia's mouth curved, this time with more bitterness. "I wasn't very happy with myself a year ago. You could say I was wallowing. Not pretty."

"Understandable," Suzanne said, images from her own past clustering in her mind.

Two little girls in white frocks ran by rolling hoops along the gravel. Cordelia watched them vanish down a tree-lined walkway, their nurse trailing behind. A stir of wind brought the scent of the orange trees planted in wooden crates about the garden. A scent almost too intense in its sweetness. "There are hours at a time when I forget the past," Cordelia said. "Even whole days occasionally. But it never really goes away. It's folly to think it can."

Livia's boat had got stuck against the stone edge of the fountain. Blanca, Colin at her hip, Livia by the hand, was walking round the fountain to retrieve it. Livia looked over her shoulder to wave at her mother. Cordelia waved back.

"One has to learn to live with it," Suzanne said.

"Johnny came to see me yesterday," Cordelia said, watching her daughter. John Ashton had been married to Cordelia's sister Julia, who had been killed just before Waterloo. "He paced about the salon and kept adding milk to his tea. At last he blurted out that he wants to ask Violet to marry him, though they can't announce anything formally yet. He wanted to know if I thought it would be an insult to Julia's memory."

The investigation into Julia Ashton's death had revealed a great deal about Julia and her relationship with her husband. Suzanne studied Cordelia. "What did you say?"

"That if we'd learned nothing else in Brussels it was that it's folly not to seize happiness when we can."

Blanca had retrieved the boat. Livia held it aloft, then with great concentration set it in the water. Colin clamored to be put down. Livia held out the boat, and they set it to sail across the basin of the fountain together.

"No sense in hiding," Cordelia said in a bright voice. "Edmond and I didn't part on bad terms. Do you want me to talk to him?"

"Cordy—," Suzanne said, her mouth dry.

"I might as well put my past to use." Cordelia gave a wry smile. "The truth is I'd like to be of use." She watched Livia and Colin run round the fountain to catch the boat as it bobbed against the opposite side. "I know how Harry feels stuck behind a desk. Those days in Brussels when we were nursing the wounded—I've never been through anything so horrible. And yet there was a wonderful sort of—'exhilaration' I suppose is the best word—in doing something of such substance. It seems sadly trivial to be back to paying calls and sipping champagne and changing our dresses five times a day."

"I feel much the same," Suzanne said, recalling how empty she'd felt when she told Raoul she was stopping the work that had sustained her for more than five years. "It's odd after life-and-death stakes that suddenly a seating arrangement is a matter of great moment."

"You? You've never just paid calls and ordered champagne."

No, but now instead of being a spy on her own she was a spy's wife. A distinction she could not explain to Cordelia. "Cordy—" She looked at Cordelia—the experience in the curve of her mouth, the worldly wisdom in the blue eyes beneath her blackened lashes—and was swept by an unexpected wave of protection for her strong-minded friend. "The work Malcolm does. The work Malcolm and I do. Probing people's pasts, uncovering secrets. It's often not very pretty." How odd. In the old days she'd have made use of an asset with no qualms and quibbles about anyone's feelings.

"I know." Cordelia returned her gaze, her eyes steady with understanding. "I saw enough of that in the investigation into my sister's death. But I'm not the sort to need to be wrapped in cotton wool."

"And Harry?"

Cordelia gave her a bright smile that at once defied the past and acknowledged its risks. "Harry and I can live with the past. Or we're going to have to learn to do so."

*   *   *

Annina Barbera looked up from her café au lait. "Monsieur Rannoch."

"Annina." Malcolm dropped into a chair across from her. "Don't you think you might begin to call me Malcolm?"

Her mouth curled. "Only a man born to your fortune and position can pretend social distinctions don't matter."

"Well, I could begin to call you Mademoiselle Barbera, but I think I'd have a difficult time remembering. I've got in the habit of calling you Annina. Humor me."

"You can't make inequality go away with a word."

"No, but I can level the ground between us."

"Very well, Malcolm. At least in private." Annina smiled. Beneath a stylish chip straw bonnet her delicate face was brighter than it had been in Vienna last autumn.

"You look well," Malcolm said.

Annina smiled. "The Duchess of Sagan is a kind mistress. I've been fortunate. I have you to thank."

"You have your own quick wits and hard work to thank." Malcolm signaled to a waiter to bring him coffee. "I'm glad things are working out."

Annina's gaze flickered over his face. She might look less haggard than she had just after Tatiana Kirsanova's death, but her eyes were as sharp as ever. "What's happened?"

"Do you think I'd only come to see you if something had happened?"

"No. But in my years with Princess Tatiana, I learned to read your face rather well."

"Annina—" Malcolm broke off as the waiter set a cup of coffee in front of him. He curled his fingers round the warm porcelain and considered and abandoned a dozen approaches. "Did Tatiana have a child?"

Annina stared at him, blue eyes dark as agate in a face drained of color. "Dear God. What do you know?"

Fear, horror, and a strange sort of hope settled within him. "Nothing conclusive."

Annina cast a quick glance round the café. Three Prussian soldiers had just come through the door. The crowd of Parisians eyed them askance. No one was paying attention to the corner where Malcolm and Annina were seated. Annina leaned forwards, voice lowered. "What do you know that's not conclusive?"

"Just a suggestion that Tania may have had a child."

Annina drew a long breath. "From the time she engaged my services, I was never away from her for more than a fortnight. I helped her in and out of gowns, I laced her corsets. I'd have known if she was with child. She never was."

"But?" Malcolm asked, gaze trained on Annina's face. Behind him, he heard the Prussians asking for beer in loud, badly accented French.

Annina took a careful sip of café au lait. "I once found her packing a parcel. She was kneeling beside the box, with the oddest look on her face. As though her thoughts were miles away. She was holding a bit of fluff and blue ribbon in her hand. At first I thought it was a pincushion. Then I realized it was a stuffed dog. I walked closer—she didn't seem to realize I was in the room—and saw that the box was filled with toys. Stuffed animals, carved wooden horses, blocks, picture books. I must have gasped because the princess looked up suddenly. She slammed the lid on the box and sprang to her feet. Her eyes—" Annina shook her head. "She was in a temper, but it was more than that. She was frightened."

"What did she say?"

"That I must never mention what I'd seen. She actually made me swear, which would have been comical, given that neither of us held much sacred to swear by, save that she was so serious. I asked if she wanted me to help, but she said no, she'd take care of it."

"Did she ever mention it again?"

Annina nodded, fingers curled round her cup, brows drawn together. "That night when I was helping her dress for dinner. She laughed—a bit too brittle a laugh, if you see what I mean. And she said she was sorry she'd overreacted earlier, that it was just that she'd been packing the parcel for a friend, but that it would be awkward for the friend if there was talk about her sending gifts to a child. Then she laughed again, a laugh like broken crystal, and said, 'Children's nonsense, what a nuisance.' Later that night—"

"What?" Malcolm asked.

"When I went in to help her undress. Her eye blacking was smeared and her eyes were a shade too bright. I'd swear she'd been crying. And you know the princess. She almost never cried."

"I think the only time I saw her do so was when I told her our mother had died." For a moment Malcolm could see Tatiana, turned away from him to hide her grief, hands fisted against her face. He picked up his coffee and choked down a sip. It burned his throat. "When was this?"

"Four years ago. No, it must be five now. The spring of 1810. April, I think."

"Did she ever again—?"

Annina shook her head. "Perhaps I should have told you, after she died. But she made me promise. And I had no proof of anything."

Tatiana had been determined to keep the secret of her child's birth. Just as their mother had been determined to keep the secret of Tatiana's birth. A great deal of harm could come from secrets, as he had learned last autumn. Yet he could understand the need to keep them. Sometimes truth in the open air was worse.

He reached across the table and squeezed Annina's hand. "It's difficult, deciding where one's loyalties lie. One can tug against another. And with Tania loyalty was a particularly complicated thing."

Annina's face relaxed into a smile. "Thank you. For understanding."

"Thank you for protecting her."

Annina's gaze flickered over his face. "But you're going to find the child?"

"I have to."

"You never know where the princess's secrets may lead."

"Which makes it all the more imperative for me to find the child."

Annina's fingers tightened round his own. "Be careful, Malcolm. Madame wouldn't have been frightened without good cause."

* * *

Cordelia Davenport turned in the midst of fastening a bracelet as her husband appeared in the dressing room doorway. "You look remarkably cheerful."

Harry dug his shoulder into the doorjamb, his face relaxed into a grin that was uncharacteristically open. "I spent the afternoon with Malcolm Rannoch."

"You've been investigating."

"Helping out round the edges." Harry hesitated. An intelligence officer didn't share information idly, even with his wife. Malcolm, she knew, didn't tell everything to Suzanne, and Harry had far less reason to trust her.

"It's all right," Cordelia said. "I already know a bit. I spent the afternoon with Suzanne. She was asking me about Bertrand Laclos."

"Of course. You knew him in England."

"A bit." Her fingers moved over the diamond links of the bracelet. It had been a gift from Harry early in their marriage, when they scarcely knew each other. "Growing up. I didn't realize he was friendly with Edmond Talleyrand when he first came to France. Which may put me in a position to help Suzanne with her inquiries."

"Why should—" Harry's face went still. His gaze settled on her, his eyes dark and opaque. "Oh."

Behind that shuttered gaze, Cordelia saw the pain of every past betrayal. As clearly as if it were yesterday, she could see the look on his face when, a year into their marriage, he'd discovered her in the arms of her childhood sweetheart. "I'm sorry," she said.

"It's not as if I didn't know."

Her fingers tightened. The filigree clasp on her bracelet cut into her palm. "It's one thing to know in the abstract. It's another to be confronted with evidence."

Harry crossed to her side, took the clasp from her nerveless fingers, and snapped it closed. "A year ago our marriage was dead."

"Because I'd killed it."

"Oh, I think we both played a role." He lifted her hand and

pressed his lips to her knuckles. "The point is a year ago we hardly had a marriage to be faithful to."

"I was still your wife."

He retained hold of her hand. "You've never asked me about my own behavior the years we were apart."

Her gaze flew to his face. His eyes were dark and a little challenging. Unaccustomed jealousy sliced through her. She flushed. "I never thought I had a right to."

"Then don't be harder on yourself than you are on me."

"Damn it, Harry." Regret over a thousand actions that couldn't be undone tore through her. "There must be times when you hate me."

His face turned hard. His eyes had a bleak look that twisted her heart. "Not you. But I confess at times I hate myself."

"Why on earth—"

"For marrying you for the wrong reasons. When I scarcely knew you. For being so eager to possess you, I was blind to what you needed and wanted."

She saw the intense gaze of the broody, awkward young scholar who had offered her marriage. At a time when she was so desperate to escape, so sure she would never love again, that she'd jumped at it. "For God's sake, Harry—"

"You can't deny I was a fool. Perhaps it's arrogance, but I hate the thought of being a blithering idiot."

"Harry." She tightened her fingers over his own. "If you hadn't offered for me, we wouldn't be where we are now. We wouldn't have Livia. You may think you got a bad bargain, but I'll never be anything but grateful."

A smile softened his face. "How could I not be grateful when I have you?"

When he looked at her like that, happiness washed over her. Followed by the conviction that she couldn't possibly deserve it. "I'm sorry. I've still forced Edmond to your notice."

"Yes, well, I assume it was unavoidable at one point or another."

"Harry!"

"Don't be missish, sweetheart. I know your reputation." He brushed his fingers against her cheek. "Talk to Edmond Talleyrand. Learn what you can for Suzanne and Malcolm."

"You don't have to do this to prove something, Harry."

"I don't need to prove anything. You're my wife. I trust you."

Cordelia drew a breath and buried her face in his shoulder to hide the tears prickling behind her eyes. His arms tightened round her. Yet she knew this was a test, a test they had always been going to have to face at some point or another. She had just hoped it wouldn't be so soon.

CHAPTER 7

Malcolm let his hands linger on his wife's waist as the last notes of a waltz died away. He could feel the warmth of her skin through the kid of his gloves and the fragile stuff of her gown. The scent of her perfume washed over him, a riot of roses and vanilla and an elusive, aromatic scent. Her side curls were disarranged from the dance and her eyes bright with laughter.

"Darling," Suzanne said, "it's unfashionable enough that we danced together. If you ogle me on the dance floor we'll be positively beyond the pale."

"And why would that be a problem?"

"We have your career to think about."

"Ogling my wife will get in the way of my career?"

"Being thought unconventional will."

He disengaged a curl from her diamond earring and tucked it behind her ear. "Then my career was hopelessly compromised long before I met you."

"Besides, blending in is a vital technique in investigation."

"Well, there you may have a point." He loosed his hands on her waist, oddly reluctant to let her go. He wasn't quite sure what had come over him. Perhaps it was the champagne or the particular lilt of the waltz that had been playing or the way the candlelight glowed in his wife's eyes. Nonsensical.

Suzanne put up a hand and smoothed his cravat. "We have work to do, dearest."

He kept his fingertips at her waist. "How's your wound?"

"Darling. I just danced a waltz. More strenuous than anything else I'll be doing tonight. Let me go. The game's afoot."

She moved off with a rustle of silk and a last smile over her shoulder. Malcolm felt an answering smile break across his face. Suzanne at work was even more seductive than Suzanne waltzing.

He moved to the edge of the dance floor as new couples took their place for the *boulanger* that was forming.

"Rannoch," Granville Leveson-Gower called to him.

Malcolm turned to greet the former ambassador to St. Petersburg, who had offered him some sound advice when he first joined the diplomatic corps.

"Watching you with your wife I'd swear you'd turned into a romantic," Granville said.

"Surely a diplomat with your experience has learned not to believe everything you see in an embassy ballroom," Malcolm returned.

Granville's gaze slid along the edge of the dance floor to where his wife, Harriet, quietly gowned in claret-colored crêpe, her dark hair swept back in a simple knot, stood talking with her cousin Lady Caroline Lamb. "Marriage has a way of changing one."

Granville Leveson-Gower had been known for his libertine behavior in Malcolm's youth—including a long-term affair with Harriet's aunt. Yet since Granville's marriage Malcolm had heard no whisper of scandal about him, and the gaze that now rested on his wife was soft with tenderness. "Yes," Malcolm said, thinking of the myriad ways marriage had changed him and the challenges it still posed. Marriage had changed him and challenged him and forced him to confront his own inadequacies. "So it can."

Granville grinned and clapped him on the shoulder. "Glad to hear it. I think we're both more fortunate in our marriages than some." His gaze settled for a moment on Wellington, who was standing between the lovely blond Lady Frances Webster and the equally lovely Lady Shelley. "I imagine Wellington isn't in a hurry for the duchess to join him."

"She's certainly been delayed in London for whatever reason."

"Wellington waited for years to get her father's consent to the marriage, you know," Granville said. "By the time Pakenham agreed, Wellington's ardor had cooled. But he kept his word and married Kitty all the same."

"She might have been happier if he hadn't," Malcolm said. The Duchess of Wellington was a sweet woman but not suited to public life.

"Perhaps." Granville cast a glance about and lowered his voice. "What's this I hear about the Frenchman who was killed last night?"

"Devil take it, is the news all over the ballroom?"

"Just about. Though as a diplomat myself I have a bit of inside knowledge." His gaze swept the diplomats and royals filling the ballroom. "I just saw a French undersecretary and an Austrian attaché nearly come to blows over whether or not to return foreign art treasures Napoleon filled the Louvre with. Paris is a tinderbox. And the most unexpected incident could set it alight."

"Granville." Malcolm hesitated, but he knew Granville could be trusted. "Do you remember the Laclos affair?"

Granville's brows drew together, though he didn't appear as surprised as Malcolm might have expected. "Castlereagh mentioned you were looking into it. A bad business. I didn't know much. But to own the truth, I always thought Stewart acted precipitously. We could have watched Laclos, intercepted his communications. An ally deserves more consideration."

"Spoken like a diplomat, not an agent. Which is a compliment."

Granville smiled. "Bertrand Laclos was a good man. Never quite fit in, like so many émigrés. I wondered if that was why he returned to work for the French. If—"

"He really did work for the French?"

"You said it, Malcolm, not me."

Malcolm swallowed, his worst fears settling in his chest. If a temperate man like Granville could admit they might have been wrong about Laclos—He nodded at Sarah Lennox and moved on, focusing his mind on his quarry.

He found him by the doorway to the card room, moving off from a conversation with Count Nesselrode.

"Malcolm." Prince Talleyrand extended his hand. He was, as usual, faultlessly arrayed, in a frock coat that would have been quite at home in the ancien régime, a frilled shirt, a starched satin cravat, and diamond-buckled shoes. "I saw you dancing with your exquisite wife. You make a charming couple."

"I thought you had far more important things to observe in a diplomatic ballroom."

Talleyrand turned his walking stick so the diamonds on the handle flashed in the candlelight. "I'd scarcely have survived as long as I have could I not observe more than one thing at once. I'm glad you dance more than you used to."

"Even if it is with my own wife?"

Talleyrand's thin mouth curved in a smile that also lit his pale blue eyes. "On the contrary. Unfashionable, perhaps, but then you've never been one to care about the fashion. It's good to find you circulating instead of spending the evening in the library."

Malcolm had been four when he first met Talleyrand. It was both an advantage and a disadvantage in their relationship. It gave Malcolm inside knowledge of the prince, but it also gave Talleyrand inside knowledge of Malcolm, and Talleyrand was a master at using it. "I'm not quite such a recluse, sir," Malcolm said. "Though as it happens I was hoping I could have a word with you in private."

Talleyrand's shrewd gaze slid over him, but the prince merely said, "Of course. I confess I frequently find society stifling myself these days."

They moved along the edge of the dance floor, Talleyrand stopping several times to exchange greetings, and at last reached a white-and-gold antechamber, empty though the candles were lit. "To what do I owe this pleasure?" Talleyrand asked.

"Do I need an excuse to talk to you?"

"These days none of us does anything without an excuse." Talleyrand dropped into a gilded armchair. "Is it to do with Rivère's death last night?"

"What do you know about Rivère?" Malcolm asked, settling into the chair across from the prince.

Talleyrand leaned back in his own chair, stirring a faint dusting of powder from his hair. "I'd hardly be doing my job if I wasn't aware that Rivère was selling information to the British."

"You didn't tell anyone. Did you?"

"By the time I acquired the knowledge I was dealing with the British myself."

Malcolm set his hands on the arms of his chair, his gaze steady on Talleyrand's face. "Who killed him?"

"My dear boy. I'm not as omniscient as you think." Talleyrand smoothed his frilled cuff over his fingers. "I assume Rivère wanted you to get him out of France?"

"Was he about to be arrested?"

Talleyrand pressed a crease in the frill. "You'd have to ask Fouché."

"Rivère's cousin had been pressuring to have him arrested."

"Yes, I believe so." Talleyrand crossed his clubfoot over his good leg. The diamond buckle on his shoe flashed in the light from the branch of candles. "What did he threaten if you didn't help him?"

"Vague claims to wreak havoc on the British delegation. What did Rivère have to do with Bertrand Laclos?"

Talleyrand's brows drew together. His hooded eyes were suddenly more hawk-like than usual. "What did Rivère tell you?"

"Nothing specific. But his threats of havoc centered on Laclos."

Talleyrand stared at his signet ring. "Laclos was an embarrassment. We were so proud when he returned to the fold. We should have suspected he might be a British asset from the first. I should have. I pride myself on knowing how the British think."

"But in the end he wasn't."

Talleyrand frowned. "As is often the case, you're too quick for me, Malcolm."

Malcolm swallowed. Unease coiled within him. "Laclos was a

double. I intercepted the communication that betrayed his work for the French myself."

Rare surprise shot through Talleyrand's blue eyes. "My word. So his death—"

"He was deemed to know too much."

Talleyrand settled back in his chair. "Either I am a lamentable fool—which is entirely possible—or you've been deceived."

Unease gave way to sick certainty. "You didn't know Laclos was a double?"

"No. Of course I scarcely know the name of every French agent, but I like to think I would have done with someone so high profile."

Guilt tightened Malcolm's throat. "When did you learn he'd been working for the British?"

"Not until after his death. I could hardly fail to investigate with so important an asset. I had someone go through his papers. There was evidence he'd been working for the British. Given the embarrassed ripples that sent through French intelligence, if he'd actually been one of ours someone would have spoken up."

Malcolm pushed himself to his feet and strode to the unlit fireplace. "I was afraid of this."

He could feel Talleyrand's gaze on him. "You blame yourself too much, Malcolm."

Malcolm spun round and looked at the man he had known since boyhood, his grandfather's and mother's friend. "An innocent man may have been killed because of me."

"And in your line of work, I highly doubt he was the first. Or the last. You reported the evidence, Malcolm. Evidence which must have been fabricated."

"By whom?"

"A fascinating question." Talleyrand tented his fingers together. "I must say this is interesting. I can certainly understand Rivère's claims that he could shake the British delegation."

"I'm glad our difficulties amuse you, sir."

"You must allow me to take my amusements where I can, Malcolm. There are few enough of them these days."

Malcolm crossed back to Talleyrand. "Laclos was friendly with your nephew."

"So he was."

"Did you arrange it?" Malcolm dropped back into his chair and leaned towards the prince.

"My dear Malcolm. I choose my agents with care, for their keen understanding and discretion. Which is why I've always regretted I couldn't have you for an agent. And why I'd never want Edmond for one. I did suggest it might be a good idea for Edmond to show Laclos round Paris."

"And you got reports on Laclos from him."

"I found it useful to get Edmond's rather unsophisticated view of Laclos. Later when I learned Laclos had been working for the British, I wondered if Laclos had encouraged the friendship because Edmond was my nephew. Perhaps he thought my avuncular affections went further than they do."

"You got Edmond his wife," Malcolm said, perhaps unwisely.

"So I did." Talleyrand's fingers tightened. He unclenched them and curved them round the arms of his chair. "Speaking of actions which haunt one."

"Actually knowing Dorothée makes it clear she's not a chess piece?"

"Regrets come with age. God knows what that means lies in store for you, considering the number you already appear to have at—what? Eight-and-twenty?"

"Come October."

"When I was eight-and-twenty—" Memories drifted through Talleyrand's eyes. "I thought I knew a great deal, but in many ways I think I was much younger than you. I certainly hadn't yet learned the meaning of regret. Or of love."

Malcolm watched the prince for a moment. "Sometimes the two go hand in hand."

"Yes." Talleyrand's fingers tensed on the chair arms. "So they do."

"Rivère said one thing more." Malcolm drew a breath, his throat raw. "Sir, is it possible Tatiana had a child?"

Talleyrand went still. His eyes became even more hooded than usual. "Rivère knew how to wound."

"Is it—"

Talleyrand folded his hands together. "It's possible Tatiana did any number of things."

Malcolm studied the man his grandfather had trusted with the secret of his unmarried mother's pregnancy thirty-some years ago, the man his mother had trusted to keep an eye on her secret daughter in France. The man who had made Tatiana his agent. "Are you saying you knew—"

"My dear Malcolm. If I'd known your sister had a child I'd have told you."

"Would you?"

"After Tatiana died." Talleyrand's gaze was now unusually open.

"You might have thought I was better off not knowing. You might have made a promise to Tania."

Talleyrand's mouth curved in a rueful smile. "I'm not as protective as you think me. And I've learned to take a flexible attitude towards promises."

Malcolm pushed himself to his feet, crossed the room in two strides, and leaned over the prince's chair. "What *do* you know?"

Talleyrand looked up at him with the same open gaze. "A few stray comments that might, in retrospect, mean something."

"What comments?" Malcolm's fingers bit into the fabric of the chair.

"An uncharacteristically wistful look in her eyes when she saw a small child once or twice. A comment, on hearing of a courtesan or actress who'd found herself in a delicate situation, that at least she herself had learned the value of precautions. And—"

"What?" Malcolm tightened his grip on the chair, holding Talleyrand's gaze with his own.

"She asked me to help arrange time away from Paris for her. She needed a rest, she said. She needed not to be troubled by any of her various lovers. She was gone for about five months."

"When was this?" Malcolm did calculations in his head.

"The spring of 1807."

Malcolm straightened up and paced across the room. "More than three years after Tania left Russia. So the father couldn't have been Tsar Alexander. Who could have fathered the child?"

"My dear boy. No offense meant to your sister—I hardly consider such behavior offensive—but keeping track of Tatiana's conquests would have left me quite without time to tend to the business of France. I was still foreign minister at the time."

"And Tatiana was your agent. Whom else did you have her collecting information from?"

"You can't be so crude as to think the only way of collecting information—"

"Perhaps not the only but certainly one of the most likely with a beautiful woman like Tatiana."

"She was establishing herself in Parisian society. She was indulging in flirtations with attachés from the Austrian and Prussian embassies. I don't know if they went further. Even if they did, I see no reason for a child born of such a liaison to be kept secret."

Malcolm locked his gaze on the prince's own, trying to see behind that enigmatic stare. "Is there any chance Tania was involved with Napoleon Bonaparte that early?"

Talleyrand hesitated a fraction too long before he answered. "Not that I know of."

"Not that you *know* of?"

Talleyrand smoothed his ruffled shirt cuff over his fingers. "I'd be lying if I said Bonaparte hadn't noticed her. And it was like Tania to set her sights on men in the highest positions of power. It's possible something had begun and she had reasons for keeping it from me. But even if it had, even if he was the father of her child, there'd have been no need then for such excessive secrecy. Bonaparte was generous with his bastards."

Malcolm paced back to Talleyrand's side and stood looking down at him. "What else?"

Talleyrand looked up at him, gaze bland as butter. "I don't believe there is anything else."

"Doing it much too brown, sir. You admit yourself you suspected Tania had had a child. And that she might have been Bonaparte's mistress. You can't expect me to believe you didn't ask her about the child's parentage."

Talleyrand's mouth curved with appreciation. "I could deny it, but I suppose there's no point now. Yes, as it happens I did ask her.

Tatiana didn't deny there was a child. But she went as serious as I've ever seen her. She begged me not to ask any questions about the baby's parentage. Not for her sake, but for the child's." He shook his head. "I've never been the sort to take vows seriously."

"She made you swear not to ask more about the child's parentage?" Malcolm asked.

"She made me swear not to tell anyone there *was* a child." Talleyrand met Malcolm's gaze, his own deceptively clear and direct. "Especially you."

"Suzie." Simon Tanner slipped through the crowd with the ease allowed by his height and theatrical background. "You look exquisite. No one would guess you hadn't had hours to prepare for the ball."

"Darling Simon." Suzanne gave him her hand and leaned forwards to accept his kiss on her cheek. "But how on earth do you know I wasn't chained to my dressing table all afternoon?"

Simon's dark brows lifted over his sharp blue eyes. "Because I know you. You've never been chained to your dressing table in your life."

"And because we know about the Rivère affair." David Mallinson, Viscount Worsley, moved through the crowd after Simon.

Suzanne gave David her hand. David as well leaned forwards and kissed her cheek, which was a sign of what degree of intimacy they had achieved. The heir to an earldom, who carried the weight of all that entailed on his shoulders, David had treated her with careful formality when they first met in England a year ago, for all she was his best friend's wife. But their time in Britain had broken much of his constraint, and then she, David, Simon, and Cordelia had been in Brussels together during Quatre Bras and Waterloo. With wounded and dying men on pallets in the hall, the house shaking from the cannonade, and Malcolm, Harry, and many of their friends risking their lives, any last vestiges of formality had fled. She could still remember Simon and Cordelia scrambling eggs in the kitchen and David coming through the front door, his hair dripping wet, his arms full of rolls of lint and bottles of laudanum.

"I can't imagine what the Rivère affair should have had to do with my dressing for a ball," Suzanne said, though she permitted a smile to play about her lips.

"My dear Suzanne," Simon said. "We may be civilians, but we aren't that slow. When put together with the fact that you and Malcolm were off on an errand last night—"

She laughed. "You know us too well."

David ran a sharp gaze over her. "You're all right?"

"Perfectly." That wasn't entirely true. She had chosen a gown with pearl-buttoned sleeves of satin and gauze that stretched down to her elbows, concealing the fresh dressing Malcolm had put on her right arm before they left for the ball.

"And Malcolm?" David asked. "I haven't seen him except across the room."

"Preoccupied, but unhurt." David and Simon were Malcolm's closest friends, but it was up to Malcolm to decide what, if anything, he told them about Tatiana Kirsanova and her possible child.

Simon's gaze lingered on Suzanne, and she thought he sensed her reticence. Simon had a way of sensing entirely too much. She loved him, but she knew it made him dangerous to someone in her position.

He turned away and cast a glance round the room. "I still can't quite grow accustomed to hearing people speak French all the time. Though I remember when it was just as unusual to hear English spoken."

Simon had been born in Paris. His father, the son of a wealthy Northumbrian brewer, had gone to Paris to study painting and married an artist's model. Simon had lived on the Left Bank—enjoying a warm, chaotic childhood that sounded not unlike Suzanne's own theatrical upbringing—until the death of both his parents when he was ten sent him to England and a family who didn't understand his French words or his French ways.

"I spoke with Gabrielle Caruthers this afternoon," Suzanne said. "She was saying how at home she felt in Paris, though she was little more than Colin's age when she left it."

"It is like returning home in a way," Simon said. "And yet returning to a home that's changed. And it's not just the Royalist cockades replacing the tricolor. Paris burned with excitement in my childhood. And with fear. There's fear now, but precious little excitement, I'd say."

Simon's parents, Suzanne knew, had been supporters of the Revolution, though like many they'd lived in fear during the Reign of Terror. Simon's own politics were more Radical than David's Radical-leaning Whiggishness or even Malcolm's.

David was watching her with concern. "I'm sorry, Suzanne, it must be difficult—"

"No, it's quite all right." She put a hand on his arm. "Not that I remember Paris myself. I was only a baby when we left." After all these years, her supposed Royalist background, in which her parents had fled Paris for Spain during the Reign of Terror, was the hardest part of her cover story to maintain. "And I don't think anyone could fail to be concerned for the reprisals that are taking place now."

"Well, not quite anyone," Simon said. "Or they wouldn't be happening."

David grimaced. "I don't think this is what anyone envisioned after Waterloo."

"On the contrary," Simon said. "The risk was clear."

Simon's and David's gazes met. Nominally they had shared rooms since they came down from Oxford. In reality, they were closer than most married couples Suzanne knew. But though it was politics that had drawn the two of them and Malcolm together in their undergraduate days, politics sometimes divided them. David would always be an aristocrat. Simon would always be a revolutionary. Suzanne well understood the tension.

"I always felt a bit sorry for Gabrielle Laclos," David said. "It wasn't easy to be an émigrée. And then her cousin Étienne was killed, and his younger brother—"

"Bertrand." Simon frowned. "I'd forgot. I didn't know him well, but I liked him. Brilliant at Latin and mathematics. He never seemed like a Bonapartist, though."

"Perhaps he wanted to get his estates back," Suzanne suggested.

"Not at the expense to his family," David said.

Suzanne nodded. It was the sort of thing David would understand.

"At least Caruthers married Gabrielle," David continued. "Rupert's a good man."

"Yes," Simon said. "So he is." But Suzanne would have sworn a shadow flickered across his face before he said it.

"You know Lord Caruthers well?" she asked.

"Not particularly," Simon said. "We were at Oxford together, but he was older and moved in different circles, at least from me."

"He was more of a sportsman," David said. "While Simon and Malcolm and I were either organizing theatricals or writing political tracts. But I've known Rupert since we were children. His father, Lord Dewhurst, is a friend of my father's. I remember the family visiting us for a house party when Rupert and I were ten or so. We got up a game of cricket. I can still see Dewhurst frowning on the sidelines when Rupert bowled less well than he expected. Even my father wasn't so exacting, at least not then."

One of the footmen approached Suzanne with a question about opening more champagne. David and Simon were claimed by Harriet Granville. Suzanne turned from the footman to hear her voice called from the doorway. Dorothée, lovely and fragile in sapphire crêpe over white satin, had just stepped into the ballroom on Count Karl Clam-Martinitz's arm.

"Doro." Suzanne leaned forwards to embrace her friend and then offered her hand to Clam-Martinitz. He and Dorothée moved about Paris as an established couple.

Dorothée cast a glance round the salon. "I suppose Edmond's here."

"In the card room. It shouldn't be difficult to avoid him."

Clam-Martinitz's well-molded mouth tightened. "We don't need to—"

"Karl, please." Dorothée looked up at him, her white-gloved fingers curled round his arm. "For my sake."

Clam-Martinitz's face softened as he looked down at her. He was the picture of a hero out of a novel, with his thick dark hair and well-molded features, but what endeared him most to Suzanne for her friend's sake was the kindness in his eyes. Doro had found all-too-little kindness in her young life. "I'd do nothing to cause you distress, *ma chère*. But I won't hide from him."

"Just don't seek him out." Dorothée turned to Suzanne. "We'll find some champagne. I know you must have all sorts of things to do."

"I did promise Lady Castlereagh I'd help."

Dorothée smiled. "I imagine that's the least of it."

And yet even Doro couldn't know how very complicated her evening was. As Suzanne watched Dorothée and Clam-Martinitz move into the ballroom, she caught sight of Raoul across the room by the French windows. She didn't let her gaze so much as rest on him. She made her way across the room without haste, stopping to speak to John Ashton and Violet Chase. Raoul had been speaking with Tsar Alexander's envoy Pozzo di Borgo, but he moved away just as Suzanne approached, though he hadn't seemingly so much as glanced in her direction.

"Mr. O'Roarke." Suzanne extended her hand. "So glad you could join us."

"I wouldn't have missed it, Mrs. Rannoch."

She shook his hand, her shawl draped over her extended arm. When she drew her hand back, she held a handful of papers, concealed in the embroidered silk and cashmere folds of the shawl.

"Do forgive me, Mr. O'Roarke. I promised Lady Castlereagh I would help greet the guests."

"I quite understand, Mrs. Rannoch."

Malcolm was across the room, shoulder dug into a pillar, champagne glass half-forgot in one hand, deep in conversation with William Lamb and Fitzroy Somerset. Her husband was not as inclined to disappear into the library at entertainments as he had been when they met, but he still showed no inclination to follow her with his gaze or to pay the least attention to her actions. In fact, she doubted he was even aware of what she did or to whom she spoke in the course of a ball. Some, she knew, took it as a sign of Malcolm's lack of romantic interest in her that he appeared to pay no notice to whom she danced or even flirted with. Sometimes this lack of attention piqued her vanity. But the truth, she knew upon reflection, was that it never occurred to Malcolm that he needed to pay attention to where she was or with whom she spoke. He trusted that at the end of the evening she would find her way back to him.

He trusted that the end of the night would find her home in his bed. He trusted *her* implicitly.

Her fingers tightened round the papers beneath the folds of her shawl. Bitterness lingered on her tongue. But it was so familiar now it was like the ache of an old wound was to a soldier like Harry Davenport.

"Suzanne." Malcolm's cousin Aline Blackwell hurried through the crowd, ash brown hair slipping free of its pins. "I haven't seen you all night. I thought you and Malcolm might be off investigating again."

Suzanne looked into Aline's bright gaze, at once acerbic and innocent. "No, just minor domestic dramas."

Aline grimaced. "Better you than me. I'd never make a diplomatic wife. To own the truth, I find myself quite in sympathy with Malcolm's habit of disappearing into the library."

"It seems to be a family trait. Baby not giving you any trouble?"

Aline touched her stomach, rounded now in the fifth month of her pregnancy beneath the orange blossom crêpe of her gown. "He or she is wonderfully adaptable. Like Colin. I only hope I'm as good a mother as you."

Suzanne's throat closed. "You're very sweet, Allie."

"Rubbish, I'm not in the least sweet. But though I may have my head buried in my numbers, I am passingly good at observing people. You made me realize one can be a wife and mother without ceasing to be everything else. I used to think marriage was a trap."

"I think that rather depends on whom one's married to."

"Yes, it does help that Geoff's quite as unconventional as I am. I can't imagine being married to anyone else. I rather think you must feel the same about Malcolm."

"Until I met Malcolm," Suzanne said truthfully, "I couldn't imagine being married to anyone at all."

They might seem unusual words for a girl from a seemingly conventional background, but Aline merely nodded. Her own family were filled with eccentricities despite, or perhaps because of, their impeccable lineage. "If you do need to slip out, let me know. I won't pry, but I imagine you're caught up in this Rivère business."

"How well you know us."

"Of course. We're family."

Suzanne forced a smile to her lips, squeezed Aline's hand, then slipped from the ballroom and made her way along the gallery, towards the ladies' retiring room and on past it, down a back staircase to the first floor. She was in the less public part of the embassy now, where it would be more difficult to explain her presence. But not impossible. Still, she moved cautiously, testing the stair treads. When she heard voices that seemed to belong to two of the servants, she flattened herself against the stair wall until they had passed. A routine mission, yet a thrill ran through her that came only from risk. Dear God, it was good to be back.

At the base of the stairs, she made her way down the passage and then into another until she reached the door to Castlereagh's study. No sound, no sign of movement. She turned the handle and slipped inside.

She had only been in the study once, when Castlereagh briefed Malcolm and her about a difficulty with the Austrian delegation. She made her way to the desk by memory and lit the lamp. The foreign secretary was almost painfully neat, papers stacked precisely on his desktop, a line of mended pens on the ink blotter, books aligned precisely on the shelves. It made it easier to search. As she had suspected, several drawers in the desk were locked. She pulled off her long ivory silk gloves, fished her picklocks from the special pocket Blanca had sewn into the satin skirt of her gown beneath the gauze drapery, and made quick work of the locks. She found the seal in the second drawer. Another, unlocked drawer yielded wax. She spread Raoul's papers out on the desk, lit a taper, melted the red wax, dripped it onto each paper, and then pressed the seal into the liquid wax. Then to wait for it to dry, the most nerve-wracking part. She snuffed the taper, checked for any telltale drips of wax, returned the sealing wax and the seal to their drawers, put her picklocks back in her pocket.

A few minutes more and she touched a fingertip to the wax. No red residue came away on her finger. She pulled her gloves back on, smoothed them with care, folded the papers, and tucked them once more beneath her shawl.

She cast a last glance round the room for any detail she might have missed, turned down the lamp, and slipped back into the passage. Back the way she had come. Silly to have even felt the risk. It showed how staid she had become. If—

"Mrs. Rannoch."

The loud voice greeted her as she rounded a bend in the passage. Damn. She'd grown careless.

CHAPTER 8

A tall man with a florid face, a shock of dark hair, and an indolent mouth stood before her. Lord Stewart, Castlereagh's half-brother. Wilhelmine of Sagan's lover. The man who had ordered Bertrand Laclos's death.

He stood, blocking the passage, regarding her with raised brows and a speculative look in his eyes. The light from the candle sconces made his skin appear more ruddy than usual. Or perhaps that was an indication of the amount of wine he had drunk. "Good lord. You're the last woman I'd have thought to find slipping round the back passages in the midst of a ball." He gave a low laugh. "If it weren't for your reputation as the last faithful wife in the beau monde, I'd have a very good idea of what you were doing here."

"Nothing nearly so interesting, my lord. I had to find one of the footmen to ask him to open some more champagne, and I took a circuitous route."

"Of course." Stewart's gaze moved over her, sharp despite the brandy that wafted off his breath. She'd known fingers to probe in much the same way. "Always the perfect hostess, just as you're the perfect wife."

"You flatter me, my lord."

"I wonder."

He had that tiresome look that cut right through the ivory satin and pomegranate gauze of her gown. In Vienna, he'd nearly caused an international incident when he pinched Dorothée at a masquerade at the Metternichs' villa. Suzanne took a step forwards, conscious of the way the folds of her shawl fell over her arm, conscious of not drawing attention to it. "If you'll excuse me, my lord—"

"What's the hurry?" Stewart caught her arm as she made to move past him. "Malcolm is deep in some prosy conversation with Lamb and Somerset. I doubt he even knows you left the ballroom. I was just remarking to Gronow that your husband pays shockingly little attention to his wife. An insult to a woman like you. Can't believe you don't mind."

His hot, brandy-laced breath was close to her face. His grip was surprisingly strong on her arm. She could feel the imprint of his fingers through the silk of her glove. Her wound smarted in protest. "My husband has his ways of showing his affections, Lord Stewart. And he has a way of noticing things just when one thinks he's oblivious."

Amusement shot through Stewart's gaze. "You can drop the playacting, my dear Mrs. Rannoch. Remember, Frederick Radley is a friend of mine."

Damnation. She should have seen this coming. She had seduced Frederick Radley on a mission in Spain before she was Malcolm's wife. Radley didn't know she was a French agent, but he did know she hadn't been the innocent bride she'd professed to be when she entered British society. He'd threatened to reveal as much to Malcolm in Vienna when suspicion fell on him in the investigation into Princess Tatiana's murder. And so she had confessed to Malcolm about their affair, fully expecting it would destroy his image of the woman he'd married. But Malcolm had surprised her. He'd merely been angry at Radley for taking advantage of her at the time of her grief (her supposed grief) over the loss of her family. Radley's threat had been neutralized. But she should have realized he'd have talked to his friend Stewart.

She met Stewart's gaze, keeping her own wide and steady. "Whatever happened between Radley and me was over long before I married Malcolm."

"What's that to say to anything?"

"I'm a faithful wife." Something she could at least say with conviction in a world of pretense.

"I have yet to meet any such animal." His gaze settled on the ruched satin that edged her bodice. "You deserve a man who can satisfy you."

"Believe me—"

"Just one kiss." Stewart dragged her closer. He was holding her left arm and she couldn't move her right without revealing the papers. She could knee him in the groin, but that would cause its own set of complications. Probably more complicated complications than letting him have a kiss. It wasn't as though she hadn't let gentlemen take more from her in the past.

But she needed to preserve her veneer. "Please, my lord, if someone sees—"

"No one about." He pulled her closer. She could feel the scrape of his breath on her skin and see the pores in his chin.

"But—"

His hand slid to curve round her breast. "Spare me the decorous protests. You may have the veneer of a perfect wife, but you have the soul of an adventuress. I've seen it. And if your husband isn't man enough—"

Footsteps sounded on the floorboards. Suzanne heard them before he did.

"Charlie."

The shocked, cold voice belonged to Wilhelmine of Sagan.

Stewart released Suzanne and turned to face his mistress. "Willie." His voice rang with exaggerated bonhomie. "What are you doing in the back reaches of the embassy?"

"Looking for you." Wilhelmine came forwards in a stir of seafoam gauze and custom-blended scent. "I might ask you the same."

"I've been helping Mrs. Rannoch. She had to order more champagne."

"Obviously a job for two." Wilhelmine had a knack for keeping her voice well modulated and still making it cut like a dagger.

Stewart released Suzanne's arm, though he showed no particular discomfort. Wilhelmine's gaze moved to Suzanne. "I trust you suffered no difficulties, Suzanne?" Her gaze held concern, not censure.

"None." Suzanne met her friend's gaze. "I'm quite well able to manage these matters."

"Thank goodness for that. I imagine Charlie only complicated things for you. Gentlemen can be so tiresome."

"Nothing irreparable. If you'll excuse me, I really must be getting back to the guests." Suzanne smoothed the folds of her shawl over her arm and walked down the passage, leaving Stewart to face his mistress's wrath. On the first floor, she paused before a pier glass, tugged the gauze and satin sleeve of her gown back in place with her free hand, smoothed her bodice where Stewart had crushed the satin, pushed her disordered ringlets into place. Then she strolled back towards the ballroom, stopping to speak to Prince Metternich and Count Nesselrode, even accepting a glass of champagne from a passing footman with her free hand.

Raoul was not too far from the ballroom door, in conversation with Lord March. Suzanne joined them. When March was claimed by his sister Georgiana, to whom he'd promised a dance, Suzanne and Raoul moved to an ivory damask settee set between two pillars.

"Agreeable young man, Lord March," Raoul murmured. "Of course we couldn't be further apart on Ireland."

"Not surprising considering that as lord lieutenant his father was trying to put a stop to everything you were trying to accomplish." Suzanne turned towards the settee, her back to the ballroom, and adjusted the folds of her shawl. In an instant the papers were in Raoul's hand and then slid beneath his coat.

"No difficulties?" he asked as they seated themselves.

"Only a minor skirmish with Lord Stewart. Just to keep things interesting. It shows you how staid my life's become that a boor makes things interesting."

"I wish I'd seen you fight him off." Raoul turned a little to the side, a very correct distance away from her, but his voice pitched for her ears alone. "The supper party is arranged for tomorrow."

Her gaze skimmed over his face. "You've had to move it up."

"We began to fear it would be quite impossible to find a date that worked if we delayed. A bit spontaneous this way."

"But sometimes those are the most agreeable entertainments."

"Quite. You're still sure you can make one of the party?"

"You know I wouldn't miss such an occasion."

He held her gaze for a moment. "Your presence will mean a great deal. Ten o'clock. The Café des Arts." That meant Manon's dressing room.

Suzanne smiled. She felt alive again. God help her.

Cordelia had a glass of champagne halfway to her lips when she felt a light touch at her waist.

"Edmond Talleyrand's in the card room," her husband whispered into her ear.

Cordelia turned and looked up at him. His face was expressionless. "Are you sure about this?" she asked.

"Why wouldn't I be?" His face relaxed a trifle, though there was a hint of mockery about his mouth that she knew he employed as a defense. He squeezed her hand. "Good luck, sweetheart. Not that you need it."

She returned the pressure of his fingers and slipped away. She met Suzanne midway to the card room. "Edmond's in the card room. I'll see what I can do."

Suzanne nodded. Her eyes were bright, probably a testament to the evening's various crosscurrents. "Does Harry know?"

"Harry told me where he was. Nothing like having a husband who's quite ruthless about confronting hard truths."

"Yes, I know a bit about that. Be careful, Cordy."

Cordelia met Suzanne's gaze for a moment. Though Suzanne Rannoch was gossiped about as an émigrée who'd snared one of the beau monde's most eligible bachelors, no cloud of scandal surrounded her. Yet Cordelia recalled an exchange between Suzanne and Colonel Frederick Radley at the Duchess of Richmond's ball. Suzanne too had a past, if not as spectacular a one as Cordelia herself. "Edmond represents the sort of danger I know how to confront," she said. "You could say I'm an expert at it."

Suzanne squeezed Cordelia's hand.

Cordelia glanced in a pier glass as she moved towards the card room. Her ringlets were just slightly disarranged round her pearl bandeau, enough to suggest further abandon. Her lips were bright with rouge. She bit them to exaggerate the effect. She let her spangled shawl slither lower on her arms and tugged at the puffed gauze and silver satin of her sleeves, pulling them a half inch lower on her shoulders.

She turned and swept towards the card room, recalling a time, not so very long ago, when part of the allure of a party had been seeing how many men she could fascinate. Not that she was beyond enjoying admiration now. But it was no longer a quest.

Tobacco smoke and brandy fumes greeted her at the door to the card room. She lingered in the doorway for a few moments, taking in the scene before her and attracting more than a few glances. Edmond was at a table halfway across the room, deep in a game of faro. It was seconds before he looked up and she could catch his eye. She smiled, and he returned the smile with a surprised lift of his brows. She moved across the room at a leisurely pace, conscious of sharp glances from Fitzroy Somerset and Lord March, who were friends of Harry's. Oh, well. It couldn't be helped. Look at the people who said that Suzanne had married Malcolm for his money and that Malcolm was a cold fish of a man who obviously had no romantic interest in his wife.

She came up behind Edmond's chair and bent over his shoulder, giving the men across the table a good view down her bodice. A waste perhaps, but Edmond would have the same view when he turned round.

"You used to say I brought you luck," she murmured. "I thought I'd see if that was still the case."

Edmond turned to look over his shoulder. "Lady Cordelia. An unexpected pleasure."

"Do continue with the game. You know I enjoy watching." She rested a white-gloved hand on the back of his chair, one leg extended so his arm brushed against it when he leaned back, and observed as he continued the faro game. Fortunately, it came to an end before too long with Edmond considerably richer than he had been when it started. Flushed with victory, he got to his feet and pocketed his winnings.

"We haven't had a chance to talk for so long," Cordelia said. "Might I persuade you to drink a glass of champagne with me?"

"How could that possibly take persuading?" He gave her his arm, and they moved into the adjoining salon, where he procured two glasses of champagne from a passing footman.

Edmond lifted his glass to hers. "I must say I'm rather surprised you sought me out. I hear you're living with Davenport again. And rumor has it you've become something of a devoted wife."

She tilted her head back to look up at him from beneath her blackened lashes. "Since when do you listen to rumor?"

"It can be useful."

"Harry isn't the jealous sort." She wasn't, actually, sure if that was true. Harry kept his emotions carefully guarded. Though he'd certainly lost his temper with her former lover George. She flinched at the memory. "He doesn't expect me to give up my old friends." She took a sip of champagne. "I've got to know your wife. She's a good friend of my friend Suzanne Rannoch. I quite like the comtesse."

Edmond's fingers tightened round his glass.

"Of course," Cordelia continued, "she's bookish, like my husband. I can see how that wouldn't do for you. And it must be a bit galling to see her so publicly flaunting a lover."

Edmond tossed down a swallow of champagne. "Every man has his limits."

In the course of their affair, she had never heard such anger in his voice. Unease on Dorothée's behalf prickled Cordelia's skin. She cast a glance round the room. "Paris is an odd place these days. Enemies turned to allies and back again. You're fortunate in your uncle."

"He has his uses." Edmond took her arm and steered her to a gold damask bench set in an alcove between two pillars, shaded by a potted palm. Edmond, as she recalled, had an unerring instinct for alcoves.

Cordelia unfurled her fan and stirred the air, heavy with perfumes and scented wax tapers. "I heard you talked about recently. In the British delegation."

Edmond's brows drew together. "Why?" These days, being talked about could be a dangerous thing.

"A man named Bertrand Laclos. I understand he was a friend of yours."

"Laclos?" Edmond said with seemingly genuine surprise. "Good God. That was years ago. Why mention him now?"

"I'm not sure precisely. Apparently no one's quite clear whom he was spying for."

Edmond gave a rough laugh. "Odd fellow, Laclos. Left his émigré family in England and returned to France in a burst of drama. He was quite a hero when he arrived in Paris. The aristocratic prodigal returned to the Bonapartist fold. My uncle suggested I might take him under my wing. Show him round Paris."

"He wanted you to keep an eye on him?"

"Nothing so specific. Oh, I suppose in a sense he wanted to make sure Laclos was genuine. I certainly never saw anything to suggest he wasn't. Which is damned ironic, considering after he died we found out he'd been working for the British. I suppose that's why they're asking questions about him now? His family's kicking up a fuss with the Restoration?"

Cordelia made a vague gesture with her fan that could have been assent or simply an attempt to stir the air. "I remember him a bit in England when I was a girl. Quite handsome, but so serious." She smiled, in a way meant to indicate that Edmond had been far more amusing than Bertrand Laclos. "I can't imagine what the two of you found to talk about."

Edmond stretched his arm along the back of the sofa, his gloved fingers brushing the bare skin above the puffed sleeve of her gown. "He wasn't the liveliest of fellows. A good judge of horseflesh, though. He helped me choose a splendid pair of chestnuts. And was quite good at cards, actually—excellent instincts. Mathematical sort of mind. But gaming didn't seem to interest him overmuch. And though he'd go along for a convivial evening in the Palais Royale, his—er—his heart didn't seem to be in it."

She tilted her head back. "Not the sort to enjoy an evening out at a brothel, was he?"

Edmond grinned. "Damn it, Cordy, I forget how delightfully plainspoken you are. Woman after my own heart. No, birds of paradise didn't seem much to Laclos's taste. Of course he had an exquisite mistress. I suppose she kept him occupied." Edmond's tone doubted the believability of one woman so keeping a man ensnared.

" 'Mistress'?" Cordelia asked, careful to keep the question idle.

"Louise de Carnot." Edmond's fingers stirred against her shoulder. "Believe me, many men have tried to follow in Laclos's footsteps, but I don't think any succeeded."

Cordelia frowned, trying to put a name to the face.

"Louise Sevigny now," Edmond said. "Married the painter Emile Sevigny after her husband died. Nearly was ostracized from court circles, but the Empress Marie Louise came to her defense."

Of course. An image of a red-haired woman with a sweet smile shot into Cordelia's memory. "How long were she and Laclos involved?"

"It began a month or so after he arrived in Paris and continued until he went off to the Peninsula. Afterwards by letter for all I know."

"Was Monsieur Carnot a complacent husband?"

Edmond gave a brief laugh. "Hardly. He was off with the army himself, which gave Louise a bit more license. Rather like you."

Cordelia controlled an inward wince. "But Carnot wouldn't have been as complacent as Harry if he'd found out?"

"Wagers were laid on whether or not he'd challenge Laclos to a duel when he got back to Paris. I more than half-thought I was going to have to act as a second. But as it happened, Laclos was sent off to the Peninsula before Carnot returned."

"Did Carnot learn of the affair?"

"Not that I know of."

"If he had you think he'd have exacted retribution?"

"Most definitely." Edmond took a sip of champagne. "Of course before long Laclos was dead."

"So he was." Cordelia touched his arm. "Thank you, Edmond."

He tossed down the last of his champagne, his gaze trained on her face. "A waltz for old times' sake?"

She shook her head. "I'm not the woman I was a year ago."

Edmond ran an appraising gaze over her. "Different with Davenport here to see?"

Cordelia got to her feet. "Different because I care what he thinks."

Suzanne resisted the impulse to follow Cordelia into the card room. She would only be in the way. Cordy could take care of herself. Suzanne moved down the passage towards the ballroom to find herself face-to-face with Wilhelmine of Sagan.

"I'm sorry, Suzanne." Wilhelmine's voice and gaze held regret and sympathy with no overtones of jealousy.

"You needn't apologize, Willie. It's not your responsibility."

Wilhelmine grimaced. "Isn't it? Doesn't one in a certain way make oneself responsible for a man by taking him into one's bed? Dear God, listen to me. I used to claim I valued my freedom more than anything."

"Freedom can be lonely."

"And not as amusing as one gets older." Wilhelmine tugged at her Grecian scarf. "He can be so agreeable. But then he drinks too much and forgets himself."

"It's nothing I haven't experienced before. I was more concerned—"

"For me?" Wilhelmine shrugged. "I stopped expecting exclusivity a long time ago. He's amusing. And in a powerful position."

"I can understand the allure. For a few weeks. Or even a few months. But for anything more permanent— A wife cedes a great deal of power to her husband." A power she was fortunate Malcolm never tried to take.

"And gains a great deal of position." Wilhelmine glanced into the pier glass across the passage and adjusted a ringlet beneath her emerald circlet, a Courland heirloom. "I can manage him."

"But will you be satisfied managing him?"

Wilhelmine smoothed the embroidered folds of the Grecian scarf over her arm. "I'm more than ten years older than you,

Suzanne. It's different when one starts thinking about being old and alone."

Suzanne smiled at the glowing woman before her. Wilhelmine's complexion was nearly as fresh and unlined as Dorothée's. "You're not old."

"But I will be one day."

Suzanne was silent. Before she'd married Malcolm she hadn't thought about growing old. It hadn't seemed likely she'd survive that long.

Wilhelmine met her gaze. "It's not the life I wanted as a girl. But then I gave up expecting that life centuries ago. I have to make do with the options before me."

"Have you gone mad, Cordy?" Lady Caroline Lamb seized Cordelia's arm as Cordelia stepped into the ballroom.

Still conscious of the imprint of Edmond's fingers and the warmth of his breath, Cordelia met her friend's gaze. "I don't think so. Any more than I always have been."

"You were talking with Edmond Talleyrand. In an alcove."

"More an embrasure."

Caroline's eyes went wider than usual in her thin face. She'd looked like that in the nursery when her brother Fred insisted fairy tales were only made up stories. "I really believed you and Harry were happy. That things had changed."

For all her scandalous reputation, Caro was much more of a romantic than Cordelia was herself. Cordelia gripped her friend's hands. "We are. Truly."

"But you must realize what you're risking. Harry's trust. His faith in you. He may say he'll forgive you, but you'll never get that back. I know I never will with William." Caroline cast a quick glance across the ballroom to where her husband, William, stood with Granville Leveson-Gower. "You have no idea what it's like to look in your husband's eyes and know he'll never look at you in the same way."

"Harry never will look at me the way he did when we married. Which is perhaps a good thing—he didn't understand me in the least."

"Don't joke, Cordy."

"I'm not." In truth, she couldn't help but feel a pang for the young, intense love she had failed to appreciate and would never know again. "But Harry knows I was talking to Edmond. I was—"

Caroline's gaze skimmed over her face. "You're helping the Rannochs again, aren't you?"

"Caro—"

Caroline stepped back. "Never mind, I know you can't tell me about it. But do be careful, Cordy. You're still playing with fire."

Cordelia managed a smile. "When have I not?"

Caroline's gaze remained grave and uncharacteristically mature. "Then you should know the consequences."

Mouth unexpectedly dry, Cordelia squeezed her friend's hands and moved off in search of Suzanne, whom she found on the edge of the dance floor. Suzanne scanned her face but waited for her to speak.

"Confronting old ghosts isn't necessarily a bad thing," Cordelia said. "Though I fear I've stirred up some tiresome gossip."

"Harry's strong enough to handle gossip."

Cordelia nodded. "I think Harry will be all right. As he said himself, we were going to have to deal with this at some point. I just didn't—" She shook her head, regret twisting in her chest.

"What?" Suzanne asked.

Cordelia twisted her diamond bracelet round her wrist. "I didn't much care to be reminded of who I used to be."

Suzanne touched her arm. "We all have sides of ourselves we don't like to be reminded of. Believe me."

For a moment, Suzanne's eyes were dark with self-loathing. Cordelia touched her friend's arm. "Suzette—"

"After what you and Harry have been through, Cordy, I rather think you can survive anything." Suzanne's eyes were bright, the polished armor in place again. For the first time, Cordelia realized just how much her friend's demeanor was armor. As close as they had become, there was a great deal about Suzanne that Cordelia didn't know. She swallowed and told Suzanne what Edmond had revealed about Bertrand Laclos and his relationship with Louise de Carnot.

Suzanne smiled. "You have the makings of a capital agent, Cordy. Thank you."

"Does it help?"

"Anything connected with Bertrand Laclos helps."

"Good." Cordelia felt the knot of tension ease within her. "It's amazing how gratifying it is to feel one's done something useful. Since Waterloo, I've been oddly discontented with my usual round of idle frivolity."

Suzanne smiled. "I can't quite imagine you as idle or frivolous, Cordy. Do you think—"

"Cordy!"

The voice rang out across the ballroom, through the blur of conversation and clink of glasses and strains of the waltz. Cordelia's body tensed in response even before her mind registered whom the voice belonged to. Damnation. There was no escaping the past.

CHAPTER 9

Cordelia turned to see him ducking between a British hussar and two plumed ladies with his characteristic loose-limbed gait. His coffee brown hair still fell over his forehead with a disorder, which she'd never been able to decide was the result of natural carelessness or careful time at the mirror. His coat, midnight blue rather than black, was exquisitely cut but a bit rumpled, his neckcloth slightly askew, a diamond glinting in the linen.

"Monsieur Laclos." Cordelia drew the tattered remnants of her self-respect round her and extended a white-gloved hand.

"Such formality." Gui Laclos bowed over her hand with a grin that even now she could not deny was engaging.

"Do you know Mrs. Rannoch?" Cordelia asked, withdrawing her hand from his clasp even as his fingers tightened over her own. "Monsieur Guilaume de Laclos, Suzanne."

Gui turned the full force of his smile on Suzanne as he swept her a bow. "We haven't been formally introduced, but I could hardly fail to be aware of the beautiful Mrs. Rannoch."

Suzanne extended her hand. "You're Lady Caruthers's brother."

"Guilty as charged." Gui lifted her hand to his lips. "You know Gaby?"

"I took coffee with her just this afternoon as it happens."

"Gaby loves French cafés. She's far more Parisian than I am, though she left Paris when she was scarcely more than a baby, while I grew up here. Or rather in Provence."

"Your sister said you weren't able to flee Paris with the rest of the family." Suzanne's gaze was warm with sympathy. Cordelia knew it was one of her friend's best techniques for drawing out someone she was questioning. Which didn't mean the sympathy wasn't genuine. "It must have been terribly difficult."

"They all thought I'd died with our parents when a mob stormed our house in Provence. Gaby was with our uncle and aunt in Paris." Raw grief flickered through Gui's eyes. Those were the moments that had caught Cordelia, had made him more to her than a fleeting fancy. "Our nurse hid me before she was killed. There was no way to get me to our uncle and aunt in Paris. One of the grooms smuggled me to her cousins, who were farmers in Provence. I lived as one of their children until I was fifteen." He shook his head, drawing the familiar insouciance over the darkness in his eyes. "Sorry. Didn't mean to go on so."

"It's all right," Suzanne said. "My own family fled France during the Terror, though like your sister I was too young to remember much. I was fortunate to grow up in Spain in relative peace."

Gui gave a twisted smile. "It wasn't so bad. To own the truth, much of the time I more than half-forgot I'd ever been anything but the third son of a Provençal farmer. I scrambled round the countryside with my adopted brothers and sisters. Bit of a shock when a man came knocking at our door one night and said he could get me to my family in London." He grimaced. "I thought I was with my family. That was my first meeting with Lord Dewhurst."

"Lord Dewhurst?" Suzanne said. "I didn't realize he was the one who brought you to England."

"He and my uncle were friends from their university days in Paris. You wouldn't think it to look at him now, but apparently he lived quite the life of daring a decade ago, slipping over to France to work with the Royalists. He tracked down my nurse to see that she was all right and learned from her that I'd survived." He shook his head. "Were it not for Dewhurst I might still be in Provence."

"London must have been quite a shock."

"Quite. My cousins tried to be kind, tried to show me how to go on. I'm afraid I didn't appreciate them properly until after they were gone." He cast a quick look from Suzanne to Cordelia. "They—"

"Étienne died on a mission in France and Bertrand fighting in Spain," Suzanne said. "Your family have been through a great deal."

"Next to them I've been fortunate." Gui flashed a careless smile, bright as the crystal and gilt of the chandeliers overhead. "Life in Britain has had its compensations." His gaze lingered on Cordelia for a moment. "You look well, Cordy. I heard you'd been in Brussels during Waterloo."

"That's where I met Mrs. Rannoch." Cordelia kept her gaze on Gui's face. He deserved better from her than Edmond Talleyrand. "And where I reconciled with my husband."

Gui's eyes widened. "I heard of course—"

"That we were living under the same roof?"

"But I didn't realize—"

"I learned a number of things about Harry in Brussels. And about myself."

Gui regarded her for a moment. His eyes now held not insouciance or the scars of the past but something that might have been regret mixed with affection. "Congratulations, Cordy. I'm happy for you. And Davenport's a lucky man."

He touched her arm, nodded to Suzanne, and moved off. Cordelia drew a harsh breath. "You must think me quite indiscriminate," she said, not meeting Suzanne's gaze.

"Hardly that. He's very charming. And clever enough to hold a woman's interest, I should think."

Cordelia folded her arms, gripping her elbows. "It didn't last very long. A fortnight at a house party in Devon. The Somertons'. I don't know why I accepted. I never did well immured in the country, and then the weather was wretched. Gui made things so much more amusing."

"There's nothing wrong with amusement."

"I was married."

"And separated from your husband. And treated like a pariah by society."

Cordelia gave a bleak smile. "Are you saying I lived up to my reputation?"

"I think you lived in the society that would accept you."

Cordelia forced herself to stare into the past without flinching. "Somehow I didn't realize quite how many ghosts I was creating in the process. But then I was never very good at thinking ahead."

"Cordy—" Suzanne adjusted one of the pearl buttons on her sleeve. "Did Gui Laclos ever talk about his family?"

"Is Gui caught up in this?"

"The Lacloses are caught up in this. What happened to his cousin Bertrand could have to do with why Antoine Rivère was killed and have a whole host of implications."

Cordelia frowned, fingering the ebony sticks of her fan. She understood the questions that had to be asked in an investigation, better now than she had last June in Brussels. And she understood that Suzanne and Malcolm didn't ask those questions idly or reveal confidences if they didn't have to. But a part of her still shied away from probing into the lives of her friends. "Gui didn't talk about his family much. Except at first to tell me he was the black sheep and quite everyone's despair. Said partly as a dare, partly with little-boy ruefulness. Then later after we"—she hesitated, then wondered at her hesitation over the wording; it was nothing Suzanne didn't know—"after we became intimate," she said with determination. "The weather had cleared for a bit and we were walking along the stream bank on the estate. Gui mentioned the first time Étienne and Bertrand took him fishing after he came to England. A common enough story, but unusual, because he didn't often talk about them." She frowned, trying to remember back to that exchange. The damp chill of the air cutting through her pelisse, the tug of the breeze on her bonnet ribbons, the firmness of Gui's arm beneath her gloved fingers were all vivid, but the precise words eluded her. "I think I said something about how it must have been nice to have cousins to show him how to go on in England—trying to be innocuous. And I suppose perhaps trying to learn more about his past. Gui stopped then and looked across the water." The muscles in his arm had gone taut beneath her touch. "He said Bertrand and Étienne were quite different from him. And that perhaps he was fortunate duty and honor had never meant a great deal to him. His mouth twisted as he said it with a sort of self-derision. He added that his lack of sensitivity to the call of duty was perhaps the only reason he was still alive, while his cousins were not."

"This must have been not long after Bertrand Laclos was killed," Suzanne said.

"About six months. Most people wouldn't have described Bertrand's going to fight for Bonaparte as honorable, but one could take the view that he was serving the country of his birth." Cordelia studied Suzanne for a moment. "Or wasn't he at all?"

Suzanne returned her gaze for a moment, her own gaze still and steady. Cordelia thought she would deny that she had the least idea what Cordelia was talking about. Instead she gave a sudden smile. "Damn it, Cordy, you're much too quick. Or have you heard something?"

"There was always talk that no one could make sense of what Bertrand had done," Cordelia said, putting into words thoughts that had only been half-formulated until now. "But it was mostly that here you are implying there's some mystery about his life and death. He never struck me as the sort to turn his back on his family and fight for Bonaparte. If nothing else because of the family duty that Gui was talking about. He had to have known the burden it would place on his parents."

"Do you think Gui knew or suspected Bertrand's defection wasn't all that met the eye?"

Cordelia considered her former lover. For all his seemingly careless, open manner, there was a great deal she hadn't known about him. "I'm not sure. Perhaps. Otherwise that comment about Bertrand being driven by family and duty like Étienne doesn't make a great deal of sense."

"It must have been terribly difficult for all of them."

Cordelia rubbed her arms. "Gui was tormented. I've never been sure how much of it was growing up in a completely different world and then being transported abruptly to England, and how much was losing his two cousins. He went from being the rebel outsider to the family heir and the only surviving son in effect." She forced her mind back to those days in Devon. For all the affair had been lighthearted and agreeable, it had had moments that touched on something more serious. "Gui had nightmares. One night we both indulged in too much champagne, and he fell asleep in my bed. Which would have been problematic if my maid had found him there in the morning. Instead, I woke to the sound of Gui screaming."

"I have nightmares myself," Suzanne said. It was one of those moments when Cordelia had the oddest sense her friend had made a great admission. "Did Gui scream anything in particular?"

" 'Frémont.' I have no idea who that is. Or what. I shook him awake. He stared at me quite wild-eyed, as though for a moment he wasn't sure where he was or who I was. Then he came to and apologized profusely, He said he should know better than to fall asleep in a lady's bed. I asked if anything was the matter, and he assured me it was just the champagne talking. But—"

"What?" Suzanne asked.

"He asked if he'd said anything tiresome." Cordelia's fingers tightened on her fan. "Perhaps it's nonsense, but I had the oddest sense he thought he'd betrayed something while he slept."

"Did you ask him about Frémont?"

"No. It seemed better to ignore the whole thing. He continued perfectly charming after that, but he was more guarded than ever." Cordelia flicked her fan open and looked down at the copy of a Fragonard painting on the silk. A couple in a decorous garden obviously about to indulge in some very indecorous behavior. "I can't claim Gui and I were confidants. I certainly didn't confide in him about my life and past. But we were both outsiders in society in one way or another. He because of being an émigré and coming here late, and I because of my own scandals and folly. I think that was part of what drew us together."

Suzanne drew a breath, but Harry came up beside them before she could speak. "I've been getting the oddest number of sympathetic glances," he said.

Cordelia slid her arm through her husband's own. "Poor darling." Her voice was light. The undertone was not.

Harry grinned down at her, mockery tempered by something softer. "It's amazingly easier to take when one knows the sympathy is quite misplaced."

Suzanne touched his arm. "You're a generous man, Harry."

"Don't let it get about. You'll ruin my reputation."

Dorothée Talleyrand swept up to them and claimed Suzanne. Cordelia watched her friend move off. "Harry—"

"Mmm?" Harry was studying her face.

"Do you think that Suzanne—"

"What?" Harry's gaze turned sharp.

Cordelia watched Suzanne, a slender figure in pomegranate gauze over ivory satin, laughing with Dorothée and Lord Granville and the Russian envoy Pozzo di Borgo with just the right blend of charm and flirtation. "We shared so much in Brussels. I've confided things to her I haven't shared with anyone. And yet there are times I feel there are whole sides of her I don't know at all."

Harry's gaze narrowed as he too looked at Suzanne. "That's true of most people, I expect. And Suzanne's had a more difficult life than most of us."

"But I'm—"

"Not everyone is as wonderfully straightforward as you."

"Harry."

"It's true. You have a wonderful, dangerous knack for doing what seems right to you and damn the consequences."

"I don't—"

"Why else would you have run off with George Chase in the teeth of society?"

Cordelia bit her lip. Talking, even thinking, about George was painful. But she understood why Harry didn't shy away from mentioning him. Ignoring him would make it worse. "That was because—"

"You loved Chase, or thought you did, and that came first. It was more important than anything."

"Including my marriage."

"Well, yes." Harry returned her gaze without recrimination or any hint of softness. "You weren't in love with me at the time. And afterwards you didn't hide away—"

"No," she said, the bitterness back in her throat, "I fairly flaunted my damaged reputation."

"You have a great knack for being yourself, Cordy. It's the same knack that had you in Brussels, caring for your bitter fool of a husband when all common sense dictated you should be elsewhere. And that made you jump in to help Suzanne and Malcolm with their investigation, whatever the consequences to your own reputation."

"What you're saying is, I blunder straight into trouble. Suzanne's much more sensible. But she's not the sort to pretend simply because of what society thinks."

"No," Harry agreed. "But I think her life has taught her to foresee consequences."

Cordelia's gaze returned to her friend, now accepting a glass of champagne from Pozzo di Borgo with a smile that held just the right flirtatious edge for a beautiful woman who was also a virtuous wife. "I just hate to think—"

"What?"

"Of her hiding anything from Malcolm." Worry bit Cordelia in the throat. Suzanne and Malcolm had been an inspiration to her in Brussels when she took the seemingly impossible step of reconciling with Harry. Perhaps she needed to believe in the solidity of their happiness to believe she and Harry had a chance at making their fragile, wonderful reunion work.

"Don't you think we all hide things from the people we love?" Harry said in a soft voice.

Her fingers tightened on his arm, for she feared he was right. "But—"

"Malcolm understands his wife. Whatever's between them, he understands its limitations."

Cordelia cast a quick glance up at him. "I hate the thought of limitations."

Harry squeezed her fingers. "That's what makes you you, my darling." He looked down at her for a moment, his gaze still and neutral. "Did it go all right with Edmond Talleyrand?"

She drew a breath. Perhaps she had been worrying over Malcolm and Suzanne's relationship to avoid having to concentrate on her own. "Yes. Edmond was...Edmond. But he mentioned Bertrand was Louise Carnot's lover, which gives Suzanne a new lead."

Harry nodded. "And?"

"I didn't say 'and.' "

"No, but it's in your eyes. Not that you need tell me of course."

Cordelia closed her fan and ran her fingers over the silk and ebony. "Edmond's not— That is, he isn't the only—"

"The only one of your former lovers in Paris? I wouldn't have thought so. A matter of mathematical odds."

She looked up at him with a surprised laugh, torn between amusement, exasperation, and the sharp bite of guilt. "Damn you, Harry—"

"You needn't tell me who else if you'd rather not." His voice was level, but he seemed to be choosing his words with a trifle more care than usual. "I've no objection to hearing, but there's no need to drag out tiresome details simply to satisfy some urge of confession."

"No, I wouldn't— But it seems it may have to do with Malcolm and Suzanne's investigation. And if you hear any gossip—"

"Who?" Harry asked, in a voice of carefully calibrated disinterest.

She drew a breath and looked steadily into the eyes of the man she loved. "Gui Laclos."

Harry considered for a moment. "Yes, I can see how that could touch on the investigation. I saw you and Suzanne talking to him earlier, didn't I?"

"Were you—"

"I wasn't spying on you. But it's difficult for me not to be aware of you. It always has been."

She flushed. "Gui came up to me. So I told Suzanne, and then of course she had questions."

"I never knew him well, but he strikes me as having more wit than Edmond Talleyrand."

"Yes. And he's a nicer person." She forced her gaze to stay on Harry's face. "He wasn't— I liked him, but it never meant any-thing— Oh, poison, that makes me sound horrid. It never meant more than a fortnight's diversion, on either side. I wasn't looking for more. I didn't want to feel more. I didn't think it was possible to feel more."

He kept his gaze steady on her face. Resolutely honest and yet barricaded. "What was between us was over. You can't betray vows that are already broken."

"I was the one who'd broken them."

"I walked away." His voice turned rough. It was an admission he hadn't made before, even to her.

She touched his arm. "You didn't—"

"Think you had the least desire for me to stay? No, that's true. But it's also true I was afraid to fight for you. Easier to walk away and damn the world to hell than face the messy consequences. And then I left you to raise our daughter alone."

She drew a breath that cut through her. "That was because—"

"Because I didn't know if I was her father? But having given her my name, I was. I realized that in Brussels. Ignoring Livia is one of the things for which I'll never forgive myself."

She shook her head. "You shouldn't—"

"Berate myself now? That applies to you as well, sweetheart. We can only move forwards." He regarded her for a moment. "For what it's worth, the few times I sought consolation in the years we were apart, it didn't mean more than a momentary escape, either."

Her chest constricted beneath her corset laces. Not that she'd thought Harry had been celibate in the years they'd been apart. But she didn't like thinking of him with another woman. Which was absurd. She could lay no claim to him in those years. "I never thought—"

"That I was chastely pining? That would be a bit too clean and romantic."

Which perhaps was why he had told her. Not to punish her, but to even out the field between them.

"It's now that matters," he said. He slid his hand down her arm to grip her own and drew her onto the dance floor.

She stepped into his arms. She knew he was right. Save that it wasn't just now that mattered. She needed to be confident of the future.

CHAPTER 10

"Laclos was set up." Malcolm turned up the Argand lamp in the privacy of the bedchamber he and Suzanne shared. His fingers shook. "Damnation."

Suzanne touched his arm. "Darling—"

"Don't, Suzette." He jerked away from her touch. The lamp hissed. He turned it up again. "Don't tell me it's not my fault or I couldn't have known. I bloody well should have seen it."

He felt her gaze on him. "Are you sure?" she asked.

"Talleyrand says Bertrand wasn't working for the French." His fingers curled inwards. "As inclined as I am to take everything Talleyrand says with numerous grains of salt, I don't know why he'd lie about this." Bertrand Laclos's face shot into his memory, bent over books at Oxford, on the sidelines in a Mayfair ballroom. Dark, serious eyes, an unexpectedly infectious grin. "I fell for some bastard's deception. I fell right into the trap they laid for me, and the cost of my idiocy was the life of a man who was running incalculable risks for my own side."

"People die," Suzanne said, her voice quiet and steady. "Because of things we do. Because of things we don't do. People on our side, people on the opposing side. Sides. A death is a death.

And we have no choice but to live with them on our conscience. Or we'd go mad."

He swung his gaze to her face. Her sea green eyes were haunted and yet unusually hard, like Perthshire agate. "It has to matter. If it ever stops mattering I won't be able to live with myself."

"I know, dearest. That's what makes you you."

He strode across the room. The watered-silk walls seemed damnably close. "If I'd thought to question—"

"I know. It's rather an insult to one's intelligence."

"What?"

"Falling for a deception."

"That's not—" He spun towards her and gave a rueful grin. "Oh, all right. That's part of it. I like to think I'm above being deceived."

"We none of us are, darling. In the right circumstances."

Malcolm struggled out of his coat and tossed it over a gilded chairback. "Whoever was behind the deception knew Bertrand Laclos was a British agent. Knew his methods of communication. Knew the codes to use."

"Rupert Caruthers would have known all that." Suzanne struck a flint to the tapers on her dressing table. "Are you sure he and Laclos remained the greatest of friends?"

Malcolm frowned, seeing the anger on Rupert's face when he talked about Bertrand Laclos's death. "There's no reason to think otherwise."

"Rupert married Bertrand's cousin after Laclos's death. Could they have been rivals? Or could Bertrand have opposed the match?"

"The way you described your conversation with Gabrielle, it sounds more as though Rupert married Gabrielle because he took pity on her."

Suzanne undid the clasp on her necklace and stared at the pearls and diamonds as they glowed and sparkled in the candlelight. "Or because he felt guilty?"

"Possibly." Malcolm unwound the folds of his cravat. "So you're suggesting Rupert and Bertrand had some sort of falling-out and Rupert chose this method to get rid of him?"

"I'm only suggesting that it's possible." Suzanne set the necklace in its velvet box. "Lord Caruthers would have been ideally positioned to put the plan into place."

Malcolm dropped his cravat on top of the coat. "Whoever was behind it planned to use me."

"Because they knew your intelligence would be believed without question."

He stared at the starched white linen folds of the cravat, pristine when Addison had handed it to him, now creased and stained. "Quite."

"And they did their job well."

Malcolm grimaced. "Gabrielle's brother Gui became heir to the title with Bertrand Laclos's death, as Étienne had already died in the failed Royalist plot."

"I met Gui Laclos tonight. He came up to Cordy and me. It seems he and Cordy were once rather close."

Malcolm stared at his wife. He was very fond of Cordelia and he wasn't a prude—or so he kept telling himself—but the reality of Cordelia's past still brought him up short. "Poor Davenport."

"I don't think it was very serious. But Cordelia seems to have been fond of him. And he of her. Cordy said he was an outsider, like her, because he came to England so late in his growing up and had been separated from his family for so long. He seems to have felt a great deal of guilt at having survived when both his cousins had lost their lives."

Malcolm tugged at his waistcoat buttons. "Understandable."

"But apparently it was more than that." Suzanne unfastened one of the diamond earrings he had given her for her birthday last year and held it swinging from her fingertips. "Cordelia said Gui Laclos had a nightmare one night and called out, 'Frémont.' Does that mean anything to you?"

"No." Malcolm shrugged out of the waistcoat. "Cordelia didn't know what it meant?"

"No. Only that when Gui woke he seemed afraid he'd betrayed himself somehow in his sleep."

"Interesting." Malcolm perched on the chair arm and started on his shirt cuffs. "I've never known Gui well. We ran in different crowds."

Suzanne removed the second earring. "Gabrielle said her brother has a weakness for gambling."

"So rumor has it. I've never been one to haunt gaming hells."

"Except in the line of duty." Suzanne's mouth curved in a smile.

"Quite."

Suzanne began to pull the pins from her hair. "Perhaps he was indulging himself and making up for lost time all those years living in Provence." She twisted a hairpin between her fingers. "Or perhaps he was trying to distract himself from whatever he felt guilty about."

"Perhaps." Malcolm frowned at his shirt cuff. He'd got a spot of red wine on it at some point in the evening. "Rupert dismissed the idea that Gui might have tried to get rid of Bertrand. But then Gui is Rupert's brother-in-law, and Rupert's the sort who wants to think the best about everyone." He pulled the shirt over his head. There was more he had to say, though he was oddly unsure how to put it into words. "Talleyrand revealed more than that Bertrand Laclos was framed. Apparently Rivère was telling the truth, at least in part. It looks as though Tania did have a child."

"Oh, Malcolm." His wife's voice was warm with a sympathy that threatened to undo him.

He moved to the bed and wrapped himself in his dressing gown while he told her, as matter-of-factly as possible, about his conversations with Annina and Talleyrand.

"So it sounds as though Tatiana became pregnant in late 1806 or early 1807," Suzanne said.

"Yes." He tightened the belt on the dressing gown. His fingers were shaking. Damnable not to be in more control. "I just can't understand—"

"Why she didn't tell you?"

"Why she didn't at least leave a message for me." The burgundy silk slipped through his fingers. He tugged at it and heard a stitch give way.

"She wouldn't have been expecting to die, Malcolm." Suzanne

hesitated, and he knew she was thinking of the letters he'd written to her and Colin in case he didn't survive their various adventures. The letters that were still in his dispatch box. He never knew when they might be necessary. "Not everyone plans for contingencies as carefully as you do, darling. And she wasn't going into a battle as you were at Waterloo."

"She was—"

"Your sister. I know." Suzanne crossed the room, her half-unpinned hair falling over one shoulder, and dropped down on the bed. "It sounds as though she was concerned for her child's safety. God knows I can understand that."

Malcolm sat beside his wife. He saw Colin, curled in his bed when he and Suzanne had looked in on him a quarter hour before. Relaxed in sleep, one arm curled round his stuffed bear, the other flung up beside his head. So content. So vulnerable. "That's just the point. I would have—"

"Protected Tatiana's child? She may have been trying to protect you as well." Suzanne touched his back, her fingers warm through the silk of his dressing gown.

"She made Talleyrand swear to keep his knowledge of the child from me in particular." That revelation still hammered him, a blow from which he'd never recover.

"I don't think it means she didn't love you or trust you, darling. I think it means quite the opposite."

Myriad fears sliced into his brain. "If she thought the child represented a danger—"

Suzanne hesitated a moment. "If her affair with Napoleon began earlier than we thought—"

"Quite. But Talleyrand's right. Even that wouldn't have seemingly needed to be so secret at the time. But if the father was someone less exalted—" He shook his head.

"Do you know who else she was involved with about that time?"

"No. I didn't see her when she was in Russia or when she first came to Paris. I went to Paris secretly in early 1807 to tell her of our mother's death. She must have been with child then. But she gave no hint of it. If I'd been able to guess—" Malcolm stared at his hands and saw Tatiana's fingers moving over the keyboard of the pianoforte in her rooms in Paris. With her cropped hair and plucked brows and carefully applied cosmetics, she'd seemed so much more elegant and self-assured than the girl he'd last seen at her school in France. Until her eyes had lit in a familiar way over a favorite passage in the Beethoven sonata and he'd known she'd always be his sister.

"It was early in the pregnancy, darling. You couldn't have known." Suzanne hesitated, her fingers spread on the crimson silk embroidery on the counterpane. "I didn't want to mention this until I knew if anything would come of it. I talked to Doro about Edmond's friendship with Bertrand Laclos. Doro said she could hardly account for Edmond's friends. But Cordelia offered to have a word with Edmond."

"Why should Cordelia be able to—"

"Apparently she was acquainted with Edmond Talleyrand in Paris last year." Suzanne looked steadily at him. "Rather well acquainted."

"Oh." Sometimes, he thought he was a great deal too simple. "Edmond Talleyrand and Gui Laclos. Poor Harry."

"Cordelia was a bit concerned. But she said she and Harry had to learn to live with the past."

Malcolm grimaced, seeing the guarded cynicism on Harry Davenport's face in Brussels last June. Both the Davenports had changed amazingly in the past two months, but everyone had their limits. "I hate to see them face this so soon. Though I doubt Harry would thank me for my sympathies."

"Cordelia spoke to Edmond at the ball tonight. He said his uncle had asked him to keep an eye on Bertrand Laclos when Laclos first came to Paris. He also said he and Laclos didn't have a great deal in common, which is hardly a surprise. But he did reveal that Laclos was the lover of Louise Carnot. Louise Sevigny now."

"The painter's wife?" Malcolm recalled meeting her at an exhibition of Emile Sevigny's work a fortnight or so ago. Sevigny was a talented artist. As a favorite of Bonaparte and Josephine, he was on thin ice in Restoration Paris, like so many others.

"Apparently her first husband, Carnot, was an aristocrat and a soldier and not one to take kindly to his wife's infidelity. Edmond wasn't sure if Carnot had ever learned of Louise's affair with Bertrand Laclos. But if he had—"

"It would have been harder for Carnot to set up Bertrand than someone British, but it's possible."

"I'll talk to Louise Sevigny. Simon's friends with Emile Sevigny—he can help me." Suzanne smoothed the crumpled gauze of her overdress. "Cordelia said her talk with Edmond stirred some uncomfortable gossip. We should be on the lookout to deflect it."

Malcolm recalled the self-hatred he'd glimpsed in Cordelia's eyes so often in Brussels and still caught flashes of. He might not understand the life Cordelia had lived, but he knew the bite of self-hatred all too well. "How was Cordelia afterwards?"

"A bit unhappy to be reminded of her past. Having Gui Laclos come up to us just after didn't help. But Harry seemed to have things well in hand. They'll cope."

"I hope so."

She cast a quick look at him. "Darling, you don't think—"

He kept his gaze steady on her face. "I think marriage is difficult. I think love is difficult. I think Harry and Cordelia are two complicated people with complicated pasts. I don't think being married comes easily to either of them. That doesn't mean they won't succeed. But it does worry me when they go through something like this."

She shook her head, her hair falling over her face. "I can't help but think—"

"I know." He reached out and slid his fingers down her arm. "That's because you're much more of a romantic than I am."

She gave a rough laugh. "I lost my capacity for romance years ago, Malcolm."

Rage at the French soldiers who had raped her and killed her family and at the very English Colonel Frederick Radley who had seduced and abandoned her blurred his vision for a moment. "Not lost, I think. Just buried it beneath some very hard-earned realism."

She looked up at him. The candlelight slid over her face. "I don't know that I was ever a romantic even . . . before. I just—"

"Believe people can be happy."

Her fingers curled into the coverlet. "I believe happiness is possible, in fits and snatches if nothing else. Perhaps it's precisely because it's rare that I believe in grabbing hold of it."

When he was growing up, watching his parents, happiness had never seemed like much of a possibility. He lifted his hand and pushed the loose strands behind her ear.

She smiled but then went still, her hand on his back. "Darling—" She broke off. He could feel the question in the tension of her fingers through the silk of his dressing gown.

"Don't tell me there's something you're afraid to ask me."

"No." Her gaze moved over his face. "Not afraid. But I'm not sure it's my place—"

"For God's sake, Suzette, since when do you worry about what it's your place to do or not do?"

"I don't think marriage should entirely strip one of privacy. But—" Her gaze flickered over his face. "Have you thought about telling Willie and Doro about Tatiana's child?"

He checked the instinctive denial. His fingers dug into the coverlet. His mother had trained him to secrecy when it came to his sister. But she was Wilhelmine's sister as well, and he knew Dorothée felt a responsibility towards her. Tania and Dorothée did not share a biological father, but the man Dorothée had grown up calling father had fathered Tania. Questions of parentage and sibling relationships were complicated among the aristocracy. "You think they'd want to know?" he asked, his voice harsh to his own ears.

"I think so. I think I would in their place. And I think they could help."

"We don't—"

"Help can always come in useful, dearest. I think one's wise if one learns to accept it when it's offered. I know I'm trying to do so. There've been a lot of secrets where Tatiana's concerned. Perhaps it's time—"

"For honesty? That's what I was just saying to Wellington and Castlereagh."

Suzanne drew back against the bedpost as though to give him

space to make his choice. "It's your decision, darling. There's no right answer. But for what it's worth, I think you can trust Willie and Doro. I think we learned that in Vienna. After all—"

"I owe Wilhelmine my liberty and quite possibly my life." Malcolm saw the heavy door of his Vienna prison cell swing open to let in his wife and the Duchess of Sagan. And Prince Metternich. "And without Wilhelmine and Dorothée we might not have been able to save the tsarina. You're right. One should be grateful for help where one finds it."

"I know I'll be forever grateful to them."

For a moment in Suzanne's eyes he saw the fear of the time he had spent in prison. It was still odd to think of such fear being focused on him. Of his safety mattering so much to someone.

Suzanne leaned forwards, her dark ringlets stirring about her face, her silk gown rustling. The roses and vanilla and exotic tang of her perfume teased his senses. Her hand slid behind his neck and her lips met his own.

He closed his arms round her and returned her kiss with an urgency that took him by surprise. With the portion of his brain that could still think, he knew that she was trying to comfort him for his discoveries about Tatiana. Part of him rebelled against needing comfort, while another part craved it as a wounded man craves laudanum.

His fingers sank into her hair. She pushed his dressing gown off his shoulders and slid her hands over his back with familiar witchcraft. They fell onto the coverlet and pillows, and the last vestiges of coherent thought fled.

Stewart strolled across Wilhelmine's salon. "Damned fine evening. Though I thought Count Nesselrode would never stop talking. And Emily should do something about the quality of the brandy." He picked up a decanter from the lapis lazuli–inlaid table and splashed cognac into a glass. "I must say you looked particularly lovely, my dear."

Wilhelmine dropped her velvet cloak over a chairback. "You aren't seriously going to try to pretend it didn't happen, are you?" she asked her lover.

Stewart had the grace to flush, but he merely said, "What didn't happen?"

"For heaven's sake, dearest. Suzanne Rannoch is a very beautiful woman and over a decade younger than me. You wouldn't be human if you didn't notice her. I can scarcely blame you. But I do take issue with your pawing one of my friends. Or any woman for that matter."

His chin jerked up. "I didn't—"

"I saw you." Her hand closed on the giltwood of the chairback. "Plainly."

"My darling, you misinterpreted—"

"You had one hand on her bottom and the other down her dress. You're lucky Suzanne didn't choose to take stronger evasive action. She can be quite lethal."

Stewart lurched towards her. Cognac spattered on the delicate blue and pink of the Aubusson carpet. "Those things don't mean anything. You know that. You aren't an innocent. You must realize it's nothing to do with you, my dear. Men are different from women. We have our . . . harmless amusements."

Wilhelmine stepped back out of the way of his hands and his brandy-laced breath. She had every intention of reconciling with him before the end of the evening, but she wasn't prepared to do so yet. "Women are quite capable of harmless amusements. What I object to is your amusing yourself with women who don't find the flirtation welcome."

"Mrs. Rannoch is—"

"Suzanne Rannoch is very much in love with her husband."

Stewart's chin jutted out and his eyes hardened. "Perhaps you don't know your friend as well as you think, Willie. Mrs. Rannoch knows how the game is played. I would think you'd understand that." He gave a brief laugh. "If you could have heard Radley's stories back in Vienna—"

Wilhelmine grimaced at the mention of the British officer who was one of her lover's friends. Frederick Radley was a handsome man, with his golden hair and well-made body, but he rated his charms rather higher than the reality. "I have no particular desire to hear any more from Frederick Radley than I have to."

"Radley knew Suzanne Rannoch," Stewart said with delibera-tion. "In Spain. Before she was married. When she was supposedly an innocent victim of war. Knew her quite well to hear him tell it."

That was interesting, though not altogether surprising. Wil-helmine had long suspected Suzanne Rannoch had a more compli-cated past than she admitted to. "That's Suzanne's business. But I'm quite sure that now she has no interest in any gentleman other than her husband."

Stewart flung back his head and gave another, deeper laugh. "Lord, Willie. Who'd have taken you for a romantic? Don't tell me you're taken in by the perfect-wife veneer. You of all people."

Wilhelmine pulled the folds of her scarf about her shoulders. "I think I'm enough acquainted with both the Rannochs to see be-neath the veneer."

Stewart tossed back the last of the cognac and put the glass down on the lapis table with a clatter. "You can't expect me to be-lieve a woman like Suzanne Rannoch is satisfied with a cold fish like Malcolm Rannoch."

"Perhaps you're the one who isn't seeing Malcolm Rannoch properly."

Stewart regarded her through narrowed eyes. "Good God, Willie. Did you—"

Her fingers tightened on the delicate silk of the scarf. It had been a gift from Alfred von Windisgrätz. "No, I have no personal reason to know about Malcolm Rannoch's skills in the bedcham-ber. But I've seen the way he looks at his wife in unguarded mo-ments."

"It takes a lot more than looking to satisfy a woman." Stewart closed the distance between them and reached for her. "Cry friends, Willie. The night is still young."

She leaned into him and lifted her face, because kissing was something he did quite well. And all the accompanying acts that proceeded from it.

Much later, when they were lying in her bed in a tangle of Irish linen sheets and embroidered coverlet, Stewart turned his face into her hair and said, "Suzanne hasn't said anything to you about this investigation of her husband's, has she?"

Wilhelmine pushed herself up on one elbow. "The investigation into Antoine Rivère's death?"

"Er—yes." Stewart sat up in bed and reached for the half-full glass of brandy on the night table.

"Why on earth should you— Oh." Wilhelmine propped a pillow behind her shoulder and studied her lover. "Because of the accusations Rivère made about the Laclos affair? You were the one who ordered Bertrand Laclos's death, weren't you?"

Stewart tossed down half the remaining brandy. "The man was a traitor."

"Not according to Antoine Rivère. Or Malcolm Rannoch now."

Stewart's fingers tightened on the glass. "Rannoch was sure enough at the time."

"He feels guilty about it." Wilhelmine studied Stewart in the light of the single candle they'd left lit. At times like this, she thought she could mold her lover into something interesting. "Is that it? Do you feel guilty?"

Stewart drained the last of the brandy. "I'm not the sort to brood on the past like Rannoch."

"It wouldn't bother you if you were wrong?"

"We weren't wrong, damn it." He pushed himself from the bed and padded naked across the room to refill his brandy glass from the decanter on a pier table.

Wilhelmine sat up straighter so she could watch him. "You never once questioned it?"

"No." He clunked the decanter down and drained half his second glass.

Wilhelmine watched him through narrowed eyes, his body outlined by the candlelight. The body she knew intimately. A chill shot through her that had nothing to do with her bare skin. Stewart was not a complicated man. Which at times was useful. She could read him well.

And just now, she was quite sure he was lying.

CHAPTER 11

Malcolm relaxed his hands on the reins, letting his mare, Perdita, lengthen her stride to a trot. He cast a sidelong glance at his wife beneath the shadows of the overhanging branches in the Bois de Boulogne.

Suzanne returned his gaze. "Are you sure about this?"

"Not in the least. But then that's true of most important decisions." Off to the side he could see the tents where British soldiers were encamped and flashes of red uniform coats, but this path was open for riding and largely empty at this unfashionably early hour of the morning. Up ahead he glimpsed a lady in a blue riding habit on a white horse and another in a green habit on a chestnut, galloping with the abandon afforded by the empty path. Malcolm exchanged another look with his wife, and they touched their heels to their horses and galloped forwards.

Wilhelmine and Dorothée looked round at the sound of the approaching horse hooves and slowed their own mounts. "Well met," Wilhelmine said. "How pleasant to find only friends abroad."

"You're out early after last night," Malcolm said, reining Perdita in beside the Courland sisters.

For a moment, Wilhelmine seemed to grimace, though it might have been the way the shadows fell over the blue velvet brim of her riding hat. "Sometimes early morning air is just the thing to clear one's head after a night of dancing and dignitaries."

"It often seems to be the only time of day one can have any peace," Dorothée added. "Worth getting up early for."

"And yet," Wilhelmine said, her gaze moving between Malcolm and Suzanne, "somehow I don't think it's entirely coincidence that you happened to ride up beside us."

Malcolm felt a smile cross his face. "You're a perceptive woman, Wilhelmine. I've been hoping to speak to you." He glanced at Dorothée. "Both of you."

Wilhelmine regarded him with amusement tinged with wariness. "More about this business with Antoine Rivère? I scarcely knew him. And Doro's already told Suzanne all she knows."

"No. At least not directly." Malcolm hesitated. Once he spoke there was no going back. The instinct to hold his family's secrets close was ingrained from childhood. And yet he and Wilhelmine and Dorothée shared a sister. Willie and Doro came from a different world, the majestic, feudal world of Courland. Yet in a sense they were family. He could feel Suzanne's gaze on him, steady but without pressure. He knew she'd say nothing if he chose to turn the conversation and make for home. He drew a breath. The air was crisp and redolent of damp grass. "Just before he was killed, Rivère made a number of claims involving information in his possession. The first concerned the Laclos affair, which Suzanne asked Dorothée about because Laclos was friends with Edmond Talleyrand. But he also claimed to have information more personal to me."

Wilhelmine and Dorothée exchanged glances. "And you're telling us because—?" Wilhelmine said.

"He claimed Tatiana had a child."

Wilhelmine went stone still.

Dorothée drew in her breath. "Do you believe him?"

"I wasn't sure at first. But I've since spoken with Annina and with your uncle. And what I've learned confirms it."

Wilhelmine's gloved hands tightened on the reins. She had borne a child in secret herself, Malcolm had learned in Vienna, at the age of eighteen. A little girl her family had compelled her to surrender to her lover's relations in Finland. A child she was desperately, and so far unsuccessfully, seeking to have restored to her. "Did she have contact with the child?"

"I don't know. She seems to at least have sent gifts."

Wilhelmine nodded, her gaze clouded with her own regrets. "How old—"

"Probably about eight as far as I can tell."

"Is it a boy or a girl?" Dorothée asked.

"I don't know. Any more than I know who the father is. Tania was at some pains to keep everything secret."

"You're going to find the child," Wilhelmine said.

It wasn't a question. "Whatever it takes," Malcolm said.

Wilhelmine nodded. "I'll render any assistance you need."

"Thank you. I don't know—"

"Malcolm, please." Wilhelmine leaned across the gap between their horses and put a hand on his arm. "My family—my father—treated Tatiana abominably. And I can't bear to think of a child who shares my blood alone in the world. I'm sure I seem like a frivolous woman to you, but I assure you I can be remarkably resourceful."

Malcolm looked into her eyes, bright and steady behind the black lace veil on her hat. "I saw that in Vienna. And I don't think you frivolous at all. But you must know I don't know where this investigation will take us. Or whom it will anger."

Wilhelmine's chin jerked up, fluttering the veil. "You think I'd abandon my sister's child to keep a man?"

"I think you're entitled to know the risks you're running."

"Leave Lord Stewart to me. Unless you have reason to think he fathered Tatiana's child."

"No. Though knowing Tatiana, I can't rule anything out."

Wilhelmine inclined her head. "What have you learned?"

"Don't keep me out of this, Willie," Dorothée said. "Just because I had a different father doesn't mean I don't feel a sense of obligation. I think of myself as a Courland. Tatiana was our responsibility. Besides, we're talking about a child."

"That's what it comes down to, doesn't it?" Wilhelmine said. "One's own concerns scarcely matter beside a child's safety."

Dorothée looked from Suzanne to Malcolm, her fingers curled tight round the reins. "What does my uncle know about this?"

"He arranged for Tatiana to leave Paris," Malcolm said. "Presumably to have the child. He says she wouldn't tell him the father's identity."

"Says," Dorothée repeated.

Her gaze was wide and steady, worldly wise and yet vulnerable as that of a schoolgirl. Malcolm reached between their horses and touched her wrist between her kid glove and braided cuff. "I know Talleyrand was fond of Tatiana." It was more than he'd always been willing to admit, but in that moment Dorothée might have been his teenage sister home in England and his first impulse was to offer comfort.

"But that doesn't stop him from playing games with people," Dorothée said, her gaze on his face.

"No, it doesn't."

Dorothée nodded, fingers flexing on the reins. "I've always known it," she said in a low voice. "But it's different when it comes to a child. I'll learn what I can to help you."

"Talleyrand is important to you. I'd never ask you to risk your relationship with him."

Dorothée lifted her chin. She seemed to be aware of her sister watching her. "You didn't. I'm risking it myself."

Lord Stewart set down his smoking pistol and studied the point where his bullet had pierced the target.

"A capital shot," Malcolm said from the sidelines in Napier's shooting gallery.

"Could have been worse, I suppose. Come to try your hand, Rannoch? My brother says you're a crack shot."

"Then Castlereagh exaggerates, which isn't like him. I do better when faced with necessity."

Stewart ran his gaze over Malcolm, as though it had only just occurred to him that while Malcolm might not be a soldier he wasn't a stranger to action. "Just pretend the target's a Bonapartist agent."

"Actually, I was hoping for a word with you, sir."

Stewart set the pistol in its tooled leather case. "How did you know I'd be here?"

"It's common knowledge you frequent Napier's." In fact, Wilhelmine had told him, but however unworthy Malcolm thought Stewart was of her, he saw no reason to create trouble between them if it could be avoided.

"More about this Rivère business?" Stewart asked.

"In a roundabout sort of way."

"Oh, well, I could do with a glass of wine. The café across the street serves a decent Tokay and the Parisian girls tend to show a bit of ankle."

Malcolm had a great deal of respect for Stewart's brother, Castlereagh, despite the fact that they were diametrically opposed on many of the major issues of the day, from Catholic Emancipation to the future of Poland. Still, he recognized Castlereagh's keen understanding and dedication to his work. Stewart possessed neither the understanding nor the dedication. And it didn't help Malcolm's opinion of the man that he had a tendency to ogle Suzanne.

Stewart chose a table in the café with a good view of another table where three Parisian girls sat with shopping parcels round their feet. He ordered a bottle of the most expensive Tokay the café offered, then flung himself back in his chair. "All right. I suppose we must turn to work."

"Your brother told you Antoine Rivère made accusations about the Laclos affair just before his death?"

Stewart gestured to the waiter to hurry with the wine. "He mentioned it. Rivère was the sort to say anything if he thought it would get him what he wanted."

"But in this case he appears to have been telling the truth. Talleyrand says Bertrand Laclos wasn't reporting to the French."

Stewart stared at him. The waiter set a bottle of Tokay and two glasses on the table. Stewart continued to stare while the waiter uncorked the bottle and filled their glasses. Then he snatched up his glass and took a long swallow. "Talleyrand may not have known."

"Very little goes on in France about which Talleyrand doesn't know."

"It's possible—"

"According to Talleyrand, the revelation that Bertrand Laclos was working for us sent shock waves through French intelligence. Someone would have spoken up if he'd really been working for the French."

"If—"

"For God's sake, sir." Malcolm slammed his hands down on the table, rattling the glasses and bottle. "I gave you the information. I thought it was incontrovertible, too."

"It was." Stewart steadied the bottle and his glass. "It was incontrovertible. Damn it, Bertrand Laclos was a traitor. Every moment he was on the loose he was endangering British lives. We had to deal with him as soon as possible."

"Was there a particular reason you were quick to rush to judgment?"

"I didn't rush."

Stewart had taken immediate action against Laclos while Malcolm had urged caution, but there was nothing to be gained from arguing that now. "Sir, we were all taken in. But did you have any reason to be suspicious of Laclos before?"

Stewart's gaze strayed to the few inches of ankle displayed below the flounced muslin skirt of a blond girl at the adjoining table. "Laclos never quite fit in. He was French, of course. But it was more than that. He was a good sportsman, but he didn't seem to enjoy it much. Wouldn't take more than a drink or two. Always thought he didn't have the head for it. And he wasn't much of—"

"A womanizer?"

Stewart's gaze shifted from the ankles of the blond girl to the low-cut, lace-edged bodice of a brunette. "Didn't even seem to enjoy the girls at the opera. Odd, that."

"Perhaps he had a mistress he loved."

"No reason for that to—" Stewart bit back the words.

"Are you saying all this made you more inclined to believe in his treason?"

"No." Stewart swung his gaze back to Malcolm's face. "I believed in his treason because of the evidence you brought me."

"Fair enough." Malcolm took a sip of wine, guilt raw in his throat. "Did you talk to anyone before you decided Laclos had to be eliminated? Did anyone encourage you to make that decision?"

"There was no other decision to make. Even after I saw that letter—"

Malcolm clunked his glass down, sloshing the wine. *"What letter?"*

Stewart snatched up his glass and took a long drink. "Doesn't amount to anything."

"I think you should let me be the judge of that."

"Damn it, Rannoch—" Stewart splashed more wine into his glass and took another swallow. "After Laclos was killed a letter from him was delivered to me at Headquarters. Sent before his death."

"And?" Malcolm held Stewart with his gaze.

He set the glass down with a sigh of frustration. "Laclos said he was going to abandon his mission and return to his family in England."

Dorothée pushed open the door of Talleyrand's study. The smell of fresh ink, leather, hair powder, and eau de cologne wrapped her in familiar comfort. She stepped into the room to meet his gaze. He was looking up, pen clutched in one hand, as though he'd been aware of her step on the stairs. For a moment, the air between seemed to tighten with something she could not put into words save that it reminded her of an experiment she'd once seen with an electrical current. "Did you enjoy your ride?" he asked.

She pushed the door to and paused, fingering a fold of her green velvet riding habit. "Willie and I met Malcolm and Suzanne Rannoch in the Bois de Boulogne."

For an instant she'd swear she saw a flicker of concern in Talleyrand's eyes. Then it was gone and he said, "Always pleasant to encounter friends. Malcolm has been a superb rider from childhood."

Dorothée drew a breath. For a moment every nerve in her body rebelled against putting it into words. An illustration of Pandora opening the box from a favorite nursery book hung before her eyes. Once spoken, the words could not be called back any more than Pandora could stuff the evils back into the box. She would have to live with the consequences. "Malcolm told us." She crossed the room to stand in front of Talleyrand's desk. "About Princess Tatiana's child."

"I see." Talleyrand leaned back in his chair, the pen tilting between his fingers. "That was a great admission for him to make. Malcolm holds his family's secrets close."

"He recognizes that Princess Tatiana is our family, too. Of course Willie and I said we'd help them."

His gaze skimmed over her face, watchful as always. "You have a kind heart, Doro."

"I recognize my responsibilities."

"And you have the courage and the kindness not to shirk them." Talleyrand's eyes softened in that way they sometimes did when they rested on her. It was very different from the glow she saw in Karl's gaze when it met her own, yet it stirred her in a way Karl's gaze did not. A way that was less easy to define but that cut deeper.

She swallowed, realizing she had not yet fully lifted the lid from the box. "Did you know?" She blurted the words out, as she would have done when she was an awkward schoolgirl.

He tilted his head back, somehow managing not to disturb his wig by so much as a fraction of an inch. "Surely Malcolm told you that Tatiana eventually admitted to me there was a child but made me swear not to inquire into the identity of the father."

"Yes, that's what Malcolm said." Dorothée fingered her riding crop. She stood before the desk instead of perching on the edge as was her usual practice when talking to him. Somehow that represented an intimacy that seemed inappropriate now.

"But you don't believe it." Talleyrand gave a faint smile.

She lifted her chin. "I don't believe that's all of it, no. Any more than I imagine Malcolm does."

His smile deepened. "You both know me well."

"We both know you wouldn't hesitate to withhold information if you thought it important."

"Certainly not." He picked up the pen and tapped it against the gilt-embossed burgundy leather of the blotter. "But that doesn't necessarily mean I possess such information."

"Damn it, Uncle." Dorothée bit her lip, more at the word "Uncle" than at the curse. It felt odder and odder to call Talleyrand Uncle. "You had to have been curious about the father's identity. How can you talk about it so coolly?" She took two quick steps forwards and gripped the edge of the desk. "You must have cared about her."

His gaze moved over her face with a curiosity that seemed quite genuine. "What makes you think so?"

"You'd known her since she was a child. Her mother and grandfather were friends of yours."

He lifted his brows. "Your point being?"

"I know you. Enough to know that that relationship couldn't have left you entirely unmoved."

"My dear child. You're developing a healthy cynicism, but your faith in humanity is still touchingly naïve. You remind me a bit of Malcolm."

Dorothée pushed aside a stack of papers and perched on the edge of the desk. "Don't try to change the subject. You always say I'm a good observer. That also applies to observing you."

He ran the pen through his fingers. "Touché."

"Which brings us back to the question from which you've adroitly managed to divert me." She rested one hand on the desktop and leaned towards him. "What did you learn about Tatiana Kirsanova's child's father?"

He set down the pen and rested his jeweled hands on the ink blotter. "You're right of course that I made inquiries. Rather exhaustive inquiries. But Tatiana covered her tracks well. I had trained her, and she was a brilliant student. I spoke the truth when I told Malcolm I learned nothing conclusive."

" 'The truth.' Such an elusive word, as you're always saying. I'm wary when you use it."

"And yet sometimes even I mean what I say."

Dorothée searched his face, his hooded eyes, the lines in his forehead, the curve of his full-lipped mouth, which could be at once ironic, mocking, and warm. She drew a breath of frustration. She knew he revealed parts of himself to her that he didn't to anyone else. Yet there were still untold layers to him she couldn't read. A source of frustration. And fascination. And fear. "This is different. This isn't politics—"

He gave a brief laugh. "*Ma chère.* Everything Tatiana did had to do with politics, one way or another."

"But we're talking about a child who made no such choices. A child no different from my own boys. Or little Anne." For a moment the face of her little daughter who had died a year ago hung before her eyes.

Talleyrand touched her hand. His fingers were gentle, but when he spoke his voice was unyielding. "I'm not entirely insensible of that. But in this world children are victims of their parents' intrigues."

"And yet you've gone to great lengths to save Flahaut."

Talleyrand's gaze darkened. The Comte de Flahaut, his illegitimate son, had fought for Napoleon at Waterloo and then found himself on the proscribed list. Dorothée had seen the concern in Talleyrand's eyes over him and a few moments of naked fear such as she had never before glimpsed on her uncle-by-marriage's face. "I take my responsibilities seriously."

Dorothée put her other hand on the desk. "So do I. This is my responsibility."

"The child of—"

"A woman my family should have protected and didn't. And by lying you're preventing me from meeting my responsibility."

"You can't be sure I'm lying."

"I know you're withholding something."

"My dear child. First you credit me with finer feelings than I would ever admit to. Then you accuse me of not having a care for Tatiana and her child."

Dorothée straightened up. "I believe you couldn't help but care for Tatiana and for any child of hers."

"And?" Talleyrand asked, gaze trained on her face.

She got to her feet, the full horror of what she'd unloosed from the box washing over her. "And I don't think that would stop you for a moment from sacrificing them to your ends. If you thought it was important enough. I don't think you hold anyone inviolable. Even me."

CHAPTER 12

"Thank you for coming with me," Suzanne said to Simon as their fiacre clattered through the cramped, twisting maze of the Left Bank. Colin bounced on her lap, face pressed to the grimy window.

Simon grinned. "I'm always pleased when you and Malcolm let civilians assist you." He leaned back in his corner of the cracked leather seat and studied her across the fiacre. "How are you?"

Suzanne steadied Colin as he squirmed on her lap. "You mean besides investigating another mysterious death?"

"I haven't asked you in a while. You look a bit less haggard than you did in Brussels."

"Aren't we all?" Her mind went back to their house in the Rue Ducale in Brussels, the black-and-white marble floor tiles lined with pallets on which wounded soldiers lay, the smells of laudanum and beef tea and sickness in the air and Waterloo had touched all of them, but in addition the investigation into Julia Ashton's murder had been a strain, not just on Suzanne and Malcolm and Cordelia and Harry, but on Simon and David as well. The secrets uncovered had scarred all of them.

"Quite," Simon said. "But I don't think you're finding Paris entirely easy, either."

Simon understood her confoundedly well. Which meant he saw

far too much. She often thought it was because like her he was an outsider in the beau monde, so the usual assumptions didn't apply. "You have to admit the atmosphere in Paris is rather fraught."

"And the politics not what one could call convivial."

Simon was a Radical. He hadn't supported war when Napoleon escaped from Elba. The politics in Paris now weren't convivial to him or to Malcolm or to David. It didn't mean he had any special knowledge about her and her past. She had to remember that. "Scarcely."

Simon tilted his head back. "Just remember that I'm here to listen if ever needed."

Colin bounced in her lap. "Dragons," he said, his face pressed to the glass.

Three British dragoons had stopped before a bakery to flirt with a couple of Parisian girls. Colin had become good at spotting different types of soldiers in Brussels. Simon gave an ironic smile. "Even on the Left Bank." He glanced out the window. "I grew up only a few streets over. One saw more tricolor in those days. And then Republican soldiers."

They pulled up in a narrow winding street before a blue-shuttered house with a riot of violets spilling from the window boxes. Emile Sevigny himself opened the door to greet them, a wiry man in his early thirties with a bony face and a shock of disordered dark hair. His neckcloth was carelessly tied and a spot of blue paint showed on the shirt cuff peeping out from beneath his rumpled blue coat. "Simon, we got your note this morning. Splendid to see you."

When Simon introduced Suzanne and Colin, Sevigny said, "Forgive the informality. Simon and I've known each other since we were boys. His father was my mentor."

Emile Sevigny took them through a hall with walls hung with bright watercolors, charcoal sketches, and vivid oil portraits, and floorboards strewn with blocks and tops and a toy wagon, and out into the back garden. Louise Sevigny came towards them. She'd been fashionably dressed when Suzanne met her at the exhibition at the Louvre. Now she wore a simple muslin gown and her red-brown ringlets slipped from their pins beneath a gypsy straw hat.

"Simon. It's been too long since you've come to see us." She lifted her face for his kiss and then held out her hand when he introduced Suzanne and Colin. "Of course. Madame Rannoch. Your husband is the dashing man who does all sorts of secret things for Wellington."

"My husband would say not to listen to gross exaggerations. Colin, make a bow to Madame Sevigny. You saw some of her husband's pictures when we went to the Louvre."

Colin bowed and shook Madame Sevigny's hand. Louise Sevigny called over her own children, two boys of about eight and two, and suggested they might like to show Colin their fort. The three boys at once darted across the garden to the fort, a paint-spattered tablecloth draped over two bushes. Louise and Emile Sevigny smiled. It was a good thing, Suzanne thought, that most spymasters didn't realize how wonderful children were at creating diversions and putting suspects at their ease.

Louise Sevigny waved the adults towards a wrought-iron table set in the shade of a lilac tree. A maid emerged from the house with a tray of chilled white wine and almond cakes.

Emile cast a glance at the children as he poured the wine. "Simon and I were like that once at his parents' house."

"Save that Emile always dragged me off to the studio." Simon accepted a glass of wine. "He found the sight of my father at work much more entrancing than I did."

"It meant a lot, having someone take my youthful paint smears seriously." Emile returned the wine bottle to its cooler. "I've started a new painting. The conspirators in the capitol after the assassination of Julius Caesar."

Simon stared at him. "Good God, you madman."

Emile gave a grin that turned him into a mischievous schoolboy. "It's a classical subject. Something of a tribute to your father's style."

"My father could be a madman, too, when it came to running risks with the authorities."

"And you're a model of sober caution? I read the reviews of your plays, Simon. You've had the government censor close you down more than once."

"There's a big difference between risking a theatre being closed and risking—"

Emile shot a glance at Louise. She was watching him with a steady concern that reminded Suzanne of the moments she watched Malcolm go into danger. Knowing that to give way to any impulse to stop him would be to deny who he was. Not to mention who she was. Emile settled back in his chair. "People can take from the painting what they will. The assassination of a general who aspired to be an emperor could easily be a commentary on Bonaparte. A way of atoning for having painted the Bonaparte family."

"My father would be proud of you," Simon said.

"I hope so."

"The truth is Emile has to do something other than society portraits or he'd go mad," Louise said.

Simon took a sip of wine. "You both seem more at ease than the last time we met."

Emile exchanged a look with his wife again. "We've just learned to laugh in the face of adversity. Forgive me, Madame Rannoch," he added quickly. "These aren't easy times for someone who painted the Bonaparte family."

"I quite understand, Monsieur Sevigny. My husband deplores what's been happening in Paris. As do I."

Emile inclined his head. "It's worse for others. Men like St. Gilles, who were more outspoken."

"Including against Bonaparte." Simon glanced at Suzanne. "Paul St. Gilles is a committed Republican."

"So he was equally disgusted with Bonaparte and Louis?" Suzanne recalled a striking seascape by Paul St. Gilles she'd seen at the Louvre.

"He thought Bonaparte was the lesser of two evils," Emile said. "Which is enough to render him anathema to the Ultra Royalists."

Louise shivered. "I keep thinking about Paul and Juliette and the children. Dreadful." She cast a glance at her own children, whose shiny black shoes and white-stockinged ankles peeped out from beneath the tablecloth fort.

"But I'm far less important than St. Gilles," Emile said.

Louise turned her gaze to him, frowning.

Emile touched her hand. "My wife has an inflated sense of my importance." He leaned back in his chair. "It hasn't stopped the commissions, thankfully."

Simon brushed crumbs of almond cake from his fingers. "I'd like to see what you're working on. Particularly this Julius Caesar piece."

"Of course." Emile turned to the ladies.

"I'd best stay out here." Suzanne glanced at the tablecloth fort from whence high-pitched chatter now emitted. "You wouldn't think it, but ever since Waterloo Colin gets a bit nervous when I'm out of sight."

"It will give us a chance to talk," Louise said with an easy smile.

Emile refilled the ladies' wineglasses before he and Simon went into the house, already deep in a conversation about capturing the quality of light.

"Simon's a dear friend," Louise said, looking after them.

"One of the first of my husband's friends I felt at ease with," Suzanne said. "I often think it's because he knows what it is to be an outsider."

"Yes, that's it precisely." Louise gave her a quick smile. "And that makes him at home anywhere."

"It's quite a knack." Suzanne settled back in her chair in the sort of pose that invited confidences. "I can't say being an outsider has quite done that for me. I certainly didn't feel at home when Malcolm took me to Britain last year."

"I know precisely what you mean. Marriage is supposed to make one belong, but sometimes it just makes one feel hopelessly lost and lonely." Louise glanced round the garden. "Though it doesn't seem to have done that for me." She took a sip of wine. "I was married before Emile."

"To the Comte de Carnot."

"Yes." Louise stared into the pale gold wine, as though looking into a troubled past. She must have been in her midtwenties, but her wide blue eyes and soft-featured face made her appear younger than her years. "A very different life. I'd say it seems like a dream now, save that it's more like a nightmare."

Sometimes honesty was the best way to discover information.

Which was rather a relief. Suzanne took a fortifying sip of wine and set down her glass. "Madame Sevigny. I confess I've been hoping for a word with you."

"With me?" Louise's brows—which looked as though they had once been carefully plucked but now received less attention—rose, but her voice betrayed no alarm.

"My husband's latest unofficial exploit is looking into the death of Antoine Rivère."

"Good heavens." Louise Sevigny adjusted the brim of her hat. "I thought he died in a tavern brawl."

"It may have been a bit more complicated. And in looking into the Comte de Rivère's past, Malcolm has come across the name of a friend of yours."

Louise's frown deepened. "A friend of mine? Who?"

"Bertrand Laclos."

Louise Sevigny drew a breath and then sighed. "I might have known the gossip would still be in circulation." Her voice held no denial or outrage, merely weary acceptance. Years of experience showed beneath her ingénue features. She leaned back in her chair. "What have you heard?"

"Merely that you and Monsieur Laclos were close when he was in Paris."

"Yes. You could say that." Louise gave a bleak smile. "I miss him." She drew a sharp breath. "Madame Rannoch, you said Rivère's death had led you to Bertrand's. Do you have reason to suspect Bertrand's death was also not what it appeared?"

"Do you?" Suzanne asked.

Louise stared at the bits of almond cake on the plate before her. "There was always something odd about it. Bertrand was a careful man. Not one to get caught in a tavern brawl. He didn't fight—at least not for sport—and he didn't drink to excess. I've often wondered—" A shadow crossed her face.

"I understand your first husband was jealous," Suzanne said.

"Odiously so, though he didn't seem the least bit burdened by the marriage vow himself." Louise crumbled a piece of almond cake between her fingers. "I grew up in the country, in Normandy.

Our family name is old, but our fortune negligible. I was only sixteen when my parents married me off to Carnot. He looked quite dashing in his military uniform. But the glamour was gone before dawn broke on our wedding night."

"From what I've heard of Bertrand Laclos, I can see how he'd have been a refuge."

"Yes, but not in the way you think." Louise Sevigny cast a glance at the children. Colin and her younger son lurked behind the fort, a fringe of hair showing above the sheet, while her elder son appeared to be standing guard. "I used to worry that Jean would be like his father, but he's far too sensitive to take after Carnot. Jules, on the other hand, is very like my Emile." She turned her gaze back to Suzanne, open and direct. "I've loved Emile for a long time. I first met him when he painted my portrait, the autumn after my son was born. Emile was making a name for himself as a society portraitist and names mattered to Carnot. I went to Emile's studio every day for a month. With my maid, of course, but during the sittings we could talk. Such a novelty to have a gentleman listen to one."

"How very true," Suzanne said. "My husband's ability to listen is one of the reasons I fell in love with him."

Louise Sevigny shot her a quick smile. "You understand then. It was so lovely. The hopes, the foolish fears that keep one awake at night, the relief when those fears dissolve, the unexpected discoveries. The brush of fingers that affects one more than a kiss. Everything one thinks a first love ought to be. Except that I was already married."

"An uncomfortable situation."

"Beastly." Louise smoothed her hands over the primrose-sprigged muslin of her skirt. "Eventually the painting was done. For a time I thought that would be the end of it. I can't tell you how desolate I felt. Then I encountered Emile at an exhibition. We talked. And the next thing I knew, I sent him a note, and we arranged to meet." She flushed, though the wonder of it still showed in her eyes.

"I'm glad you were able to snatch some happiness," Suzanne

said. That sort of wonder had never been part of her life. She'd been long past it by the time she met Malcolm. Even by the time she met Raoul.

"It was dangerous." Louise pushed aside the plate, her eyes darkening. "I didn't know how to navigate Parisian society as a bride. How to dress, what to say, what not to say. Carnot found me embarrassingly naïve. Worldly gentlemen may be entranced by innocent young girls from the country in novels, but in my experience it isn't that way at all in real life. They far prefer their women as sophisticated as they are themselves." She jabbed a curl beneath the brim of her hat. "I knew about my husband's mistresses. He was scarcely discreet. And I knew other ladies with lovers—well, my husband's mistresses were all married to other men. But one night Carnot caught me flirting—just flirting, laughing over a glass of champagne—with a young officer at a party, and he dealt the young man a blow that sent him crashing into a vase of roses. That was when I learned a man can feel no desire for a woman and yet still think he owns her."

"So you knew you had to be discreet," Suzanne said, wondering where Louise's affair with Bertrand Laclos fit in with her early love affair with Emile Sevigny and her later marriage to him.

Louise nodded. "Some men are more complacent after their wives have given them an heir. But Jean's birth didn't change Carnot. Emile was dependent on commissions from the Bonaparte family and officials like Prince Talleyrand for his livelihood. Carnot could have ruined him. I lived with the dread of that, even when Carnot was away with the army."

"Is that why you ended it?"

"Ended it?" Louise said on a note of surprise. "Oh, I never ended it. I tried once, but I couldn't bear it. That was where Bertrand was so helpful."

Suzanne frowned, looking into the artless face of the woman before her. "Are you saying Monsieur Laclos—"

"He found me crying in the garden at Madame Rémusant's one night," Louise said. "He said it couldn't possibly be that bad. And I said what did he know about being trapped in a horrid marriage and in love with someone else—I do have a shockingly indiscreet tongue, I always have, it's a wonder I don't get myself into more trouble. But in any case, I found myself spilling the whole story out to him. Which only made me cry more. Bertrand put his arm round me. And just then—isn't that the way it always happens—Madame Décazes walked by. Of course she's the worst sort of gossip. I told Bertrand how sorry I was, and that now there'd be all sorts of talk about us. Bertrand smiled and said it would only enhance his credit to be thought to have such a mistress." Louise flushed again. "Well, he said 'a beautiful mistress,' he was always so kind. And I said for that matter, if people thought he was my lover, there'd be less likely to be talk about me and Emile. Bertrand looked at me for a moment and said, 'Why not?' "

"How very gallant of him," Suzanne said.

"Yes, wasn't it? At first I said I couldn't let him risk himself, but he said there was precious little Carnot could do against a fellow officer, and if he challenged him to a duel—which would be dangerous, given that the emperor had forbidden them—he would quite enjoy the chance to cross swords with him. Though, truthfully, I don't think Carnot would have risked a duel. He was a dreadful coward."

Suzanne studied Louise Sevigny beneath the brim of the gypsy hat. Amazing how the most seemingly guileless person could prove a master of deception. "So you and Monsieur Laclos encouraged comment about your supposed liaison."

"It's not that we flaunted it. It's just that we let there be just enough talk that no one would ever suspect about Emile and me."

"And Monsieur Laclos?" Suzanne asked. "What did he gain from it?"

Louise frowned as though this was something she was still puzzling over years later. "He said he was tired of being dragged to brothels or having beautiful women thrust at him. He never said so in so many words, but I thought he'd left someone behind in England whom he loved. He was very loyal."

"Did he ever refer to this person?"

Louise shook her head. "No. Except that once he said something about his heart already being given." She met Suzanne's gaze. "I know infidelity is the way of the world, but some men are constant. Bertrand was. Emile is."

As was Malcolm. Suzanne took a sip of wine, the tang of guilt sharp in her mouth. "Your relationship with Monsieur Sevigny must have been more difficult after Monsieur Laclos died."

Louise nodded, the memories stark in her gaze. "We had to be doubly careful. I tried to end things again. Bertrand's death was so dreadful. But then Carnot fell at Salamanca." She drew a sharp breath. Her cheeks were flushed with color, her gaze at once dark with guilt and bright with defiance. "I sound the horridest person on the planet to say I was glad. And I wasn't precisely. But for the first time in my life I felt free."

"Given your circumstances, I don't see how you could but feel a bit relieved."

"Do you?" Louise cast a quick glance at her children. "He's my son's father."

"You weren't responsible for his death. And it got you out of an intolerable situation."

Louise rubbed her arms. "I can scarcely believe how it's all turned out. How hopeless everything seemed when I used to cry on Bertrand's shoulder. Now he's dead, and I have everything I wanted. Do be careful, *chéri*," she added, as a shriek of delight carried across the garden. Colin and Jules were dueling with sticks.

"Monsieur Laclos must have been a good friend to you," Suzanne said.

"It was so splendid. I could talk to Bertrand about Emile, which was heaven. And about other things." Louise paused a moment. "I think he was the best friend I've ever had."

"And in many ways a friend is a rarer thing than a lover. I'm sure you were a good friend to him."

"I hope so." Louise's brows drew together. "After I heard he'd been killed, I couldn't help but wonder—" She turned to Suzanne, her gaze haunted with a guilt Suzanne understood all too well. "I couldn't help but wonder if perhaps Carnot did find out and was more willing to take revenge on a fellow officer than I'd thought."

"Did he ever say anything to you about Monsieur Laclos?"

Louise shook her head. "No. Well, once after Bertrand's death he made a comment about my not having a new cavalier."

"Could you read anything behind it?"

"I couldn't be sure. I went petrified and changed the subject." Louise leaned forwards across the table. "Madame Rannoch, that's why I told you all this. Because I have to know. If Carnot had anything to do with Bertrand's death—"

"We don't know that. And even if by any chance he did, Monsieur Laclos was a grown man who made his own choices." Suzanne hesitated. A gust of wind ripped through the garden, bringing the scent of lavender. "Madame Sevigny, guilt has a way of lingering. And corroding. But it's a poor foundation for a life. And it will do no good to your husband and children. You need to let go of it. For their sake if not your own."

Louise Sevigny met her gaze, her own wide with surprise and understanding. "You sound as though you understand so well."

"Personal experience," Suzanne said. It was a far greater admission than she normally made about her life.

Louise gave a faint but heartfelt smile. "Thank you."

Suzanne took a sip of wine. "Madame Sevigny, was there anyone Bertrand ever indicated he was afraid of?"

Louise's gaze darted over her face. "So you do think someone was behind his death?"

"It seems likely. But by no means does that mean it was your husband."

Louise reached for her own wine. "Bertrand would never have admitted it to me if he had been afraid. He had a ridiculous protective streak. And yet—" She took a sip of wine. "I never connected it with his death—perhaps because I was so preoccupied worrying about Carnot. But he wrote me an odd letter just before he was killed. He said he'd discovered something unexpected. That he hoped to be back in Paris soon so he could learn more."

"Did he give any indication what this was about?"

"No." Louise set down her glass and stared at the shadow it cast on the table. "But he said if he was right it could change everything."

*　*　*

"Étienne Laclos was a very gallant man," Suzanne said, when she'd finished telling Malcolm about Étienne's arrangement with Louise de Carnot.

"Rupert told me about a girl in Spain but not about Louise." Malcolm glanced out across the stream. "I wonder if Rupert was protecting Louise's reputation or if he knew the truth of the relationship or if he didn't know about it at all."

"What he'd discovered that he told Louise changed everything—do you think that's the same reason he wrote to Stewart he was going to return to England?"

"It's certainly suggestive." Malcolm's brows drew together. "Stewart may be slow, but when he got that letter even he had to have wondered why a traitor would have been thinking about returning to the country he was betraying. And yet he said nothing."

"He didn't want to be the man who'd ordered the death of a man who might be innocent."

"Quite." Malcolm's fingers curved inwards as though he'd like to smash them into Stewart's face. "Precisely what Bertrand had discovered remains open to question."

"Malcolm—" Suzanne glanced down the gravel walk in the Jardin des Tuileries where Simon and David were walking with Colin between them. With the clarity of an image on the stage, she saw Simon's expression when she'd talked to him and David about Rupert Caruthers. How could she be so blind to a truth that was staring her in the face? "I never asked you— With David and Simon, did you know immediately? What they meant to each other, that is?" she concluded, feeling unwontedly awkward.

Malcolm frowned a moment, as though sifting through the past. "I was there when they met. At Oxford. In a dusty hall, where we were rehearsing *Henry IV Part I*. I can't say I knew instantly. But by the end of that rehearsal, I was making conversation with Oliver Lydgate and doing my best to appear invisible so David and Simon could talk." He hesitated. Malcolm didn't talk about anyone's feelings easily. "I can't pretend to know precisely how and when the relationship progressed, but the spark was clear from the first." He gave a faint smile. "Though it was more than a year later before Oliver asked me if I thought there might be something between

David and Simon, and even then I don't think he'd have said it if he hadn't been three sheets to the wind."

Gleeful laughter carried back on the breeze. Colin was giggling as Simon held him up to examine a bird's nest in a tree overhead. "But you already knew that David—" Why was she having trouble saying it? She could be perfectly frank about most love affairs. But then most love affairs didn't risk getting the participants arrested. "You'd known that David was attracted to men for some time."

Malcolm shot a look at her. "I can't remember not knowing. No, that's not quite true. We were boys when we met at Harrow. I didn't think about it one way or another. Even as we got older, as David showed little interest in girls or inclination to talk about them, I thought he was just reticent as I was." He glanced ahead at their son, as though hoping Colin navigated the shoals of adolescence better than he had himself. "But then I remember one day in a maths lecture seeing David glance at another boy. Just glance. There wasn't anything between them. David was as slow to develop in such matters as I was. But somehow I knew. And it wasn't like discovering something surprising. It was acknowledging something I should have seen long since." He studied her face. "Why?"

Suzanne drew a breath, fragrant with fresh cut grass and orange trees. Even now she hesitated to put it into words, because it was based so much on intuitions and impressions. "Because Louise Sevigny said she thought Bertrand loved someone in England. And I'm wondering if perhaps it should be blindingly obvious to us who that person is."

CHAPTER 13

Malcolm moved through the elm trees in the Jardin du Luxembourg, planted by Marie de' Medici some two centuries ago. Rupert Caruthers was slumped on the ground, his back against a tree trunk, his gaze fixed on the leaf-strewn ground, though Malcolm suspected whatever he was seeing had more to do with memory than with what was presently before him. Malcolm took a half step forwards, letting the toe of his boot crunch over a pile of fallen leaves.

Rupert looked up with a start of surprise. "Malcolm. I didn't realize—"

"You were lost in thought."

"I come here, sometimes, when I want to get away." Rupert hesitated, then, his face oddly vulnerable, added, "Bertrand wrote to me about it. It was his favorite spot in Paris."

Malcolm dropped down on the ground beside Rupert. The smell of damp earth brought a memory of boyhood rambles. "You were right to have faith in Bertrand. He wasn't working for the French."

Rupert's gaze shot to Malcolm's face. Relief, triumph, grief, and anger did battle in his eyes. "You're sure?"

"As sure as I can be. Talleyrand says the French were shocked to learn Bertrand had been working for us."

"By God—" Rupert started to push himself to his feet.

"Rupert." Malcolm gripped his friend's wrist. "I'll do everything in my power to learn the truth. I swear it. But rushing off in anger won't solve anything."

"It will—"

"Vengeance is singularly corrosive. And you don't know whom to wreak vengeance on."

"Stewart is—"

"An arrogant fool and a danger to his own people. But he's not the man who set Bertrand up. And if we're going to learn who did, we need to keep our wits about us."

Rupert hesitated, his wrist taut in Malcolm's grip. "If only I'd—"

"Don't, Rupert. For God's sake don't blame yourself. Therein lies the way to madness."

"I owed it to him—"

"You owe it to him to try to discover the truth. And not to ruin your life."

Rupert drew a harsh breath. "My life was—" He bit back the words and collapsed back beside Malcolm on the ground.

"You must miss him a great deal," Malcolm said.

The vulnerability was gone. Rupert's face turned as guarded as the Hofburg Palace. "He was my best friend."

"I think one's childhood friends sometimes know one as no one else does. I know that's true for me with David Mallinson."

A question flickered in Rupert's eyes. He must know about David's relationship with Simon. Was he wondering if Malcolm had brought David up to test the waters? For a moment Malcolm thought he'd pushed it too far and Rupert would close up completely. Then, as though he had a compulsion to speak, Rupert said, "I don't make friends easily. Not the sort one confides in. Losing someone like that— It's like a window shutting. A part of one's life closed off forever."

"A horrible feeling," Malcolm said. "I find it difficult enough to share things myself. I've learned I can talk to my wife. Better than I ever thought I'd be able to. But sometimes I think I'm afraid if she sees too much it will change the way she feels about me."

Rupert's gaze shot to his face, as though he was surprised by how much Malcolm had revealed. In truth, Malcolm was surprised himself. "You're fortunate in your marriage, Malcolm. Gaby and I— I'm fond of her. And I think she is of me. But we're not confidants."

Malcolm stretched his legs out in front of him and contemplated the toes of his boots. "For a long time I never thought I'd marry at all. I hadn't seen a particularly good example from my parents, and I doubted I'd be good at sharing my life with anyone. I suppose the truth is I didn't think it was fair to inflict myself on anyone. Then I met Suzanne, who'd been left alone in the midst of a war. That gave me an excuse."

"Gaby needed protection," Rupert said. "It had always been hard for the family as émigrés and with the scandal about Bertrand it had grown intolerable. And of course I needed—"

"You needed a wife. As heir to an earldom. A burden I didn't share. I imagine you were under considerable pressure from your parents to marry."

"Isn't everyone?"

"My mother died years ago, and my father never paid much interest to me. Not an ideal relationship with a parent, but there are certain advantages."

Rupert gave a bleak smile. "My parents wanted me to marry, of course. It got worse as I got older. Gaby was in difficult straits, and I've always been fond of her. It seemed the right time—"

"Did Gabrielle understand?" Malcolm asked.

"Understand what?"

"What you were offering her?" His own proposal to Suzanne rang hollow in his ears.

Rupert hesitated.

"I warned Suzanne," Malcolm said. "That I hadn't thought to marry and didn't think I'd be very good at it. I made it very clear what I was offering. And what I wasn't." He drew his knees up, scraping his boots over the ground. Hot shame washed over him.

"I didn't— That is, I never said—"

"I suppose it rather has to do with how Lady Caruthers feels about you. I had no illusions about how Suzanne felt about me." He could see the wide-eyed surprise in her gaze that night on a balcony overlooking the river Tagus when he proposed. "And yet I wondered often after we married if I'd done an unfair thing to her. Because however much I've come to care for her, I can't make myself into something I'm not."

"That's just it." The words burst from Rupert with sudden force. "I care for Gaby, but I can't be—" He bit back whatever he had been going to say and swung his gaze away, his face set hard.

"Rupert." Malcolm touched the other man's arm. "David and Simon Tanner are two of my best friends. I've known what was between them since we were at Oxford. I've known it was the sort of relationship David wanted for longer than that. I value what they share tremendously. To own the truth, I've been jealous of it."

Rupert swung his head round to meet Malcolm's gaze, defenses slammed into place. "What's between Mallinson and Tanner is irrelevant—"

"You loved Bertrand," Malcolm said. "That's relevant. And I can't imagine the hell it must have been for you to lose him and not be able to talk about it."

Rupert jerked away from Malcolm. "Damn it, Rannoch—"

"Please, Rupert. I wouldn't have pried if I didn't need to learn the truth about Bertrand's death. I think you want to learn it, too. But more than that I think you need to talk."

Rupert's fingers curled inwards, pulling the leather of his gloves taut across his knuckles. For a moment he looked like a trapped animal. Malcolm felt a stab of self-hatred. Then Rupert released his breath in a rough sigh. "I've never talked about it. I've never told . . . anyone."

"Love's difficult enough without having to keep it secret."

Rupert stared at the interlaced leaves of an elm tree. "I didn't know when we first became friends. We were only children. I only knew he understood me as no one else seemed to. Then it was as if . . . we both discovered it together." His gaze held a wonder of a discovery he'd never put into words. Young, intense, delirious love of the sort Malcolm had never known. "We were able to spend so much time together. We never talked about the future, save that we both knew I was expected to marry. Somehow I thought we could go on as we had before. Share rooms in London when we finished up at Oxford. But of course my parents pressured me to take a wife. Of course ultimately it had to change. I sometimes think Bertrand saw that better than I did. And that it was because he saw it that he volunteered for the mission in France. It made the decision for both of us."

"And allowed you to continue to work together."

"That's what Bertrand said." Rupert turned his gaze to Malcolm. "I told you the truth yesterday. Bertrand didn't tell me anything about the mission until he'd already volunteered his services to Carfax."

"It must have been a shock," Malcolm said. He worried enough when Suzanne went into danger, but at least she'd never volunteered her services to Castlereagh or Wellington without telling him. Not that he wouldn't put it past her to do so or put it past them to use her without telling him.

"I was furious. I said Bertrand had no right to take such a decision without consulting me. He pointed out that we had no claim on each other."

"That must have hurt."

"You have no notion. And yet I couldn't deny it." Rupert scraped a hand through his hair. "I told him it was too dangerous. He said danger couldn't stand in the way of duty. He accused me of thinking him a coward. I said I only wanted to protect him."

Malcolm gave a rough laugh. "I've had remarkably similar conversations with Suzanne on more than one occasion."

Rupert looked at him in surprise, then nodded. He picked up a fallen elm leaf and twirled it between his fingers. "That's when Bertrand pointed out we could work together, that it was an adventure we could share. We argued until dawn. But in the end I couldn't talk him out of it, and if he was set on it, I wanted to be part of things. Once I agreed, I got caught up in the mission. Even when we were apart we shared something. Something secret. That made a difference. And we could meet from time to time. It's amazing how little one can learn to get by on."

Malcolm nodded, thinking of the times he'd been separated from Suzanne. A prosaic note with no mention of love could still speak volumes.

Rupert went still, gaze fixed on the leaf in his fingers. "I was in Lisbon on leave at some damned embassy dinner when he—when it all happened." He dropped the leaf. His hand curled into a fist. "When they killed him. I didn't know until I got back. I couldn't believe— Wellington showed me the proof. Even then— I couldn't believe Bertrand would betray his country, but more than that, I couldn't believe—"

"That he'd betray you?"

Rupert turned and looked Malcolm full in the face. "Yes. To trust someone so thoroughly— I'm not sure I ever will again."

"And yet it seems you were right to trust him after all."

Rupert squeezed his eyes shut. "I'll never forgive myself."

"You didn't know what was happening. You couldn't have prevented—"

"Not for not preventing it. For doubting Bertrand. For believing for even a moment that he could have been a traitor. Love isn't supposed to have doubts."

"Love is complicated." Malcolm studied his friend in the shadows of the overhanging branches. "Tell me about after Bertrand was killed. What did you do?"

"You mean after I came close to calling Stewart a liar and nearly got myself cashiered for insubordination?" Rupert gave a bleak smile. "Bertrand was dead. And I wasn't sure I'd ever even known him. To be honest I didn't care much if I lived or died."

Malcolm nodded. "There was a time in my life when I felt much the same. I stumbled through the motions."

Rupert looked at him for a moment and nodded. "I went home on leave. Bertrand's parents were devastated. His father had a stroke, and the family had already been suffering the social repercussions of him being assumed to have gone over to the French. We were stupid not to have thought of that. Gaby was trying to hold things together for her uncle and aunt. She missed Bertrand as well. We could talk about the good times."

"It's natural you were drawn together."

Rupert grimaced. "And I knew what I owed to my name. It seemed one of the few things I had left to hang on to. Gaby was in precarious straits with no fortune and a family scandal. I could offer her protection. I could help Bertrand's family, and do my duty to my own."

"So you offered for her."

Rupert nodded. "I thought— No, it's foolish to say I thought we could be happy, because I didn't think happiness was a possibility for me. But I thought we could rub along. I didn't realize—"

"That perhaps Gabrielle's feelings for you ran deeper than yours for her?"

Rupert's mouth twisted. "I haven't been— I haven't been unfaithful to her. But as I said before, I can't be what I know she wants me to be. And now she's tied to me."

"She has her child and a secure position. That counts for a lot."

Rupert looked sideways at him. "Is that what you tell yourself about Suzanne?"

Malcolm drew a breath. "I love Suzanne." The words echoed oddly in his head. It wasn't something he voiced very often. "But that doesn't mean I can be what she wants or needs. Whatever the novelists say, love doesn't transform one. I'm still the man I was before I met her, with the same scars and flaws and inadequacies. Love doesn't sweep away all obstacles. In fact, sometimes it creates them. There can be a great deal to be said for rubbing along amicably."

"But one misses—" Rupert scanned the trees that stretched before them, memories shifting through his eyes, at once painful and sweet.

"Yes," Malcolm said.

"Who?" Rupert's voice was rough. "Who did this to Bertrand?"

"I asked you before who his enemies were. Does your answer change now I know the truth?"

Rupert's brows drew together.

"I take it the girl in Spain you told me about was a fabrication?"

"The girl existed. But the hopes were all on her side."

"Who knew about your relationship with Bertrand?"

"No one."

"You're sure?"

"My God, you can't think it's the sort of thing we'd share."

"Not willingly. But secrets can get out."

Rupert shook his head. "We were careful. We both knew the consequences. We were both conscious of our families. And once Bertrand went to France and then Spain, we only saw each other in secret. For reasons of the mission more than our relationship."

"What about Gui?" Malcolm asked.

"Malcolm, I told you yesterday, Gui's a bit feckless, but you can't think—"

"In investigations, I've learned never to rule anyone out." Even his closest friends. "And money and a title are an obvious motive."

"But there wasn't any money then. Or estates. And the title was only a dream émigrés clung to. The family were in desperate financial straits. You can't think Gui somehow foresaw Napoleon's downfall and strategized to get rid of Bertrand so he could have the title and fortune after the Restoration? Morality aside, I don't think Gui's that organized or forwards thinking."

"Did he know about Bertrand's work?"

"No. Only Bertrand's parents did. They never told Gaby. I'm sure they didn't tell Gui. Other than his parents, only I knew."

"And his masters."

"Yes." Rupert's frown deepened. He wasn't as used as Malcolm to the idea of finding betrayal on one's own side. "But as I told you, I don't know of any particular enemies he had."

"Did he ever talk to you about the Comte de Carnot?"

Rupert shifted on the ground. "Bertrand was friendly with his wife."

"Bertrand let it be rumored that he was Louise Carnot's lover so her husband wouldn't learn about her affair with Emile Sevigny. It's all right, I know you're trying to protect Louise, but she confessed the whole to Suzanne. She was quite frank. Also concerned that her husband might have had something to do with Bertrand's death."

"Bertrand was very fond of Louise. He always said he could handle anything Carnot tried. But for Carnot to have framed

Bertrand, he'd have had to know Bertrand was reporting to the British."

"Surprising," Malcolm said. "But not impossible."

Rupert stared at him. "I'll keep my temper in check. I won't do anything rash. I won't impede your investigation. But in turn— I want you to tell me the truth. I want to know who did this. I know it won't bring Bertrand back, but I owe him that much at least."

Malcolm, thinking of his own reaction to Tatiana's death, could only nod.

Dorothée fingered an ivory kid glove edged with cerise ribbon. "This could be quite dramatic with my new crêpe. I think it's the right red." Her fingers stilled on the glove. "It seems horrid to be talking about clothes. Worse than in Vienna somehow."

"We still have events we have to dress for." Suzanne cast a glance at Colin, asleep in the baby carriage Malcolm had specially designed to make it easier to take him about with them. Colin had his arm curled round Figaro, the stuffed bear they'd given him in Brussels for his second birthday.

"Poor Princess Tatiana." Dorothée picked up a pair of wrist-length gloves of dove-colored kid. "When I think how I disliked her in Vienna for your sake. And now all I can think is how different her life would have been if my father had acknowledged her."

"Tatiana Kirsanova had a taste for adventure. That wouldn't have changed."

"But she would have had security. She wouldn't have had to be so grasping." Dorothée gave a wry smile. "It's easier to be a nice person when one doesn't want for anything. Perhaps she wouldn't have had to hide her child away."

"Willie did."

Dorothée's delicate brows drew together. "I still find it hard to look my mother in the face, knowing what she did to Willie."

"It can't have been easy for your mother, either." Gustav Arm-felt, the man who seduced the eighteen-year-old Wilhelmine, had been her mother's lover for several years.

Dorothée drew the gloves through her fingers. "No, I know

that. But to have pressured Willie to give the child away so Willie may never see her again—"

Suzanne cast another quick glance at her son. When a marriage ended in separation or divorce, the father almost always retained custody of the children. One of her greatest fears about her past coming to light was the possibility of losing Colin. Tonight's rescue of Manon Caret hung before her, a challenge and a risk.

Dorothée set the gloves down abruptly. "I'm not in the mood for trifles. Let's go."

They left the glovemaker's and stepped out into the bustle of the Boulevard des Italiens. Sunlight spilled onto the broad, cobbled expanse of the boulevard, a marked contrast to most Paris streets, where the light leached through a narrow sliver between tall, close-set buildings. Fiacres, cabriolets, wooden carts, and crested private carriages rattled over the road. Suzanne and Dorothée threaded their way along the pedestrian walkway in a throng of ladies in muslins and silks, ribboned bonnets and flower-trimmed hats, and gentlemen with high, gleaming shirt points and fashionably cut coats.

And of course soldiers. Fair-haired Prussians in coats of blue or brown or green. Cossacks in short red jackets and billowing trousers. Dark-mustached Hungarian grenadiers in fur caps. Dutch-Belgians in blue or green. And a sea of red-coated Englishmen, here and there relieved by the blue of a dragoon, the dark green of a rifleman, the kilt of a Highland regiment. Colin wakened, pushed himself up in the baby carriage, and glanced from side to side with wide eyes.

Dorothée gathered up her French-worked skirts as they brushed past three ladies with shopping parcels, relaxing in wooden chairs on the pavement hired out from a white-haired man in a worn black coat. "Karl wants me to go back to Vienna with him," she said, her gaze fixed on two British dragoons up ahead.

Suzanne swung her gaze to her friend. Dorothée's delicate profile was set as stone beneath the quilted yellow satin of her poke bonnet. "Paris is difficult for you."

"Yes." Dorothée's gloved fingers moved over the carved ivory handle of her parasol. "It's odd, I'm happier than I was before Vienna. I used to be so desperately lonely. Vienna changed that."

"You have Karl," Suzanne said. It was almost a question.

Dorothée hesitated a fraction of a second. "Yes."

A husky voice drifted across the street. A ballad singer in a flowered shawl stood on the opposite walkway singing a Gluck aria. Eurydice lamenting for her husband.

"Edmond never used to seem to pay the least attention to what I did," Dorothée said. "I'd swear he didn't even know where I was half the time. Whom I spoke with or danced with. Whom I slept with or the fact that I slept alone."

Suzanne took a biscuit from her reticule and leaned forwards to give it to Colin. "There's nothing like a wife's infidelity to arouse a husband's interest."

"He's never paid so much attention to me the entire time we've been married. Now when I see the way he looks at Karl—"

"Doro." Suzanne laid a hand on her friend's arm. "You can't blame yourself for Edmond's idiocy."

"Isn't a wife supposed to be able to manage her husband?" Dorothée shook her head.

"A wife shouldn't have to manage her husband."

"*Ma chère* Suzanne, you're talking like a revolutionary."

"*Dix sols pour chacun!*" "*Sept sols seulement, madame!*" Shouts from open-air tables offering bottles of scent, carved wooden toys, gaudy glass jewelry, and all manner of trifles rose above the strains of Gluck.

"In Vienna Karl and I could go about as a couple quite openly," Dorothée said, "as my sister Jeanne does with Monsieur Borel. Without fear of Edmond. I'd feel at home there, in a way I don't think I ever will in Paris."

They moved past a café. The smell of coffee and fresh-baked bread, roast meat and wine drifted into the street. "And yet?" Suzanne asked.

Dorothée bent over the baby carriage and touched her fingers to Colin's hair. Colin grinned up at her. "Tante Doro."

"*Mon cher.*" Dorothée straightened up. "My little boys. Edmond would lay claim to them."

A chill cut through Suzanne's jaconet gown and twill silk mantle. "Children are considered a father's property."

A thin-faced girl darted through the crowd and ran up to them. *"Que voulez-vous, madame?"* She reached into the basket over her arm and held up a handful of toothpicks. *"Deux sols, madame. Mon pauvre père, il est malade."*

She looked no more than eight. The age Suzanne's sister had been when she lost her life. Suzanne reached into her reticule and pressed some coins into the girl's hand. "Get yourself a decent meal," she said in French.

"I doubt her father really is ill," Dorothée said.

"No, but she looks underfed." For a moment, Suzanne was back alone and hungry on the streets of Léon. And she at least had been fifteen. A world away from the court of Courland, where Dorothée had grown up with a private orchestra and their own theatre company and house parties overflowing with royal guests.

"Willie and Princess Tatiana had to give up their children," Dorothée said. "I don't know how they did it. But they were babies. They'd barely had a chance to know them. When I think of my boys—"

Suzanne leaned down to brush biscuit crumbs from Colin's shirt. Colin grinned at her. "It's every mother's nightmare."

"Perdita!" Colin's gaze fastened on a wooden horse in the stall they were passing.

"Yes, it does look like Daddy's horse," Suzanne said. "But you already have two horses—"

"There's always room for another horse in a stable." Dorothée opened the steel clasp on her reticule.

"Doro—," Suzanne protested.

"No, please, I'd like him to have it." Dorothée purchased the horse and gave it to Colin, who curled his hands round it with delight. "It's lovely at this age when the smallest thing can make them happy," she said, watching Colin turn the horse over in his small hands. "One must enjoy that."

"You're a good honorary aunt, Doro. And a good mother."

"I don't know about that. I often feel as though I'm fumbling to find the right way to go on."

"Doesn't everyone? I know I do. I wasn't even sure how to hold a baby when they first put Colin in my arms." For a moment she could feel the small weight of his newborn body cradled against her, his limbs squirming, his small head bobbing about, so insubstantial and yet at the same time so tangible it sent a shock through her. And then she saw Malcolm sitting on the edge of the bed, drawn back a little as though he feared to intrude, yet looking at both of them with an expression that cut her soul in two.

"You make it look effortless," Dorothée said.

"If so, it's only because I'm a good actress."

A sizzling sound cut the air. They moved round a crowd surrounding a man frying sausages in a pan. "Some couples are able to come to an amicable arrangement over children," Suzanne said. "If you could find a way to share the boys with Edmond—"

"I can't imagine that," Dorothée said. "But even then—"

She broke off. Suzanne heard the trouble in her friend's voice even before she turned her head to see the line of worry between Doro's delicate brows. They moved past a boy polishing boots. The earnest voice of a young man discoursing on Descartes washed over them. "There are other considerations that would keep you in Paris?" Suzanne asked in a soft voice.

Dorothée frowned. "Vienna changed so much for me. I never thought I fit in as a girl in Courland. The sallow little younger sister who trailed after Willie and Jeanne and Pauline. I never felt I could compete with my dazzling sisters. Or with Maman. And God knows I didn't fit into Parisian society as a bride. I went tongue-tied whenever I went into company. It was as though I came alive in Vienna. Among new society I didn't have the baggage of my childhood hanging over me. I could be a different person. Karl— Karl changed a lot for me. But it wasn't just him. I was able to use my mind as I hadn't since my girlhood lessons."

"You helped Monsieur Talleyrand with communiqués and correspondence," Suzanne said, watching her friend carefully.

"He genuinely seemed to listen to me and value my opinion." Dorothée's eyes lit in a way they hadn't all day. "He said I was an invaluable help, and I actually believed him, though I'm sure it was partly just that he was being kind." She looked at Suzanne as Suzanne smiled. "Yes, I know, most people would laugh at the idea of Monsieur Talleyrand being kind, but he is kind to me."

"I know he is," Suzanne said. "I've seen it."

Dorothée turned her gaze away. They had neared another stall. It contained engravings, but not the views of Paris and copies of old masters displayed elsewhere. These pictures showed men and women in a variety of positions. A number of which Suzanne had attempted, though some appeared physically impossible. The artist was not without talent, and Suzanne could not deny the effect quickened her blood. "The French are so wonderfully frank about these things," she said.

Dorothée's gaze darted to Colin.

"Much better not to make a fuss over it," Suzanne said. "As though there's something wrong. It's a perfectly natural act after all." She cast another glance at the engravings. "At least most of them are."

Color flooded Dorothée's cheeks beneath the brim of her poke bonnet. "I didn't grow up an innocent. Not in Courland. I never thought— I hadn't— It's not that I was ignorant, but I didn't understand what all the fuss was. I had few illusions about fidelity, but there seemed no point. I couldn't imagine enjoying— Until Karl."

Suzanne swallowed. It had been that way for her in the brothel. A way of survival, a game at best, but not something she'd enjoyed. Not until later. "Learning that is worth a great deal."

"Yes, but it's not—"

"Enough to build a life on? Not on its own."

"I love Karl or I could never be his mistress. But—" Dorothée cast a quick glance about. "Oh, the devil, I'm tired. Let's go into a café."

She said nothing further until they had repaired to the nearest café and were seated by a sparkling glass window, supplied with cups of café au lait and a mug for milk for Colin. Dorothée stared into her frothing cup. "I think my uncle would miss me if I went to Vienna."

Suzanne took a sip from her own cup. "I'm sure he would."

Dorothée picked up the silver spoon and frowned at it. "I'm not blind or deaf. I know what people are saying. That he's besotted with me. That he's lost track of the negotiations with Britain and Russia and the other powers. As though personal feelings could ever make Talleyrand lose track of anything."

"No. Though I do think you've upset his equilibrium more than has happened to him in many years."

Dorothée fixed her gaze out the window. Two ladies in flowered bonnets were passing on the pedestrian walkway, accompanied by two British infantry officers. "Some people say I've been his mistress since Vienna." She cast a quick glance at Suzanne. "I'm not. We've never—"

"I didn't think you had."

Dorothée studied her with a mixture of relief and curiosity. "No?"

"One notices such a thing about one's friends."

Dorothée reached for her cup again and blew on the steam. "Not that— It's not the same as Karl, but I don't think of Monsieur Talleyrand as— I don't precisely think of him as an uncle," she said in a rush, not meeting Suzanne's gaze.

"He's not your uncle. He's your estranged husband's uncle. He's no blood connection to you at all."

Dorothée took a careful sip of café au lait. "No. He isn't." She set down the cup. "At times I feel years older than Karl for all he's more experienced than I am in many ways. I wonder sometimes—"

"If you'll outgrow him?" Suzanne picked up the mug of milk and held it so Colin could take a careful sip.

"No. Yes. Perhaps. I think Talleyrand will fascinate me forever." Dorothée hunched her shoulders, as though she felt a chill despite the warmth of the day. "I feel so safe with him. And yet sometimes the way he looks at me almost frightens me."

Malcolm's gaze, in rare moments of naked vulnerability, shot through Suzanne's memory. "It can be scary, being cared about that much."

"Yes. That is, I don't know that he— But it feels that way."

Dorothée picked up the spoon again and turned it between her fingers. "I worry about Talleyrand if I go to Vienna. But sometimes I think if I don't leave him now, I'll never be able to do so."

"Do you want to leave?"

Dorothée looked at her with stricken eyes. "I'm not sure."

Suzanne stared at the swans floating on the surface of the pond in the Jardin des Tuileries. "I should have guessed sooner. About Bertrand Laclos and Rupert Caruthers."

"In the end you did guess," Malcolm said. He was sitting in a chair beside her.

"Not until I talked to Louise."

"I don't see how you could have worked it out sooner."

"The way Gabrielle Caruthers described her marriage. This makes so much sense of it. But at the time I merely thought—"

"That they were like us?" Malcolm asked, his voice soft and neutral.

She swung her gaze to him. "How could you—"

"Because I thought the same thing when Rupert was talking to me about his marriage. English—Scots—man comes to the rescue of penniless émigrée and offers her the protection of his name and fortune. A pleasing fairy tale. Only he can't share himself as easily as he can share his position and worldly possessions."

Her throat closed. "Malcolm—"

"You can't deny it has a familiar ring."

Regret tore at her throat. "I never asked—"

"For anything. That doesn't mean you didn't deserve it. Or want it. I've learned to read you rather well."

She put her hand over his own. His skin was cool beneath her gloved fingers. "The similarities are superficial. Gabrielle was in love with Lord Caruthers when they married."

"And you weren't in love with me." It was a statement of fact.

She looked steadily at him. "Not then."

He swallowed. "Yes. Well, we've both changed."

"And though we danced round it, in light of what Gabrielle told me and certainly what Rupert Caruthers told you I doubt the Carutherses' marriage is particularly passionate." She kept her gaze fastened on his face. "That's one place we've never had any problems."

An unexpected smile shot into his eyes. He took her hand and lifted it to his lips. "I don't deserve you."

"That's silly, darling. I often think the same about you."

He laced his fingers through her own. "The irony being that of the two it's Rupert who's been faithful. Though I suspect that's because he doesn't think he'll ever fall in love again. Some people are like that."

She tightened her grip on his hand, holding on to the moment. Pushing aside the time, only a few hours away, when she was going to slip away from her British husband to assist in the escape of a Bonapartist agent. "Do you think Lord Caruthers had any idea about his wife's affair with Rivère?"

"I doubt it. He only expressed guilt where she was concerned. If he killed Rivère in a fit of jealousy he's an exceedingly good actor."

"He was an Intelligence Agent."

"True. I still doubt it. Rupert takes his code and his vows seriously and has difficulty imagining anyone else doing otherwise, whether it's his military colleagues or his wife. He's a bit like David that way." Malcolm was silent for a moment. "Rupert and Gabrielle's situation is exactly what I've always feared for David if he ever married."

Suzanne drew a breath. Her chest hurt, as though her corset laces were pulled too tight. "Simon isn't going anywhere. And David's strong enough to hold out against pressure."

"There's no pressure quite like that of aristocratic family tradition. And love's a complicated thing. It doesn't sweep aside all problems. Sometimes it creates them. That's what I told Rupert."

Suzanne watched her husband in the dancing shadows as the breeze stirred the leaves of the tree overhead. "That love's complicated?"

"That it doesn't sweep aside obstacles or miraculously turn one into a better person." He turned his head and met her gaze. "I know that full well because I love you."

She looked back into his gray eyes, open and vulnerable, in that way they so seldom were. "Complicated or not," she said, "I'd take it over the alternative."

"Yes, so would I. Terrifying as I often find it."

She rested her head against his shoulder, thinking how well she knew him and at the same time of the corners of his mind and soul that were still barred to her. "You make me very happy, Malcolm." *Even though I know full well I don't deserve you.*

"Rank flattery, my darling."

"As a good investigator, you should recognize the truth when you hear it."

He slid his arm round her shoulders, uncharacteristically heedless of anyone who might walk by. "To own the truth, I've been envious of David and Simon since we were all at Oxford. To be that sure of another person."

"I know." She thought back to her first visit to England just over a year ago. "I felt the same way when I first met them. Even before that, exchanging letters with Simon."

He looked down at her. "I never told you—"

"About their relationship? Not in so many words. But I can read between the lines rather well. Cordelia figured it out a half hour after they arrived in Brussels. If she hadn't guessed earlier. One just has to be open to the possibility."

He smiled, then his gaze went serious. "But even as I envied them, I worried about them. Love isn't easy in the best of circumstances, and they face greater obstacles than many of us."

"The weight of family and tradition."

"Particularly with Lord Carfax for a father." Malcolm grimaced at the thought of his spymaster. "He's a man willing to go to any lengths to achieve his objectives, as I know full well. I don't know that he'd object to the relationship continuing, but he wants David to marry and produce an heir."

"And that sort of marriage would tear David in two. Aside from the fact that I can't imagine Simon standing for such a pretense."

Malcolm nodded. "I think Carfax has been biding his time,

hoping David will grow out of it. I wonder when Carfax's patience may run out, what he may try—"

Malcolm broke off, gaze fixed on the pond.

"Darling?" Suzanne asked.

"Dear God," he said in a rough voice. "It's so obvious. Why didn't I think of it sooner?"

CHAPTER 14

Lord Dewhurst, the footman informed Malcolm in the entry hall of Dewhurst's hired house in the Rue de Richelieu, was engaged. With Lord Caruthers. Malcolm bit back a curse. It was just as he had feared. He brushed past the footman, ignoring his gasp of surprise, and took the stairs two at a time.

He pushed open the study door without knocking to find Rupert with his hand round Lord Dewhurst's throat, pressing Dewhurst against the cherrywood and gilt paneling. Dewhurst's face was red.

"Rupert, no." Malcolm ran across the room and caught his friend by the arm.

"Damn it, Malcolm, stay out of this. You don't know what he's done."

"Yes, I do. He's responsible for the death of the man you love."

"Then get out of my way. If it were Suzanne—"

"I hope to hell you'd stop me."

Dewhurst wrenched himself away from his son and collapsed against a chair, breathing hard. "You don't understand, Rupert."

"On the contrary, I understand very well. You wanted me married. You wanted me to produce an heir. You thought you had to get rid of Bertrand to ensure that. The wonder is I didn't see it sooner."

"Damn it, boy, that fellow had you bewitched."

Rupert lunged at his father again. "Don't you dare—"

Malcolm ran between father and son. Rupert's fist caught him on the jaw. He grabbed hold of the desk to keep from falling, sending a bronze paperweight thudding to the floor. "Lord Dewhurst, do you admit you were behind the forged papers that made it look as though Bertrand Laclos was a double?"

Dewhurst put his hand to his throat and tugged at his cravat. "I admit nothing of the sort."

"Don't add lies to your other sins, Father." Weary disgust edged Rupert's voice. "We know Bertrand was set up. Who had a better motive than you? The hell of it is, I fell right into your trap. If I'd known I'd have done anything rather than marry and fall in with your plans."

"Gabrielle's a good woman. You can't quarrel with how things turned out there."

"Gabrielle deserves better than me. Thanks to your machinations and my stupidity, she's trapped in a marriage to a man who can never give her what she deserves."

Dewhurst regarded his son as he might a diplomat from a minor country who was refusing to see the British perspective. "You're irrational, Rupert."

"On the contrary. For the first time in my life, I see things clearly."

Something wavered in Dewhurst's gaze. He took a half step towards his son. "You're a good father, Rupert. You've given me a grandson to be proud of."

"Don't you dare come near Stephen." Rupert's shoulders tensed as though he would deliver another blow. "So help me God, I may not be able to repudiate the title, but I can damn well keep my son away from you."

"For God's sake, Rupert. He's my grandson."

"No." Rupert's gaze was ash cold. "Stephen can't be your grandson because you aren't my father anymore." He strode to the door. "Malcolm. Thank you for discovering the truth. I'm sorry you were dragged into our sordid family drama."

He went out, pulling the heavy door to behind him with a sharp click. Dewhurst stared at the gleaming door panels, a wounded man who could not yet quite feel the extent of the injury he had been dealt.

"Lord Dewhurst—," Malcolm said.

Dewhurst spun towards Malcolm, his gaze hard. "I'd advise you not to spread these outrageous stories any further, Malcolm."

"Wellington and Castlereagh have charged me to discover the truth."

"Wellington and Castlereagh wish to avoid scandal. They won't thank you for causing one."

That, Malcolm feared, was all too true. "They're neither of them one to shirk the truth."

"But they both know enough to realize at times one has to be flexible with it. Something you need to learn yourself, Malcolm. And to acknowledge what's due to your position."

"I'm more concerned with what's due to Bertrand Laclos's memory."

Dewhurst twitched his shirt cuffs straight beneath his coat. "Bertrand Laclos was a traitor who preyed upon my son's friendship and did incalculable damage to the country. Thank God you uncovered his crimes before he wreaked more havoc."

"Believe me, sir, I will never forgive myself for the part I played in this affair."

"You're a clever man, Malcolm." Dewhurst made this sound like a backhanded compliment. "But you have difficulty understanding where your loyalties lie. That's a dangerous quality in Paris these days. Don't be foolish. You too have a young family to consider."

"What the devil are you suggesting, sir?" Malcolm asked, voice hard with the fear that shot through him.

Dewhurst returned his gaze, his own level and hard and stripped of vulnerability. "Merely that you should be prudent."

"It sounded more as though you were telling me to watch my back. Which you may be sure I will do."

* * *

Wellington swore with the same vehemence Malcolm had heard in the duke's voice at the Duchess of Richmond's ball when he announced that Napoleon had humbugged him. "Damn fool Dewhurst. Should have known better than to let family matters intrude on politics."

Castlereagh's fine-boned face was drawn into a frown, as though he were forcing himself to look at something distasteful. "Accusations of such a relationship could have destroyed young Caruthers's career."

"And in acting as he did, Dewhurst has just drawn attention to that relationship."

"You believe it then?" Castlereagh asked, still frowning.

"What? That Caruthers and Bertrand Laclos were lovers? That Dewhurst was behind the accusations against Laclos?"

"All of it."

Wellington took a turn about the room, hands clasped behind his back. "I don't give a damn who Bertrand Laclos and Rupert Caruthers were sleeping with. As to Dewhurst orchestrating the Laclos affair— Malcolm presents a convincing case."

"But there's no definitive evidence," Castlereagh pointed out. "Dewhurst denies the whole. Perhaps the French used Laclos's unnatural relationship with Caruthers to blackmail him into working for them."

"Talleyrand says he wasn't working for them," Malcolm pointed out.

"Hardly the most reliable of sources," Castlereagh returned.

"But in this case I believe him. And if you'd seen Dewhurst's reaction to the accusations, it was as good as an admission."

"The question," said Charles Stuart, who had been listening to the whole with a somewhat bemused expression, "seems to be what we do next. The Ultra Royalists are difficult enough without something like this to hold over us. If this becomes public—"

"It can't," Castlereagh said. "Even if we were certain, to admit that one of our senior diplomats destroyed the son of a noble French family who are close to the Comte d'Artois— Not to mention what it would do to Caruthers."

"Caruthers can take care of himself," Wellington said, striding back to the center of the room. "But we can't risk the story getting out."

"We may not have a choice," Stuart said.

"We can damn well do everything we can to ensure it doesn't get out."

"The Lacloses deserve to know Bertrand didn't betray his British allies," Malcolm said.

Wellington took a step towards him. "You'll say nothing to them. That's an order, Malcolm." His mouth twisted. "How the hell did Rivère know about this? And whom might he have told?"

"I don't know how he knew." Malcolm met the duke's gaze, wondering again at what lay behind Wellington's own confrontation with Rivère. "I doubt he told many people—he understood the value of information." He glanced from Wellington to Castlereagh to Stuart. "Do any of you know what the surprising news might be that Bertrand wrote about to Louise Carnot just before he was killed?"

"If it was something in Paris, it's more likely to have had to do with French intelligence," Castlereagh said. "Perhaps he suspected they were on to him."

"Odd he'd have written to Madame Carnot about that, though," Stuart pointed out. "And odd he'd have wanted to go back to Paris to investigate."

"And then there's the fact that eventually he planned to return to England," Malcolm said.

Castlereagh's mouth tightened. "My brother was wrong to conceal that."

Wellington, continuing to frown, said nothing at all. Stuart examined his nails.

"I've just heard from Davenport that he's located a former mistress of Rivère's," Malcolm said. "We're going to talk to her tonight. Hopefully she'll be able to shed some light on what Rivère knew and whom he told."

"Just be careful that in questioning her you don't reveal more," Wellington said.

"Of course."

The duke gave a curt nod. "God save us from careless words spoken across a pillow."

Movement flickered in the dressing table looking glass as Suzanne fastened her second diamond earring. Malcolm stood leaning in the open doorway of their bedchamber, watching her. She met his gaze in the mirror. She could read fresh intelligence in his eyes. "What?" she asked.

"I found Rupert trying to strangle his father."

"I take it you stopped him?" Suzanne turned round on the dressing table bench to face him.

"Yes, though I have to admit I was sorely tempted to strangle Dewhurst myself." Malcolm closed the door behind him and moved into the room.

"Did Dewhurst admit to setting Bertrand up?"

"Not in so many words. But he may as well have done." Malcolm dropped down on the edge of the bed. He moved as though his limbs ached. "Rupert stormed out of the house and told Dewhurst he couldn't come near his grandson again. It's not easy, hating one's father."

Suzanne saw Alistair Rannoch's mocking, sardonic face and heard the lash of his tongue. "Rupert had to know the truth."

"Of course. And Dewhurst deserves the enmity." Malcolm frowned at the pale flowers in the Aubusson carpet. "God knows I've never been able to summon filial love for Alistair Rannoch—"

"With good reason."

"With reason certainly. But nothing like this. If I learned he'd been responsible for your death—" Malcolm's fingers curled round the bedpost. "I don't know that I'd be able to refrain from strangling him."

It was one of those rare, oblique admissions of feeling he made that always took her breath away. But it would never do to draw attention to it. "Then we're fortunate your father largely ignores me," she said.

"Ignoring passes for good parenting with Alistair."

Suzanne leaned forwards on the dressing table bench, hands on her gauze skirt. "What happened after Rupert stalked out?"

"Dewhurst blustered a great deal and tried to deny the whole. Threatened me if I went to Wellington and Castlereagh."

"With what?"

Malcolm's fingers tightened on the fluted wood. "My family. I think it was bluster, but we need to watch him carefully."

"I'm always careful."

He shot an amused gaze over her face. "You can be distinctly reckless, sweetheart."

"Not without carefully calculating the odds." She smoothed down a snagged thread in her skirt. "I don't suppose this stopped you from going to Wellington and Castlereagh?"

"No. And Stuart. Stuart took it the most calmly, jumped right to the consequences. Wellington cursed Dewhurst for mixing personal matters with politics. Castlereagh seemed surprisingly distressed by the suggestion of the relationship between Rupert and Bertrand."

"He's a conventional man, darling."

"But a man of the world. I'd have thought—"

"I think sometimes you overestimate how many people see the world as you do, dearest."

"I'm well aware Castlereagh and I see the world through different lenses. But I wouldn't have thought Rupert and Bertrand's relationship would trouble him so deeply." Malcolm frowned. He respected Castlereagh, Suzanne knew, and despite his words it troubled him that their views diverged so strongly over issues that mattered passionately to him. And this one touched on his closest friends.

"Do they believe Dewhurst set up Bertrand Laclos?" she asked.

"They seem at least willing to consider it. Wellington insisted it has to remain secret, at least at present."

"The Lacloses—"

"Need to learn the truth. Whatever Wellington said. Of course there's nothing to stop Rupert from telling Gabrielle. It's difficult to tell what will happen between them. But honesty can only improve matters."

Her breath caught. "Sometimes honesty can make things worse."

"Than living a lie?" He shook his head. "Difficult to imagine."

Her throat closed as though someone had tied a noose round it. "That's because you're so wonderfully honest, darling."

"Lies have a way of corroding the soul. And it's never good to live in ignorance."

Unless one could stay that way forever. Her fingers curled inwards, nails biting into her palms. Malcolm leaned against the bedpost, watching her. "There's more, isn't there?" she said.

He hesitated a moment. She could see him searching for the right words. It took her back to the early days of their marriage, when they'd both walked on eggshells round each other. "I saw Harry Davenport on the way to Headquarters," Malcolm said. "He's traced the Christine we found reference to in Rivère's things. An opera singer who plays minor roles and is known more for her list of protectors than her vocal accomplishments."

"Harry's quite brilliant at his work."

"And quite pleased to have work to do besides pushing papers."

Suzanne adjusted one of her earrings. "And, being Harry, I imagine he knows where to find this woman?"

"We think she'll be at the Salon des Etrangers tonight," Malcolm said, his voice carefully neutral.

Suzanne pulled the earring free of an escaped tendril from a ringlet. The earrings had tiny fleurs-de-lis above the diamonds. Malcolm had chosen the design because it was French and could not possibly appreciate the irony. "Harry's going with you?"

Malcolm nodded, watching her with a steady gaze.

She smoothed a crease from the gauze ruffle at the neck of her gown. A strangled laugh rose up in her throat. Here she had spent the afternoon constructing an elaborate scenario to explain her absence this evening to her husband, and this new information—and Malcolm's protective instincts—rendered it irrelevant. "And you don't want me to come with you."

His gaze shifted over her face. She had a feeling he'd thought this scene through in advance, but he was still choosing his words with care. "How could I possibly not want you with me? But the Salon des Etrangers isn't like Frascati's, where ladies can eat ices and gamble with no fear for their reputation. The Salons des

Etrangers is like a London gaming hell. Respectable women aren't seen there."

"So odd to think of myself as a respectable woman." Even to Malcolm she could say that, though he didn't know the half of it.

"It's a favorite haunt of Allied soldiers and diplomats. It will be thronged with people we know. Even if you wore a disguise there's a good risk you'd be recognized."

Suzanne leaned back on the bench and smiled at her husband. "I love the moments where you turn protective."

"I'm not trying to coddle you, Suzette." He gave a rueful grin. "God knows there are times when I want to, but this is different. To own the truth, if there's gossip about you it won't be so easy for you to get women like Gabrielle Caruthers and Louise Sevigny to confide in you."

"And it would be tiresome for your diplomatic career."

"I don't give a damn about—"

"No, but I do." She reached behind her for her scent bottle. "I quite agree with you, Malcolm."

"You do?" The suspicion in his voice at once made her want to laugh and it choked her throat.

"You should go with Harry to the Salon des Etrangers. I'll go to the Russian embassy with Cordelia." She removed the crystal stopper and dabbed her custom-blended scent on her ears and wrists. One of the few vestiges of her former life she still carried with her. She'd worn the same scent as Raoul O'Roarke's agent in the Peninsula. "Don't look so surprised, darling. Do you imagine I've lost all common sense?"

"No, but I know how you dislike—"

"Being left out of things? Of course I do. But not to the point where it jeopardizes an investigation." Though the truth was she probably would have protested a bit more if it weren't for Manon Caret's escape being set for tonight. Suzanne's role as a former French agent and her loyalty to her comrades was making her more prudent and a more conformable wife. That ought to be funny. "Just don't let the Marquis de Livry invite you to one of his Sunday evenings."

Malcolm laughed. Livry, the proprietor of the Salon des Etrangers, was known for the Sunday evening parties he gave at his villa at Komainville where the wine flowed freely, cards were dealt, and the gentlemen present—including some of the most powerful men in France and other countries—mingled with actresses, dancers, and opera singers. "Even if it proves necessary to the investigation? Though I don't think I'd fit in very well."

She returned the scent bottle to the dressing table. "You could fit in anywhere, dearest. In the service of an investigation. Though in that case we might have to revisit my staying behind."

"I wouldn't have expected anything less."

Suzanne studied her husband's face. "You look as though you were set for a battle."

"I was."

She got to her feet and shook out her ruched satin and gauze skirts. "Disappointed you didn't get to fight it?"

"Hardly. I know better than to waste my energies." He continued to study her. Not with suspicion—she'd never known Malcolm to be suspicious where she was concerned—but with the sense that he didn't fully understand. Malcolm was far too clever to take her at face value.

She moved to the bed and put a hand on his shoulder. "Dearest, our life is different now. The war's over. We're running fewer risks. Or the risks we run are more insidious. I'm trying to learn how to go on in a civilian world. For your sake. For Colin's sake. For my own."

He reached up and put his hand over her own. "I don't want you to be—"

"Stifled? I don't think there's any danger of that." Though oddly, it was one of the things she'd worried most about when she stopped working for Raoul. She'd gone from being an agent to a wife, not a role she'd ever envisaged herself in. She lifted her other hand and ran her fingers through his hair. "Usually you're the one trying to keep me out of danger."

"Only when—"

"Absolutely necessary?"

He gave an abashed grin. "I was going to say when I can't help myself."

"And I promise to continue to resist your chivalrous impulses. But tonight I'll see what I can learn at the Russian embassy." She bent down and brushed her lips over his own. "And I charge you to remember this conversation the next time you have one of your Hotspur moments."

He returned the kiss, holding her against him for a moment, his grip unexpectedly tight. "I'm more a Brutus than a Hotspur."

"It's the same thing, dearest. Both of them are equally misguided when it comes to informing their wives of their plans."

He took her face between his hands. His eyes searched her own for a moment. "There's one way I'm not like Brutus. Sometimes I'm not at all sure I could manage to go on without you as Brutus does without Portia."

Her chest constricted. She was all too afraid he'd have to go on without her one way or another. It went without saying that they both risked their lives. But an even greater risk was that he would learn the truth and not be able to go on living with her. "You would, you know," she said, smoothing his hair off his forehead. "You would because you'd have to. Eventually you might marry again. You might even fall in love."

"No," he said in a flat voice. "Once was unexpected enough."

"I'm touched, darling, but—"

" 'Doubt thou the stars are fire—' " He pulled her close and kissed her again, sliding his fingers into her carefully arranged hair. "It's all right, beloved. I learned early on to take advice from Shakespeare."

CHAPTER 15

Harry cast a sideways glance at Malcolm as they walked to the Salon des Etrangers. "I more than half-expected Suzanne to be with you, probably in some sort of clever disguise."

"So did I. I spent most of the time after we spoke thinking up clever arguments about why it didn't make sense for her to accompany us. No one was more surprised than I when she agreed with them so readily."

"Surprised and a bit disappointed?"

"No. Yes. Perhaps." Malcolm frowned at the cobblestones, blue-black in the moonlight. "I'm not used to such ready acquiescence from my wife."

"Wives can surprise one. Though I imagine yours does less than most."

"Not really." A host of memories tumbled through his mind. "That is, in many ways I still feel I'm coming to know her."

Davenport shot a look at him. "You don't give that impression. At times I'd swear you can communicate just by looking at each other."

"About some things. We've always been our closest when we share a mission. But we'd only known each other for a few weeks when we married." He saw her wide, startled gaze the night he proposed, and then felt her hand trembling in his own when he slid the wedding band onto her finger. His own hands had been like ice and none too steady. "And even after two and a half years—"

Harry snorted. "Cordy and I've been married five years. Of course we were apart for four of them. Even so I feel I'm still coming to know her. For instance—"

Malcolm turned to look at his friend. Harry's face was a study in lack of obvious emotion. "If you mean the help your wife has given us in the course of the investigation—"

Harry's features relaxed into a rueful grin. "Of course you would know. God knows why I'm being reticent. God knows why I care. I've heard enough stories about Cordy's lovers through the years. And I faced down the only one she cared about when I confronted George Chase in Brussels."

Harry was a master at disguising emotion. But Malcolm, no novice at it himself, could spot the technique. "It's one thing knowing in theory. It's another being confronted by the actual person."

"It shouldn't be. The past is in the past. I told Cordy that in Brussels."

"Harry . . ." Malcolm hesitated, because as close as he and Harry Davenport had become, they rarely touched on personal topics. "Jealousy is perfectly normal."

"You think I should be jealous of a man my wife dallied with years ago when she and I were estranged?" Harry's voice was taut with self-mockery.

"I don't think 'should' has anything do with it. I think you might be, logic be damned." Malcolm pictured the arrogant face of Suzanne's former lover Frederick Radley. Was he jealous of Radley? Not precisely. He was conscious of a keen desire to throttle the man. But then of course he hadn't even met Suzanne when her affair with Radley had occurred.

"And yet I pride myself on logic," Harry said. "It's the only thing that's saved me from madness on more than one occasion."

"But that was taking Cordelia out of the equation."

Harry stared at a pool of yellow lamplight on the cobblestones ahead. "Cordy told me in Brussels that she could make me no promises. I believe she cares for me. I believe she means to make our marriage work. Just as I do. But I know there are no guarantees. Not in anything in life, and perhaps particularly not where Cordy and I are concerned. Last night was just one of any number of tests. There was no point in making more of it than there already was. It was bad enough for Cordy in any case. I just hope to God she never knows—"

"Never knows what?" Malcolm asked, watching Harry's set profile in the lamplight.

Harry drew a breath that scraped against the warm evening air, like a rock dragged over porcelain. "That seeing her with Edmond Talleyrand hurt like the very devil."

Malcolm touched his friend's arm. "I don't think you'd be human if it didn't."

"Damn it, Rannoch, do I have to admit to being human? I pride myself on being above such things."

"There's nothing like love to pull one back to earth," Malcolm said, surprised the word "love" had come so easily to his lips.

Harry paused in front of the Salon des Etrangers. The kid of his glove pulled tight over his fingers. "I still remember my first glimpse of Cordy, across the Devonshire House ballroom. God knows why I was even there that night. Usually I avoid balls like the plague. But when I looked at her I thought I'd never seen anyone so beautiful or so alive. I wanted her as I've never wanted anything or anyone, before or since. And I was sure she'd always be out of my reach. Part of me still feels that way."

Malcolm had an image of Suzanne, sitting at her white and gold dressing table a few hours before. For a moment as he'd watched her, surrounded by gilt and porcelain and crystal, framed by the tapers with their flames glowing in the looking glass, she'd seemed as ethereal as a vision. "I know the feeling. I'd never have had the courage to offer for Suzanne if she hadn't needed me. But though I agree one can never know what the future may hold, I'd swear Cordelia is yours now."

"For a man who claims not to believe in love, you can be damnably romantic, Malcolm." Harry turned to the door. "None of us can really belong to anyone. But most of the time I believe what's between Cordy and me is real. I think perhaps that's the most any of us can ask for."

A liveried footman admitted them to the gilded magnificence of the Salon des Etrangers. Crystal chandeliers glittered in gilt-edged mirrors. Marble gleamed. Laughter and the clink of glasses and the sound of champagne corks popping drifted down the stairs.

A portly man approached them. For a moment, Malcolm was thrown back to his visit to the prince regent's reception at Carlton House the previous summer. The Marquis de Livry, proprietor of the Salon des Etrangers, might have been the prince's twin.

They had only met once, but the marquis greeted Malcolm and Harry like old friends. "Monsieur Rannoch. And Colonel Davenport. This is the first night you have honored us with your presence."

"Wellington and Castlereagh keep us busy," Malcolm said, shaking the marquis's hand.

"They should realize you'll work the better for indulging yourselves for an evening," Livry said, shaking Harry's hand as well. "I thought it was perhaps that the duke disapproved. Or that your charming wives did."

"Wellington doesn't control us," Harry said. "Nor do our wives if it comes to that."

The marquis smiled. "I'm glad to hear it, Colonel Davenport. So many of your compatriots find themselves at home here that we have begun to feel quite like a little island of Britain in Paris." He waved a hand towards the stairs. "I'm sure you'll find something to tempt you."

They laughed with what Malcolm hoped was a fair imitation of gentlemen out for an evening of sport and climbed the stairs. This was hardly Malcolm's first visit to a casino, but nearly all had been in the service of an investigation. He associated the whiffle of cards, the rattle of dice, and the smells of champagne and brandy with work.

Glowing wax candlelight spilled over the broad stairs. Numerous salons opened off the landing, offering a seemingly endless vista of gilt chairs and tables of hazard and *rouge et noir*. A fair-haired lady in a clinging white gown stood beside a pier table surrounded by two dragoons, a Prussian captain, and three men in civilian coats. She had stripped off one of her gloves and was holding out a shapely arm to one of the dragoons, who appeared to be taking snuff from her wrist.

"Never understood the allure of that trick," Harry said. "But then I've never had a taste for snuff." He regarded the woman for a moment. "Christine Leroux is supposed to be a petite brunette."

They moved into a salon. Green baize–topped tables were strewn about the Aubusson carpets. Candlelight and voices bounced off the gilt ceiling. English, a variety of German dialects, Russian, and of course French, much of it badly accented. A number of elegantly gowned ladies moved through the crowd, but though they received appreciative glances, many of the men present focused with hot-eyed intensity on the cards and dice on the tables before them.

"So many familiar faces we could almost be in London," Harry murmured.

He was right. Malcolm saw Lord Apsley, Punch Greville, the Duke of Devonshire. No one from Wellington's staff, but then Wellington was known to disapprove of gambling.

A cry cut the air, followed by the scrape of a chair being pushed back from a table. "Damn you. Isn't it enough you overrun our city? Must you cheat at cards as well?" The speaker, who spoke in French-accented English, wore civilian dress. He lurched towards a sandy-haired man in the uniform of a British lieutenant.

"That's a damnable accusation." The British lieutenant pushed himself to his feet.

"You couldn't have drawn that hand by accident."

"How dare you—"

"I saw the card up your sleeve."

"By God, sir." The British lieutenant strode towards the Frenchman. The Frenchman caught him by the arm and landed a blow to his jaw. The lieutenant went reeling back but did not fall to the ground.

A thin, dark-haired man in a black coat moved between them with quiet economy. "You both forget yourselves."

It was Raoul O'Roarke, Malcolm realized with surprise.

The Frenchman whirled on O'Roarke. "Stay the hell out of this."

"Difficult to do so when you've held your quarrel so publicly."

"You're not even French."

"No. But I love this country."

"And you fought on the opposite side." The Frenchman lunged at the lieutenant again.

O'Roarke's arm shot between them. "You'd both be wise to remember the uniform you once wore. You owe your countries better than this."

All round them, the salon had gone silent. Not even a card turned in the stillness. Malcolm was ready for violence to break out, but O'Roarke's voice held both men.

The Frenchman tugged his coat smooth. "If you'll excuse me, I think I will take the air."

"A wise choice." O'Roarke glanced at the red-faced lieutenant. "I suggest a cup of coffee. I believe you may obtain one in the salon across the passage."

Slowly, play resumed. The Frenchman and the lieutenant moved to separate doors with what dignity they could muster.

O'Roarke started across the room himself and stopped at the sight of Malcolm. "Well played," Malcolm said. "I think you missed your calling as a diplomat."

O'Roarke gave a faint smile. "Those I've worked with would scarcely agree with you. But there's been enough madness these past months. These past years. I hate to see it continue."

"It's a rare thing to hear such sanity in Paris these days," Harry said.

O'Roarke cast a glance round the salon. "In truth, we're closer to twenty years ago than I ever thought to see again." He turned back to Malcolm and Harry. "I must be off, I'm promised to look in at the Russian embassy. Enjoy your evening. Though I rather suspect it has more to do with work than pleasure."

He was off with a smile and a nod. Harry looked after him. "O'Roarke was in Paris twenty years ago?"

"He was an early supporter of the Revolution," Malcolm said.

"Speaking out in coffeehouses, writing pamphlets, organizing protests. Then he was imprisoned in Les Carmes during the Terror. He was nearly guillotined. Only a matter of days according to my mother." Malcolm had only been six, but he still recalled his mother's white face and the way she'd scanned the Paris papers, fingers taut on the newsprint.

"He was a friend of your family?" Harry asked.

"He used to visit quite a bit, particularly in Ireland where my grandfather has estates. I saw a lot of him growing up, especially before the United Irish Uprising. He had a knack for talking to a confused boy as though he were an adult. "

"We could use more like him."

"I've often thought—"

"Rannoch," a voice called out. "What are you doing here?"

It was Freddy Camden, who had been two years ahead of Malcolm at Harrow. His younger brother had fought at Waterloo and come through with minor wounds. Freddy had come to Paris during the peace with other expatriates.

"What else does one do at the Salon des Etrangers?" Malcolm said, relaxing his posture. "Seeking diversion."

"You don't seek diversion, Rannoch." Freddy threaded his way between the tables. "You're always working. Even at school. You've just traded books for dispatches."

"He has hidden depths," Harry said.

"You come here often?" Malcolm asked.

"Lord, yes." Freddy pushed his lank fair hair back from his eyes. "That is, where else is one to go in Paris? Feels just like home."

"What else would one want in a foreign capital?" Harry murmured.

"Yes, quite," Freddy agreed, the irony lost on him.

"We're looking for someone specific as it happens," Malcolm said. "Have you met a woman named Christine Leroux?"

Freddy stared at him for a moment. "Good lord, Rannoch. And here I actually believed the talk that you were happily married." He clapped Malcolm on the shoulder. "Good for you."

Malcolm sent a mental apology to his wife, while at the same time wishing she were present. She'd appreciate the scene. "I don't suppose you'd believe I want to interview her?"

"Call it whatever you like. Mademoiselle Leroux is rather out of my league, but you never know. She's in the salon across the passage. In a green gown."

Christine Leroux stood at a *rouge et noir* table. She wore a gown of bronze green satin, cut along elegant lines and low at the neck. Her hair, a dark, rich brown, was drawn into a simple knot with artful tendrils escaping about her face. She held a glass of champagne in one hand. As they watched, she stepped forwards and leaned over the shoulder of a Highland captain to whisper encouragement.

Harry went still halfway across the room.

Malcolm cast a glance at him.

"Sorry," Harry murmured. "For a moment I saw a ghost. Cordelia last night, with Edmond Talleyrand."

Malcolm and Harry proceeded across the room. The dragoon leaned forwards to make his play. Christine straightened up. Then she turned round, quickly but still with grace, and looked Malcolm directly in the eye. "Not that I don't enjoy being looked at, but I confess I'm a bit curious as to the reason."

She had a low, musical voice with the resonance of a trained singer. "We haven't met, Mademoiselle Leroux," Malcolm said. "I trust you will forgive the informality of the introduction. My name is Rannoch, Malcolm Rannoch. My friend Harry Davenport."

Christine Leroux regarded them from beneath artfully darkened lashes. She had a thin, fine-boned face, dominated by a pair of wide, expressive brown eyes. "What may I do for you gentlemen?"

"Perhaps we could talk somewhere quieter?"

She gave a throaty laugh. "About?"

"I believe we have an acquaintance in common," Malcolm said. "Or rather had."

Her brows lifted, darkened and strongly marked. "Oh?"

"Antoine Rivère."

For a moment Christine Leroux's face went still. Faint lines stood out about her eyes and mouth beneath carefully applied paint. "Yes, I knew Antoine. The Comte de Rivère. A bit. It was tragic what happened to him."

"So it was. We are endeavoring to learn the truth."

"He died in a tavern brawl."

"It may have been more complicated. Perhaps if we could go to another room?"

Christine Leroux cast a glance at the dragoon, who had won the last hand, and gave a quick nod. She led the way across the room, drawing a number of glances, and down the passage to a small sitting room hung with cream-colored silk. She swept forwards, leaving it to them to close the door, and took up a position in front of the unlit fireplace, where the light from the two braces of candles fell at a flattering angle across her face. Every movement carefully controlled, an actress setting the stage. She was only an inch or so over five feet tall, but she dominated the scene. "The champagne in the cooler on the table should be chilled. Perhaps one of you gentlemen could pour us all a glass? I don't know about you, but I find myself in need of fortification."

Malcolm uncorked the bottle—which was indeed well chilled—and filled three glasses, while Harry leaned against a chair, his gaze on Mademoiselle Leroux. Mademoiselle Leroux held her position. She might have been the lady of the house, waiting for her footmen to serve her.

"I assume you mean to explain further," she said at last, when Malcolm put a glass into her hand.

"Colonel Davenport and I found your name in a letter in Rivère's rooms." Malcolm carried a second glass over to Harry. "It appears you were more than acquainted."

Mademoiselle Leroux studied him for a moment, then gave a faint smile. "Surely you realize there are different degrees of acquaintance, Monsieur Rannoch."

Malcolm returned to the table and picked up the third glass. "As a friend, I'm sure you wish to learn what happened to him."

For a moment, something flickered in her eyes that might have been grief. "Of course." She took a sip of champagne. "But I don't see how I can help you."

Harry turned his glass in his hand, studying the play of candlelight on the crystal. "In this letter, Rivère makes certain comments about his future. About a fortune he expects to come into."

She kept her gaze steady on his face. "I wouldn't know about that."

"You didn't know he was a blackmailer?" Malcolm asked.

Mademoiselle Leroux twisted the stem of her glass between her fingers. "Rather a harsh word. If you mean did I know he made use of information, yes. Most people do. A way to help one's self to a role, a preferment. To solve an investigation."

Malcolm took a sip of champagne. It was a superb vintage, dry and yeasty. "Point taken. Had Rivère's use of information made him any enemies?"

Mademoiselle Leroux gave a low laugh. "Does anyone get past the age of eighteen without making enemies? At least anyone whose life hasn't been a complete bore."

"Any enemies who'd have wanted him dead?" Harry asked.

She frowned in apparently genuine consideration. "His cousin wanted the title. But he was going to have Antoine denounced, not killed. Though it might well have led to the same thing."

"And so Antoine was going to leave Paris," Malcolm said.

Mademoiselle Leroux took another sip of champagne. "Was he?"

Malcolm knew gesture as prevarication when he saw it. "Did you know Rivère was meeting me the night he was killed?"

She opened her mouth as though to deny it, then gave a sudden laugh. "There's little point in denying it, is there? For what it's worth, he told me you were clever. I suppose he told you he wanted safe passage out of France?"

"Was he planning to take you with him?" Harry asked.

Her gaze shot to him, bright with amusement. "Antoine? Take me off to England to live in luxury off the charity of the British government? Hardly. There are all sorts of lovers. That isn't the sort we were. It's not even as though I was his only—"

"His only mistress?" Malcolm asked.

"Any more than he was my only lover."

"Did you know the names of the others?"

"There was a dancer at the opera—Ninette. A bit annoying that he chose someone so close to home. And..." She hesitated a moment, then shrugged, fluttering her gauze scarf over her shoulders. "I don't know why I feel any particular reason to protect another woman's reputation. Antoine was involved in an affair with a married lady. Lady Caruthers." Her gaze flickered between them, taking in their reaction. "You already knew."

"As it happens, yes," Malcolm said. "What did you know about the affair?"

"It seemed to amuse him. He said dallying with married women could be dangerous, but fortunately she took it no more seriously than he did. Than I did. The secret to a successful love affair, don't you find?"

"But he confided in you," Malcolm said.

"A bit." She moved to a gilded chair and sank into it, still commanding the room.

Malcolm dropped into a chair across from her. "Why was Rivère so convinced the British would support him in luxury in England?"

She twisted the stem of her glass between her fingers. "Surely he told you when you met the night he was killed?"

"Mostly he made vague threats."

Mademoiselle Leroux leaned back in her chair. The silk of her gown slithered over her legs. "Are you sure you want to know?"

"We want to learn why Rivère was killed."

She tilted her head back. "No matter where it takes you?"

"You intrigue us, mademoiselle." Harry moved to a third chair at the table. "I think you'd best elaborate. Rannoch and I promise not to faint with shock."

She gave a reluctant smile. "There was some past scandal. To do with Lady Caruthers's cousin. Bertrand Laclos."

"So Rivère told me," Malcolm said. "What did Rivère tell you about Laclos?"

She hesitated, weighing the value of information. "That his death wasn't what it appeared."

"Who did he say was behind Laclos's death?" Malcolm asked in a casual voice.

"He didn't." She shifted in her chair. "Antoine talked to me, perhaps more than he should. But he wasn't a fool."

"What else did he say he had to bargain with?" Harry asked.

"Who says he told me anything?"

"He couldn't have conveyed such confidence based on something so vague."

Malcolm could see the carefully masked calculation in Mademoiselle Leroux's eyes. Then she smiled and held out her half-empty glass. "A refill?"

Malcolm crossed the room, took the champagne bottle from the cooler, and refilled the glass. Mademoiselle Leroux smoothed a crease from her glove. Harry leaned back in his chair and kept his gaze on her.

"You're very obliging, Monsieur Rannoch," she said when Malcolm brought her the refilled glass. "I can only wonder what you'd do for a woman with whom you were intimately involved."

"You flatter me," Malcolm said as he put the glass into her hand.

"But then of course I've learned men are generally obliging when they want something from one, one way or another."

"What else did Rivère have to use against the British?" Malcolm asked.

"He knew something about you." Mademoiselle Leroux sipped her champagne. "I suppose he told you?"

"Yes," Malcolm said, his gaze steady on her. He could feel Harry looking at him. "But he was too astute to think any hold he had on me would guarantee his safety."

"He said you always underestimated what you could accomplish," Mademoiselle Leroux murmured. "But no. He did have more information."

"About?"

She tilted her head back. "How much do you know?"

"Enough prevarication, Mademoiselle Leroux." Harry clunked his glass down on the table. "What did Rivère have on Wellington?"

CHAPTER 16

The smell was instantly recognizable as Suzanne stepped through the stage door. Greasepaint, smoking oil lamps, sweat, dust, and excitement. The smells of backstage at the theatre, the smells of her childhood. She nodded at the porter. In a plain dark blue dress and gray cloak, a blond wig over her hair, a basket on her arm, she could pass as a seamstress come to assist Manon Caret's dresser. The porter jerked his head to the right.

"Thank you," Suzanne said, her voice roughened into the accents of Montmartre. "I know the way."

She turned to the right and started down the maze of passages. Raised voices sounded as she neared the wings. Sonorous, rolling, intense. Racine. *Baj a zet.* A French play that made her think of her mother performing in Spain.

A stagehand leaned against the wall nearby. Bearded, pot-bellied, smelling of tobacco. Suzanne skirted a basket of swords and shields, which forced her to nearly brush against the stagehand. He didn't move out of her way.

"Men have it easy," she murmured. "A beard hides so much."

"A woman's hair color makes for a great change," Raoul returned, in a Breton accent. "Two of Fouché's agents are at the stage door," he continued in the same tones. "And two more at the front of the house."

"Are you telling me to go home?"

"On the contrary. You know I never indulge in regrets in the midst of a mission. And your help is more vital now than ever. But go carefully."

"I always do."

He gave a snort that could pass for the stagehand making a flirtatious pass at the seamstress. He hesitated a moment, as though debating the wisdom of further speech. "I was at the Salon des Etrangers before I came here."

Her heartbeat quickened. "Did you see Malcolm? He was going there tonight with Harry Davenport."

"I saw them both. I also broke up a fight between a British lieutenant and a former soldier of the Empire." His mouth twisted. "Not that I don't understand the impulse to lash out at the victors, but there's been too much death as it is."

His gaze held ghosts. Suzanne scanned his face. "It was good of you to save the combatants from themselves. If perhaps not wise to draw attention to yourself."

"I can't abide waste. Malcolm said I'd make a good diplomat. Of all the names I've been called, that's perhaps the most unusual." He rested his hand on her shoulder for a moment, again in a gesture that could pass for flirtation, though the current that ran between them held no echo of romance. "I'm glad you're too young to remember twenty years ago. This is closer to the Terror than anything I'd have ever wanted you to see."

A bitter taste welled up on her tongue. "But I'm one of the victors."

"For which I'm eternally grateful. You should be as well, for your son's sake if not your own."

"I try. In between bouts of self-disgust. Which is why I'm here."

His hand tightened on her shoulder. "Look after yourself, *querida*."

Suzanne nodded and moved on down the passage. Actors in gaudy robes and seamstresses and dressers with arms full of costumes brushed past her. Strange, from her few visits to the Comédie-Française the direction was imprinted in her memory. But then she had a good memory for direction. It was a survival skill. She reached the door, rapped once, and turned the handle.

Manon Caret's signature scent, tuberose and violet, greeted her, along with the smells of face powder and greasepaint. Manon herself was not in the dressing room. A brace of candles flickered on the dressing table. A blue silk dressing gown edged in Valençiennes lace had been flung over the dressing table bench. An elaborate cloth of gold gown lay on the sofa. More costumes hung from strings of clothesline from the ceiling. Paste jewels spilled from a box on the dressing table. Wigs stood on stands round the room. Masks hung from the wall. Trunks and hatboxes were stacked indiscriminately about the room. Programmes and playbills adorned the walls. A stack of scripts stood on a spindle-legged table.

A light shone from the open door to the adjoining sitting room. Suzanne glanced through and met the gaze of the tall woman with honey-colored hair standing there. Berthe, Manon's dresser. Berthe inclined her head. A small blond head showed on the arm of the sitting room sofa. That must be Clarisse, who would be four now. She'd been a baby when Manon came to Suzanne's rescue. Roxane, who must be about seven, sat in a worn damask armchair, white-stockinged legs crossed at the ankles, a book in her lap. She looked up at Suzanne, leaned forwards as though to spring to her feet, then at a look from Berthe bit her lip and waved silently. Suzanne waved back.

For a moment she was a girl again, falling asleep on a sofa in her mother's dressing room or on cushions on the floor, the sounds of actors' chatter, the rustle of silk as her mother swept in and out of the room, the jangle of jewels, the stir of a quick costume change all round. Her father poking his head in to confer with her mother about how the performance was progressing. It had been so much a part of her life, she had dozed through the noise and commotion, secure in the happy, chaotic world of whichever theatre her parents' traveling company was playing in.

Her gaze moved back to Roxane. She'd been just about that age when her mother died giving birth to her sister. Her life had begun to change, though even then the security of her theatre family had continued for some time. Until she was fifteen and her father's and sister's deaths had changed everything.

She set down her basket, perched on top of a brass-bound chest, and waited.

"What did Rivère have on Wellington?" Harry asked.

Christine Leroux met his gaze. "Ah. I should have realized you knew. Though I'm rather surprised you'd discuss it with me."

"I told you," Malcolm said. "We want the truth."

She tightened her gloved fingers round the glass. "A brilliant man, they say, your duke. A number of my countrymen and women will never forgive him, but I can't but admire the man who brought down the emperor. But then I've never been one to pay much attention to politics." She gave an elegant shrug and sipped her champagne. "I sometimes wonder what Napoleon could have accomplished if he'd been able to avoid some of his unfortunate entanglements. Though your Duke of Wellington seems to share the failing. She's quite pretty, I admit, in a rather insipid way, though it's a bit odd, as she's only recently given birth to a baby. And apparently her husband is not precisely compliant." She set her glass on the table with care. "Antoine had come into possession of an indiscreet letter the Duke of Wellington had written to Lady Frances Webster."

Malcolm suppressed a curse while a part of his mind screamed, *Of course,* and another part darted over myriad disquieting questions.

"Do you know the exact contents of the letter?" Harry asked in a tone that told Malcolm his reaction was much the same.

Mademoiselle Leroux shook her head. "But I know it was enough to convince Antoine he had a strong hold on the duke. And to render the duke extremely angry." Her gaze darted between Malcolm and Harry. "The duke is a powerful man."

"Wellington isn't the sort to be driven by personal motives," Malcolm said.

"All men can be driven by personal motives when it comes to questions about women. And honor." Her mouth curled round the last word. "I suppose this rather changes your quest for justice."

"On the contrary, mademoiselle," Malcolm said. "Davenport and I are determined to learn the truth wherever it may lead us."

She regarded him for a moment. "Do you know, Monsieur Rannoch, I have the oddest inclination to believe you. Which no doubt means I am a fool."

"Did Rivère quarrel with anyone else recently?" Harry asked. "Or was there anyone else he was blackmailing?"

"Isn't this enough?"

"We need to explore all options."

"And you'd like your duke not to be guilty of murder."

"We'd like to be certain."

Christine Leroux frowned for a moment, fingering a fold of her silk gown. "About a week ago. I passed a man on the stairs when I was going to Antoine's lodgings. He was storming out, and he looked angry. I asked Antoine if this man owed him money. Antoine merely smiled."

"This man is a gamester?" Malcolm asked.

"He's here nearly every night. Including tonight."

"Then you must know his name."

"Gui Laclos."

Malcolm exchanged a quick glance with Harry. "Rivère had a distinct interest in that family."

"So he did," Harry murmured.

"I did wonder if the quarrel was about Lady Caruthers," Mademoiselle Leroux said. "Antoine said no, but I couldn't be sure. Laclos doesn't look the sort to fuss about those things, but gentlemen can be funny when it comes to their sisters." She took another sip of champagne and set her glass down. "I've enjoyed our tête-à-tête, gentlemen, but I fear I should not be gone from the salon much longer. It might be considered rude."

They returned to the passage to the sounds of an altercation from the open door of one of the salons.

"Take your hands off me, you damned frog!" a British voice yelled. "Can't you accept that you lost?"

"You mistake," another voice replied, in English with just the faintest undertone of French. "My family have spent the past twenty years in England. So we considered Waterloo a victory. And I fear my frog blood runs pale."

Malcolm, Harry, and Mademoiselle Leroux stepped through the open doorway to see a dragoon major pushing a dark-coated civilian away from him.

"I might have known it," Mademoiselle Leroux murmured. "He has a temper."

The civilian was Gui Laclos. His voice was steady, but his eyes were bright with one too many glasses of champagne or brandy.

"So you're one of the émigré bastards who've been overrunning our country," the major said.

Gui smoothed the sleeve of his coat with exaggerated care. "I assure you, we're glad to be back in our own country."

"Which far too many of my comrades died to get back for you." The major eyed Gui as though he were something unpleasant he'd discovered under a rock. "While you sat snug in England, living on our charity."

Gui's mouth tightened. "I can't claim to have fought myself. But my family—"

"You're Laclos." Another dragoon sprang to his feet. "Your brother's the traitor who fought for Bonaparte."

Rage flared in Gui's eyes. "My cousin as it happens. And while his actions could be called misguided, I don't believe fighting for one's own country can be considered treason."

"Might have known you'd make excuses," the major said. "You pampered blighter—"

Gui's fist connected with the major's jaw. The other dragoon knocked Gui into the table. Cards thudded to the floor. A brandy decanter upended and crystal glasses smashed. The tension simmering below the surface, which O'Roarke had managed to defuse earlier, flared to the boiling point once again.

Even as a half-dozen other men sprang to their feet, a man in a superbly tailored evening coat moved between the combatants. "I think perhaps it's time you left, gentlemen."

The dragoons began to argue. Gui pushed past Malcolm and

Harry and staggered into the passage. Malcolm and Harry followed to find him being sick into a Sèvres vase on a pier table. He spun round at the sound of footsteps and wiped his hand across his mouth. "Rannoch," he said, as though confirming to himself that it was indeed Malcolm he was looking at. He seemed unaware of Harry's presence. "Sorry. Not sure if it's the drink or the disgust."

"You had great provocation," Malcolm said.

Gui's mouth twisted. "Those bastards had a point. I didn't fight at Waterloo. Or anywhere else."

"Your cousins did," Malcolm said. "Both of them."

Gui gave a short laugh. "Bertrand—"

"Bertrand fought in his own way. You're right, what he did can hardly be called treason."

Gui regarded Malcolm for a moment, as though trying to blink him into focus. "You always had an odd way of looking at the world, Rannoch."

"I'll take that as a compliment."

"It was meant as— Oh, God." Gui spun round and threw up into the vase again. "Sorry," he said, breathing hard. "Usually have a better head."

"It's been a difficult few days," Malcolm said.

Gui gave a crooked smile. "I hardly have a right to say so. My life is ridiculously easy."

"How well did you know Antoine Rivère?" Malcolm asked.

Wariness shot through Gui's posture for an instant. Then he relaxed into exaggerated insouciance, one hand braced against the gilded molding on the wall. "Rivère? The chap who was killed two nights ago? Is it true you were there—"

"Yes. How well did you know him?"

"Not at all. That is, I suppose we'd been at some of the same entertainments these past weeks, but one could say that of half of Paris."

"Half of certain circles in Paris perhaps. You were seen storming out of Rivère's lodgings a week ago."

Gui drew a breath, then released it. "Walked right into that, didn't I? But then I told you I'm not myself." He glanced at the toes of his boots. "This isn't the first night I've come to the Salon des Etrangers. By any means. I've lost rather a lot. A great deal of it to Rivère. My family may have a chance at recovering our estates, but we've hardly recovered our fortune yet. I couldn't bring myself to go to my uncle once again. Rivère wasn't inclined to be accommodating."

"A simple explanation," Malcolm said.

Gui met his gaze, his own unexpectedly steady in his ashen face. "Sometimes simple explanations happen to be the truth."

"Sometimes," Harry said.

Gui spun towards him. "You're—"

"Davenport. Harry Davenport."

Gui's eyes focused. He stared at Harry for a moment. "Cordelia's husband."

"Yes." Harry's voice was scrupulously casual. "I understand you and my wife are acquainted."

"A long time ago." Gui scraped a hand over his hair. "I saw her last night. She looked happy. I'm glad." His gaze moved back to Malcolm. "I was angry at Rivère, but I didn't kill him. Though I don't expect you to believe that. Any more than you believe my explanation in the first place. After all, my family are given to deception."

Manon Caret swept into the dressing room with a rustle of pearl-stitched velvet and a waft of scent. "Lucille stepped on my train again, devil take the girl. I'm trying to glide with regal authority, and I get jerked back like a fish on a line. And I have Marvaux breathing down my neck. He eats too much garlic." Her gaze fell on Suzanne as though she'd never seen her before. "Who are you?"

"The new seamstress, madame."

"I trust you're deft with quick repairs. This gown has a tear in the train thanks to Lucille. Berthe!" Manon pushed the door closed on the passage, smiled at Suzanne in a very different way, and blew a kiss to Roxane. Berthe came through the door from the dressing room and began to deftly unlace the purple velvet gown. Clarisse continued to sleep on the sofa, as deaf to the noise as Suzanne had been as a child.

"You look well," Manon said to Suzanne. "I've often wondered how you got on."

"I've often remembered your kindness."

"Rubbish, I'm not in the least kind, but one must help out where one can. One never knows when one will be in need of help oneself," Manon said. Berthe pulled the purple velvet gown down. Manon stepped out of it in her corset and chemise. "You married, Raoul tells me. An Englishman."

"I married him for work." At a nod from Berthe, Suzanne picked up the cloth of gold gown from the sofa and handed it to the dresser. "That isn't why I'm still married to him now."

Manon's mouth curved in a smile. "I never thought much of the married state, but for some it proves to work out remarkably well." She stepped into the new gown and slid her arms into the slashed sleeves. "And you have a child?"

"A little boy, Colin. He's two."

Manon cast a glance at her own daughters as Berthe laced her into the gown. "It changes one, being a mother. As I believe I once told you."

"And I said it seemed highly unlikely I ever would find out." Had that only been four years ago? "That was how I felt at the time."

"Life has a way of taking us by surprise." Manon regarded her for a moment while Berthe stripped off her pearl necklace and earrings and replaced them with paste diamonds. "You're in a fortunate position now, married to an Englishman."

Guilt bit her in the throat. "I've been more fortunate than I have a right to be."

"Don't apologize, *ma chère*. We have to take good fortune where we find it." Manon picked up a jeweled fan from the dressing table and moved back to the door. "Only four scenes more, thank goodness."

Manon swept out of the room, letting in chatter, the rustle of stiff gowns, and the jangle of ornamental swords. Berthe began to tidy the dressing table, then stopped, as though aware that too much uncharacteristic tidying would give the game away. She returned to the sitting room. Suzanne dropped back down on the chest. In the dressing room, Roxane had set down her book and picked up a doll with yellow hair. She was changing the doll's dress.

A short time later, Manon swept back into the room, letting in a babble of voices from the passage. "Five curtain calls. Not bad." She paused for a moment, her back to the door. In her blue eyes, usually so brilliant, Suzanne saw the stricken realization that this would be her last curtain call for goodness knew how long.

"I'll help you, madame." Suzanne unlaced the cloth of gold gown, while Berthe removed the luxuriant dark wig and held out Manon's dressing gown. Manon went behind the gilded screen, keeping up a light flow of chatter. The door to the passage was still ajar. "I'm far too tired for supper. All I want is to go home. Clarisse was complaining of a sore throat, she needs her sleep." Manon tossed her corset and chemise over the side of the screen and emerged swathed in the foaming lace dressing gown. "Yes, yes, I'll take a few minutes for visitors. Once I'm presentable. What a wig does to one's hair." She tugged at hairpins and ran her fingers through her blond curls, leaving them as artfully tousled as if a hairdresser had worked at them for hours. "All right, I'm ready to receive."

Berthe moved to the door. Suzanne sank down on a different chest, deep on one corner. A stream of guests spilled through the door, mostly young gallants with high shirt points, Byronic hair, and ribbon-tied bouquets clutched in their hands.

Manon extended a beringed hand to be kissed, gestured to Berthe and then Suzanne to take the flowers, and accepted the compliments with a careless smile. "I'm so glad you enjoyed it. Truthfully, I prefer Phèdre. Well, I would, she's the main character. Though I quite like playing vengeance and I did name my daughter Roxane. Well, it was my first success. I won't tell you how many years ago that was. No, I'm afraid I couldn't possibly manage supper tonight. I'm run ragged. Café des Etoiles? It's tempting, but no, my younger daughter isn't feeling well. Perhaps another night. No, you must go before I weaken. I'm determined to be a good mother for once. Berthe, do get rid of them."

Berthe shooed the gallants out. Manon kept up her stream of chatter until five minutes after the door had closed behind the last of them. "Thank goodness," she said at last in a quite different tone. She still wore the lace and ribbon–trimmed dressing gown, her hair still tumbled down her back, yet she looked like an entirely different person. "One part of being an actress I won't miss."

"No?" Berthe asked with a raised brow.

"Well, perhaps the flowers. And the compliments. A bit. But one can't seem to have them without the accompanying silliness. Suzanne, are you ready for your costume?"

Suzanne had already undone the ties on her cloak and was unbuttoning the blue gown, which fastened down the front. Manon went behind the dressing screen again. "Help Suzanne, Berthe. My change is easier. It's Suzanne who has to be me."

Berthe helped Suzanne into a cinnamon-striped sarcenet gown and a swansdown-trimmed cloak, then unpinned the simple knot her blond wig was arranged in and pulled it into a loose chignon. She plunged the curling tongs into the lamp on the dressing table and created a mass of ringlets round Suzanne's face, which had the added advantage of offering concealment.

"Splendid. Even I could almost believe it's me." Manon emerged from behind the dressing screen. She wore a man's breeches, shirt, waistcoat, and coat and her body was padded round the middle, so that not only were her breasts disguised, but she also appeared rather stout. "The dark wig, I think," she said, gesturing towards a stand in the corner. "The one I wore in *As You Like It.*"

Berthe pinned her mistress's hair close to her head again and set the wig over it. Manon inclined her head. "Spectacles and a bit of makeup and I will do. Make sure the girls are ready, Berthe."

Berthe moved back to the sitting room. Suzanne perched on the sofa, while Manon returned to the dressing table and began to apply shading to her face, making her jaw appear stronger, her nose sharper. "Odd. Just as I leave the theatre for God knows how long, I play one of the most important roles of my career."

"I sometimes think I've done more acting since I stopped performing onstage than before," Suzanne said.

Manon studied her for a moment in the lamplit looking glass. "I should also imagine the role of a British diplomat's wife is one of the more difficult you've ever played. For the sheer duration of it if nothing else."

Suzanne gripped her hands together. Manon's rings shone on her knuckles. For the first few months of her marriage, there had been moments when it had choked her, the realization that there was no end to her masquerade in sight. She remembered waking suddenly, Malcolm asleep beside her, her heart pounding, her body as tense as though she were caught in a snare. "It grows easier," she said. "Sometimes I forget it *is* a role." And yet if she was honest, lately some of the moments of panic had returned. "But now—"

"Perhaps the role is all the more difficult now you're no longer working for Raoul."

Suzanne drew a breath. Manon had hit it exactly, though she'd scarcely been able even to articulate it to herself. It was as though without her work as a spy to define her, she had lost all track of where she left off and the role she was playing began. Much as her meetings with Raoul had tugged at her loyalties, especially those last days in Brussels, they had been moments when she could cease pretending. Now she was so lost in pretense she sometimes felt she had lost track of her self. "I don't regret my decision," she said, fumbling for the right words. "But sometimes it feels as though I've lost my sense of purpose. Before—when I was deceiving Malcolm—at times I hated myself. But I knew who I was. Now I'm not sure. Being a French agent defined me for so long."

Manon turned her head to look at Suzanne directly. "We all play different roles. I do myself, offstage as much as on-. The actress, the agent, the lover, the mother. It's hard sometimes to know which is the most real. And it's a rare thing to find someone who sees one for oneself."

Suzanne hunched her shoulders. "Malcolm sees me for myself. At least at times I think he does. I sometimes have a lowering feeling that what he sees and loves is the character I created for him, not the real me at all. I doubt he'd ever get past how I've deceived him, but even if he could, I sometimes wonder if he'd like the real me at all."

Manon turned back to the dressing table and picked up her

rouge brush. "And yet sometimes a role tells me something about myself. Didn't you find that?" She brushed color over her cheeks, somehow making them appear fuller. "When you were an actress, I mean?"

"Oh yes," Suzanne said. "Only sometimes it's difficult to tell where the role leaves off and oneself begins."

"Or perhaps it's that the role itself changes one." Manon peered at her face and added some rouge to her left cheekbone. "My most brilliant lovers were also the most exhausting. Amusing but always seeming to need to be catered to. I couldn't abide being married to a fool. But I imagine it isn't easy being the wife of a complicated man."

Suzanne drew a breath to deny it, then bit it back. So much of her life revolved round Malcolm. Helping draft documents, sifting through invitations and knowing which to accept, making sure meals were served and appointments kept, coaxing him out of the library at entertainments, packing and unpacking their things and making a home in various lodgings, smoothing feathers he had ruffled, smoothing his own ruffled feathers when his frustration with Castlereagh, Wellington, Metternich, and others threatened to get the better of him.

"It's been that way from the first," she said. "But somehow— It's absurd, but somehow it was easier before."

"Of course." Manon turned her face from side to side to regard her handiwork. "Before you catered to him in the service of your work. In the service of your own ends. Now you do it simply—"

"Because I love him." Which should matter more than anything. And yet— "I *have* dwindled into a wife."

Manon smiled as she added some shading to her forehead. "I can't imagine you dwindling into anything, *ma chère* Suzanne."

Suzanne stared at her hands. "When we were first married, I simply did what seemed to be required. That's what one does when playing a role. And then I suddenly realized Malcolm needed me." She remembered the look of relief on his face when he returned home from a long day at the embassy to find supper waiting and she handed him the draft of a memorandum he'd forgot he needed to write. *What would I do without you?* he'd said. And she'd been shocked to realize how much he meant it. "It's a rather remarkable thing realizing one is needed. Especially when one's used to being on one's own." Since her father's and sister's deaths, she couldn't really say anyone had needed her until Malcolm. Raoul needed her talents, but he didn't need *her*. He was entirely self-sufficient. She gripped her hands together, conscious of the absence of her wedding ring. "Dwindling into a wife is scant enough recompense for what I've done to him."

Manon picked up a comb and coaxed the hair of her wig closer round her face. "Recompense is a poor foundation to build a life on."

Suzanne looked up and met Manon's gaze in the mirror. "It's more than recompense."

Manon's mouth curved in a smile. "Good. That's the only reason I can imagine to get married."

"But loving Malcolm doesn't make me want to lose myself." It felt like an almost shameful admission, yet it was a relief to make it.

"And so you're here." Manon set down the comb.

"I'm here because I'm your friend."

"Friends are a rare thing. Far rarer than husbands. Or lovers." Manon settled a pair of spectacles on her nose. "There." She turned round on the dressing table bench to face Suzanne. "If I deepen my voice and remember how to walk, I think I'll pass for a tutor."

"The girls—?"

"Are traveling as Raoul's daughters. I'm going as their tutor. Berthe as their nurse. Once we get out of Paris we'll change to a different set of costumes and Raoul will return to the city." She regarded Suzanne for a moment. "We couldn't have done it without the documents you procured. At considerable risk."

"I've run greater risks anytime these past two years."

"But you no longer have to."

"One's loyalty to one's friends doesn't go away."

Manon pushed herself to her feet and then went still. She glanced round the dressing room slowly, taking in the details of a room she saw every day but to which she probably paid little heed.

She touched her fingers to a peasant bodice hung from the clothes-line above, and then to a paste tiara resting on top of a hatbox. "Was it difficult, leaving your old life behind?"

Suzanne hesitated, searching for honesty. "I didn't have the least idea what I was doing when I went into my marriage. I saw it as a challenge. A game. When it hit me that there was no end in sight, I felt trapped. It's grown easier. I've made friends. I have whole days now where I feel at home. But . . ." She hesitated. "One stays an exile. I don't think my husband will ever entirely under-stand that."

Manon nodded slowly. "I'm used to making my home different places. But I never thought— Well, all one can do is go forwards and explore the next role offered." She moved to the sofa beside Suzanne. "Now we merely have to wait."

CHAPTER 17

"Gui Laclos was right," Harry said, as they descended the steps of the Salon des Etrangers. "I don't believe his explanation." He paused a moment, gaze fixed straight ahead. "Though I don't know that I'm the best judge."

"For what it's worth, Gui Laclos never slept with my wife that I know of, and I'm not inclined to believe him, either," Malcolm said. "As Mademoiselle Leroux said, he and Rivère could have quarreled about Gabrielle Caruthers."

"You didn't confront Laclos with that."

"He may not know about his sister and Rivère. The circumstances didn't seem to warrant betraying Lady Caruthers's secrets."

Harry shook his head. "You have a soft heart, Rannoch."

"You've only just discovered that?"

Harry gave a twisted grin. "Would Gui Laclos have killed to protect his sister's honor?"

"I wouldn't have thought so. But then it's also possible that the quarrel was about something else. That Rivère was blackmailing him as well. He could have learned something about Gui from Gabrielle."

"I don't know Gui Laclos well, and as I said I'm not inclined to have a good opinion of him. But from tonight, I'd say he has a temper."

"He does." Malcolm stared at the moonlight bouncing off the cobblestones. "As does Wellington."

Harry shot a look at him. "Can't imagine what a man with Wellington's understanding sees in Frances Webster." He paused a moment. "Go carefully, Malcolm."

"You think Wellington wouldn't stoop to killing a blackmailer?"

"I think Wellington's a dangerous opponent. And if he's guilty of murder, he's even more dangerous than I credited."

It was Malcolm's turn to stare at his friend. His throat was tight with possibilities he didn't want to articulate. "You think it's possible?"

"I pride myself on not having illusions, remember?" Harry said.

"So do I, in theory."

"Don't fool yourself, Malcolm. You have a remarkable capacity for believing in people."

"Is it quite that bad?"

"And I've always envied you for it." Harry was quiet for a moment. "We both agreed in Brussels that Wellington wouldn't cavil at having a double agent killed. Wellington doesn't think it would have been wrong to have had Bertrand Laclos killed if he really had been a double agent. How much of a jump is it from that to having a British agent killed when he tried to blackmail a British commander?"

Harry's words cut all too close to what Malcolm feared might be the mark. "One compromise after another until one looks over one's shoulder and integrity is gone."

"Quite."

Manon cast a glance round the dressing room. "Odd I didn't realize until now how much I'd miss Paris. I've rather taken it for granted. Like a lover one doesn't properly appreciate until he's not there to pay one silly compliments or open the carriage door."

Suzanne had only spent small snatches of her life in Paris, but the city seemed to run through Manon's blood. She'd always been a font of information, for she knew everyone and everything.

"Manon," Suzanne said on sudden impulse. "Did you ever hear any talk about Tatiana Kirsanova?"

Manon gave a dry laugh. "Could anyone in Paris fail to hear talk about Tatiana Kirsanova?" She hesitated a moment, fiddling with one of the buttons on her coat.

"It's all right," Suzanne said. "I know. That is, I know about the rumors. The rumors that Princess Tatiana was Malcolm's mistress. She wasn't as it happens."

Manon turned to look at her. "You sound very confident."

"I wasn't for the longest time, but I am now."

"Because?"

"Because Malcolm told me, and I believe him."

Manon's brows rose above her spectacles. "You do have a remarkable marriage."

"Trust grows easier with time," Suzanne said, and then bit her lip because Malcolm trusted her far too readily. "But Malcolm was close to Princess Tatiana," she continued. "He'd worked with her—"

"Worked with— I should have known."

"That she was an agent? Yes, I felt quite foolish for not knowing it myself."

"I heard your husband looked into her murder in Vienna."

"He did. And though no one could be publicly charged, he learned a great deal. But Malcolm takes his responsibilities hard. I don't think he'll ever stop blaming himself for not having been able to save Princess Tatiana." Suzanne hesitated, studying Manon's artfully made-up face, then made a leap of trust. "It seems Princess Tatiana may have had a child."

Manon's eyes widened in seemingly genuine surprise. *"Mon Dieu."* Her gaze flickered to the sitting room. "Hidden away?"

"Apparently. But Tatiana seemingly knew where. We think the child would have been born about eight years ago. Did you hear anything about who might have been Tatiana's lover nine years ago or a bit less?"

Manon's brows, thickened with blacking, drew together in consideration. "I remember the swath Princess Tatiana cut through Parisian society when she first arrived. I wasn't invited to her parties, of course, but she was pointed out to me at the theatre. When she was present, the gentlemen in the crowd had a distressing tendency to look at her box instead of at the stage. And there'd be less of a crowd in my dressing room because a throng of gentlemen would follow her when she left. She had a group of us put on a private theatrical at one of her parties. It would have been the autumn of 1806. *Love's Labour's Lost*. A bit of a surprising choice."

Suzanne said nothing, though she wondered if Tatiana's fondness for the play had come from Malcolm or from their mother.

"I must say she was quite generous with her payment and she encouraged us to mingle with the guests afterwards," Manon continued. "It was a bit lowering to realize I couldn't dislike her as I could when she was simply a glamorous stranger distracting the crowd."

It was a simpler version of what Suzanne had gone through the previous autumn, peeling away the complex layers of the woman she had been prepared simply to dislike as her husband's supposed mistress. "Princess Tatiana was a complicated woman."

"So she was. She had a throng of gentlemen about her that night of course. But as I recall she divided her favors quite evenly." Manon cast a quick glance at Suzanne.

"Whoever fathered the child, Princess Tatiana seemed to feel secrecy was of the utmost importance."

"A bit odd, that. Not that a woman can afford to flaunt children born out of wedlock— Well"—Manon glanced at the sitting room again—"an actress can, but it's more difficult for a lady. Still, there are plenty of widows with by-blows who are known about. As long as they don't actively flaunt them, they can get away with it. Tatiana Kirsanova didn't strike me as a woman who would frighten easily."

"No."

"You should talk to Paul St. Gilles."

"The painter?" Suzanne had seen his work at the Louvre, and Louise and Emile Sevigny had mentioned his anti-Royalist writings. "Was he her lover?" It seemed an unlikely pairing.

"Not her type, you think? Princess Tatiana seemed to have eclectic tastes. And I think there was a difference between the lovers she chose for expediency, because they were powerful men, and the lovers she chose simply to amuse herself. She and St. Gilles were certainly close. If he didn't father the child, he might know who did."

"Do you think—"

The door swung open on Suzanne's words. Raoul entered, no longer the stagehand but a stout gentleman with graying hair and side-whiskers, modest shirt points, and a coat of sturdy wool. A prosperous bourgeois. He looked from Manon to Suzanne. "An admirable transformation. I'd have expected no less of either of you."

Another man followed him into the room, stoop shouldered, with straggly hair. He was dressed as a coachman. "Best hurry," he said in a slurred voice.

Raoul glanced at him and from their interaction Suzanne realized this must be the Kestrel. She suspected the hair was a wig. She wondered how old he was. Not so old as the seventy or so he was portraying, but he could be anywhere from five-and-twenty to five-and-fifty.

Manon moved to the sitting room door and looked at her daughters. For a moment, the other roles were gone and a mother's concern and quiet assurance suffused her face. Roxane got to her feet and nodded. Manon bent over the sleeping Clarisse and murmured to her.

Raoul and the Kestrel moved two large trunks from the welter in the dressing room to the sitting room. The girls climbed inside, wrapped in soft blankets. "Just until we're away from the theatre," Manon murmured to them. "Then you'll ride in the carriage with Oncle Raoul and me."

"Suzanne should leave first," Raoul said. "Or rather Manon Caret should. That should draw off the watchers."

Suzanne pulled on a pair of kid gloves, glanced in the looking glass to make sure her ringlets still fell about her face, and then raised the hood of her cloak. She bent down to touch her fingers to Roxane's and Clarisse's hair, then stood and regarded Manon. "One way or another, I'll see you again. Perhaps in England. My friend Simon Tanner is a part owner of the Tavistock Theatre. I'll find a way to recommend you."

"I'd be most grateful."

"I think you'll find the theatre community in England easier to navigate than the beau monde." She embraced Manon. Manon clung to her for a moment, fingers tight, then stepped back with a smile that seemed designed to hold tears at bay.

Raoul squeezed Suzanne's hand."No unnecessary risks, *querida*."

"The same goes for you." Suzanne hugged Berthe, then turned to the Kestrel and inclined her head. He returned her nod, his dark gaze veiled.

Two stagehands, old friends of Manon's, came into the room and picked up two bundles, blankets wrapped round pillows with blond wigs peeping out from the top. Close enough to the sight of Roxane and Clarisse being carried from the theatre to fool watchers.

Suzanne cast a last glance at her friends, then followed the stagehands down the passage, moving with Manon's unique combination of languor and impetuous speed.

Manon's cherry red barouche was drawn up in front of the theatre. "Do try not to wake them," Suzanne called in Manon's accents as the stagehands settled their burden in the carriage. "Clarisse isn't well."

Pausing to give a careless wave to any denizens of the Palais Royale waiting for a last glimpse of Manon Caret, Suzanne moved to the carriage, aware of the two men lingering in doorways on either side of the street, though she didn't risk looking at them directly. She leaned into the carriage to adjust the blankets over her supposed daughters, murmured, "Shush, shush," then climbed in the carriage herself. "Home, Jacques," she called to the coachman.

The carriage clattered off down the street. Suzanne fell back against the squabs. No way to tell if the watchers followed the carriage. She leaned forwards a few times to tuck the blankets round the girls, just in case anyone should glance through the windows. It would be hours, if not days, before she knew if her friends were safe. Worry was tight within her. But with it, she could not deny, a thrill of excitement.

Flashes of lamplight pierced the gloom as they swept over the cobblestones. At last they pulled up before Manon's elegant house in the Rue Vivienne, with fanciful plaster moldings and gilded wrought ironwork. A footman hurried down the steps. He handed Suzanne down from the carriage, then reached inside to lift one of the blanket-wrapped forms. The coachman lifted the other. "Clarisse has a sore throat," Suzanne murmured. "I should have left her at home."

"Where's Berthe?" the footman asked, cued to his part.

"She had plans with her young man. I couldn't ask her to stay back, not with everything she does for me."

The footman grinned, as if to say his mistress was softhearted beneath her sometimes imperious exterior. They climbed the steps to the columned portico, Suzanne fussing over her two supposed daughters. Inside the house, the footman and coachman carried the blanket-wrapped bundles up the curving staircase to the nursery. Suzanne lit a lamp, bent over the two bundles in the beds, smoothed the covers, kissed their wig hair, all for the benefit of any-one watching the windows. Then she cast a last look round the room, drew the curtains, turned down the lamp, and went down the passage to Manon's bedchamber.

The room still smelled of jasmine and tuberose. She lit a lamp and the tapers on the dressing table. A dressing case still stood on the table, pots of rouge and powder, a crystal scent bottle, velvet jewel boxes, a silver-backed brush with hairs caught in the bristles. Manon would only have been able to take a few essentials. Suzanne stretched her arms, unpinned her hair with Manon's leisurely grace, then drew the blue watered-silk curtains over the windows. All the while she saw the dolls and stuffed animals that had still stood on the shelves and beds in the nursery, Manon's toiletries and jewels, embossed stationery and pens and inkpot. The bits of a life. Manon and the girls would only have had time to pack essentials. Suzanne had had to make some quick departures of her own, but she'd never had a settled-enough life to have a great deal to leave behind. It would be different now. She shuddered as she laid Manon's cloak on the bed and tugged at the strings on the gown. Not that she ever would flee the life she had now. Unless Malcolm fled with her. And that would mean he would know what she had done and accept it, which was also unthinkable.

Pounding came from the street outside. Her senses quickened even before she had made sense of the noise. She moved to the windows, straining to hear. "Manon!" a man's voice yelled in the street. "Let me in, damn it."

The voice was slurred with drink and sharp with feeling. Manon's latest lover? Suzanne realized she had no notion of his identity or of what he had meant to Manon. He sounded like a native French speaker. She daren't risk a glance into the street. But impossible for her to slip from the house while he was outside.

A pounding sounded, like a fist beating against polished door panels. A low-voiced murmur that must be the footman, another cry of "Manon," then a crash and the wrench of tearing hinges. Dear God. He'd pushed the door open. Suzanne ran to the bedchamber door, Manon's half-unlaced gown slipping from her shoulders, and shot the bolt home.

Feet pounded on the stairs. "Manon!" the voice yelled again. The brass door handle rattled. "For God's sake, Manon, let me in."

She crossed to the connecting door to the dressing room and bolted it as well. To speak or not to speak? She was good at imitating voices, but this was a lover. But then she'd survived this far by trusting her instincts, not doubting them. *"Chéri,"* she said, in Manon's tones, back by the bed where her voice would carry less clearly. "I told you tonight would not work." A risk, but surely Manon would have given him some excuse about tonight.

"You can't still be cross about Yvette." His voice shook with desperation. "You know that ended months ago. I haven't had eyes for anyone else since I met you."

"That isn't how it looked." Suzanne stripped off the gown and pulled the pins from her wig.

"She's a friend. She was in trouble. I couldn't turn my back on a friend in trouble."

Suzanne gave an imitation of Manon's snort as she stuffed the wig into the wardrobe and grabbed the plain black gown Manon had left for her.

"I settled her debts. That doesn't mean I took her to bed. I don't want to be in anyone's bed but yours. Can you doubt that after all that's passed between us?"

"Fine words." She pulled on the black gown, which mercifully fastened up the front.

The handle rattled again. The door shook in its frame. "Have you got a man in there? Damn it, who is he—"

"Don't be silly, *chéri*." She stowed Manon's silk-rosetted slippers in the wardrobe and pulled on a pair of plain black ones.

"You witch! They warned me you wouldn't be faithful, but I was mad enough to trust you."

"Because of course I love you, *mon amour*." She softened her voice as she moved to the dressing table and grabbed some pins to tidy her hair.

"Then why—"

"Because tonight I am tired and the performance was difficult and Clarisse was ill and you hurt me with your silly attentions to Yvette."

"Mon ange!" His voice had softened as well and turned husky. "Let me in. I won't tease you, I swear it. I only want to hold you in my arms."

Oh, poison. "Not tonight, *mon cher*. I look wretched." Suzanne tucked the last strand of hair into place. "You know I can't bear for you to see me when I'm not at my best."

"As if I care. We're beyond that."

"Oh, *chéri*. A woman is never beyond that."

"Mon Dieu. You do have a man in there." The door shook. "By God, Manon, I'll call the fellow to account."

"If I did have a man in here—which I don't, I'm in no mood to see any man—that would hardly be the action to win me over. Do go home and go to sleep, *chéri*."

"As if I could sleep tonight. As if I could leave." A thud sounded against the door. "If you won't let me in now, I'll wait here until you will." Another thud as his body slid to the floor.

Damnation. Suzanne cast a glance round the room. Manon's gown and cloak could stay tossed across the bed. That looked very like Manon. So did the hairpins strewn on the dressing table and the scattered jewels. No other signs of her own presence remained.

"Oh, have it your own way," she called.

She crossed the room, pushed back one of the curtains on a side window, and eased up the sash. Thank God it was well oiled. Outside was the dark stillness of a side garden, and the shadowy mass of another house beyond, mercifully unlit. She climbed onto the sill and reached out an arm, feeling round for the grout between the stones. She found a purchase with her toe, drew a breath, slid her other foot from the ledge. *Inch by inch, focus, don't think about the drop down.* Carriage wheels rattled and horse hooves clopped in the street, but surely no one could see into the shadows of the side garden.

Fingers stinging, she felt the molding of the dressing room window frame. Her hand closed round the molding, and then she was standing on the sill, breathing hard, her face pressed to the glass. She crouched down, pulled a pin from her hair, and worked at the window latch. Not as quick as her picklocks, and her smarting fingers made it more difficult, but at last she got the latch open. She pushed up the sash, slid through, and dropped onto the dressing room floor.

Another breath of relief, the window closed. She found and lit a candle, looked in the dressing table looking glass long enough to smooth her gown and once again tidy her hair. Then she took an embroidered cushion and a cashmere blanket from the striped satin chaise-longue, blew out the candle, and slipped into the passage.

He was slumped on the floorboards against Manon's bedroom door, dark hair disordered, cravat askew, coat rumpled. He had pale skin and finely molded features. A handsome man, though he looked to weigh a stone or so more than might be ideal. Suzanne walked briskly down the passage and held out the blanket and cushion. "Madame says if you insist on staying here, you might as well have these."

He blinked at her out of burning dark eyes. "Who the devil are you?"

"Odette, monsieur." Suzanne made her voice slightly husky and roughened it with the accents of Gascony. "The new housemaid. Madame hired me last week."

His brows, dark and dramatic and standing on end, drew together. He pushed himself to his feet. "Didn't say anything to me."

"No, monsieur." Suzanne lowered her gaze to the blanket and pillow in her hands. "I don't expect madame is in the habit of discussing her domestic arrangements with you."

He gave a short laugh. She could feel his gaze moving over her face. "See here, Odette. Is your mistress— Is she alone in there?"

Suzanne lifted her gaze to his face. "Of course, monsieur."

"You'd say that in any case." He scraped a hand through his hair, cut in a Byronic crop. "Damnation."

His eyes held genuine torment. Whatever their history, whatever had happened with this woman Yvette, it was clear he loved Manon. And Manon? Did she return his feelings? Suzanne suppressed a shiver. There was a time when she had believed she could walk away from Malcolm. She had gone into their marriage thinking as much. Thinking she could not only leave but also take her—their—child with her. Now it was unthinkable. Or rather, she could imagine it, but only in the nightmare sense she could imagine cutting out a part of herself and going on living.

"Monsieur—" Suzanne stretched out a hand but did not quite risk touching him. She made her eyes very wide, in that way that signaled openness and invited trust. "There is no man in madame's bedchamber. I swear it."

He met her gaze for a long moment, then drew a harsh breath and gave a shaky nod. Suzanne pressed the blanket and pillow into his arms. His fingers closed round them, as though he were clutching on to his beloved, and he slid down against the door panels again. Some of the tension had left his face. He leaned against the doorjamb, the pillow behind his head, the blanket spread over his knees, his cheek pressed to Manon's door. God help him in the morning.

But she could not afford to think about that now. Suzanne walked briskly to the green baize–covered door at the end of the passage that led to the service stairs. Down three flights to the kitchen, where the smell of bread lingered in the air and coals glowed in the range, but no one stirred. She listened at the area door while carriage wheels rattled past, then opened the door and went up the area steps. The street was dark and still, save for the glow of street lamps and lights in one or two houses. A cabriolet clattered by, but the shades were drawn and it did not slow. She didn't think it held unseen watchers.

The man was still in his position across the street, but he didn't stir. Suzanne paused beneath a street lamp, long enough to let her dark hair and plain dark gown show. A maid slipping out for a rendezvous with her lover. Sometimes it was safer to be in plain sight. She walked down the street, making no attempt to hide herself, and turned at the first corner. She doubled back twice and paused once in a doorway, but she could detect no sign of pursuit. Soon she was lost in the throng of Parisian nightlife.

She turned down a narrow side street, cut through an alley to another, and opened a side door to a glover's. The door was unlatched. She was in a storeroom. Her evening gown, cloak, stockings, shoes, and reticule were where Raoul had said they'd be, on the third shelf down on the left, behind a box of evening gloves. She dressed in the dark by instinct, a trick Raoul had made sure she mastered years ago when he trained her. Her strand of pearls, her diamond earrings, and her pearl bracelet were tucked into the reticule. And her wedding ring. She slid it onto her finger and gripped the solid metal for a moment. Then she pulled her side curls loose from their pins and wound them round her fingers. An approximation of the coiffure she'd left the house with, but she hoped the night breeze would be enough to account for the change.

The maid's clothes tucked behind the box, her gloves pulled on, her silk-lined velvet cloak round her shoulders, her reticule in her hand, she stepped back into the side street, raised the hood of her cloak so she wouldn't be too obvious, and made her way towards the Rue du Faubourg Saint-Honoré. She avoided the impulse to linger too far in the shadows.

She didn't know the exact time, but thanks to Manon's lover she must be close to an hour later than she'd meant to be. Malcolm might well be home before she was. Well, she would deal with that. She'd dealt with countless unforeseen turns of events since their marriage, including one memorable night when he'd caught her climbing through their bedroom window with a stolen British dispatch tucked into her corset. She might no longer be actively spying for the French, but she couldn't afford to grow rusty. Her pulse quickened, partly at the risk, but partly at the thrill of the challenge.

She moved past cafés bright with candlelight. Talk and laughter and flirtatious giggles came from open doors and from tables set out on the pavement in the warm evening air. The smells of wine and tobacco drifted in the breeze. In another life she could have slipped into one of those cafés, ordered a glass of wine, and lost herself in the crowd. But not as Mrs. Malcolm Rannoch. Playing one role limited the other roles she could take on.

The door of a café swung open when she was only a few paces away. The pop of a champagne cork and a medley of voices spilled out. Two young men in silk hats and evening cloaks staggered from the café, drew up short to avoid colliding with her, swept elaborate bows, and then stared. "Good lord. Mrs. Rannoch?"

The round face, pale blue eyes, and straight flaxen hair showing beneath the hat belonged to Freddy Lyttleton, a junior attaché whom she'd danced with last night at the British embassy. Suzanne extended her hand. "Good evening, Freddy. It was so wretchedly hot at the Russian embassy, and I didn't want to wait to call for my carriage. It's such a pleasant evening, I thought I'd walk."

Freddy stared at her as though she'd taken leave of her senses. His companion flung back his head and laughed. Bobby Gordon, Suzanne realized, another junior attaché, dark haired, shorter than his friend Freddy, and with rather more wit. "You're a regular out-and-outer, Mrs. Rannoch," he said. "But you can't walk alone in the streets of Paris, you know. It simply isn't done. Not by an Englishwoman in any case."

"But I'm not an Englishwoman, Mr. Gordon. Everyone knows about Continental eccentricities."

"But your husband's an Englishman," Freddy said, as though he could still not quite make sense of her presence in the street.

"Scots."

Freddy waved a hand as though centuries of contentious history and border warfare might never have occurred. "British. We'll see you home, Mrs. Rannoch."

"That's very kind of you, Freddy, but I assure you—"

"No, we insist." Bobby's voice was firm and less slurred than Freddy's. "Malcolm would never forgive us if we let you go on alone."

There was no help for it. Suzanne smiled and said it was too kind of them. The two men walked, rather unsteadily, one on either side of her, to the Rue du Faubourg Saint-Honoré.

And of course they would not simply leave her at the door. Suzanne rang the bell. Valentin, the footman who had come with them from Brussels, opened the door. They stepped into the entrance hall. There, just beyond Valentin, was Suzanne's husband.

CHAPTER 18

"Darling." Suzanne walked forwards. "Mr. Lyttleton and Mr. Gordon were kind enough to escort me home. Wasn't that splendid of them?"

"My thanks," Malcolm said with an easy smile. "Although my wife is quite capable of looking after herself, you know."

"Walking in the street alone. Wouldn't do. Dangerous. Besides, people might talk." Freddy coughed, as Bobby nudged him in the ribs. "Not that Mrs. Rannoch could know that, of course."

"Quite," Malcolm said. "May we offer you some refreshment?"

Freddy opened his mouth as though to agree, but Bobby grabbed his arm. "No. Thank you, but we won't impose. Rannoch. Mrs. Rannoch."

The young men withdrew. Valentin, who had been pretending to be deaf, closed the door behind them. Malcolm and Suzanne climbed the stairs to their bedchamber. Suzanne could feel her husband's amused gaze on her. He was waiting for her explanation. But he had no doubt there would be a simple, logical one.

"Cordy left the Russian embassy early," Suzanne said, tugging at the ties on her cloak. "I stayed. I was hoping to talk to the Lacloses or learn more about them. But I was singularly unsuccessful. Though I did hear an interesting piece of gossip. Apparently Tatiana may have been the lover of Paul St. Gilles around the time the child would have been conceived."

Malcolm's brows rose, though he did not appear as surprised as she'd have expected. "Tania and a Radical painter. I've heard stranger things. Though it's hard to see why his being the father would occasion such secrecy."

"No. But we should talk to him. He may know more about her life at that time." She dropped the cloak on the dressing table bench. "After I left the embassy, I thought with my cloak on I could stop in at a café and perhaps learn something more." She glanced at her husband. "Yes, I know it was a risk, but I thought—"

"That I was off in the thick of things and you didn't want to be behindhand?"

"No. Well, yes, perhaps. A bit. But again, no success. So I thought I'd walk home. I'm sorry."

"Why should you be sorry?"

"I try not to cause unnecessary talk for you."

"Having a wife who is the toast of the junior attachés is more likely to make me envied than talked about." He was smiling. Malcolm was a master at deception, but it had never occurred to him that his own wife would deceive him. A sign of his love and trust in her. Which made the champagne and cold salmon from the embassy rise up in her throat.

She pushed aside the folds of the cloak and perched on the bench. "I trust you had a more productive evening."

"You could say that." Malcolm's smile faded, and Suzanne noticed the strain in the set of his mouth.

"You found Christine Leroux?"

"Oh yes. Rivère is to be congratulated. A woman of spirit and intelligence. And quite capable of lying to us, though I don't think she was. At least not the whole time. She admitted Rivère engaged in blackmail." He dropped down on the edge of the bed across from her. "Apparently Rivère had come into possession of an indiscreet letter Wellington wrote to Lady Frances Webster."

Suzanne pictured the duke sitting beside the lovely blond Lady Frances at the Duchess of Richmond's ball in Brussels. "It's hardly secret there's something between them. Though I'd have thought—"

"That the man who defeated Napoleon Bonaparte would have had the wit not to put it in writing? So would I. Whatever the devil was between them, Lady Frances was already seven months pregnant at the time of Waterloo—"

"That isn't a bar to all sorts of activities. As we well know."

Malcolm flushed. Her husband could be delightfully prudish. Of course during her own pregnancy she'd had to persuade Malcolm that it was no imposition on her to engage in those activities. "I'll speak to Wellington in the morning," he said. "As I told Harry, this explains his quarrel with Rivère but not what he did about it."

"I'm sorry," Suzanne said. "I know this can't be easy. You're fond of him."

Malcolm gave a wry smile. "It seems almost presumptuous to be 'fond' where Wellington's concerned. God knows I disagree with him about enough political matters. But I suppose—" He stared at his hands for a moment. "Intelligence is a messy game, with its double crosses and betrayals. I long since accepted I'm not sure I know the limits of what Carfax is capable of. I suppose I liked thinking Wellington was above that."

Her heart twisted. "You're much too decent for the intelligence game, Malcolm."

"Carfax often says the same. It's not meant as a compliment."

"I meant it as a compliment." In truth, Malcolm's empathy often allowed him to see things other agents would miss. It just burdened him with an intolerable load of guilt.

"But then you possess far more tact than Carfax. Not to mention a kinder heart." Malcolm shifted his position on the bed. "There's more," he said. "Apparently Rivère also quarreled with Gui Laclos last week."

Suzanne drew in her breath, Cordelia's confidences sharp in her mind.

"I know," Malcolm said. "About Gui and Cordelia. Harry told me."

"So Cordy told him. I'm glad of that at least."

"Yes," Malcolm said, but she heard the slight hesitancy in his voice.

"Darling? What is it?"

He hesitated a moment. "Merely that confronting his wife's past is a bit harder for Harry than he'd admit to anyone. Particularly Cordelia."

She swallowed. "Yes, I imagine it would be. But he must realize—"

"I think at times he still finds it difficult to believe Cordelia loves him."

"Rubbish. He has to know—"

"Not because he doesn't trust her. Because he has difficulty believing a woman like her could love him. I can understand that."

Suzanne fixed her husband with a firm stare, her throat torn by conflicting impulses. "Men," she said, "sometimes can't see what's directly in front of them."

"Oh, that's undoubtedly true." He grinned, though his eyes were vulnerable as spun glass. "For what it's worth, I am glad Cordelia told Harry about Gui. And about Edmond Talleyrand. However painful the truth may be, it's infinitely preferable to have it in the open rather than keeping it concealed."

Her fingers dug into the padded satin of the bench. "Just so." She drew a breath. "So now you know what Wellington quarreled with Rivère about."

"Quite. Which doesn't mean Wellington didn't—"

Questions he couldn't quite put into words lurked in his eyes. She was fond of Wellington, but she had no such loyalty to the British commander. "You think Wellington would have killed to keep this letter secret?"

Malcolm's brows drew together. "Wellington can be ruthless, but I'd like to think not for personal reasons. He's not the sort to put much stock in what others say about him. But he also has a temper. We don't know what was in the letter. It mattered enough to him for him to withhold information from me."

The concern behind his eyes belied his even tone of voice. Suzanne got to her feet and crossed to the bed. "Whatever he's done, darling, it's not on your conscience."

He looked up at her with a quick smile. "That's my Suzette. No false reassurances."

"You wouldn't believe them if I tried." She rested her hand on his shoulder. "If anyone can get Wellington to talk it's you."

A bleaker smile pulled at his mouth. "I'm not sure that's reassuring."

"But it's true." She bent down and put her mouth to his.

His arms came up to circle her shoulders. She sank down onto his lap and tangled her fingers in his hair.

She could not have said which of them she was trying to comfort.

Harry eased open the door of the bedchamber he shared with his wife, trying not to wake her. Sharing a bedchamber was still new territory for them. There were times when he entered the room shocked to find her there or to smell the whiff of her perfume. And others when he woke stunned to feel the warmth of her beside him. Or the weight of her arm flung over his chest.

Candlelight spilled over the floorboards. Cordelia was sitting up in bed, her knees drawn up beneath the coverlet, a book in her hands.

"Harry." She smiled at him. Her hair tumbled loose over her shoulders. Her eyes had that open look they got when she removed her eye blacking, though she still wore her sapphire earrings. "Did everything go all right?"

"I wasn't sure you'd be awake." He pushed the door to. "Is Livia all right?" Their daughter had been sickly as a baby, and though she seemed perfectly sturdy now, the worry still haunted him, despite the fact that he hadn't seen Livia in those early years. Or because of it.

"Livia's fine. Sound asleep when I got home with her face squished up against Portia." Portia was Livia's stuffed cat. "But I find it difficult to sleep when you're on a mission."

"A visit to a casino is a hardly a mission."

"You're investigating a murder." She put a hand on the embroidered silk coverlet, a sort of invitation.

He dropped down on the edge of the bed. A ridiculously domestic action. If anyone had suggested three months ago that he'd be in such a position with his wife— "Rivère's mistress might be called a dangerous woman, but hardly in that sense."

Cordelia's gaze shot over his face, her eyes lit with amusement. "She intrigues you."

"Of course she intrigues me. She has information."

"And she's an intriguing woman."

"Well, I'm hardly blind."

"Thank goodness for that. Did she tell you anything? No, it's all right if you shouldn't talk about it. I won't tease you."

Harry looked into his wife's blue eyes, open and trusting in a way he'd never thought to see them. The temptation to say nothing, to lean over and kiss her, to sink back into the pillows and blot out past knowledge and present questions, was almost overmastering. But for all his sins and fears, he'd known from the first that the only chance they had lay with honesty.

"We saw—" He almost said "a friend of yours," but that would sound too arch. "We saw someone you know—" He was as tongue-tied as he'd been when he first met her at the Devonshire House ball, a callow young scholar dazzled by her glittering beauty.

"Edmond or Gui?" Cordelia asked in a level voice.

He met her gaze. She looked back at him, her own steady. He wasn't the only one who understood about uncompromising honesty. "Gui," he said. "Apparently he's a regular at the Salon des Etrangers."

Cordelia settled back against the pillows. She'd have looked relaxed to anyone who didn't know her as well as her husband. Or perhaps one of her lovers. "Hardly a surprise. He once told me perhaps it was as well the family fortune had been left in France or ten to one he'd have gambled it away."

"You liked him." He could hear the memories in her voice.

"He was kind. It's amazing how many of the men I—how many of my lovers weren't."

"You shouldn't sell yourself short, Cordy."

She gave a brief laugh, brittle as old paper. "I didn't like myself very well. Perhaps it felt more convivial to be with someone I didn't like very well, either."

"But not Gui Laclos."

Cordelia pleated a fold of the coverlet between her fingers. Her wedding band flashed in the candlelight against the apricot silk. "Not Gui. Though I rather think one of the things that drew me to Gui was that he suffered from as much self-disgust as I did."

"Over what?" Harry kept his voice even, though he couldn't quite manage a conversational tone.

Cordelia's gaze skimmed over his face. "Did you just happen to encounter Gui tonight or does he have something to do with the investigation? You don't have to answer that. But if you want me to help you—"

"Quite. Apparently Gui quarreled with Antoine Rivère a week ago."

He saw the surprise that ran through Cordelia's eyes. Surprise and a jolt of concern. "Do you know what the quarrel was about?" she asked, her voice taut as a bowstring.

"Gui says he'd lost money to Rivère at the gaming table."

"But you think it's more than that."

"So does Malcolm. Who's a more unbiased judge." Harry hesitated a moment. "Rivère dealt in blackmail."

"And you wonder if Gui—" She was silent for a moment. He thought she might refuse to say more. "I can't say the source of his self-disgust. Perhaps in part that he was safe in England while both his cousins had died fighting for France one way or another. And yet—"

"You think there was something more?"

"I think there was a great deal about Gui I didn't know. But—"

"You're sure he couldn't be a killer?"

She swallowed. "I learned in Brussels I couldn't be sure of that about anyone."

He caught her hand. "I'm sorry, Cordy. That was unpardonable. I didn't—"

"You were doing your job." Cordelia put her other hand against his face, her eyes dark and fragile as stained glass. "What I meant to say is there are things about Gui I'm quite sure I didn't know. I can't say they have anything to do with Antoine Rivère. But if Rivère was blackmailing him—"

"Just so."

She swallowed. Without eye blacking and rouge, her face framed by wispy bits of hair, she looked unexpectedly like a school-girl. "Do you want me to see what I can learn?"

He kept his gaze steady on her face. "It's not a pretty thing, looking into people's pasts. Especially people one cares for. I wouldn't ask that of you, Cordy."

"I know. But I'm offering."

"You don't need to do this to prove something." His voice turned rougher than he intended.

"I'm not. I'd be a fool to think I could prove certain things to you. Those things can only be accepted with time, if at all. But you know I can't bear to hang back once questions have been raised. I need to know."

"You may not like the answers," he said, in the tone he'd used with young intelligence operatives he was training.

"I daresay I may not. But avoiding the answers won't make the questions go away."

He seized her hand and lifted it to his lips. "I have a remarkable wife."

"For a man who claims to despise flattery, you're indecently good at it, Harry." She leaned forwards, her dressing gown slithering from her shoulders, and put her mouth to his.

After two months her kisses still sent a shock of wonder through him. He closed his arms round her, carefully, because his impulse was to crush her to him as though she might be gone at any moment. They fell back against the pillows. There might still be ghosts between them. Perhaps there always would be. But this was the surest way he knew to drive them from thought.

Rupert stopped in the doorway of his wife's bedchamber. She was at her dressing table, wrapped in a frothy dressing gown of blue silk and cream-colored lace, her hair already unpinned by her maid. Absorbed in unfastening her moonstone earrings, Gabrielle didn't seem to be aware of the opening of the door. He stood watching her for a moment, memories and regrets tugging his mind in a dozen different directions.

He must have moved, because Gabrielle gave a sudden start. "Rupert, I didn't hear you come in."

He stepped into the room and closed the door behind him. After three years of marriage, his wife's bedchamber was still alien territory. "We need to talk, Gaby," he said quickly, lest she should think he had come for something else. There hadn't been anything else for some time.

Gabrielle swung round on the dressing table bench, eyes wide with inquiry. "What is it? Rupert, you look dreadful."

"I had a scene with Father."

"Oh dear." She put out a hand, touched his arm, then let it fall as though she feared she'd pushed too far. "I knew living so close to him would prove difficult."

"And it's going to get more so." Rupert pulled a scroll-backed chair away from the escritoire and drew it up beside the dressing table. "I've told Father he's no longer welcome in our home. Nor is he to have any contact with Stephen."

Gabrielle's eyes widened. "Darling, I know how your father can anger you—"

"This goes beyond that." The desire to smash something, to smash his father, roiled through him. "After what he's done I'm severing all contact with him."

Gabrielle drew a confused breath. "Rupert, whatever it is—"

"Father was responsible for Bertrand's death."

Shock flared in Gabrielle's eyes. "How on earth—"

"Gaby—" Rupert sought for words that would be anywhere approaching appropriate. "I've done you a great wrong."

"Rupert. Darling." Gabrielle sprang up from the dressing table bench, dropped down on the floor beside his chair, and took his hands. "You aren't making any sense. You and I don't have anything to do with what happened to Bertrand. And you didn't wrong me. You gave me everything. I'm afraid I haven't been nearly as grateful as I should have been."

He looked down at her face, familiar since childhood, lovely, deserving of so much more. "I should have told you before I offered for you. I should have made it clear that I couldn't—"

"You never promised anything you couldn't give, Rupert." Gabrielle sat back on her heels. "I know what marriage is in the beau monde. Or I should. If I had expectations that were . . . unrealistic . . . it's my own fault."

The words of his proposal echoed in his head with bitter clarity. He'd been mad. Too caught up in his grief to see anyone's feelings but his own. "You expected what you had every right to. You deserved a man who could pledge you his heart without reserve. Not one who gave his away long since."

Her gaze moved over him with an understanding that was almost like relief. "I never realized— I never thought to ask. Was it someone in Spain? Was she already married? Or—"

"Gaby, no. Yes, it was someone in Spain. Someone I knew in Spain. But not in the way you're thinking." He swallowed, every instinct of secrecy tight in his throat. "Bertrand— Bertrand was my friend. But it was more. I—" He sought for words and realized there was only one way to say it. "I loved him."

Confusion filled Gabrielle's clear blue gaze and slowly gave way to understanding. He waited, braced for horror or disgust. Instead Gabrielle touched his hand. "Oh, Rupert, I'm so sorry. I should have seen it."

"You couldn't possibly—"

"Don't be silly, Rupert." Gabrielle's mouth curved in a smile, the sort of smile she gave when she was thinking about France in her days of exile or her lost parents or anything out of reach. "I'm hardly innocent of such things. I hear gossip. I know there are men who— I just never thought—"

He pulled his hands from her clasp. "That I was so depraved."

"Rupert, no." Her eyes widened in what seemed to be genuine shock. "You can't think— Is that how you see yourself?"

He swallowed, the past roiling in his head. Careless comments, confused thoughts. "I—" He straightened his shoulders. "No." The conviction in his own voice shook him. "What Bertrand and I felt for each other— It was nothing but good." The memories tugged at his senses, and he smiled despite everything. "But I didn't think—"

"That anyone else could accept you? Or that I could?" Gabrielle got to her feet, but instead of drawing back, she touched his hair with tentative fingers. "How poorly you must think of me. I'm so sorry you couldn't talk to me. You must have so needed a friend. And whatever else we were, I thought we were always that."

"Always. But I've asked far too much of you as it is. I should never have offered for you."

Gabrielle shrugged her shoulders, one of those moments when she looked unmistakably French. "If you hadn't, God knows where I'd be now. And we wouldn't have Stephen." She dropped back down on the dressing table bench but leaned towards him, as though not to break contact. "You were in touch with Bertrand even though he was working for the French?" Her brows drew together. "Or—?" Another question flickered in her eyes that she could not quite put into words.

He gave a faint smile. "I'm not a French agent, Gaby. And neither was Bertrand."

Gabrielle drew a sharp breath. "But—"

He told her in as quick and controlled a tone as he could. Bertrand's work for the British, the supposed revelation that he had in fact been a French double agent, his death on the orders of the British.

Gabrielle gave a strangled cry.

"I couldn't believe it," Rupert said. "But I had no proof. And God help me, even I had doubts. Until Malcolm Rannoch began asking questions."

"Why—?"

"He's looking into the Comte de Rivère's death. And Rivère claimed to have information about Bertrand."

"Suzanne Rannoch talked to me." A shadow flickered through Gabrielle's eyes. "Rupert—"

"I owe Rannoch a debt of gratitude," Rupert said, determined to get the rest of the story out. "He learned what I couldn't. What I should have learned four years ago." Guilt and anger bit him in the throat, a rank taste he would never be rid of.

"But who—"

"Father."

Gabrielle stared at him with growing horror as the picture formed in her eyes. "You can't know—"

"I can. He admitted it." Rupert pushed himself to his feet and strode across the room. The violence he hadn't been able to unleash on his father coiled within him. He wanted to sweep the porcelain figurines off the mantel, hurl the lamp across the room, crush the crystal girandoles on the candle sconces beneath his heel.

Gabrielle rubbed her arms. She had charmed Dewhurst from the first and had always seemed more at ease with him than Rupert was himself. "He hated Bertrand so much—"

"He hated what Bertrand was to me." Rupert's hands curled into fists. To know that the person one had loved above all others would still be alive if one had only kept one's distance.

Gabrielle's sharp breath sliced through the room. "He wanted you to marry."

Rupert spun round and took a quick step towards her. "It's nothing to do with you, Gaby."

She pushed herself to her feet as well, her hand to her mouth as though she were about to be sick. "But we fell right in with his plans. When I remember him congratulating us—"

"Gaby—" He crossed to her side and took her by the shoulders. "It's not your fault. It's thanks to me you were mixed up in this sorry business. But you must see now why Father is no longer welcome under our roof."

She gave a jerky nod. "At least now I know why you could never—" She drew a breath, her gaze turned away from him. "Why you could never love me as I loved you."

He looked down at her, the strands of hair falling against her cheek, the delicate line of her brows, the curve of her jaw, and saw the girl she'd been before Bertrand left England. Before everything went wrong. "I didn't realize at the time— I should have known. I was too caught up in my grief to see you properly." He lifted a hand and pushed her hair back from her shoulder, easier with the gesture than he had been for some time. Amazing the difference now the truth was in the open.

Gabrielle caught his hand and took a step back. "Rupert—"

She squeezed his fingers and released him. "You aren't the only one with reason to feel guilty."

He studied the familiar face he felt he'd so rarely looked at. Or so rarely seen properly. "Gaby?"

She folded her arms in front of her. "I was lonely. And I'm no saint."

For a moment he could simply stare at her, his brain refusing to make sense of it. He could not quite name the emotions that coursed through him. Surprise. Relief. And a bite of jealousy. A jealousy he had no right to feel.

Gabrielle looked into his eyes, her own dark and steady. "I wasn't in love with him. But I needed to be noticed. I needed to feel like a woman. I needed a person with whom I didn't have to pretend I had a perfect life."

He swallowed, parched for something he could not name. "Who?" He had to know, at the same time he didn't want to.

She drew a breath that felt rough against his skin. "Antoine Rivère."

He took a step backwards. "He—"

"He never gave me the least hint he knew anything about Bertrand, Rupert. I swear it."

"Did you talk to him about Bertrand?"

Gabrielle glanced away, chewing on her lower lip. "I said that I missed Bertrand. That I still couldn't believe he'd gone off as he had. Antoine never gave the least sign he knew more."

Rupert touched her shoulder. "I'm sorry, Gaby."

"Sorry?"

"That you lost him. And that he lied to you."

She gave a rough laugh. "It was hardly a deathless love." She looked at him, face etched with guilt. "Rupert—"

"I betrayed the marriage first, Gaby. Before I even offered for you."

"A fine pair, aren't we?"

CHAPTER 19

Malcolm stared at Wellington over the silver coffee service on his desk. "For God's sake, sir, why didn't you tell me?"

Wellington returned his gaze. He wore civilian dress as he often did, a light blue morning coat, buckskin breeches, and riding boots, but he held himself with military precision. "That should be self-evident."

"I could hardly fail to be aware that you were close to Lady Frances in Brussels. And in Paris. How far the relationship went is your own affair. And Lady Frances's."

Wellington's mouth tightened. "Quite."

"But her husband made it his affair as well? What was he threatening you with?"

Wellington reached for his coffee cup and took a deliberate sip. "Wedderburton-Webster quite misinterpreted the whole affair—matter." He returned the cup to its saucer with a clatter. "The damned puppy hasn't the sense to see that talk only makes things worse for Frances."

"But perhaps that was his intention?"

Wellington pushed back his chair, scraping it against the thick pile of the Aubusson carpet, got to his feet, and took a turn about the room. "How a woman like Frances ever chose such a man— The only thing to do with such accusations is to ignore them."

"But Rivère was making it difficult to do so?"

"I never said—"

"No, but Rivère's mistress did."

Wellington whirled on him with a gaze like a cannonade. "You talked about this with Rivère's mistress—"

"I needed to learn the truth. And you wouldn't tell it me."

"Damn it, Malcolm, you can't think I'd have given way to the threats of a man like Rivère."

"Then why not simply tell me?"

Wellington looked him straight in the eye. "I should think that would be obvious. A gentleman doesn't reveal such things about a lady."

"But surely that would have been precisely the result of your refusing to accede to Rivère's demands. Rivère would have made the letter public. With all the attendant embarrassment for Lady Frances. And for you."

A muscle twitched in Wellington's jaw. "That would have been Rivère's choice."

"And you simply planned to stand back and let him do his worst?"

Wellington put up a hand to his neckcloth. "I've never given a damn what people say about me."

"But this isn't just a question of your reputation. It concerns that of a lady you . . . care for. Where is the letter now?"

"I sent someone to retrieve it from Rivère's rooms. The night he was killed."

"While I sat strategizing with Suzanne. And before Rivère was conveniently killed? Are you asking me to believe you didn't even consider ways to stop him yourself?"

Wellington's mouth whitened. "If you're accusing me of killing Rivère, Malcolm, you should have the guts to do so outright."

Malcolm looked steadily at the victor of Waterloo. "I don't make accusations without more information at my disposal."

"And?" For the first time in their long association, Malcolm had the sense that Wellington was measuring him as an opponent.

And for the first time Malcolm looked back at Wellington as an antagonist. "And I give you fair warning that I will attempt to discover whatever information may be at hand."

"You've learned something." Malcolm regarded Wilhelmine of Sagan across the salon in the Rue du Faubourg Saint-Honoré. He had returned from his visit to Wellington to find she had just called.

"No. Yes. Perhaps." Wilhelmine set down the cup of tea Suzanne had given her. Such prevarication was uncharacteristic of her. She swallowed. Her face was pale beneath the brim of a bonnet lined with gathered blue silk and festooned with forget-me-not ostrich feathers. She folded her hands in her lap and sat up very straight. "I believe . . . I suspect . . . I think it's possible that Stewart is concealing—that he knows more than he is admitting about the death of Bertrand Laclos."

Malcolm felt the quick look his wife shot at him. "What makes you think so?" he asked.

Wilhelmine reached for her cup again and took a sip of tea. "A woman can read these things in a man she is . . . intimate with."

Malcolm studied the set face of his sister's sister. She was wasted on a man like Stewart, but he'd seen them together enough to guess at what Stewart meant to her. Love could be quixotic. And he understood the lure of security. "Stewart received a letter from Bertrand Laclos after Laclos's death. Bertrand wanted to return to England. If Stewart had told us about it sooner we might have questioned Bertrand's guilt sooner."

Wilhelmine's gaze flickered over his face. "Stewart admitted this to you?"

"Yesterday."

She shook her head. "I wish to God that was all there was to it, but I fear there's more. He all but ordered me to stop working with you the night of the British embassy ball. I can't believe he'd have turned round and confessed the whole to you." She drew a breath. "My suspicions were roused the night of the embassy ball. I spent a day mulling over what to do. But I can't abide the idea that wrong could have been done to an innocent man. And Bertrand Laclos is connected to Antoine Rivère's death, and Antoine is connected to Tatiana's child."

"Yes."

She gave a quick nod. "That was what decided me. My own concerns seem petty beside a child's safety." She set the teacup in its saucer and turned the gilt handle. "Stewart's not— He can be foolish, and he doesn't like to own to mistakes. But I don't think he'd deliberately harm an innocent man." She picked up the silver spoon, stirred the tea, set it down. "At least that's what I've been telling myself. But of course one doesn't like to think such things about a man who is sharing one's bed. And I've scarcely proved myself the best judge of men in the past."

"For what it's worth," Malcolm said, "four years ago I was convinced of Bertrand Laclos's guilt as well."

"But you didn't order his death." Wilhelmine met his gaze as though she were facing down a loaded pistol.

"No."

She nodded. "If I learn more I will bring it to you. I won't ask you to share your discoveries with me. But if you learn anything you think it would be of use for me to know—"

"Of course," Malcolm said.

"Willie, there's more." Suzanne leaned forwards. "I learned last night that Princess Tatiana may have been the lover of Paul St. Gilles."

"The painter?" Wilhelmine asked.

"You know him?" Malcolm said.

Wilhelmine gave a deep-throated laugh, a sudden break in the tension. "You don't think I know anyone without a title? He painted my portrait last year. One of my favorite likenesses. To my eye it looks like me, yet also beautiful. Metternich was particularly fond of it." She took another sip of tea, her eyes bright and her color returning. "An interesting man. St. Gilles, I mean. I wouldn't go so far as to say he considers me a friend, but I think I can help you get him to talk."

The concierge at the house on the Left Bank where Paul St. Gilles had his studio let them in without question. People weren't in the habit of denying Wilhelmine of Sagan. Rank had its uses. Much as he might deplore it, Malcolm had made use of his ducal grandfather's name and position on more than one occasion.

Wilhelmine led them up two flights of narrow stairs to a low-ceilinged passage and knocked at a door with peeling red paint. When no answer was forthcoming, she turned the handle. Malcolm had an impression of a wall of windows letting in a surprising amount of light for the cramped streets of the Left Bank, canvases stacked against the walls, sketches strewn across tables. A man with thinning sandy hair wearing a paint-smeared smock sat at an easel and wielded his brush as though there'd been no interruption.

"I'm sorry, Paul," Wilhelmine said, advancing into the room and stripping off her gloves. "I hate to interrupt an artist at work, but I'm afraid we have rather pressing business."

Paul St. Gilles set down his paintbrush and blinked as though getting her into focus. His eyes were blue-gray and surprisingly sharp. "*Madame la duchesse.* An unexpected pleasure."

Wilhelmine gathered up her flounced skirts as she navigated round a pile of canvases. "I must tell you that your portrait is by far the most talked of I've sat for."

"Which I hope is a good thing," St. Gilles said.

"Oh yes, I assure you. I quite like being talked about. Especially when the likeness is so flattering."

St. Gilles got to his feet. He was a tall man, lean and fit. "I never flatter, madame. I represent the truth."

"The perfect thing to say, Monsieur St. Gilles. May I present Monsieur and Madame Rannoch?"

St. Gilles inclined his head. "You're interested in a portrait?" His gaze moved between them and settled on Suzanne with an admiration that was more that of a connoisseur appreciating something rare than a man admiring a beautiful woman. "I should very much like to take your likeness, Madame Rannoch."

"And you claim not to flatter, Monsieur St. Gilles," Suzanne said with one of those smiles that could disarm anyone.

"Surely you realize I don't. You look to be a woman of keen understanding, Madame Rannoch."

"Simon Tanner's a good friend of ours," Malcolm said. "Perhaps you knew his father?"

"Roger Tanner? Yes. A formidable talent, lost far too young. And Simone was exquisite. Their son's quite a talent in his own right." St. Gilles looked at Malcolm and hesitated a moment, as though taking his measure.

"So he is. Simon says things I don't quite dare put into words, far more eloquently than I could myself."

St. Gilles met Malcolm's gaze and slowly inclined his head, as though in acknowledgment of a hit.

"I've read your pamphlets," Malcolm added. "You're quite eloquent yourself with words as well as paint. Not to mention daring."

"Or foolhardy, depending on whom you listen to. I imagine 'foolhardy' would receive considerably more votes."

Malcolm moved to the canvas on the easel. A fair-haired woman sitting on a stone bench in a garden. A common enough subject and setting, but something in the way her head was tilted back and her hand lifted to tuck a gold ringlet beneath the brim of her straw hat captured her personality, a bit imperious, a bit impulsive, warmhearted, quick-witted. While the sunlight glowing against the white stuff of her gown fairly leaped off the canvas.

"The Duc de Renaud's mistress," St. Gilles said. "The sort of commission one can't turn down. It helps pay for my more esoteric subjects." He gestured towards canvases leaning against the wall in the corner. A ruined ship, its sails tattered, on a wind-tossed sea, pierced by moonlight. A rocky seascape in what looked like Brittany, the blues and greens vivid against the gray of the rocks, gulls circling overhead. The roofs of Paris dusted by snow, blues and grays and vivid white.

"I'd give a great deal to have you paint my wife," Malcolm said with perfect truth. "But as it happens we're here for information."

"Not the most comforting words in Paris these days," St. Gilles said in a mild voice.

"I'm employed at the British embassy," Malcolm said, "but this is unofficial. I believe you were acquainted with a friend of mine."

St. Gilles's brows rose. "I doubt we move in the same circles, Monsieur Rannoch."

"Tatiana Kirsanova."

St. Gilles's eyes narrowed. "Yes, I knew Tatiana. The princess. I suppose you could say we were friends. We met first when she sat for a portrait. Shortly after she came to Paris. Perhaps that accounts for our friendship. She didn't know many people in Paris." St. Gilles glanced round. "I suppose I should offer you refreshment. A glass of wine?"

Wilhelmine started to demur, but Malcolm said that would be splendid. He wanted St. Gilles at his ease. St. Gilles moved stacks of canvases from two frayed velvet chairs, pulled up a folding stool, retrieved a ladder-back chair from behind a dressing screen, then pulled a bottle and glasses from a cabinet stacked with yet more canvases.

"I was a good friend of Princess Tatiana's myself," Malcolm said, accepting a glass from St. Gilles. "My wife and I looked into her death in Vienna last autumn."

St. Gilles's hand stilled as he set down the bottle. "They never caught her killer."

"Not officially."

"But he was brought to justice," Wilhelmine said.

That was a matter of debate, but Malcolm let it pass. Better for St. Gilles to trust him and see him as Tatiana's protector. However he'd failed her. "I'd known Tatiana since we were both young," he said. "I thought I knew her well. But since her death, I've realized more and more her capacity for secrets."

St. Gilles was regarding him, his wineglass forgot in his hand. "She talked about you."

"She mentioned my name?" Such carelessness would have been unlike Tania.

"No." St. Gilles twisted the stem of his glass between his fingers. "But she said she had a childhood friend who was almost like a brother. Who could cap any Shakespeare quotation."

Malcolm kept his fingers steady on his glass as a shock of surprise ran through him. If Tania had admitted that much to St. Gilles, they had been close indeed. Closer than she'd been to most of her lovers. It was more than he had told Suzanne about his half-sister, until well after her death. "Tatiana trusted you."

St. Gilles took a sip of wine, his gaze on the glass. "We were friends."

"A word that can cover a multitude of sins, as Tania would have said."

St. Gilles looked up at Malcolm, then flung back his head and gave a shout of laughter. "For God's sake, Monsieur Rannoch. Do I look like the sort of man who would have appealed to Tatiana Kirsanova?"

"Tania had eclectic tastes."

St. Gilles put up a hand to his thinning, gray-streaked hair. "Not that eclectic."

"And she liked artists," Wilhelmine said.

"Dramatic, romantic artists. Not middle-aged curmudgeons. Besides, I'd already met Juliette then. My wife," he added. "My wife now. At the time she was steadfastly refusing the bourgeois bonds of matrimony. I was doing my best to talk her out of it."

"You're married to Juliette Dubretton," Suzanne said.

"You know my wife?"

"I've read her books. In England she's called the French Mary Wollstonecraft. Which rather shows a British perspective."

St. Gilles smiled. "It's an apt comparison. Like William Godwin with Mary Wollstonecraft, I had a damnable time convincing Juliette to marry me. Tania was very kind about my crying on her shoulder."

Malcolm took a sip of wine. "You confided in Tatiana."

"Is that so hard to imagine?"

"No. Tania could be disarming. And a good listener when she put her mind to it. I'm wondering if she also confided in you."

"We were friends," St. Gilles said in an even voice. "We talked."

Malcolm hesitated. When it came to Tania, the instinct to secrecy was still deeply ingrained. Suzanne and Wilhelmine were silent, leaving the decision to him. "Did Tania tell you she was pregnant?" he asked.

St. Gilles flung back his head and gave another laugh. "Tania? Pregnant? Don't you think all Paris would have known?"

"Not if she'd gone away and had the child in secret."

St. Gilles went still. "My God. You're serious."

Malcolm leaned forwards and held St. Gilles with his gaze, the look he'd used to win confidences from everyone from diplomats across the negotiating table to murder suspects. "We have reason to believe Tania left Paris and gave birth to a child in the country. She gave the child up, but she appears to have known where he or she was and sent gifts. She was at great pains to keep the child's existence a secret."

St. Gilles ran a hand through his hair. "That would have been—"

"The child would have been conceived in late 1806 or possibly early 1807," Suzanne said.

St. Gilles picked up the bottle and splashed some more wine into his glass, frowning at the pale gold liquid. "It's not as though she gave me a list of her conquests."

"But—," Malcolm said.

"One couldn't but notice the court that surrounded her. She'd tell amusing stories about her cavaliers. I never knew which, if any, shared her bed."

"But there was someone else, wasn't there?" It was Wilhelmine's turn to lean forwards.

St. Gilles frowned at the splotches of paint on a canvas across the room. "It may mean nothing. One can make a child as easily in one night with a chance acquaintance as one can in the arms of the love of one's life." He took a thoughtful sip of wine. "Not that I'd necessarily say he was the love of her life."

"But he might have been?" Malcolm asked, gaze trained on St. Gilles.

"She said once that she thought he might be. I laughed, because I was sure she was making a joke. Tatiana laughed as well. But from the look in her eyes, I suddenly wondered if perhaps she hadn't been joking after all."

"Who?" Malcolm said. His breath seemed to have caught in his throat.

St. Gilles took another sip of wine. "He called himself Jean Leblanc."

"Called himself?"

"Claimed to be a law student from Provence. By the time I'd

shared a bottle of Burgundy with him and Tatiana I was sure that was a fabrication. I went so far as to warn Tania about him. But she kissed my cheek and told me not to be silly. Which I took to mean she knew who he was. And Leblanc seemed a decent sort. Far more decent than—" He bit back the words.

"Than Tania?" Malcolm asked with a smile.

St. Gilles met his gaze squarely. "You knew her."

"Just so. Though I wouldn't have said a decent man was the sort to appeal to her."

"No." St. Gilles frowned, as though turning over memories. "This was different, as I said before. Leblanc seemed a serious sort. Always a bit preoccupied. But quite charming. And obviously in love with Tania. Unlike Tania, he made no effort to hide it. I decided there wasn't anything significant to worry about and Tania could take care of herself." His fingers tightened round his glass. "More fool me. It was weeks before I learned who he really was."

"Who?" Malcolm asked.

"Laclos."

"Bertrand Laclos?" Wilhelmine said with a gasp of disbelief. "But he wouldn't have been in Paris yet."

"Not Bertrand. His elder brother."

"Tatiana was in love with Étienne Laclos?" Malcolm said.

St. Gilles gave a faint smile. "The closest she came to admitting it was that joke that may not have been a joke. But Tatiana was Étienne Laclos's lover, yes. Not that I knew him as Étienne Laclos at the time."

"He was in France in secret, wasn't he?" Suzanne said. "Involved in a plot against Napoleon."

"So I later learned. I—" St. Gilles broke off at the opening of the door. A tall, dark-haired woman stepped into the room and paused on the threshold. She wore a gown of brown-spotted muslin and her hair was drawn back into a simple chignon. Her brows were strongly marked, her cheekbones high, her mouth full lipped, her eyes radiating shrewd intelligence. An attractive woman who employed no obvious arts to attract.

"I didn't realize you had guests," she said.

"I fear we arrived unexpectedly and have been quite monopolizing your husband, Madame St. Gilles," Wilhelmine said. "Or do you prefer 'Mademoiselle Dubretton'?"

"I answer to both." Juliette Dubretton stepped into the room. She looked to be in her midthirties, with deepest dark eyes, fine-boned features, and tawny skin that suggested Spanish origins.

Wilhelmine introduced Malcolm and Suzanne. "I'm an admirer of your writing," Suzanne said, shaking hands.

"You're very kind, Madame Rannoch. But I wonder if your husband would thank me."

"Actually, it was my husband who introduced me to your books."

Juliette Dubretton ran a frank gaze over Malcolm. "You're evidently an intriguing man, Monsieur Rannoch."

"Merely a man who recognizes good sense when he reads it."

Juliette's gaze moved from Malcolm and Suzanne to her husband. "Flattered as I am, I seem to have interrupted. Shall I leave?"

"No, no," St. Gilles said. "It's not as though we have secrets, and you may be able to help. They've come in search of information about Tatiana Kirsanova."

"Poor Tatiana." Juliette perched on the arm of her husband's chair. "She was very kind to Paul when I fear I was being rather tiresomely prickly about how I couldn't compromise my principles with matrimony. Is this about her death?"

"More about her life," Malcolm said. "It seems she may have had a child."

Juliette's dark eyes widened. *"Mon Dieu."*

St. Gilles caught his wife up on the discussion. Juliette listened in frowning silence. "I only met Leblanc—Laclos—once or twice, but he seemed to me a man quite out of his depth. With Tatiana and with whatever had brought him to Paris. But I think Paul is right. Tatiana did seem to care for him." Her fingers twined round her husband's. "When one's in love oneself one notices such things."

St. Gilles shot her a smile and lifted her hand to his lips. "Not that you'd have gone so far as to admit you were in love at the time."

Her smile was a private sort of answer. "Well, perhaps not to you."

"Did Tatiana know about Étienne Laclos's plot?" Malcolm asked.

"I'm not sure," St. Gilles said, returning the pressure of his wife's hand. "She and Leblanc—Laclos—kept their liaison secret. They met at my studio often, but naturally I took care to make myself scarce when they did. Then one night they hammered at the door at three in the morning. I slept in the studio in those days. Tania said Leblanc was in trouble and could I hide him. He left the next morning disguised as an old woman with bits of costume I keep for my pictures. By evening he'd been arrested and thrown in the Conciergerie. Though I didn't realize the Étienne Laclos who'd been arrested for plotting against the emperor was Jean Leblanc until Tania came to see me again and spilled out the whole. Surprisingly effusive for Tania. I suppose her desperation could be taken as yet more proof that she loved him."

"She tried to save him?" Malcolm asked.

"After being so determined to keep their liaison a secret, she used every bit of influence she had. And then she tried to plan a rescue. She asked me to help." He gave a wry smile. "You can appreciate the irony. I got in a fair amount of trouble with the Bonaparte government, but if there was anything to push me back to being a committed Bonapartist it was a Royalist plot." He glanced round the company. "No offense meant."

"None taken," Malcolm said.

"I painted most of the Bonaparte family," St. Gilles said. "Bonaparte, Josephine, Hortense and her children, Eugène, Jerome, Pauline twice. There's nothing like trying to capture someone on canvas to make them seem like a real person. Which rather complicates the idea of violence against the state."

Juliette shivered. "I was never much of an admirer of Bonaparte, but murder is murder. At the time of the plot, Hortense had just lost her little boy and come to Paris with her younger son. They would have been at Malmaison. If the plan had succeeded it could well have killed not just Napoleon but Josephine and Hortense and her child— Once I had children of my own, I could understand

Bonaparte's determination to exact vengeance." She hesitated, her gaze on Malcolm.

"I'm aware British gold funded the mission," Malcolm said. "Not our finest hour." He looked at St. Gilles. "But somehow I don't think you refused to help Tania when she asked you to assist Étienne?"

"Oh no. I agreed, as Tania knew I would. What are principles when one has desperate friends before one?"

"What happened?" Suzanne asked.

"The jailer she'd bribed came down with a fever, Laclos was moved to a different cell. A tragedy of errors."

"She must have been angry. Tania hated to lose."

"So she did. But this was more than anger. I'd never seen her so devastated, before or since. She stayed with me for two days."

"I still remember the sound of her sobs," Juliette said. "I doubt she cried often."

"She didn't," Malcolm said.

St. Gilles took a long swallow of wine. "After the night Étienne Laclos died, she never talked about him again."

"And then she left Paris?" Wilhelmine asked.

"A few months later."

Wilhelmine set down her wineglass. "Long enough for her to have discovered she was with child."

"Possibly. But— Forgive me, but even knowing Tatiana, even if she loved Leblanc—Laclos..." St. Gilles hesitated, glanced from Wilhelmine to Suzanne to Malcolm. "I doubt he was the only man whose bed she was sharing."

"But perhaps the only man she cared for enough to forget to take precautions," Suzanne said.

St. Gilles gave her a look of surprise and slowly nodded. "Perhaps."

Juliette reached for her husband's wineglass and took a sip. "It's true. Tatiana wasn't the sort of woman to run risks in the service of passion."

"If the child was Étienne Laclos's, do you know why Tatiana would have been at such pains to keep it secret?" Malcolm asked.

"Aside from the fact that its father had died a traitor?" St. Gilles said.

"The Bonaparte régime may be accused of overzeal, but I haven't heard of them avenging themselves on the children of traitors."

"No. That's true."

"Do you know of anyone else she might have confided in?"

"Not Tania," St. Gilles said. "She wasn't the confiding sort, as you must know yourself. As to Laclos, I'd tell you to ask his confederate in the plot. Save that he's no longer here to ask."

"His confederate?" Malcolm leaned forwards. "He was also executed?"

"No, he escaped detection. I only knew of his involvement thanks to Laclos himself. But he died three days ago. It was Antoine Rivère."

CHAPTER 20

"I hate coincidences," Suzanne said. "They always make me feel as though I'm missing something."

"We're undoubtedly missing a damned sight too much." Malcolm took a sip of coffee. The two of them and Wilhelmine had repaired to a café when they left St. Gilles's studio to collect themselves and talk over what they'd learned.

"If Étienne Laclos was the father of Tatiana's child, this could explain how Rivère knew of it," Wilhelmine said, stirring her café au lait. "Étienne could have confided in Rivère about the affair. He might even have known Tatiana was pregnant." She looked at Malcolm. "She didn't—"

"Tell me any of this? No." Malcolm's mouth hardened.

Suzanne reached across the table to touch his hand. "You weren't here. And she couldn't very well have written to you about it. She'd have put Laclos at risk. Besides, I doubt she was the sort to write confiding letters. Any more than you are."

Malcolm thought of the handful of letters, most of them coded, that were all he had left of his sister. "True enough."

Suzanne squeezed his fingers. "But even granted that's how Rivère might have learned of the child, we still have the coincidence of Rivère also knowing about Étienne Laclos's brother being framed for treason five years later."

Malcolm sat back in his chair, sifting the pieces in his head. It was like a chessboard that had been scattered midgame, so that the strategy of the players was indecipherable. "According to Rupert, Lord Dewhurst instigated the plot. Étienne had been working as Dewhurst's secretary and Dewhurst provided the funding. And Dewhurst was also behind Bertrand's returning to France as a British agent."

"You aren't suggesting Lord Dewhurst was somehow trying to get rid of both the Laclos brothers, are you?" Wilhelmine asked.

She had stumbled startlingly close to the mark, at least in Bertrand's case. Malcolm couldn't think of why Dewhurst would have wanted to get rid of Étienne. "No," he said. "But I do think I need to talk to Dewhurst."

"Malcolm—" Wilhelmine took a sip of café au lait and frowned into the cup. "Do you think Tatiana was involved in a plot to assassinate Napoléon Bonaparte?"

Malcolm checked the instinctive denial that rose to his lips. True, Tatiana had been Talleyrand's creature. But not exclusively. She played all sides, and she was quite capable of making her own choices for personal ends. He drew a breath. "With Tania, I can never be sure of anything."

Juliette Dubretton listened to the sound of their guests' footsteps fading down the stairs. The scrape of the door opening and closing. These days in Paris caution was ingrained in one. She leaned against the wall between two canvases and surveyed her husband, who was still standing beside the door. "I like them. I wouldn't have thought I would."

Paul turned from the door to face her. "Wilhelmine of Sagan is unquestionably an aristocrat, but an interesting woman. The Rannochs are more surprising. It's rare to meet a man who can laugh at his world."

"And she doesn't come from that world at all."

"How do you know?"

"Observation. Madame Rannoch has eyes that have seen things no gently bred girl observes." Juliette watched her husband for a moment, a host of considerations shifting in the scales in her mind. "You must be thinking what I'm thinking."

Paul lifted his brows. "Romantic as the idea of two minds being in tune is, I haven't the least idea what you're talking about. Which perhaps isn't surprising given that I'm scarcely a romantic."

"You're the world's last romantic, *mon cher,* but don't try to change the subject." She drew a breath, because even to put it into words was one step down an irreversible course. "You have to be wondering if we should have told them."

She saw the jolt of tension that ran through her husband before he strolled across the room and picked up his wineglass. "You're suggesting I've given way to madness as well as being a romantic?"

"It's not funny, Paul." She locked her hands together behind her back, gripping the hard gold of her wedding band. The bond she'd resisted, the bond that now anchored her life. "We can't keep the secret forever."

"For God's sake, Julie." Paul spun round to face her. "That's exactly what we have to do. What we agreed to do. There's too much at stake."

She studied his face, the father of her children, the man for whom she had abandoned her principles, the best man she had ever met. "This changes things."

He tossed down a swallow of wine. "Just because they like your books—"

"That damn well has nothing to do with it." She crossed the room and caught his arm. "I don't like what the lies are doing to me. To you. I can see where this is leading us."

He looked down at her, his eyes unexpectedly dark with fear. Paul was not a man who frightened easily. "And if we told the truth? Where would that lead us?"

She swallowed, because she wasn't sure herself and the question made her throat go tight and her blood run colder than the Seine in winter. But she kept her gaze on her husband's face, because she wasn't one to shirk hard truths. "I don't know. But I think we have to take the risk."

"Not with this." He took an impatient step across the room. "Christ, Juliette—"

"Paul." She closed the distance between them and caught his face between her hands. "Every breath we breathe is a risk these days."

"All the more reason—"

"I didn't know," she said. "I didn't understand the implications and how it could affect others. It now seems very selfish—"

He put up his hands to cover her own. "That's foolishness, *ma belle*. You have nothing to reproach yourself with. If I hadn't—"

"It's not the time for regrets, *mon amour*."

He ran a hand over her hair. His fingers trembled against her scalp. "You're a remarkable woman, Juliette."

"Hardly." She looked into his eyes, seeing the man she'd met ten years ago in Café Belles Lettres, a sketch pad in his lap, a notebook at his elbow. "But I think I'm strong enough to face the past. And I think the man I fell in love with is as well."

He looked down at her for a long moment. She could feel his breath warm on her face and words of acquiescence trembling on his lips. Then he wrenched away from her and strode across the room. "I know what I owe you, Juliette. I'd give my life for you. But I can't do this. Don't ask it of me."

Lord Dewhurst looked up at Malcolm from behind the mahogany and brass of his desk. His gaze hardened. "If you've come to make more damned accusations, Rannoch, I have nothing to say to you. Rupert can talk to me to my face if he wishes."

"Rupert didn't send me." Malcolm closed the door and advanced into the office. It smelled of good ink, old leather, and older brandy and was heavy with gilt and expensive fabric. "I don't believe he has any wish to talk to you at all."

"If it's about Laclos—"

"It's not." Malcolm stopped three paces from the desk. "At least not about Bertrand."

Dewhurst's brows lifted. "What the devil—"

"Nine years ago, you were behind a plot to bring down Napoleon."

Dewhurst's gaze flickered to the side, then narrowed. "We were at war with France at the time. Damn it, if we could have removed Bonaparte—"

"I didn't come here to argue the morality of covert operations. Wellington may have caviled at shooting Bonaparte on the field at Waterloo, but this was hardly the only plot our government financed to bring him down. You sent Étienne Laclos as your emissary."

Dewhurst grimaced. "Étienne was an able young man. A bit too much of an idealist, perhaps, but he'd have grown out of that. It was tragic what happened. Why do you care?"

"Because I've just learned that Antoine Rivère was his confederate."

Shock shot through Dewhurst's eyes. Shock but not surprise. "Who told you that?"

"Are you saying it isn't true?"

Dewhurst gave a short laugh. "You wouldn't believe me if I did."

"No. That's true enough."

Dewhurst pushed his chair back and got to his feet. "Damn it, Malcolm, you can't think—"

"I think anything to do with Rivère may have a bearing on why he was killed."

Dewhurst spun away.

"I didn't realize Rivère reported to you in his work as a British agent," Malcolm said.

"He didn't." The words seemed to be dragged from Dewhurst's throat. "He reported to Carfax. Carfax suggested him for the mission."

"So you and Carfax devised the plot against Bonaparte together?"

"Has there been any British intelligence mission in the past thirty years that Carfax hasn't known about?"

"A point. Did the plot start with you or him?"

"As it happens it started with Étienne." Dewhurst leaned against a marble-topped pier table that supported a candelabrum and a globe. Some of the tension left his shoulders. He seemed to almost enjoy reliving the planning of the mission. "His cousin had written to him that Bonaparte could be vulnerable."

"His cousin? Not Gui?"

"No, Gui had been sent to England long since. Christian. His father was the third Laclos brother. That branch of the family had stayed in France and managed to survive the Terror. In fact, Christian was employed in the foreign ministry. He and Étienne corresponded secretly. Christian wrote to Étienne that he'd been sent to Malmaison with papers and it was amazing there wasn't more security. Étienne repeated it to me. I don't think either he or Christian saw the operational implications."

"But you did."

"I could hardly fail to do so. It isn't often something drops into one's lap like that. I went to Carfax. He suggested Rivère would be a good source and that he was practical enough to keep the two Laclos cousins in line."

Malcolm moved round the side of the desk to where he could once again face Dewhurst directly. "So you packed Étienne off to Paris with British gold."

"Naturally we funded the mission."

"Was anyone else involved besides the three of them?"

"Not to my knowledge." Dewhurst flicked a piece of dried wax off the candelabrum. "It seemed safer to keep it small."

"What went wrong?"

Dewhurst's brows drew together. "I don't know. Someone betrayed them."

"They didn't make a mistake and betray themselves?"

"That's what I thought at first. Étienne and Christian were both untried. But they'd managed quite well until that point. Everything was proceeding apace. Then all hell broke loose."

"But Étienne was the only one caught."

"He didn't break and betray his comrades. A splendid young man, as I said."

"And perhaps in this case being an idealist served him well."

"Perhaps." Dewhurst frowned at the dried wax on the marble of the table. "There was one thing."

"What?"

"The gold we'd sent with Étienne to fund the mission. It disappeared."

"Into someone's pockets?"

"One can't but wonder."

"Rivère?"

Dewhurst swept the wax fragments into his hand, then crossed the room to dump them into a bin beside the desk. "If so, there's no record of him ever spending it. You didn't find it when you searched his rooms, did you?"

Malcolm shook his head.

"There's no record of Christian Laclos spending it, either."

Malcolm hesitated, weighing risks and rewards, then said, "Did you know Étienne was involved with Tatiana Kirsanova?"

Dewhurst straightened up from the bin and stared at him. "The Russian princess? The one who was murdered in Vienna?"

Malcolm swallowed. "Yes. She was also an agent."

"For us?"

"For Talleyrand. He sent her to work with us in the Peninsula."

"Talleyrand sent a French agent to work with us during the war—"

"She wasn't a French agent, she was his personal agent. And he was out of power and making overtures to the British at the time. But T—Princess Tatiana also struck out on her own and worked for the highest bidder."

"You think she was working with Étienne?"

"I don't know. It's possible she was merely his lover. Though Princess Tatiana was rarely merely anything."

Dewhurst tapped his fingers on the desktop. "I never heard that Étienne had a mistress. Though it's not the sort of thing he'd have communicated with me about. Do you think it was Tatiana Kirsanova who betrayed the plot?"

That possibility had, of course, occurred to Malcolm from the first, but he kept his face impassive. "There's nothing to suggest that."

"If she's as good as you say there wouldn't be." Dewhurst leaned against the desk, facing Malcolm. "Someone betrayed them.

You say Princess Tatiana was Talleyrand's creature. Perhaps he put her up to the affair to keep tabs on the conspirators."

"Assuming he wanted to protect Napoleon. At that point in Talleyrand's career, it's difficult to say what he wanted when it came to the emperor."

"Or perhaps someone else put her up to it. The woman was obviously an unscrupulous adventuress—" Dewhurst bit the words back, though Malcolm doubted the other man could have actually seen his nails digging into his palms. "Forgot the talk about the two of you. But damn it, Rannoch, even if she was your mistress you can't have illusions about her."

"No. That is, no, she wasn't my mistress, and no, I'm quite free of illusions where Tatiana Kirsanova is concerned." Though he wasn't entirely sure that was true.

"Well then."

"She hid Étienne Laclos the night the plot was discovered."

"But he was caught all the same." Dewhurst rested his hands behind him on the desk, a man in command of the setting and the situation. "Perhaps she led the conspirators right to him. Hiding him would be a good way of making sure she knew where he was."

That, of course, had also occurred to Malcolm when St. Gilles first told them the story. "And reportedly she was devastated by his death."

"She wouldn't be the first woman to feign grief over a lover. Or perhaps she really did feel it. Never held much call with it myself, but agents have been known to be struck by guilt. I'd have thought you knew quite a bit about that."

"As it happens." Far more than Tatiana, actually. But even Tania hadn't been entirely immune to twinges of guilt. Malcolm remembered the suspicious streaks of damp on her face after a young French lieutenant she'd seduced had died in an ambush in Spain. An ambush she had instigated.

"Nothing to be done about it, I suppose," Dewhurst said. "She's dead and beyond retribution. But I'm relieved to have the mystery solved."

"If it is solved."

Dewhurst shot him a look. "Not as free of illusions as you claim, are you, boy?"

"Perhaps. I've also learned it can be a mistake to accept the obvious explanation."

The scent of orange trees wafted from the orangerie as a breeze rippled across the Jardin du Luxembourg. Gabrielle Caruthers sat with her sketch pad by the Medici Fountain, Marie de' Medici's fanciful re-creation of Renaissance Florentine style, set in a statue-filled grotto. Gabrielle's little boy twirled a top nearby under the watchful eye of his nurse. Gabrielle looked up at Suzanne and Colin's approach and to Suzanne's relief smiled. "Mrs. Rannoch. And Colin. Would you like to play with Stephen? I know he'd be glad of company his own age."

Colin grinned and ran forwards. He and Stephen were soon happily engaged taking turns with the top. "It's a gift to make friends easily," Gabrielle said. "I don't think I ever quite had it."

"Colin seems to take everything in stride," Suzanne said, settling her muslin skirts as she sank into a chair beside Gabrielle. "I think it's a happy side effect of the unhappy fact of spending his early years in a war-torn country. It reassures me that we weren't horribly selfish to drag him about with us."

"Children are amazing." Gabrielle rested her chin in her hand, watching the boys. "Whatever becomes of a marriage, one knows one will always have them."

Suzanne had thought much the same herself on more than one occasion. What she hadn't anticipated properly was how Malcolm's tie to Colin would tie her to Malcolm as well. "It's a bond I had no conception of," she said. "Not until Colin was born."

Gabrielle turned her head and looked into Suzanne's eyes, her own clear and open in the afternoon sunlight. "You know, don't you? About Rupert and Bertrand?"

Suzanne returned the other woman's gaze. "I'm afraid murder investigations dredge up all sorts of secrets. Your husband told you?"

Gabrielle nodded, as though she didn't trust herself to speak.

"I'm glad he told you. But it must have been a shock."

Gabrielle gave a dry laugh. "Everyone keeps behaving as though I'm a sheltered girl still in the schoolroom. It's not as though I've never heard of such things. To own the truth, once Rupert told me I couldn't believe I hadn't seen it before."

Suzanne thought of the weeks last autumn when she'd been convinced Tatiana Kirsanova was Malcolm's mistress. "It can't have been easy."

"Easier in some ways than having a woman as a rival. At least now I understand why he never—" Gabrielle swallowed. The pulse beat rapidly in her throat just below the blue satin ribbons that fastened her bonnet. "Why he never could desire me."

Suzanne gripped her hands together. That at least was something she had never found lacking in her relationship with Malcolm. For a moment, the startling intimacy of her wedding night was vivid in her mind. She had been playacting, years of experience subsumed into the role of a girl who had known only violence, yet she had rarely experienced desire that was so honest. "You were caught in an intolerable situation."

"That's what Rupert said. But knowing about him and Bertrand doesn't change my gratitude to Rupert for coming to my rescue." Gabrielle looked down at her hands, ungloved and smeared with pencil. "I'll own at times thinking it over I've been angry. I smashed one of my scent bottles, and I nearly broke a jewelry casket Rupert gave me for our first anniversary. But even then I was angrier at the situation than at Rupert. He's as trapped as I am, and he's actually been faithful to his vows. I think because what he felt for Bertrand was so strong he can't bring himself to seek such intimacy again. I only wish—" She drew a breath, as though parched for something she could not name. "I could see the depth of what he felt for Bertrand. I should like to experience that myself, not the pale counterfeit I found with Antoine."

Suzanne had often felt the same, looking at David and Simon and other couples who shared startling intimacy. Now, at moments, she wondered if perhaps she and Malcolm had it themselves. "It's a rare thing," she said. "And something not many find in their marriages."

"But you did."

"Perhaps."

Gabrielle looked up as her son gave a sudden shriek of delight. "Rupert won't let his father see Stephen now. I can still scarcely take it in. That Lord Dewhurst was behind Bertrand's death—"

"You were fond of your father-in-law?"

Gabrielle twisted a stray blond ringlet round her finger. "He was always kind to me. It was rare to find an English aristocrat so welcoming to an émigrée. Now I understand that it wasn't me at all. He was relieved to see Rupert married to a woman, any woman." She swallowed and jabbed the ringlet back beneath the chip straw brim of her bonnet. "I hate that I helped his plans along, however unwittingly."

"Your cousin Étienne had worked for him as well."

"And went off to his death on Dewhurst's orders. No, I suppose there I wrong Dewhurst, much as I despise him. Étienne was eager enough—filled with thoughts of honor and dreams of glory. I'll never understand men. Women are much more practical."

Suzanne nodded, though she knew full well what it was to be driven by a cause. "Did you correspond with Étienne at all after he went to France?"

Gabrielle fortunately didn't appear surprised by the question. "Yes. He had a courier system to report to Lord Dewhurst, and he was able to include letters to us. He wrote to me more than to anyone in the family, actually. Somehow he seemed to find it easier to talk to me."

"Perhaps that had to do with what he wanted to talk about."

Gabrielle drew a breath, then hesitated. The splash of the fountain against the elaborate stone of the grotto echoed through the garden.

"Lady Caruthers," Suzanne said, "was your cousin in love with a woman in France?"

Gabrielle's blue eyes widened. "How did you know?"

"From something Malcolm and I've learned, it seems Étienne may have become involved with a woman called Tatiana Kirsanova. She was murdered in Vienna last autumn. She was a friend of Malcolm's."

Gabrielle nodded. "I've heard—" Confusion shot through her gaze. "That is—"

"You've heard the gossip about Malcolm and Princess Tatiana. But I'm sure you know better than to believe all the gossip you hear. As it happens they weren't lovers. Though for some weeks I believed they were."

"That must have been beastly."

"Yes. It was hellish. I scarcely realized my own capacity for jealousy until then. And yet when she was murdered I was more concerned for Malcolm than anything."

Gabrielle nodded. "Last night when Rupert told me about Bertrand, I could only think that I hadn't been able to comfort him properly." She folded her sketch pad. "Étienne never said— He never told me the woman's name."

"So he did confide in you about a love affair?"

"Yes. I can't believe—" Gabrielle's gaze fastened on the white marble statue of Venus in her bath that the architect Jean Chalgrin had recently added to the fountain's grotto. "He said it was the last thing he'd ever expected, to meet the love of his life in Paris. That he couldn't forgive himself for dragging her into danger. That it was a terrible irony that they'd met when so much was at stake. You know the sort of thing young men say when they fancy themselves in love. But I never thought the woman he wrote about was an—" She bit back the word.

"An adventuress?"

Gabrielle flushed. "I'm the last person who should be using such words about another woman. But Étienne was more the sort to fall for a helpless ingénue than a powerful woman. And the tone of his letters was that of a man in love who truly believed the feeling was returned."

"From the stories I've heard, Princess Tatiana gave the impression she was very much in love with your cousin."

"A penniless émigré who, much as I loved him, would have probably appeared callow to an experienced woman?"

Lord Stewart's incredulity at her marriage to Malcolm echoed in Suzanne's head. "Love can take people by surprise. Do you think the woman your cousin loved could have been involved in the plot against Napoleon?"

Gabrielle gave a surprised laugh. "My cousin Étienne was the sort to want to protect the woman he loved, not expose her to danger."

"My husband occasionally has those tendencies, but fortunately he overcomes them. I doubt such behavior would have found favor with Princess Tatiana, either."

Gabrielle frowned. "Étienne said— He said she was brave. Which surprised me. That wasn't the way I'd have expected him to talk about the woman he loved."

"Did Antoine Rivère say anything to you about Étienne's lover? Or about the plot?"

Gabrielle stiffened. For a moment, Suzanne saw the defenses slam into place in her eyes. Stephen's and Colin's giggles echoed across the garden in the stillness. Then some of the tension drained from Gabrielle's shoulders. "You know. Though I suppose there's no need for secrecy now that Antoine is dead. He was concerned about the repercussions if it became known he'd been plotting against France's government. Even by the Royalists."

"How long have you known?"

"Antoine told me. It was how we first—how we first became acquainted." Gabrielle picked up a pencil that had fallen beside her chair and tucked it into its case. "He came up to me at the opera and told me he'd had the good fortune to know my cousin and that he was a brave man. At first I wasn't sure if he was talking about Étienne or Bertrand. Then I realized he must be the third man who had worked with Étienne and our cousin Christian. I was surprised he admitted it to me, given his worry about his involvement getting out."

"I expect he had his reasons for wanting to find favor with you."

Gabrielle flushed, then smiled. "Perhaps. He seemed to trust me, which was a bit seductive in itself. Rupert isn't much in the habit of confiding in me. At least he wasn't. And I liked being able to talk about Étienne."

"What did Rivère tell you?"

Gabrielle pleated a blue-sprigged muslin fold of her skirt between her fingers. "That at first he'd taken Étienne for something of an idle fribble, a spoiled young aristo with dreams of glory. But that Étienne had surprised him with his determination and his ingenuity."

"Did he mention Étienne's mistress?"

"I asked about her." Gabrielle hesitated a moment, waved to the boys, who were now running races in front of the fountain. "He said that without her, they might have pulled it off."

"Did he mean she was a distraction?"

"What else could he have meant?" Gabrielle's gaze skimmed over Suzanne's face. "You think Princess Tatiana is the one who betrayed them?"

"There's no evidence to suggest that."

"But you think it's a possibility." Gabrielle watched Suzanne closely.

"There are a number of possibilities."

"Someone betrayed them."

"Who did Rivère think it was?"

"He didn't know who. Or why it was only Étienne who was betrayed. Only that he'd be forever grateful to Étienne for not betraying him and Christian." Gabrielle rubbed her arms, bare below the puffed sleeves of her gown. "I didn't always believe the things Antoine said to me. But that had the ring of truth."

"Do you think your cousin Christian knows more?"

"Perhaps. To own the truth, I don't know Christian well. Until these past few weeks I hadn't seen him since I was a baby. I confess I find it hard to imagine him involved in a secret plot. He's a great admirer of a friend of yours."

"Of mine?"

"Dorothée Talleyrand."

CHAPTER 21

Malcolm rapped at the door of Talleyrand's study once and then strode into the room. He stood on less ceremony with the prince than he had in Vienna.

"Malcolm." Talleyrand looked up from the papers on the desk before him with so little surprise that Malcolm wondered if the prince could recognize his step on the stairs. He wouldn't put it past Talleyrand for a minute. "An unexpected pleasure."

Malcolm pushed the door to and advanced to stand before the desk. "Did you put Tatiana up to her affair with Étienne Laclos?"

Talleyrand stared at him for the length of a half-dozen heart-beats, then raised his brows. "My dear boy—"

"You've rather exhausted the feigned innocence, sir. Particularly where Tania is concerned."

Talleyrand gave him a smile of acknowledgment. "Étienne Laclos wasn't a trained agent. He had adequate cover for slipping into France, but it was obvious early on he'd been sent by your government. I needed to find out what he was up to."

"And when you did know?"

The brows lifted again, this time with pretension-dampening hauteur. "They were plotting to take my sovereign's life."

"Quite."

Talleyrand gave a laugh and waved a hand towards a shield-back chair beside his desk. "God knows Bonaparte and I had our disagreements, but I don't recall anyone ever accusing me of having designs on his life."

"Nor do I." Malcolm dropped into the chair, not taking his gaze from Talleyrand's face. "Which doesn't mean—"

Talleyrand adjusted a crystal paperweight that anchored a stack of papers beside his elbow. "I won't ask you to have faith in my morals, Malcolm, but you should have the wit to believe me when I point out that assassination of a leader leaves a dangerous vacuum. I've seen enough of chaos in my life to deplore a vacuum."

Malcolm scanned Talleyrand's face. His only prayer of keeping up with the prince was to keep all his wits about him, and even then Talleyrand had the edge. "So it was you and Tania who put an end to the plot."

"No, as it happens." Talleyrand's fingers curled round the paperweight. "We planned to, if they ever got so far as putting it into action. But someone else betrayed them first."

"Who?"

"I don't know. Nor could I ever find out. Tania was furious. She'd developed quite an affection for Étienne Laclos. She'd made me promise that when we put an end to the plot, Étienne be allowed to escape."

"She tried to hide him."

"Yes, I know. And when he was arrested, she begged me to intervene. Begged, entreated, threatened, wheedled. I've never seen even Tania run such a gamut of emotions. But of course there was a limit to what I could do. I could hardly let it be said I'd come to the aid of a traitor in the pay of the British with designs on the emperor's life." He stared down at the sunlight bouncing off the crystal of the paperweight. "I think it was one of the worst quarrels Tatiana and I ever had. She wouldn't speak to me for weeks afterwards."

"And then she asked you to help her leave Paris quietly."

"A few months later, yes."

Malcolm drew a breath. "Do you think Étienne Laclos was the father of her child?"

Talleyrand's eyes narrowed.

"You can't tell me you never considered it."

"No, it was an obvious possibility. The strongest argument against it was that it's difficult then to see the reason for such over-whelming secrecy. For the actual birth, yes, she wouldn't have wanted open scandal. But to fear any whisper of mention of the father's name—?"

"Perhaps she didn't want it known she'd been the lover of a traitor."

"That would have garnered her sympathy in some circles. Especially after Bonaparte was exiled."

"Could she have feared vengeance?"

"From whom? The Lacloses were in England. Christian Laclos was hardly the sort for anyone to fear, let alone Tatiana, who could run rings round him without trying."

"Could she have been afraid it would come out that she'd betrayed Étienne?"

Talleyrand's brows lifted. "I told you, we didn't—"

"You didn't. Could Tania have done it on her own?"

Talleyrand didn't give the quick denial Malcolm more than half-expected. He sat back in his chair, fingers loose on the ink blotter. "I won't deny I've thought of it. But if you'd seen her concern for Laclos—" He shrugged his satin-clad shoulders. "Then again I'm the last to put store in emotional outbursts."

"You didn't take Rivère into custody."

"No. As I told you, I found it useful to watch Rivère. I was rather annoyed that whoever exposed the plot had disrupted one of my best sources. At least the damage was contained to Étienne Laclos."

"What about the gold?"

"Gold?"

"Dewhurst told me the gold to fund the plot was never recovered."

"And you're asking if it found its way into French coffers?"

"Can you blame me?"

"No. Any more than I can expect you to believe me when I deny it."

* * *

"We're not going to see Manon Caret." Aline looked up as Suzanne dropped into the chair beside her at the rail of their box in the Comédie-Française. "Apparently she's ill. Such a pity. She even makes me enjoy all that declamation in Racine, and I've never seen anyone I liked so much as Countess Almaviva."

"Sometimes an understudy can surprise one," Suzanne said in a steady voice. She still didn't know if Manon had made it safely out of Paris. Or if Raoul had safely returned.

"I imagine there are gentlemen sighing all over the theatre." Cordelia settled her skirts—black opera net over seafoam satin—as she seated herself beside Suzanne.

"Yes, I think even Geoff isn't immune to Mademoiselle Caret's charms," Aline said. "She's rather a thinking man's Aphrodite."

"Have you heard?" Dorothée brushed through the curtains at the back of the box.

"That Manon Caret is ill?" Aline asked.

"But she isn't." Dorothée dropped into a chair in the row behind them in a swirl of jade crêpe and Pomona green satin. "At least not according to the gossip I've been hearing. They say the management's put it about that she's ill, but in fact she's disappeared from Paris. There are even odds on whether she's run off with a lover or disappeared to escape her creditors."

"I would think it would take something more serious for an actress to forego her profession," Cordelia said, glancing down at the programme in her lap. "I doubt a mere man would do it and surely a woman in her position could evade creditors. Don't you think, Suzanne?"

"Quite." Suzanne was scanning the boxes with her opera glasses. She caught sight of a familiar graying dark brown head and sharp profile across the theatre. The constriction in her chest eased. Raoul had made it back to Paris.

"But plenty of people have reason to flee Paris these days," Aline said. "Was Mademoiselle Caret political?"

"Not particularly," Dorothée said. "She was rumored to have a liaison with Jerome Bonaparte, but then any number of actresses have been connected to the Bonapartes. Look at Mademoiselle Georges's success, and she was linked to the emperor himself."

"Perhaps it was something that wasn't common knowledge," Aline said. "Suzanne, have you heard anything?"

"No," Suzanne assured her husband's cousin. Why did lying seem more of a strain these days? This was the sort of deception that should be second nature to her. "But then I'm hardly in the confidence of the minister of police. Doro, I'm glad you're here. There's something I've been wanting to ask you. I understand Christian Laclos is one of your cavaliers."

"Yes, that's why I came. That is, I wouldn't call Christian a cavalier, but he comes to my salons. He's quite sweet in a bumbling sort of way. Willie told me. That you might want to talk to him. . . ." Dorothée hesitated.

"Don't mind us," Aline said. "We're used to secrets with Malcolm and Suzanne."

"And it's not exactly surprising that Suzanne would want to talk to a Laclos cousin," Cordelia said.

"Can you help me talk to him at the interval?" Suzanne asked Dorothée.

"Yes, of course. You know I've been longing to help."

Malcolm, Harry, and Geoffrey came through the curtains from the anteroom, and Dorothée left to go to her sister's box. Her thoughts with Manon, wherever she might be, Suzanne settled in to watch *Phèdre*. With the part of her mind that could focus on the stage, she noted that the understudy was giving a quite creditable performance but lacked Manon's sparkle and fire.

Dorothée found her in the salon during the first interval. "Stewart's already drunk," Doro said, slipping her arm through Suzanne's. "I don't know how Willie stands it."

"Love can cloud the mind."

"I can't believe Willie loves him." She glanced up at Suzanne. "I wasn't sure how much Lady Cordelia and Aline knew."

"They don't know about the child."

"I'm honored Malcolm told Willie and me. There's Christian."

"Madame la comtesse." Christian Laclos pushed back his chair, getting his feet tangled up with the rungs. He made a grab for the

gilded chairback, knocked the chair forwards, and jostled the table, spattering champagne from his glass onto the marble surface. "Terribly sorry." He righted the chair and stepped away from it as though it were a dog liable to bite. "Won't you sit down?" He pulled out two more chairs from the table, with great care.

"Thank you." Dorothée sank into one of the chairs, settling the crêpe and satin folds of her skirt with care. "You know Madame Rannoch, don't you?"

"Yes, of course. That is, I don't know that we've been properly introduced, but one can't fail but to be aware of Madame Rannoch." Christian sketched a bow and nearly collided with the table again. He had disordered brown hair cut into a fashionable Brutus crop and wore a well-cut coat and high shirt points.

Suzanne sank into a chair beside Dorothée. "I'm sorry we've interrupted you."

"No. Not in the least." Christian tugged a handkerchief from his sleeve and blotted the spilled champagne. He turned to summon a waiter, but Dorothée had already done so with a simple lift of a finger.

The waiter brought Suzanne and Dorothée champagne. Christian returned to his chair without mishap. "Jolly good show, as the British would say. Pity about Manon Caret, but the actress is charming. Of course not quite as much of a spectacle as the Waterloo ballet at the opera last week."

Suzanne's gloved fingers tightened on the beaded strap of her reticule. The ballet had re-created the battle in great detail and had ended with an English officer presenting a French officer he had taken prisoner to the Frenchman's mistress, who had believed him dead. They had knelt and kissed the hem of the English officer's garment before dancing the finale. The French audience had gone wild with applause. Suzanne hadn't known whether to laugh or to cry.

"Certainly memorable, though to me it didn't seem in quite the best taste." Dorothée took a sip of champagne. "You must be wondering why we wanted to see you," she said with one of her charming smiles.

"No. Yes. That is, always a pleasure to see you of course, *madame la comtesse.*"

"I fear it's about your cousin."

"Gabrielle? Is anything the matter with her? Just saw her across the theatre. Looked perfectly lovely. Or Gui? Has he got himself into some sort of trouble?"

"No." Dorothée set down her glass. "Étienne."

Christian's champagne glass tilted in his fingers. Dorothée righted it before it could spatter over the table again. "It must have been very hard to lose him."

"Yes. That is— I didn't know him well. Just a boy when they all left Paris. And I didn't realize—"

"It's all right, Christian." Dorothée squeezed his hand. "We know about the plot. We know you were part of it. It's nothing to hide now. You should be proud."

Christian dragged his glass closer and took a quick swallow. "Seems mad now. But we thought it could work. Étienne was fearfully clever. I just mentioned about a line about the security at Malmaison in a letter to him. No one was more shocked than I was when Étienne said he was coming to France in secret and had to see me. He arrived with the whole plot worked out." Christian stared into the glass for a moment, then took another swallow. "To own the truth, I was more than half-inclined to refuse to get involved. Wanted Bonaparte gone as much as the next man, of course. Well, the next Royalist. But never thought to take a hand personally. Not really my thing. Had a job, an income. Managing to get along. Which isn't easy in Paris. Wasn't easy. Well, still isn't for that matter." He shifted in his chair.

"But—?" Dorothée said gently.

"Family, you know. Étienne was family, for all we hadn't seen each other since we were boys. And he was so sure he could make it work. Change the future of France. Bit hard not to get caught up in that."

"And Monsieur Rivère worked with you as well," Suzanne said.

"Étienne had been put in touch with him. Good thing. Rivère seemed to know what he was doing. Felt better about the whole thing after I met him."

"Did you see a great deal of Étienne after he came to Paris?" Suzanne asked.

"Not overmuch." Christian took a sip of champagne. "Had to keep up the appearance of our regular lives. Used to meet in secret in a room above a café. Les Trois Rois. Had to go round in the dark, up the stairs, knock three times. Felt as though I was in a novel."

"But you would have been one of the few people Étienne could confide in," Suzanne said in the tone she'd used to draw confidences from young ensigns and seasoned diplomats. "Did he talk to you about a woman he'd become involved with?"

Christian shifted in his chair. "Besotted. Étienne played his cards close to his chest, but he couldn't seem to stop talking about her." He shook his head. "Got a bit tiresome, I confess. Though of course I tried to listen."

Suzanne reached for her champagne glass. "Did you meet her?"

"Once. I got there early. To the café. She was with him. Wearing a cloak, but I could see her face was beautiful. Made a bit more sense of why Étienne couldn't stop talking about her. Of course I saw no reason not to trust her."

"Then?" Suzanne asked.

Christian took another sip of champagne and stared into the glass. "Couldn't figure out who betrayed us." He twisted the glass between his hands. "Bertrand came to see me when he came to France. Wanted to know what I knew about Étienne. Couldn't tell him much. Then he wrote to me again just before he was killed."

"About Étienne?" Dorothée asked.

"No." Christian frowned into his champagne glass. "It was odd, because I hadn't seen him since we were in the nursery and then of course he'd been gone—that is, we all thought he was dead—"

" 'He'?" Dorothée prompted.

"Gui." Christian set his glass down. "Bertrand wanted to know what I knew about Gui before he'd been sent to England."

"Madame Rannoch." The quiet, lethal voice stopped Suzanne as she moved into the passage to the boxes. Dorothée had been claimed by Clam-Martinitz.

"*Monsieur le duc.*" Suzanne extended her hand to the minister of police, now Duc d'Otrante, though she would always think of him as Fouché, and willed her fingers to remain steady as he bent over it. She was not generally given to fancies and she had dealt with—and on more than one occasion spent the night with—people she found quite repellant. But Fouché always sent a chill through her. His quiet demeanor radiated menace. Or perhaps it was the knowledge of the number of people he had tortured and sent to their death, whether Bonapartist or Royalist. Or that he didn't even pretend to have principles.

"You are enjoying your time in Paris?" the minister of police asked. Somehow she was in an embrasure between two pier tables and he was blocking the egress.

"Yes." Suzanne tugged at the embroidered rose silk of her shawl, drawing the cloak of demure war bride turned diplomatic wife tight about her. "I don't remember it as a child, of course. I was only a baby when my parents and I left. But it feels oddly like coming home."

"Almost as though you'd been here before."

Suzanne kept her gaze wide and steady on his face. "Precisely. It's as though it's in my bones."

"Remarkable." Fouché's gaze shifted over her. With many men that sort of gaze would cut through layers of clothing. With Fouché it seemed to slice into her soul.

"My felicitations on your betrothal," Suzanne said. Fouché had recently become engaged to a young woman from one of the most aristocratic families in France. Louis XVIII himself witnessed the marriage contract of the man who had helped send his brother to the guillotine.

"Thank you. Marriage can come as a surprise to one. As I suspect you understand." Fouché shifted slightly, as though to get a better view of her face. "Your husband has been very busy in Paris as well."

"There's a great deal for diplomats to do these days."

"Just so. But Monsieur Rannoch's work has always moved beyond diplomacy. You can't think me so uninformed as not to know about that."

"I would never think you uninformed, Prince."

He gave a dry smile. "I'm relieved to hear it. And of course from an enemy I had to keep track of Monsieur Rannoch has now become an ally." Fouché took a step to the side, slightly more into the shadows from the wall sconce above. "Lately your husband has been singularly preoccupied with the death of one of our own."

"Do you mean Antoine Rivère?" Suzanne asked, and immediately wondered if she had opened her eyes too wide. She had to step into the candlelight to keep eye contact with Fouché.

"If he's looking into the death of another French civil servant, his behavior borders on obsession."

"Malcolm—"

"Was there when Rivère died." Fouché's clipped voice brooked no argument. "Yes, I know. As were you. Don't look so shocked, my dear. I didn't know you were meeting Rivère. But after his death I was able to put the pieces together. Remarkable the things you and your husband share. You obviously complement each other well. But whatever misguided overtures Antoine Rivère had made to the British before his death, his death is a matter for the French. Your husband would be wise to leave the investigation to us."

Suzanne willed her face to innocence. "I'm sure Malcolm would never interfere with your investigation."

"By running his own, he's likely to stumble over my men."

"Malcolm isn't the sort to get tangled up with anyone."

"Your husband's a clever man, but he hasn't learned restraint. He's stumbled into the midst of a great deal more than he bargains on."

"Malcolm can take care of himself."

"A clever wife could protect him from himself." Fouché's gaze again shifted over her, dark in the shadows. "I imagine you're an exceedingly clever wife, my dear."

"You flatter me."

"I think not." Fouché regarded her for a moment. Once again she had the sense he was cutting through layer upon carefully constructed layer. "In a word, Suzanne, if you know what's good for your husband, not to mention yourself, you'll get him to stop this ill-judged investigation."

Tension shot through her. She willed it from her body. "I generally find it more conducive to a happy marriage to let Malcolm make such decisions for himself."

"My dear Suzanne." Fouché's hand shot out and closed round her wrist. His grip was like an iron shackle. "You wouldn't have survived so long in this business if you did not have a strong practical streak. You will stop your husband's investigation because I'm quite sure you don't wish him to know the truth of why you married him. Or the myriad ways you've betrayed him in the short span of your marriage."

For a moment she thought she was going to disgrace herself and be sick. The gilt and white plaster and gold silk of the passage swam round her while the polished floorboards seemed to open at her feet. Yet when she spoke her voice came out surprisingly even. "Malcolm already knows a great deal about me."

"But not the full extent of the truth." His voice was now so gentle it chilled her to the bone. "You wouldn't risk it. And though Rannoch may be a remarkable man, if he knew the truth he wouldn't still be living with you. Or look at you in the way he does."

That, Suzanne knew, was all too true. "Perhaps I don't care."

"I think not. I've also observed the way you look at him. Stop the investigation, Suzanne. If you want your charming, duplicitous life to have a prayer of continuing."

CHAPTER 22

She forced herself to breathe. One breath after another, driving air into her lungs, forcing more air in, pressing against her corset laces. Experience had taught that if she went on doing that she would avoid vomiting or fainting or sinking to the floor and curling into a ball while she sobbed into her knees. Not unlike the way she had got through the pangs of childbirth. She made her way down the passage, willing herself to keep her steps measured, though her every impulse was to hurry, as though she could outrun what had just happened.

She stepped back into her box, smiling at Malcolm as she moved past him to the front row. He caught her hand and squeezed her fingers. She wondered if he could feel how cold her skin was. From the look in his eyes, it seemed not.

She dropped back into her seat between Aline and Cordelia. If she couldn't manage to force her attention to the play, at least she managed to laugh and clap at the appropriate times. She even sipped a glass of champagne in the second interval, while listening to Lady Caroline Lamb's animated chatter. Through the third act and then she was in a carriage with Malcolm and the Davenports and Blackwells, and they were at Mrs. Heywood's, a haunt of the

British expatriates that Wellington had made fashionable. And there, across the room, was Raoul, engaged in a game of whist.

Malcolm was claimed by Count Nesselrode. Cordelia touched her arm. "I see Gui. I'm going to talk to him."

Suzanne squeezed her friend's hand. "Are you sure—"

"I told Harry I would. It's all right. In for a penny..."

It was good to remember that she wasn't the only one with a complicated marriage. Suzanne watched Cordelia move towards Gui, then strolled forwards, nodded to William Lamb and Freddy Lyttleton (who grinned at her, as though last night had given them a shared secret), and at last let her gaze drift casually over the card room until it met Raoul's own. Not a muscle moved in his face, but she read at once that he'd received her message. She stopped to ask after Jane Chase's children and to trade baby stories with Fitzroy and Harriet Somerset, then wandered into the adjoining salon and drifted towards a sofa set between two columns. Much safer to talk in public than to take refuge in an anteroom. In all the years they had worked together, she and Raoul had rarely risked that.

A few moments later, Raoul's voice sounded just behind her.

"Mrs. Rannoch."

"Mr. O'Roarke." She managed a smile. "I trust you had a profitable evening at the card table."

"Hardly that, but I didn't lose too egregiously. I remembered that you'd been asking me about the Fernandezes."

"Yes, I've thought about them often since we left Spain, but I wasn't sure where to write. I'd so like to hear if you have news." She sank down on the sofa.

Raoul seated himself beside her. A potted palm half-concealed them. The buzz of conversation and strains of a pianoforte washed over them, creating admirable cover.

"No difficulties," Raoul said. "They should be at the coast in another day or so. Roxane and Clarisse think it a great adventure."

"Thank God."

He scanned her face. "And yet something has you distressed."

She met his gaze with a bright smile. "Fouché knows. About me."

Raoul's expression held steady. "You're certain?"

"He left no doubt about it." She locked her gloved fingers together, because she wasn't entirely certain she could keep them from trembling. "He threatened to tell Malcolm if I don't convince Malcolm to abandon the investigation into Rivère's death."

"Damnation." Raoul ran a hand over his hair. "I'm sorry."

"It's hardly the first time I've heard you swear."

"I'm sorry I didn't protect you from Fouché." His voice was still conversational, but the undertone was like iron.

"It's never been your job to protect me from anything."

"Can you convince Malcolm to stop the investigation?"

She tightened her fingers. "I wouldn't."

"No, you wouldn't, would you?" Raoul gave a faint smile. "We'll have to make Fouché *think* the investigation has stopped."

"It's not your problem to solve."

"Of course it is. I got you into this."

"I got myself into it. You always said we had to extricate ourselves from trouble." Though Raoul had rescued her more than once in the past, most notably from a group of bandits who had been within hours of killing her. She'd never forget the harsh tone of his voice or the gentleness of his hands lifting her onto his horse as she sagged into unconsciousness.

"I could have—"

"Stopped it?" She looked up at him. Despite her tightly clenched hands, she was shaking. Terror chilled her blood and scalded her insides.

His fingers tensed, as though he would touch her, but he didn't move. "I won't let Fouché destroy your marriage, *querida*."

"You can't promise that, Raoul. Not even you." She drew a breath, forcing the air from her lungs. "Perhaps I should tell Malcolm."

"For God's sake, Suzanne. A grand sacrifice won't solve this."

"As long as he doesn't know, I'm a liability. People can use it to force my hand—"

"No one's forced you to do anything yet, have they?"

"I've been lucky."

"You've been clever and resilient. *Querida...*" He hesitated, and she sensed that once again he forced himself not to touch her hand. "If Malcolm knew, you'd just put the risk of someone using the information onto him. He'd have his enemies threatening his wife to manipulate him. And he's not as trained to combat manipulation as you are."

She met Raoul's gaze, forcing herself to look into a bleak future. "If Malcolm knew, I wouldn't be his wife anymore."

"Don't talk foolishness. You can't think—"

"You can't seriously think Malcolm could know the truth and still want to go on living with me." She couldn't quite picture what would happen, but she could see the love fading from his eyes. The love she had barely begun to realize was there.

Raoul returned her gaze, his own at once gentle and uncompromising. "I don't know. But I know he wouldn't let the mother of his child and the woman with whom he's shared his life face arrest and imprisonment. Whatever was between you in private, I'm quite certain he'd do everything in his power to protect you."

She opened her mouth to protest, but for all the fears roiling inside her, she knew Raoul was right. Malcolm took his responsibilities seriously. Even if he knew the truth, even if he hated her, he'd consider her his responsibility. They might not share a bed or even a roof, but he'd risk his career, his reputation, even his own safety to protect her.

"I'll handle Fouché," Raoul said.

"You can't—"

"I may not be the man I once was, but I think I'm still a match for Fouché."

"It's not your—"

"My dear girl. Malcolm isn't the only one who takes his responsibilities seriously."

Gui staggered into the passage before Cordelia could reach his side. She followed and found him being sick into a Sèvres vase on a console table. She touched her fingers to his shoulder. "Gui."

He started and spun round. His face had a greenish cast and his eyes were hollow. "Sorry. You know me. A tendency to over-indulge."

"I don't remember it hitting you this hard."

"I'm not as young as I once was."

"Rubbish. You can't say that without making me feel old, and you're much too gallant for that."

He gave a faint smile. She took his arm and steered him to a settee. He put a hand on the gilded back and lowered himself carefully. "Aren't you concerned for your reputation?" he asked with a glint of the old Gui.

"It's already in tatters."

"And your husband?"

She swallowed. "Harry's understanding."

"I met him at the Salon des Etrangers. From my observation he's very much in love with you."

"My dear." The raillery in her voice sounded forced to her own ears. "I didn't think you were given to such romantic fancies."

"I'm not. But I'm also not entirely unobservant." A smile drove some of the shadows from his face. "I'm happy for you, Cordy. You deserve it."

"I don't think I deserve it in the least. But I know how fortunate I am."

"You're too hard on yourself."

"On the contrary. I let myself wallow in bad behavior for far too long." She studied his face, searching for the right opening. But with Gui, directness had always seemed best. "Gui. Harry told me you were seen at Antoine Rivère's rooms two nights before he was killed."

Fear shot through his gaze, but he was too clever to deny it. "I should have realized. A man who trusts his wife would confide in her. Did he tell you I'd gone to talk to Rivère about gambling debts?"

"He said that was what you'd told him."

"But he didn't believe me."

"It's his job to ask questions."

"And yours?"

Cordelia swallowed. "Gui— I can't claim to know the workings of your mind. But it's evident you're in torment."

He gave a brief laugh. "Now who's using overblown language?"

"That's just it. I don't think it is overblown." She looked into his haunted eyes. "What's Frémont?"

For a moment he went absolutely still. Then he laughed again. "For God's sake, Cordy. You're not placing credence in my midnight ravings years ago."

"Yes. I think it was important."

He pushed himself to his feet, then dropped back down on the settee, his head in his hands.

Cordelia touched his back again. She could feel the lines of tension through the superfine of his coat. "For years I didn't like myself very much. There are still times when I don't. But I'm trying. I'm trying to be someone my daughter can be proud of. Someone my husband can love. Someone I can like myself. I didn't want to confront my past. I was running from it when you met me. In Brussels circumstances forced me to face it or I don't know that I ever would have. But it was only that that let me move forwards."

"You're romanticizing commonplace dissatisfaction."

"There's nothing commonplace about you, Gui."

He shot a look at her. "You think I killed Rivère?"

She swallowed. "No, actually. But I'd like to be able to explain my certainty to Harry and Malcolm."

"Sometimes confronting the past doesn't solve problems. Sometimes it makes them worse." He stared down at his hands. "And yet it's hard to see how the Laclos family could come to worse straits." He spread his fingers in his lap. He wore a signet ring with the Laclos crest on his right hand. "I used to think it didn't matter so much that I was such a disappointment because my uncle and aunt had Étienne and Bertrand. Two sons to be proud of. Poor Oncle Jacques and Tante Amélie. They were nothing but kind to me from the moment I first came to live with them. They never berated me for my exploits. They never had the least idea they harbored a cuckoo in their nest."

Cordelia stared at her former lover, not sure she'd heard correctly.

Gui turned his head and met her gaze. His own was level and completely focused. "Frémont is the name I was born with. Victor Frémont. The name I bore until I was fifteen and brought to England in the guise of Guilaume de Laclos."

CHAPTER 23

Cordelia had the sense she'd tumbled into a hole far deeper than anything she'd imagined. She studied the face of the man she called Gui Laclos. She'd known he harbored some secret. But she'd never doubted his identity. She knew few people were wholly what they seemed on the surface. But their names, the history written down in the family Bible, the portrait galleries of ancestors, the lists of those enrolled at Eton and Harrow, Oxford and Cambridge, those belonging to White's and Brooks's and Boodle's. Those were constants one never questioned, the warp and weft of her world. "You're—"

"My mother was Marianne Frémont, a nursery maid in the Laclos household. The household of Georges Laclos, the comte's younger brother, that is. The second of the three sons in that generation." He spoke in the quick, dispassionate tone he might use to recount the plot of a novel. "Apparently trusted and valued by the family, because when she married one of the grooms the Lacloses gave them a cottage on their estate in Provence. A short time later I came along. My mother continued to help out in the nursery, and I played with young Gui and Gabrielle. I have only the most shadowy memories. The nursery walls were a pale apple green. There was a wooden horse with a yellow mane that I liked to ride. Gui"—

his voice caught for a moment on the name—"and I used to pretend we were musketeers. Gaby used to ask me to read to her."

"You would have been—"

"Five. Gaby was in Paris with her uncle and aunt when the château was attacked. She'd had a chill and they wanted her near the best doctors. I was at the château with my mother when the attack happened. The house was set on fire. My mother tried to get Gui and me out. I... saw the falling beam that killed both of them." He swallowed, his gaze fastened on a still life of fruit that hung on the opposite wall. "The next instant another piece of timber knocked me out. I came to in the back of a cart, with sacks thrown over me. My father had died in the attack as well, but another groom who was a friend of his smuggled me off to cousins nearby. I lived with them for ten years. That part of my history is true."

"And then? Lord Dewhurst—"

"Lord Dewhurst arrived claiming I was Gui Laclos and he'd come to restore me to my birthright. I protested there was some confusion. Dewhurst persisted. Finally my foster father took me aside and told me not to be a fool. He said this could be the making of me. I'd have a life most could only dream of. That this is what my mother would have wanted for me."

"Gui." Cordelia touched his hand, still struggling to make sense of his revelations. "You were so young. Is it possible—"

"That my memories are distorted and I'm actually Gui Laclos? No," he said in a flat voice. "I was five. I remember my mother and father. I remember the real Gui. I knew I was going along with a lie when I let Dewhurst bring me to England. I've known it all these years."

"You were a child."

"I was fifteen. Boys my age fought and died at Waterloo on both sides." He scraped the toe of his evening shoe over the floorboards. "I didn't realize. What it would be like to be an outsider. An outsider as an émigré and an outsider to the family who took me in. The kinder they were, the more of an outsider I felt."

"And so since you couldn't tell them the truth, you were determined to prove how unworthy you were?"

He turned to her with a twisted smile. "A bit simplistic perhaps. A lot of it was sheer love of indulgence. But there may be a degree of truth in what you say."

"And then Étienne and Bertrand were gone—"

"And the cuckoo became the Comte de Laclos's heir. I suppose a revolutionary would approve. But Oncle Jacques would be horrified."

"Everyone knows Caro's husband, William Lamb, is most likely Lord Egremont's son. And Talleyrand as good as acknowledges the Comte de Flahaut."

"But they didn't knowingly pass themselves off as impostors."

Cordelia pressed her hands over her lap. "Rivère knew?"

"God knows how. The man had an unholy knack for uncovering secrets."

"What did he want?"

"My influence with Lord Dewhurst to convince the British to get him out of France. He seemed to think as Dewhurst's godson my pleas would hold some weight." He looked into her eyes. "I was angry. And frightened. I don't deny it. I'd lived with the secret for so long that to hear someone voice it was like the first crack that set my world crumbling. But I didn't kill Rivère. In fact, I told him I'd do what I could with Dewhurst, though I wasn't sure how much weight my pleas would carry."

"I believe you."

"You're far too trusting, Cordy."

"Perhaps. But my instincts rarely fail me." She hesitated, understanding the choices her husband and Malcolm and Suzanne regularly faced. "Gui—"

"You have to tell your husband and the Rannochs. I know. I knew that before I confided in you. Do what you must. I'm going to talk to Gaby and Rupert." He pushed himself to his feet. "It's time this comedy came to an end."

Gabrielle stared at her brother. At the man she had thought of as her brother for twelve years. "I remember you. From France. Before."

Gui's mouth twisted. They were in the study in Rupert's and her house in the Rue d'Anjou. He was sitting on a straight-backed chair, a little removed from her and Rupert, out of the circle of light cast by the branch of candles Rupert had lit. "You were only three."

"But I remember." She leaned forwards on the sofa and looked into his shadowed eyes, conjuring up memories of that dark-eyed boy with the untidy brown hair, trying to overlay his face over Gui's own. "You used to play dolls with me sometimes when I teased you. You were a deal kinder to me than Gui was, actually. I remember—" She bit back the words, stared for a long moment at the man she had called brother, then spoke them in any case. "I remember wishing you were my brother."

Gui drew a sharp breath. "Gaby—" He turned his head away.

Beside her on the sofa, Rupert had been staring fixedly at Gui. Now he pushed himself to his feet. "What did my father know about this?"

Gui's gaze shot to him, wide with surprise. "Merely that someone told him I was Guilaume de Laclos."

"Are you sure?"

"Why else would he have brought me to England and given me into the care of his closest friends?"

"I don't know. But I do know he's capable of anything."

"Rupert." Gabrielle got to her feet as well and touched her husband's arm. "This has nothing to do with—"

"You can't know that, Gaby." Rupert wrenched himself away from her. "My father sent Étienne on the mission that led to his death. He had Bertrand killed—"

"What?" Gui sprang to his feet.

Rupert met Gui's gaze directly. "Your cousin—your supposed cousin—Bertrand wasn't a traitor. My father set him up. Because he wanted him out of the way."

"Why—"

"Because he thought that was the only way to convince me to marry and produce an heir."

Gabrielle saw the realization register in her brother's—her supposed brother's—eyes. For a long moment he simply stared at Rupert. Then his gaze shot to her, filled with questions and a concern that unexpectedly tore at her chest. "I know," Gabrielle said. She reached for Rupert's hand. "Lord Dewhurst manipulated both Rupert and me."

Gui's gaze returned to Rupert. "I don't know what I've done to deserve the trust you just placed in me, Rupert."

Rupert held Gui's gaze with his own. "You knew Bertrand. I couldn't bear to have you think the worst of him. And you need to know what my father is."

Gui inclined his head. "I may not be part of this family anymore, but I don't think I'll ever stop thinking of it as mine."

"Gui." Gabrielle moved to his side and touched his arm. His muscles were taut beneath her fingers.

"Don't you think you'd better start calling me Victor?"

"I'll always think of you as Gui. You've been my brother for far too long for that to change. I don't know—" She looked at Rupert, then back at Gui. "Oncle Jacques and Tante Amélie have suffered so much. I don't know that it would serve any purpose for them to learn the truth."

"For God's sake, Gaby." This time it was Gui who jerked away from her touch. "It was bad enough that I lived a lie as a teenager. That I went on living it—" He shook his head, self-disgust washing over his face. "You can't expect me to continue to do so. I've never claimed to have much in the way of honor, but I'm not quite so far gone."

"I've always thought you had a deal more honor than you let on," Rupert said, crossing to stand beside her and Gui. "But whatever is said—if anything—we need to discover what my father's game is first. I'm done being a chess piece he can move as he wills."

Gui started to protest, then slowly inclined his head. To Gabrielle's surprise, he reached out and touched her hand, though he continued to look at Rupert. "Whatever comes of this, I'll always think of Gaby as my sister."

"I know," Rupert said. "That's a large part of why I trusted you."

Malcolm poured whisky in the salon in the Rue du Faubourg Saint-Honoré. Candlelight flickered over the sea green wall hang-

ings, the white plasterwork, the striped satin upholstery. A decorous setting for a convivial end to an evening with friends. They'd
shared many such with the Davenports in the past months. Save
that on this occasion, they were gathered together because
Cordelia had gripped Suzanne's arm with iron fingers and said
she had something she had to relate to the three of them, as soon
as possible.

Suzanne glanced at Cordelia, seated beside her on the sofa, her
face pale, her hands locked together. Soft ringlets fell about her
face, but tension radiated from the straight line of her spine and the
taut angle of her head. Suzanne's own confrontation with Fouché
still reverberated through her. Her chest was knotted and her
mouth dry. But she was used to boxing up fear and pushing it to a
place where it could be, if not forgot, at least ignored as one ignores
the ache of a troublesome wound or the nag of a headache.

Malcolm put a glass of whisky into Cordelia's hand. "Whatever
it is, sharing it probably won't worsen the situation. And it may
help."

Cordelia gave him a smile and took a quick sip of whisky. Harry
sat watching her with an intent gaze. Cordelia cradled the glass in
her hands and looked from her husband to Malcolm to Suzanne.
"Gui Laclos is an impostor."

Once the first words were out she recounted the rest of what
Gui Laclos had revealed in brisk, concise tones. She had the makings of an admirable agent. Though her hands remained locked
round the glass, white-knuckled.

Harry got to his feet and put a hand on his wife's shoulder.
"That was brilliantly done, Cordy. And it can't have been easy."

She looked up at him. "I was so proud of myself for drawing
him out. Only to discover I'd stumbled into the midst of someone
else's nightmare."

"Which unfortunately has relevance for us." Malcolm leaned
forwards in his chair. "Gui had no idea how Rivère learned of
this?"

Cordelia shook her head. "I believe Gui when he says he didn't
kill Rivère. But I don't expect you to."

Malcolm looked at Harry, then at Suzanne. "As it happens your trust in him means a great deal, Cordy."

"But you can't be sure," Cordelia said.

"No. And we have to explore every avenue. I've learned to be wary of even those closest to me."

"Rivère knew a shocking number of the Laclos family's secrets," Suzanne said. "And this one he couldn't have learned from either Gabrielle or Étienne."

Harry dropped down on the arm of the sofa, his hand still on Cordelia's shoulder. "Did Gui have any idea what made Dewhurst think he was Guilaume de Laclos?"

"Gui seemed to think it was misinformation from a relative of his mother's who was trying to do him a good turn."

"This could be what Bertrand discovered just before he was killed," Suzanne said. "What he told Louise Carnot changed everything. And why he was considering going home. Christian Laclos told Doro and me that Bertrand had written asking him about Gui just before he—Bertrand—was killed."

Malcolm nodded. "Living in France, Bertrand could have stumbled across information that cast doubt on Gui's story."

"He wasn't in France when he died," Cordelia pointed out.

"No, but he could have set inquiries in motion before he left for the Peninsula. Perhaps he'd just heard from someone with decisive information. Or perhaps he met someone in the French army who had information."

"I wonder if he could have written to Rivère for information as well as to Christian," Suzanne said. "He may have known Rivère had been his brother's confederate. Perhaps that's how Rivère learned the truth about Gui. Or perhaps Bertrand revealed enough for Rivère to ferret out the rest."

Harry flicked a glance at Malcolm. "Dewhurst doesn't strike me as the sort of man to be taken in easily."

"No." Malcolm turned his glass in his hand. "He survived working in the field with the Royalists in France for years. Though when one has lost people, one can be quick to grasp on to a shred of hope. Difficult to see what reason Dewhurst would have had to foist an impostor off on his old friends."

"Unless his old friends were in on it," Suzanne said, twisting her glass in her hand as she turned over thoughts in her head. She looked at Cordelia. "Gui told you he was born shortly after his parents' marriage, didn't he?"

"You're suggesting he was a Laclos by-blow?" Harry asked. "That he shared a father with the real Gui?"

"It would explain the generosity of the Laclos family to Gui's parents," Suzanne said. "And why Gui was allowed to mingle so freely with the Laclos children."

"In which case perhaps the Comte de Laclos has always known the Gui he took into his house isn't the real Gui," Malcolm said. "He could have set his old friend Dewhurst to look for his brother's by-blow with the idea of taking the boy into the family. Of course at the time he'd not have thought it likely Gui would become his heir."

"You think he had second thoughts about taking Gui into his family after his sons died?" Harry asked.

"Or perhaps the opposite. Perhaps he wanted to protect Gui's position as his heir."

"Which Rivère's knowledge could threaten," Cordelia said.

"Quite. If Gui were exposed as an impostor, the next heir would be Christian Laclos."

"Who is a bit of a bumbler," Suzanne said.

"Precisely. And who grew up away from the comte. The comte might well prefer Gui, whom he's come to think of as a son. Of course it's all supposition. We don't know that the comte knew Gui was an impostor or that he knew about Rivère threatening Gui. Or that Gui is a Laclos by-blow. That's the problem with pretty theories. One errant fact can knock them down like a house of cards."

"We need more information," Harry said. "I suggest a return to Christine Leroux."

Cordelia managed a smile. "You look entirely too cheerful about it."

Harry reached for her hand and lifted it to his lips. "Christine Leroux is a clever woman. But you're brilliant."

* * *

"Harry seemed to take Cordy's concern for Gui quite well," Suzanne said to Malcolm, closing the door of their bedchamber.

"Harry's testing himself. But so far I'd say he's passing the test." Malcolm tossed his coat over a chairback and struck a flint to steel to light the tapers on her dressing table and the escritoire. "I always knew Cordy had nerves of steel, but I must say even then she impressed me tonight. She's taken to intelligence work almost as quickly as you did."

Suzanne's fingers froze behind her neck on the silver filigree clasp of her pearl necklace. Because of course when Malcolm met her she'd been far from a novice at espionage. Just as she'd been far from a novice in the bedchamber. One of her greatest challenges in the early days of her marriage had been not to reveal that extent of her expertise in either area. "Cordy's a clever woman who hasn't had an outlet for her cleverness. Though I hate for her to see the ugliness of what we do. She got a taste of that uncovering Gui's secrets."

"Married to Harry, she can't hide from it. And God knows she saw enough of that ugliness in Brussels." Malcolm dropped down on the edge of the bed and began to unwind the folds of his cravat. "Talleyrand put Tatiana up to the affair with Étienne Laclos. To keep an eye on the plot."

Suzanne stared at her husband. She'd been so caught up in her own confrontation with Fouché and then Cordelia's revelations about Gui that she'd missed the shadows that drew at Malcolm's face. "He admitted it?"

"With surprising celerity for Talleyrand. But he claims he and Tania weren't the ones who betrayed the plot." Malcolm frowned at the crumpled linen in his hands. His voice was stripped of expression. "He says Tania insisted that they stop the plot without betraying Étienne."

"Darling." Suzanne set the necklace she had just unclasped down on the dressing table and moved to sit on the bed beside him. "That could very well be the truth. I don't see why Talleyrand would make it up."

"Talleyrand could have any number of reasons for making it up, each more complicated than the last. But it is possible Tania genuinely cared for Étienne." Malcolm frowned at the cravat, then tossed it across the room to the chair where he'd left his coat.

"Gabrielle Caruthers told me she had the impression her cousin was in love with someone much more—well, I suppose, innocent for want of a better word—than Tatiana," Suzanne said. It was hours since she and Malcolm had been able to talk in private, and those hours were thick with revelations. "That he seemed desperately in love and that he tended to fall for young, helpless females."

Malcolm continued to frown, as though trying to piece together his sister's past from a miasma of half-truths. "Love can take one by surprise."

"That's what I said to Gabrielle." Suzanne hesitated. For all her deceptions, she knew one couldn't comfort a man like Malcolm with half-truths. But there was honest comfort she could offer. She curved her fingers round his arm. "As I said, the fact that she became pregnant indicates she lost control enough that she forgot to take the usual precautions."

"Love isn't the only reason one loses control."

"But it is one possibility."

Malcolm frowned at the buttons on his waistcoat as he unfastened them. "Tania always claimed not to believe in love."

"So did you."

He shrugged out of the waistcoat and threw it after the cravat. "I stopped after I met you."

"Darling." She made her voice playful to hide a host of emotions that shot through her at his words. "Don't tell me you made a heartfelt confession of your feelings to anyone. I don't think you were remotely aware of them at the time."

"Quite. But I was aware enough of the conflict to stop making any claims about love at all." He fumbled with his shirt cuffs, avoiding her gaze. "Later—certainly by this winter in Vienna and then in Brussels—if Tania had still been alive . . ."

"You'd have talked to her?"

"Perhaps." He gave a reluctant grin. "Tania would have seen it and forced me to talk."

"And you think you'd have seen it if she'd fallen in love with Étienne Laclos?"

"I'd like to think I would have. But—" He shook his head. "She was my sister. I admitted things to her I didn't admit to anyone else. And she— I think she trusted me more than she did most people. But in many ways I didn't know her. I've realized that more and more since she died."

"Malcolm." Suzanne ran her fingers down his arm. "The fact that she didn't confide in you doesn't reflect any lack in you."

The muscles in his arm tensed beneath her touch. "You can't know that, Suzette."

"I know what you were to her. If she'd wanted to confide—if she'd felt able to—she'd have turned to you."

"Which doesn't change the fact that she didn't." He kicked off his shoes. "I don't know why the possibility that she betrayed a man she loved bothers me."

Suzanne swallowed a welling of bitterness. She could feel Fouché's gaze slicing into her. "But it does."

"I'm not exactly clear-sighted when it comes to Tania. I know her capacity for betrayal. But everyone has their limits. Or perhaps it's just that I like to believe so."

"That's because your own limits are so very clear." Suzanne curled her fingers round his wrist.

Malcolm gave a twisted smile. "Does any Intelligence Agent have clear limits?"

"You do." It was a large part of why she loved him. It was also why she could never fully feel she deserved him. And why she was sure he'd never be able to forgive her if he knew the truth about her past and her reasons for marrying him. "Malcolm." She rested her head against his shoulder. "We don't know that Tatiana did betray Étienne. But if she did, it doesn't necessarily mean she didn't love him. It's amazing how contradictory feelings and loyalties can coexist."

He turned his head and brushed his lips across her brow. "You're kind, Suzette."

"Kind?" It was the last thing she thought of in relation to herself. But then the woman Malcolm saw and loved wasn't really the real her.

His mouth slid to her temple. "I know how you felt about Tania during her life. And yet here you are trying to see things from her perspective."

"During her life my own perspective was distinctly colored by the fact that I thought she was my husband's mistress."

Malcolm grimaced. "And you didn't believe me when I denied it."

She swallowed. "I wasn't sure what to think. You don't lie easily, but—"

"No agent can avoid lying."

"Dearest—" She drew back and looked up at his granite-set profile beneath the shadows of the canopy. "I was jealous, but I knew I hadn't any right to be. I think the truth is I'd been half-expecting to learn you had a mistress ever since our wedding."

He swung his head round to stare down at her. "In God's name why—"

"You offered me so much when you offered me your name, but fidelity wasn't part of it."

"Did you expect me to spell it out? It's part of the marriage vow."

The sound of Malcolm's voice repeating those vows in the cramped sitting room that stood in for a chapel at the British embassy in Lisbon echoed in her head. It had been a shock of cold fire, realizing how seriously this man she had tied herself to—never expecting it to last—took those vows. "So were words like 'obey,' " she said. "Which I don't think either of us took seriously."

He grinned unexpectedly. "There are vows and then there are vows. But I never thought I needed to say— Sweetheart—" He looked away, and she could tell he was fumbling for the right words. He always did so on the rare occasions he tried to express his feelings, but as she watched the tension in his face, for the first time she realized he was terrified of putting a foot wrong. Of making a demand on her that would violate what he saw as the terms of their marriage. "I never thought much of marriage as an institution," he said, his gaze fixed across the room on a patch of candlelit blue and gold carpet between her dressing table and the chest of drawers. "But having decided to enter into it, I couldn't but feel an obligation to fulfill my side of the bargain."

"Because you take your obligations far more seriously than most people do."

"Perhaps. But—" He swallowed. To her surprise, he turned his head and looked her full in the face. His eyes were open and so vulnerable she felt she could smash them with an ill-chosen word. "The truth is that obligation scarcely enters into it. One could hardly claim I had a varied career in the bedchamber at any point, but since I met you, other women hold singularly little interest for me."

Her throat went tight, driving the air from her lungs. Something prickled in her eyes that might have been tears. "That's one of the loveliest things you've ever said to me, darling. But you can't fail to notice that other women are—"

"Beautiful? Desirable? Brilliant? No, of course not. But they aren't you."

One of the things that had shocked her, that morning in Lisbon when she'd bound her life to Malcolm's, was the realization that for the foreseeable future she wouldn't share another man's bed. A novel concept to one who was used to variety. And if that variety came in the service of her work, she could not deny that she enjoyed it. More than that. It had always been a form of escape. Even as her feelings for her husband had grown, her fidelity had been a practical part of her masquerade and later a mark of respect for the husband she had betrayed in so many ways. It hadn't really been a word in her vocabulary. Which of course had given her no right to feel jealousy but hadn't made the jealousy go away.

"Darling—" She leaned forwards and covered his mouth with her own. The surest escape when her feelings threatened to overwhelm her, the surest way to reach him.

His arms came round her with the force of still-unvoiced emotions. But when his lips slid to the corner of her mouth, her cheek, her temple, he said, "Suzette? What is it? You're crying."

"No. Yes. Damn it, Malcolm, you barely let on you're feeling anything and then you open up like smashed crystal."

"It's not the sort of thing—"

"That comes easily to you? No, I know. That's why it touched me so much." She kissed him again, lightly. "You're a remarkable man, Malcolm. I don't deserve you."

"I wasn't asking for a like declaration. If you're thinking of Frederick Radley—"

"Radley makes my skin crawl," she said truthfully. "I can't imagine what I ever saw in him." But she could not deny that at one time Radley had stirred her, in the crude way cheap wine or raw spirits could provide an escape. Lovemaking was never so complete an escape with Malcolm. He took it too seriously for that.

"It's not the sort of thing I could very well have said before," he said, in that same tone that indicated he was picking his way through a treacherous landscape of possible words. "It would have been putting another demand on you. And whatever was between us, I wanted it to have as little as possible to do with demands."

She moved back into his arms and put what she couldn't say, wouldn't ever be able to properly say to him, into her kiss. She dragged his shirt over his head with clumsy fingers, while he found the strings on the back of her gown. They fell back against the coverlet. His kiss was urgent, yet tempered as always by care. She gave a laugh that was half a sob, or the other way round, and lost herself in his embrace.

She would have sworn sleep would elude her tonight, but she must have slept, because suddenly a burst of sound jerked her awake, all senses alert to respond to whatever crisis had woken her. Not a cry from Colin. Not gunfire. Pounding. On the door.

CHAPTER 24

"Forgive me, sir. Madame." It was Valentin outside the bed-chamber door.

Malcolm was already out of bed. "Dressing gown," Suzanne said, throwing his to him, for he was stark naked. As was she. She fished her dressing gown from its spot at the bottom of the bed, beneath the tangle of their discarded clothing. She ran to the door, fumbling with her satin sash, as Malcolm opened it.

"Forgive me," Valentin said again. His eyes were sleep flushed above the candle he carried. "But the Comtesse Talleyrand has called and says it's a matter of urgency. She's in the salon."

A faint gray light leached between the curtains. Four o'clock, perhaps four-thirty. "Thank you." Suzanne touched Valentin's arm. "Perhaps you could have coffee sent in."

Dorothée was on her feet in the salon, pacing back and forth. She wore a spring green pelisse with the frogged clasps askew and a French bonnet of satin straw tied in a lopsided bow. As they stepped into the room she ran towards them and gripped each of them by the arm. "Thank God. I was so afraid I wouldn't be able to find you. I couldn't think who else to turn to. It has to be stopped."

"Of course." Suzanne took her friend's hands in a firm clasp. Dorothée's pulse beat wildly. "But first you must tell us what."

"It's all my fault. I should have kept them apart. I should have stayed in Vienna. I should never have let Karl—"

"Com—Doro." Malcolm touched her arm. "Has your husband challenged Clam-Martinitz to a duel?"

Dorothée's gaze jerked to his face. "I never said, did I? How did you—"

"It seemed the sort of idiocy to account for your concerns."

"I never thought Edmond would go so far. I never thought he cared that much—at all— Why? Why would he care about whose bed a woman shares when he has no interest in the woman herself?"

"Some men consider it a question of pride," Malcolm said. "Or honor, which is much the same."

"If only Karl had refused the challenge—"

" 'I could not love thee, dear, so much'—" Malcolm shook his head. "That would have marred his own honor."

"Of all the impossible idiots." Dorothée spun away, hands pressed to her face, then turned back to Malcolm. "I'm so afraid he'll kill Karl."

"We won't let that happen." Malcolm drew Dorothée to the sofa and pressed her to sit down. "Do you know where the duel is to happen? And when?"

"The Bois de Boulogne." Dorothée's fingers worked at the clasps on her pelisse. "This morning. I'm not sure when precisely. Karl left me a note in case—in case he doesn't return. My maid gave it to me before he told her to. Thank God."

"Does Talleyrand know?"

"Not from me. He wouldn't interfere." Dorothée swallowed. "As you say, it's an affair of honor. I should never have let Karl—"

Suzanne dropped down beside Dorothée on the sofa and gripped her friend's wrist. "Karl is a brave and able man. He makes his own decisions."

"If it were Malcolm you'd be just as worried."

"Probably more so," Malcolm said. "I imagine Clam-Martinitz is considerably more skilled with weapons than I am." He glanced at the window. The sliver of sky visible between the curtains was still only pale charcoal. "We have a bit of time, but we'd best be off. Suzette—"

"Don't you dare suggest I stay at home, Malcolm."

"I wouldn't dream of it. I suspect it will take all of us to stop this lunacy. I was going to suggest you and Doro drink some coffee while I order the carriage."

Dorothée looked at Malcolm as he moved to the door. "I didn't think— Castlereagh and Wellington won't look kindly on your interfering in a French and Austrian quarrel, will they?"

Malcolm gave her one of his unexpectedly warming smiles. "Perhaps not. But it's a family matter."

Valentin brought in the coffee as Malcolm left the room. Suzanne stirred liberal amounts of cream and sugar into a cup and pressed it into Dorothée's hand. "You need something bracing."

Dorothée forced down a sip. "I've been appallingly selfish."

"Seeking happiness isn't selfish." Suzanne gulped down a swallow of coffee herself. Black. She needed a good strong jolt.

"It is when one does it at the expense of others."

"For what it's worth, I'd never have expected Edmond to behave so."

"Of course not. You aren't a man." Dorothée stared into her coffee cup. "I was living in some mad sort of dreamworld. I used to worry about scandal. Now all I want is to see Karl again alive. I'll never forgive myself if he comes to harm."

For a moment visions of what might happen to Malcolm if the truth about her was revealed swam before Suzanne's eyes. The circumstances were different. The fear was the same.

A quarter hour later the three of them were settled in the barouche. Paris, so active in the early hours of the morning, had gone silent now, just before dawn. Street sweepers moved through the gray world and hawkers were beginning to set out their tables in the boulevards. Mist hung over the Bois de Boulogne, swirling round the tree trunks, giving the wood a desolate aspect for all the soldiers encamped among the trees.

Dawn light began to rend the gloom. Dorothée sat bolt upright, her gaze fixed out the window. Malcolm seemed to have given the coachman a predetermined route to follow. They wound along the paths, slowing occasionally. At last Dorothée gave a cry, and then Suzanne saw it as well. The gathering light clung to the white shirts of two men moving over the green and glinted off the sabres in their hands. Three other men stood to one side, one with a surgeon's bag by his feet.

Malcolm rapped on the roof of the carriage. The coachman drew up. Dorothée fumbled for the door handle before the steps could be let down and sprang onto the grass. Malcolm jumped after her and caught her arm before she could run forwards.

Suzanne jumped from the carriage after Dorothée and Malcolm. The sabres clanged, scraped, disengaged, met again. The duelists were too intent on each other to have noticed the new arrivals. Clam-Martinitz's arm shot forwards. His blade slid along Edmond's and broke Edmond's guard. The tip of Clam-Martinitz's sabre darted to Edmond's cheek. Edmond parried the blow, but blood dripped from his face.

Dorothée screamed, wrenched herself away from Malcolm, and ran forwards.

Clam-Martinitz spun round. "Doro, for God's sake—"

Edmond lunged towards Clam-Martinitz, sabre poised to drive into his opponent's back. Malcolm, already running flat out, landed on Edmond in a flying tackle and took him to the ground.

"Rannoch?" Edmond said in disbelief as Suzanne ran forwards. "What the hell are you doing?"

"Stopping you from committing murder." Malcolm kept Edmond pinned with his body.

"This is an affair of honor."

"Not very honorable to stab a man in the back."

Dorothée was clinging to Clam-Martinitz, sobbing. "For God's sake, my darling," he said. "You shouldn't have come. I'll never forgive Brigitte for giving you the note early."

"Thank God she did. Oh, Karl, how could you be so foolish?"

"This is nothing to do with—"

"Don't say it's nothing to do with me. You were fighting *over* me. Do you know how wretched that makes me feel?"

Edmond got enough purchase to land Malcolm a blow to the face.

Malcolm sat up, nose streaming crimson. "Satisfied now you've drawn blood?"

"You bastard—" Edmond pushed himself to his feet, looming over Malcolm.

"Don't be an idiot, Talleyrand." Malcolm sprang to his feet, putting himself between Edmond and Clam-Martinitz. "Don't you realize it makes you look more an idiot to fight a duel over a woman who has no interest in you?"

"She's my wife."

"A fact of which you've seemed singularly unaware."

Edmond took a step forwards, blood spurting from the cut in his cheek. "By God, Rannoch, I'll—"

"What? Challenge me? I won't accept. Believe me, I have no fear of being branded a coward."

"You—"

"You've fought, *monsieur le comte.*" Suzanne moved between the men and gave a handkerchief to Malcolm. "Surely you can consider honor satisfied."

"Madame Rannoch, you can have no conception—"

Suzanne fished another handkerchief from her reticule and gave it to Edmond. "All that blood is making a mess of your coat. I suggest you let this very capable-looking surgeon tend to you."

Dorothée pulled away from Clam-Martinitz and took a step towards her husband. "Do let the surgeon see to you, Edmond. Before the cut becomes infected."

"What do you care?" Edmond faced his wife, sword dangling from his fingertips.

Dorothée looked into his eyes, chin lifted. "You're the father of my children. I never wanted you hurt, Edmond."

Edmond gave a short laugh. "That's a damned—"

"I never thought I had the power to hurt you."

His gaze locked on hers for a moment, angry and at the same time puzzled. Then he turned away. But he thrust his sword back into its scabbard and moved towards the surgeon. Dorothée breathed a sigh of relief. Clam-Martinitz moved to her side and touched her arm.

"There's no way this will stay secret," Suzanne said, going to stand beside them. "Not with the cut on Edmond's face, and the way gossip spreads in Paris. You shouldn't be seen leaving the park together."

Clam-Martinitz nodded. "Very wise, Madame Rannoch." His gaze moved to Malcolm. "Rannoch—"

"I'll see the comtesse safely home." Malcolm took the handkerchief down from his nose, glanced at the fresh blood, then pressed it back to his face. "As far as anyone need know, she and my wife and I merely went out for an early drive. Eccentric perhaps, but hardly scandalous."

"Thank you." Clam-Martinitz looked down at Dorothée. "I never meant to embroil you in scandal."

Dorothée reached up and touched his face. "I'm only relieved you're unhurt. You are unhurt, aren't you?"

"Not a scratch."

"I'll see you at Wellington's ball tonight."

"Are you sure—"

"It's imperative, my love. Suzanne's right. Talk will be all over Paris. We have to brazen it out."

Clam-Martinitz gave a quick nod. "See her home safely, Rannoch."

Malcolm helped Suzanne and Dorothée back into the carriage. Dorothée folded her arms, gripping her elbows. "*Sacrebleu.* If I hadn't distracted Karl—"

"If you hadn't been there, the duel wouldn't have ended when it did," Malcolm said. "And God knows what the outcome would have been."

She flashed a smile at him. "I always wanted a brother."

Rays of sunlight slanted into the carriage as they pulled out of the park. They'd be home before Colin was up for breakfast, Suzanne thought.

The carriage came to an abrupt halt, throwing them against the squabs. "What on earth—?" Dorothée said.

Malcolm opened the window and leaned out. Thuds and raised voices streamed into the carriage. Suzanne heard her husband draw a sharp breath. "Stay here," he said over his shoulder, then opened the door and sprang to the ground. Suzanne poked her head out the open window. She could only see a portion of the street ahead, but she could see enough to tell that some sort of brawl was in progress. She watched her husband run into the fray and take a blow to the chin.

"Stay here," she said to Dorothée, and sprang to the ground herself.

Five men seemed to have turned on one, a fair-haired young man who had lost his jacket and had blood spattered on his shirt. Malcolm had at least momentarily distracted them. "For God's sake—," he said.

"Stay out of this," a burly sandy-haired man said. "He's a Bonapartist."

"Then he's been dealt far worse a blow than you can deal him." Malcolm edged between the attackers and the fair-haired man.

"Filthy spy. God knows what he's plotting." A tall dark-haired man lunged towards the fair-haired man. Suzanne stuck out her foot and tripped him.

"What the devil—"

"Watch how you speak to a lady," another mumbled.

"Doesn't look like a lady."

"I fought for my country," said the fair-haired man.

"You fought for that tyrant."

Malcolm took a step forwards and took another fist to the jaw. He went reeling backwards and caught himself against the wall of the house.

"Stop."

It was Dorothée's voice. Suzanne looked over her shoulder to see her friend run up.

"Who the hell are you?" one of the men demanded.

"My uncle is the prime minister of France," Dorothée declared.

The claim did not have the desired effect. "Your uncle's the turncoat Talleyrand?" the burly man said.

Dorothée drew herself up. "Talleyrand is not a turncoat."

The burly man gave a low laugh.

"Prince Talleyrand is a patriot," the fair-haired man said.

The burly man lunged again. Malcolm moved between them. The burly man stumbled. His blow caught Dorothée on the shoulder and sent her reeling to the cobblestones.

CHAPTER 25

The men went still. "Now look what you've done," the dark-haired man said.

Malcolm strode across the cobblestones to Dorothée's still form, a fragile tangle of spring green fabric and dark hair. Blood showed at her temple. Suzanne had already dropped down beside her friend. She put her fingers to Dorothée's throat, then met Malcolm's gaze and gave a nod of relief. Answering relief coursing through him, Malcolm knelt down and scooped Dorothée into his arms. The crowd scattered save for the dark-haired man and the fair-haired man, who both ran to Malcolm's side.

"Is she all right, sir?" the fair-haired man asked.

"She will be."

Both men helped him lift Doro. The coachman had sprung down and had the carriage door open.

"You need to tend to your face," Suzanne said to the fair-haired man, when they had lifted Doro into the carriage.

"I'll do, madame. My wife's inside."

"I'll see there's no more trouble," the dark-haired man murmured.

Suzanne settled in the carriage with Dorothée's head in her lap. Doro stirred as the carriage set into motion. "What—"

"Don't move too quickly, dearest," Suzanne said. "You hit your head."

"I never thought—"

"A name isn't always protection," Malcolm said. "Sometimes it can mark one for trouble. There's a lot of anger in Paris these days."

Dorothée turned her head to look at him across the carriage. "My uncle has served France all his life."

"There are a lot of definitions of what serves France, I'm afraid."

When they pulled up in the courtyard of the Hôtel de Talleyrand in the Rue Saint-Florentin, Dorothée sat up, then swayed and grabbed Suzanne's shoulder. Malcolm scooped her up and carried her into the house. They were greeted by a wide-eyed footman and a gasp of surprise. The latter came from Talleyrand himself, who crossed the hall to their side with surprising speed for a man with a clubfoot, his walking stick thudding on the marble tiles.

"In God's name—"

"I'm all right." Dorothée turned her head on Malcolm's arm to look at Talleyrand and managed a smile.

Talleyrand's gaze fastened on the blood at her temple. Fear and anger did battle in his eyes. "Who—"

"We stumbled upon some Ultra Royalists taking out their anger on a Bonapartist," Malcolm said. "We got caught in the middle."

Talleyrand touched his fingers to Dorothée's hair as though he feared to hurt her. Or perhaps himself. "What were you doing abroad at such an hour?"

"Edmond was a fool," Dorothée said.

"Edmond—"

Malcolm glanced at the footman. "Perhaps this had best wait until we have her settled in her room."

Malcolm carried Dorothée upstairs to her bedchamber, Suzanne leading the way and Talleyrand following behind. When they had seen her settled on her bed, with Suzanne and her maid fussing over her, he and Talleyrand withdrew. Talleyrand cast a last glance at his nephew's wife from the doorway. Her bonnet was off, her dark hair spilling free of its pins, and Suzanne was dabbing at the blood on her temple. Dorothée sent him a smile of reassurance.

Talleyrand led Malcolm down to his study without further speech. "Edmond challenged Clam-Martinitz to a duel," Malcolm said the moment the door was closed.

Talleyrand grimaced. "The young fool. What then?"

Malcolm recounted the events of the morning, from the interrupted duel through their encounter with the Ultra Royalists on the drive home.

Talleyrand drew a breath. An uncharacteristically uneven breath. "I owe you my thanks, Malcolm. I owe you more than that. When I woke this morning to find Dorothée had left the house— And when I saw her when you brought her in—" He moved to the boulle cabinet and picked up a decanter of Calvados. The crystal rattled in his fingers. He set it down. "I should never have exposed her to such danger."

"Dorothée exposed herself to the danger."

"And wouldn't thank me for trying to keep her out of it?" Talleyrand gave a bleak smile. His face was ashen.

"Any more than Suzanne would me. They both take responsibility for themselves." Malcolm crossed to Talleyrand's side, poured two glasses of Calvados, and put one in Talleyrand's hand.

Talleyrand took a quick swallow, fingers white round the crystal. "Very true. But a man cannot but feel the responsibility to protect the woman he—"

He bit the word back and instead took another, deeper swallow of Calvados.

Malcolm regarded the cold-blooded schemer he'd known since boyhood. "The woman he loves?"

Talleyrand set the glass on the cabinet, as though to jostle the liquid in the slightest would be tantamount to an intolerable admission. "Dorothée is my niece by marriage. Of course I feel a responsibility towards her."

"Responsibility never made you nearly spill a decanter of good Calvados." Malcolm took a sip from his own glass.

Talleyrand reached for his glass, as though to prove he could do so. "I didn't realize how much I'd come to depend on her. Not until—"

"You faced the prospect of losing her?"

"She was never mine to keep." Talleyrand clunked the glass back down on the marble top of the cabinet. "A man would have to be blind not to be aware that she's a beautiful woman. But she has a remarkable grasp of politics and strategy. Some of my favorite moments in Vienna were when she'd perch on my desk and help me draft a communiqué."

"Suzette helps me draft dispatches." Malcolm's mind shot back to the night she had brought him a cup of coffee and ended up perched on the edge of his desk, reading the dispatch over his shoulder, taking the pen to make notes. Their relationship had shifted that night, though he hadn't recognized it until much later. "My feelings for her sneaked up on me as well."

"Suzanne is your wife." Talleyrand took a swallow of Calvados. "Dorothée is . . . my nephew's wife."

"Whom your nephew fails to appreciate."

"One of my most damnable errors, championing that marriage. But now she has Clam-Martinitz."

"That doesn't make the feelings conveniently go away."

"I don't admit to feelings, remember?"

"Neither do I," Malcolm said.

Talleyrand's fingers closed hard round his glass. His other hand tightened on the diamond head of his walking stick. He moved with deliberation across the room and sank down into a damask chair. "On the contrary, Malcolm. You may have liked to pretend you didn't have feelings. You may even have convinced yourself you didn't have them. But your feelings have always been transparently obvious to one who knew where to look. From the five-year-old boy I met who worried even then about his mother's stability."

Malcolm's fingers bit into the crystal of his glass. "You won't avoid this by bringing up my mother. Usually your strategy is more subtle than that."

"A point." Talleyrand leaned back in the chair. "The seriousness with which you took your feelings stopped you, I suspect, from indulging in one of life's most agreeable pleasures. I, on the other hand, have always taken my love affairs lightly. Including with Dorothée's mother."

Malcolm pictured Anna-Dorothea, Duchess of Courland. A beautiful, regal woman. Talleyrand had seemed to genuinely care for her, as much as Malcolm could read him. But his feelings had appeared to be within his control. As they usually were. "What you're experiencing now doesn't appear to be light."

"Nor is it a love affair."

Malcolm moved to a straight-backed chair opposite the prince. "How long do you think you can go on deceiving yourself?"

"About what?"

"That you don't have feelings."

Talleyrand took a sip of Calvados. "It will pass."

"Are you sure you want it to?"

"Nothing else is possible. However much of a fool I may be."

Malcolm settled back in his chair. "I thought for a long time that I couldn't make Suzanne happy."

Talleyrand shot a look at him. "Yes, you were quite a fool to outside observers. Unable to see what was in front of you. Suzanne is your wife. She's your age. I'm an old fool who's discovered my weakness far too late in life."

"Do you deny you love her?"

"Deny it?" Talleyrand's voice cut through the room with sudden force. Then he slumped back in the chair. "I could deny it. I should deny it, if I had any sense. But I find my flexibility with the truth does not extend so far. Or perhaps that's one blasphemy I cannot bring myself to commit."

Malcolm got to his feet and dropped down in front of Talleyrand's chair. The lines in the prime minister's face seemed more deeply scored than usual. But it was his eyes that shocked Malcolm. The shade of irony and detachment had been stripped away to reveal naked pain and longing.

"I've always foreseen a love affair's end before it began," Talleyrand said. "Not as a failure, but as a welcome escape before boredom set in. I've never imagined that having someone there as a constant presence could be a delight rather than a burden." He stared into his glass, brows drawn. "I can't imagine this ending. Senility perhaps."

"Or reality." Malcolm put his hand over Talleyrand's own on the chair arm.

Talleyrand gave a wintry smile. "I know what they say of me. That I'm besotted. That I'm a doddering fool so obsessed with a woman young enough to be my granddaughter that I've quite lost track at the negotiating table." He took a measured sip of Calvados. "For what it's worth, I don't think that's true. I've always prided myself on my ability to handle more than one situation at once. I don't see why that should change just because one of the situations begins to tinge on emotional excess." His fingers tightened on the chair arm beneath Malcolm's own. "But God knows I could be mistaken. I fully admit to having lost some of my equilibrium."

Malcolm looked into the cracks in that usually cool blue gaze and felt a welling of sympathy he'd never have thought to feel for the master schemer before him. "Even with your equilibrium disrupted, you have a keener mind than anyone else at the negotiating table."

"You're kind, my boy. But then I always knew that. Always worried it would be your downfall." Talleyrand tilted his powdered head back against the damask. "The truth is I love her as I've never loved anyone on this earth. And I have a dreadful suspicion I will carry that love to my grave."

"You'd never guess it was anything more to her than another in the summer's round of entertainments," Simon murmured. "She has the makings of a brilliant actress."

He was looking across the Duke of Wellington's ballroom . . . at Dorothée, who had just entered the room on Count Clam-Martinitz's arm. The candlelight flashed off the diamonds in the comb in her hair and round her wrist and the crystal beads on her lilac crêpe overdress. Her head was held high, her lips rouged with a steady hand, her smile brilliant as a steel breastplate. Only Suzanne would have been able to tell that the ringlets falling with careless abandon over her forehead hid the cut on her temple.

"She's grown up on a political stage," Suzanne pointed out.

"It's funny," Aline said. "No one owns to having talked about the duel and yet the news is all over Paris." She glanced at Suzanne. "Did Edmond really try to stab Clam-Martinitz in the back?"

"I haven't the least idea," Suzanne said.

"You can save your breath," Simon said. "Whoever talked, everyone knows you and Malcolm were there."

"People will say all sorts of things."

"Doing it much too brown, Suzanne," Aline said. "Even I can see through that. I must say I'm glad you and Malcolm were there to stop them being idiots."

"Poor Dorothée." Cordelia swept up beside them with a rustle of French blue tulle. "I know just what it's like to be on the receiving end of all those gazes. Though I never was quite so spectacularly the center of attention. Being a Princess of Courland has its drawbacks."

Wellington was bowing over Dorothée's hand with the genial cordiality he afforded pretty women. Not one to be shocked, Wellington. In Brussels, he'd raised eyebrows by insisting on inviting Lady John Campbell to his parties. Then again, Wellington wasn't one to listen to gossip, so it was also possible he hadn't even heard about the duel.

Dorothée and Clam-Martinitz left Wellington and moved towards Suzanne and her friends. Suzanne went forwards to embrace Doro. "I wonder if there's a soul left in Paris who hasn't heard," Dorothée said.

"There have to be a few who are deaf," Simon pointed out.

"How very true, Monsieur Tanner." Dorothée glanced through the crowd towards the pillars on the side of the room where her sister stood with Lord Stewart. They appeared to be arguing.

A few minutes later, Wilhelmine joined them. Alone.

"Let me guess," Dorothée said. "Stewart didn't want you associating with your disreputable sister."

"Even Stewart wouldn't be such an idiot."

Dorothée raised a well-groomed brow. *"Even?"*

"In any case, he can't tell me what to do. You're carrying it off beautifully, Doro. Karl, I'm glad to see you in one piece."

"Duchess." Clam-Martinitz inclined his head, his gaze grave. "I never meant to put your sister in danger."

"Oh, you needn't apologize to me, Doro can take care of herself. But you'd be wise to realize Courland women don't sit idly by when their men are in trouble. Or making fools of themselves."

Dorothée opened her mouth.

"Yes," Wilhelmine said. "I confess Stewart is likely to do the latter more often than not. Too often for me to save him from himself on all occasions."

Raoul moved along the edge of the Duke of Wellington's dance floor. Two months ago he had been in the blood and smoke of the battle of Waterloo at Marshal Ney's side, in a last desperate charge against the British forces under Wellington. Now Wellington was the victor of Paris, Ney was imprisoned, and Raoul was strolling through the duke's ballroom. Of course, if the truth of his actions came to light, he'd join Ney in prison in no time.

His quarry stood across the ballroom. In the shadows as usual. Raoul was far too seasoned an agent to feel a chill at the mere sight of Fouché's gaunt figure. At least in theory. Though he couldn't admit it even—perhaps especially—to Suzanne, he couldn't help but feel as though the wind in the Cantabrian Mountains had cut through him at the sight of the minister of police.

Fouché noticed him coming. Of course. But he didn't actually turn his head until Raoul was a handsbreadth away. "Monsieur O'Roarke. I trust you are enjoying your return to Paris."

"Paris will always be one of my favorite places on earth."

Fouché's gaze skimmed over him. "Indeed."

"Where's your lovely fiancée?"

Fouché glanced at the couples swirling before them. "On the dance floor, I believe."

"You aren't dancing with her yourself."

"No. I prefer to observe."

Raoul leaned against a pillar at an angle that gave him the best view of the minister of police's face. The candlelight accentuated Fouché's thin nose and the tight line of his mouth. "I haven't yet had the chance to offer you my felicitations."

"Thank you."

"Remarkable seeing you now to remember that once the Jacobins found you a moderating influence against Bonaparte's rage."

"We all shift with the times."

"Indeed. Fascinating where people have ended after the last two months."

"I wouldn't say anything is ended."

Raoul shifted his shoulders against the pillar, holding Fouché's gaze with his own. He remembered standing in a similar pose talking to Fouché on the edge of a dance floor in the spring of 1794. Two days later Raoul had been arrested and thrown in the Conciergerie. "I understand you spoke with Suzanne Rannoch at the theatre last night."

Fouché raised a brow. "I spoke with a number of people at the theatre."

"I don't imagine you can have forgot this conversation. Unless you now threaten so many people with ruin that they all run together."

Fouché flexed one white-gloved hand. "My dear O'Roarke. Are you admitting to a particular interest in Madame Rannoch?"

"I'm not admitting to anything." Raoul maintained his casual pose against the pillar, gaze locked on Fouché's own. "What are you afraid of coming to light about Antoine Rivère?"

"Rivère was insignificant."

"So I would have thought. And yet you threatened Madame Rannoch to get her husband to stop his investigation."

"I don't like a British agent poking his nose into our business."

"That I can well believe. Because anyone poking their nose into anything concerning you is likely to uncover a rat's nest of corruption."

"Scarcely the way to talk to an old friend, O'Roarke," Fouché said in a mild voice.

"We were never friends. Allies perhaps, but by no means always."

"By no means indeed." Fouché's gaze moved to Suzanne, her dark ringlets and silver net gown stirring as she waltzed with Granville Leveson-Gower. "It was Madame Rannoch you had break into the ministry of police to retrieve the information about Queen Hortense's child, wasn't it?"

"You can hardly expect me to answer. But for old times' sake, I advise you to leave Madame Rannoch alone if you value your own safety."

"You intrigue me. I'm sure she's an able agent, but I assure you I am quite well able to take care of myself." Fouché gave a thin smile.

Raoul recalled learning, imprisoned in the Conciergerie, that Robespierre had had Fouché expelled from the Jacobin Club. When that happened to most men, arrest and execution soon followed. But in Fouché's case, it was Robespierre himself who had fallen not long after. "I don't doubt it," Raoul said. "And like all of us who've survived the past quarter century, you have a healthy instinct for self-preservation. Which is why you will leave Madame Rannoch alone. Because if you do not I will make public exactly how much you had to do with the execution of the Duc d'Enghien."

Fouché didn't move a muscle, but Raoul saw the jolt of tension run through him and settle in his eyes. "My dear O'Roarke." Fouché's voice was even, but Raoul could hear the effort that underlay the tone. "Even if you choose to propagate lies about me—"

"You forget. I have a number of facts at my disposal that could not but give credence to my words."

"Even if you choose to do so, you can scarcely speak without exposing your own role as a Bonapartist agent."

Raoul let his shoulders sink deeper into the fluted wood of the pillar. "No," he said. "I can't."

"You'd be proscribed at once. You'd have to flee France. England would be barred to you, as would your beloved Ireland. You couldn't return to Spain without facing the wrath of your supposed *guerrillero* colleagues who would now know you'd in fact been fighting against them. You'd have to flee to South America. Assuming you could escape with your life."

"It would certainly be a challenge," Raoul conceded.

"You're not the sacrificial type, O'Roarke."

"No. But then we've all changed in the past two months. Priorities shift."

"*Mon Dieu.*" Fouché gave a short bark of laughter. "How are the mighty fallen. You and Talleyrand both bewitched by women young enough to be your daughters."

"Madame Rannoch is another man's wife."

"At your instigation. Much like Talleyrand and his niece-by-marriage." Fouché's gaze darted over Raoul's face, probing like an instrument of torture. "What game are you playing, O'Roarke?"

"You just claimed I was bewitched."

"No." Fouché's gaze was now that of a chess player trying to see the logic behind a seemingly irrational gambit. "Talleyrand may be, but you're not a lovesick fool. Or a defender of innocence. Not that Madame Rannoch is innocent. Does she have a hold on you?"

"I shouldn't waste your energy on my motives, my dear Fouché. But make no mistake, I mean what I say."

"You're going to throw your life away."

"Only if you throw away yours."

"Wellington should thank Edmond Talleyrand and Count Clam-Martinitz," Caroline Lamb said. "They've quite distracted attention from his own peccadillo." She looked from Wellington, standing with Lady Frances Webster on one side and Lady Shelley on the other, to Dorothée across the ballroom leaving the dance floor on Lord March's arm. "The comtesse looks as if this were merely another ball. If I could have learned that knack life would have been so much simpler."

"Yes, but Dorothée's trying to deflect attention," Cordelia said. "You've always wanted to provoke it."

Suzanne, looking on, was a bit startled by Cordelia's bluntness, but Lady Caroline gave a rueful laugh. "One can't hide things from friends one's grown up with. But you have to admit no one's ever fought a duel over me."

"Are you saying that with pride or disappointment?"

"Perhaps a bit of both."

"Well, I'm hardly one to talk," Cordelia said. "I liked to pretend I didn't care what people thought, but the truth is I was desperate to make some sort of mark on the world."

"You look as though you could carry it off, Mrs. Rannoch." Caroline turned to Suzanne. "Somehow I always have the sense you don't care in the least what anyone thinks of you. That is, you don't seem to mind in the least—" She broke off.

"That people claim I'm a foreign adventuress who snagged Malcolm for his fortune?"

"No, of course not." The scandalous Lady Caroline Lamb looked like an abashed schoolgirl. "That is—"

"It's all right. I can hardly be deaf to the talk. Mostly I laugh at it." Mostly.

Lady Caroline's wide-eyed gaze turned unexpectedly shrewd. And a bit wistful. "That's a wonderful knack, being able to laugh at life. Oh, I see both your husbands coming. You're going to be unfashionable and eat supper with them, aren't you? I must be off before things become too domestic."

Malcolm and Harry were indeed both approaching from opposite ends of the ballroom. Malcolm reached them first. "What happened to Lady Caroline?" he asked.

"She's afraid domesticity is catching," Cordelia said. "Poor Caro."

"William adores her," Malcolm said in a quiet voice. He didn't normally talk about his friends' private lives. It was a sign of how well he had come to know Cordelia.

Cordelia met his gaze. "Yes, I know. And Caro adores him in her way. Yet they're spectacularly unsuited. As much, I used to think, as Harry and I were."

"You and Davenport aren't unsuited."

"I hope not. Darling." Cordelia flashed a bright smile as her husband joined them. "You look as though you've learned something."

"I have." Harry looked from his wife to Malcolm and Suzanne. "I just received a message from Christine Leroux. She wants us to meet her tomorrow night. At Café de la Reine in the Palais Royale. She says she has information."

Cordelia shot a look at her husband. "Do you trust her?"

Harry's gaze flickered to Malcolm. "As much as I trust anyone in this business. Not that I'm advocating we not take precautions."

Suzanne slid her hand through the crook of her husband's arm. "I find I'm rather averse to staying behind this time."

He smiled at her. "What a surprise. As a matter of fact, I think the presence of a lady will render us less conspicuous in the café."

"Then two ladies will render you even more so," Cordelia said.

Harry regarded her but said nothing.

"I know I'm not an expert," she said. "But I'm part of this. And I think I've done enough to prove myself."

"More than enough." Harry took her hand and quite unexpectedly raised it to his lips.

"Mrs. Rannoch." Raoul stepped aside as Suzanne came through the archway from the supper room. Cordelia, up ahead, was speaking with Dorothée and Clam-Martinitz, and Malcolm and Harry had been detained in the supper room by Stuart.

"Good evening, Mr. O'Roarke. Are you enjoying the ball?"

"Very much. I've just had a word with the tiresome young man who was importuning you. Young officers often don't know when they've crossed the line with a pretty woman. You needn't worry he'll be troubling you again."

Relief shot through her, followed by concern. Because she couldn't believe Fouché could be so easily neutralized. "Are you sure?"

"Quite sure. Life is complicated enough, Mrs. Rannoch. This is one thing you don't have to worry about."

He moved through the doorway past her. Suzanne cast a look over her shoulder at him before she went to join Cordelia. Damn Raoul. It was no accident he'd told her in the midst of a crowd instead of finding a few moments for private conversation. This way she couldn't question what had transpired between him and Fouché. Or what it had cost him.

CHAPTER 26

Candlelight, gilding, and blue damask curtains looped with gold cord predominated at Café de la Reine. Tables clustered in the center of the room, beneath the diamond-bright chandelier, but more tables stood in curtained alcoves round the edge of the room. Like boxes at the theatre and just as inviting to amorous encounters. The curtains had been drawn across several.

"Quite like Vauxhall," Cordelia murmured, as a waiter showed them to a table in one of the alcoves. She had applied her eye blacking and rouge with a heavy hand and her sapphire shot-silk gown was cut even lower than her dresses were in general. Or perhaps she'd had her maid alter it. Suzanne wore a claret-colored satin with a silver-spangled overdress that she kept for occasions such as this.

"One drawback with the two of you being present," Malcolm said, holding out her chair. "Everyone's looking at us."

"Yes, but they aren't seeing agents." Suzanne dropped into the chair and settled the folds of her skirt. "And the two of you have an obvious reason for being here that has nothing to do with secret meetings."

Cordelia let her beaded shawl slither down about her shoulders. "I've always suspected courtesans have more fun than ladies of the ton. Even when I was a social outcast, the restrictions could be exhausting. Though I suppose I shouldn't speak so blithely when they have to share a man's bed for their living."

Harry settled back in his chair, easing his bad arm. "Some would say that's precisely what wives have to do."

Cordelia met her husband's gaze without blinking. "How very true. What a good thing it is Suzanne and I both have such enlightened husbands."

"And how lucky for us both that you deigned to enter matrimony, given the legal definition," Malcolm said.

"Talk about a mark of trust," Suzanne said. It was quite true. She remembered the moment, not when she agreed to be his wife nor even at their wedding but some days later, looking at him across their rooms in Lisbon, when she realized precisely what power she had given to this man by becoming his wife. Of course, at that time she had still thought she could walk away. "Juliette Dubretton would agree," she said. "In *Les Règles du Mariage* she argues quite cogently that marriage is akin to slavery, at least in legal terms."

"I wish I'd been with you when you met her," Cordelia said. "Talk about a woman with a daring mind."

"I suspect that's why she refused to marry Paul St. Gilles for so long," Suzanne said. "Not because she didn't trust the sort of husband he'd be, but because she disapproves of the whole institution."

Malcolm's gaze drifted round the café. Seemingly idle, but Suzanne knew he was scanning the uniforms, evening coats, and spangled gowns for anything out of the ordinary and searching the curtains for unseen watchers. "Manon Caret used to hold court here after the theatre," he said in conversational tones. "But she's left Paris abruptly. Rumor has it just ahead of Fouché's agents."

"So she did leave for political reasons." Cordelia cast a glance at Suzanne. "She was a Bonapartist agent?"

"So it's being said now," Harry said. "I never heard any rumors about her in the past, even when I was in Paris last year. But of course if she was that good I wouldn't have."

Suzanne forced herself not to succumb to the temptation to

pluck at her gown or fiddle with her hair or make any other obvious effort to divert attention, which with men like Malcolm and Harry would likely have just the opposite effect.

A full-throated giggle sounded from the drawn curtains of the alcove beside them. Malcolm ordered champagne. Just after the waiter had poured it, Christine Leroux approached their table. She wore a gown of bronze green satin, her hair was carefully arranged, and she had removed her stage makeup and replaced it with subtler cosmetics, but there was taut tension beneath her movements and wariness in the angle at which she held her head.

The tension palpably increased as she took in Suzanne and Cordelia at the table.

"Mademoiselle Leroux." Malcolm pushed back his chair and got to his feet, as did Harry. "May I present my wife, Suzanne Rannoch, and Lady Cordelia Davenport?"

Christine Leroux's gaze swept over Suzanne and then Cordelia. First with disbelief, then with appraisal and dawning wonder. "People are always saying the British are eccentric, but I never had the sense that meant that the ladies frequent raffish cafés. Or that their husbands escort them there."

"Cordelia and I rather push the bounds of eccentricity," Suzanne said, standing as well. "More to the point, we assist our husbands in their work."

"More and more surprising. But perhaps not quite as surprising as it would be had I not met your husbands." Mademoiselle Leroux sank into the chair Malcolm had pulled out for her.

Malcolm poured another glass of champagne and handed it to Christine Leroux. "Thank you for contacting us. You said you had information."

Mademoiselle Leroux took a careful sip of champagne, as though still debating the wisdom of speaking. "You asked me to think over everything Antoine had said to me. I've been going over it. I had been doing so in any case. One does when—" She ran her white-gloved fingers down the stem of her glass.

"When one has lost someone one was close to," Malcolm said.

She met his gaze for a moment, and the diamond armor in that blue gaze slipped. "Yes." She tossed down a sip of champagne.

"Antoine and I didn't go out together in public a great deal. And when we did it was generally in the evening. This was one of his favorite cafés." She cast a glance round the room, eyes bright with memories. "But a fortnight ago, he suggested we visit the Louvre. He said with all the debate about returning works of art to their rightful owners and countries of origin, who knew when we'd have another chance to see the collection. But I still suspected there was more to it. I teased him, but he wouldn't tell me more. When we got to the museum, I kept trying to figure out what had drawn him there. We wandered through the galleries, but there was one painting he studied in great detail. Almost covertly, as though he didn't want me to see what it meant to him."

"Which painting?" Malcolm asked in a quiet voice.

"*The Daughters of Zeus* by Paul St. Gilles." Mademoiselle Leroux cast a glance round and took a quick sip of champagne. "St. Gilles and Princess Tatiana Kirsanova were intimate."

"Yes," Malcolm said. "My wife and I spoke with him recently."

"I was rather put out that Antoine had dragged me along on this outing and then wouldn't tell me what his purpose was. I told him he was making such an elaborate pretense of ignoring the painting that it was perfectly plain to me that the painting was the reason he'd dragged me to the Louvre and what on earth was so important about it." A faint smile curved her mouth, easing the lines of strain. "Antoine looked almost rueful. He said he should have known better than to think he could deceive me, and I said let this be a lesson to him. Then he looked at the painting for a long moment and said it was quite striking in and of itself. And that you'd never guess it contained a princess's secrets."

Suzanne felt the jolt that ran through Malcolm, though they weren't so much as touching. "And then?" he asked, voice even.

"I said did he mean Princess Tatiana and was she one of the women in the painting, for I couldn't place her in it—though I knew St. Gilles had painted her. But Antoine went quiet—it was as though he feared he'd revealed too much. When I teased him, he simply took my arm in an iron grip and steered me away. And when I continued to ask questions, he said I was too wise a woman to wade into dangerous waters. Of course that made me all the more curious. But nothing I said could shake him." Her brows drew together.

Malcolm met Suzanne's gaze for the briefest moment, then looked back at Mademoiselle Leroux. "That could be . . . extremely helpful. Thank you."

Christine Leroux shrugged her shoulders as though to deny the force of her feelings. "I want to know what happened to Antoine. Anything that helps you unravel the mystery—"

Malcolm reached across the table and touched her hand. "Quite."

Mademoiselle Leroux pushed back her chair. "I must go. I have an early rehearsal tomorrow. I know most people don't credit it, but I do rely on my voice for my living." Her gaze swept them, then returned to Malcolm. "You'll let me know if you solve this?"

"My word on it." Malcolm got to his feet, as did Harry.

Mademoiselle Leroux inclined her head. "Madame Rannoch. Lady Cordelia. Colonel Davenport. You almost make me think the attractions of marriage might in some cases outweigh the drawbacks."

With a swish of satin, Christine Leroux swept into the passage between the alcoves and the main dining room.

"It appears you aren't the only one to see the freedom enjoyed by Cyprians as having advantages over marriage, my darling," Harry murmured, dropping back into his chair.

"But even the wary Mademoiselle Leroux recognized that you and Malcolm are exceptional husbands." Cordelia touched his hand. Her voice was playful, but the look in her eyes was not.

"A discerning woman in a number of ways," Suzanne said.

"Yes, her information is interesting." Malcolm's gaze followed Mademoiselle Leroux round the passage. "To say the least."

"Do you think she's right that there's some sort of clue in the painting?" Cordelia asked. "Or something hidden in the painting itself."

"That was my first thought," Suzanne said.

"Mine as well," Malcolm agreed. But for all the excitement of the discovery, his voice had the note it took on when his mind was elsewhere. His gaze shot from along the upper gallery that encircled the café. "There's a man up there who's been watching Mademoiselle Leroux since she got up from our table," he said, in the same conversational tone. "Fair hair. Side-whiskers. Prussian uniform." His gaze moved back to Christine Leroux. She had stopped to lean over the railing of one of the alcoves and speak with a gold-ringleted lady and a gentleman in a Dutch-Belgian uniform who were dining there. "And someone's following Mademoiselle Leroux. Sticking to the shadows, but I can see the movement." Malcolm was on his feet. "Suzette, Cordelia, go round to the left and intercept Mademoiselle Leroux. Move quickly, but try to act as though it's still a social occasion. Harry, see what the Prussian's up to."

"Right."

They were already all on their feet. Suzanne slid her arm through Cordelia's and they slipped into the passage and circled to the left, while Malcolm moved to the right and Harry made for the stairs.

"Who?" Cordelia murmured, her tone admirably conversational.

"Perhaps merely a jealous lover. Or someone who thinks Mademoiselle Leroux knows too much."

"You think there's danger?"

"Danger's always a possibility." Suzanne's head was turned toward Cordelia, as though she was lost in a tête-à-tête with her friend, but she managed to keep her gaze angled to take in the room. Harry was moving along the upper gallery toward the Prussian. Mademoiselle Leroux was leaning over the partition that separated the alcove where her friends were dining from the passage, laughing, dark ringlets stirring about her face. Malcolm was a shadowy form moving along the passage. The man he was following was little more than a dark blur beside a pillar near Mademoiselle Leroux.

Three more boxes to pass and she and Cordelia would reach Mademoiselle Leroux. Suzanne cracked open the steel clasp on the reticule that dangled from her wrist and closed her fingers round the silver handle of her pistol.

Mademoiselle Leroux straightened up and blew a kiss to her

friends. With a graceful swirl of skirts and ringlets, she turned and moved along the passage. The shadowy form by the pillar suddenly moved, still in the shadows, closing the distance between them. Suzanne's fingers tightened on her pistol. Two more boxes to pass now. Malcolm quickened his pace. The follower was a few feet from Christine Leroux. Movement cut the shadows, as though he had perhaps raised his arm. Malcolm hurtled through the shadows and slammed the man to the ground.

The thud of two men hitting the polished floorboards rose above the stir of conversation and the clink of glasses. A woman screamed. Suzanne dropped Cordelia's arm and ran to Christine Leroux's side.

"Madame Rannoch—"

"Get down." Suzanne pulled Christine to the floor. "Someone was trying to kill you."

Malcolm was grappling with Christine's would-be attacker, still a dark blur, on the floor of the passage. The man got his arm free and landed Malcolm a blow to the jaw. Malcolm hung on. Two waiters ran up and grabbed Malcolm by the coat, pulling him off his opponent. The man scrambled to his feet and ran the other way down the passage.

A shot whistled through the air from above.

CHAPTER 27

Malcolm went still in the grasp of the waiters, blood turned to ice. His heart went still until he saw Suzanne's arm move, still sheltering Christine, saw Christine move in response, saw Cordelia hurrying towards them.

In the next split second he took in the rest of the scene. On the upper gallery, Harry had ripped open a pair of velvet curtains. Malcolm couldn't see into the alcove behind, but the Prussian was running towards Harry, through the screaming crowd. On the main floor, screams filled the air as well, as diners sprang to their feet, glancing round for the source of the shot. Malcolm's quarry was halfway round the passage, making for the double doors that led out of the café. Malcolm wrenched himself away from the waiters and hurtled after his target.

His only chance of catching the man was to cut across the main floor. He leaped over the partition, vaguely aware of exclamations from the auburn-haired lady and British cavalry officer dining at the nearest table, dodged between an Austro-Hungarian and a Bavarian who seemed to arguing about the source of the shot, jumped over an overturned gilded chair and a fallen champagne bucket, dodged round a lady who had fainted and the three men bending over her, skirted a table overturned in a tangle of linen, silver, and broken porcelain and crystal, caught himself on another chairback to avoid skidding on the champagne-soaked floorboards, and leaped the partitions to the outer passage.

His quarry was reaching for one of the handles on the gilded double doors. Malcolm pushed between two gentlemen with gold epaulettes and sprang on the man's back again. They fell against the double doors, knocking them open, and slammed into the black-and-white marble hall tiles. As he fell to the floor Malcolm had a brief impression of silk and gold braid and heard a woman scream.

His quarry managed to land him a blow to the jaw. Malcolm caught the man by his neckcloth. With the candlelight blazing down, he had a brief impression of sandy hair, pale eyes, and freckled skin stretched over a sharp-boned face. "Who hired you?"

"Don't—" The man's breath stank of garlic and rotting teeth.

"His name."

The man jabbed an elbow in Malcolm's ribs. Malcolm lost his grip on the neckcloth. As he grabbed for the man's arm, cold fire sliced across his ribs.

"It's a wonder you don't have more scars, darling." Suzanne doused a cloth with brandy and pressed it against the cut in her husband's side. They were in a private dining room at the café, to which the proprietor had shown them after some minutes establishing that they weren't dangerous hooligans (a process helped along by the proffer of coins to pay for the damage).

"There was a man with a rifle behind the curtains in the alcove off the gallery," Harry said. He had conducted a search of the café with the proprietor. "He had the window open behind him. He got out before I could catch him. By the time I came out the Prussian was gone."

"One man with a knife, another with a rifle," Malcolm said. "Double insurance. Strikingly like Vienna last year."

"Quite," Harry agreed. "Except that was an assassination attempt on the Tsarina of Russia. This was—"

"An attack on an opera singer of middling importance." Christine rubbed her arms. She was sitting bolt upright on a gilt chair, a glass of brandy on the table before her. "Were they really after me?"

"I'm afraid there's no question," Malcolm said. "The man with the knife was making for you and the sniper shot at you."

"He'd have killed me if it wasn't for you." Christine looked up at Suzanne. "Thank you."

Cordelia dropped down beside Christine and put an arm round her. Christine was shaking and her face was as white as the lace of her shawl. Shock taking over as the reality of what had almost happened hit her.

"I still don't understand," Christine said.

Malcolm leaned towards her, then winced.

"Hold still, darling," Suzanne said, pressing a makeshift bandage made from a linen napkin against his side.

"Someone thinks Rivère told you something," Malcolm said to Christine. "Or he did tell you something and you don't realize the significance."

"By 'someone' you mean the person who killed him," Christine said.

"Yes." Malcolm regarded her for a moment. "Have you told us everything Rivère told you?"

Christine's wide eyes fastened on his face. "You'll wonder no matter what I say. But if I hadn't already I would now. I don't understand."

"Nor do we," Malcolm said. "Yet."

"Perhaps it's to do with whatever's hidden in the painting," Cordelia said.

"Hidden—" Christine drew a breath. "Of course."

"But Rivère gave you no indication of what it might be?" Harry asked.

"Not except that it related to a secret of Princess Tatiana's."

Suzanne looked up from fastening the bandage with a strip cut from an old tablecloth to see hope and fear shoot through her husband's eyes. But he merely said, "Can you leave Paris for a few days, mademoiselle?"

Christine drew a breath, then nodded. "I can go to my sister in Reims. But is it safe?"

"It will be. I'll send my valet Addison with you. He's an excellent agent in his own right."

"Meanwhile you'd best stay with us tonight," Suzanne said. "I can lend you some things and then tomorrow we can send to your lodgings for whatever you may need for your journey."

Harry went out to hire a fiacre and reconnoiter to make sure the coast was clear. Back in the Rue du Faubourg Saint-Honoré, with Christine shown to a bedroom, Suzanne, Malcolm, Harry, and Cordelia repaired to the salon. Harry poured whisky while Suzanne replaced Malcolm's makeshift bandage with a proper one from her medical supply box.

"We could go back to St. Gilles," she suggested, securing the new bandage in place.

"St. Gilles didn't tell us anything about the painting," Malcolm pointed out, pulling his dressing gown up about his shoulders. "If there's something hidden in it either he doesn't know about it . . . or he does know and made the decision not to tell us."

Harry flicked a glance at Cordelia. "I think perhaps we should leave."

"It's all right." Suzanne flipped the medical supply box closed.

"I can read enough to see that somehow this matter of Princess Tatiana and whatever the painting may conceal touches on something more personal than merely an investigation." Harry set down his whisky glass. "You'll do better exploring the topic without having to hold information back from the two of us."

"No," Malcolm said, as Harry got to his feet. "That is, we'll do better with your help. But you're right, in order to give it you need to know the whole." He looked from Harry to Cordelia, his gaze open and direct in that way it seldom was. "You're right, it is personal for me, in a way even Castlereagh and Wellington and Stuart don't realize." He drew a breath but did not falter or glance away. "Tatiana Kirsanova was my sister. And Rivère gave me reason to suppose she may have left a child behind when she died."

Cordelia drew a breath like broken glass. Her gaze went to Suzanne, then back to Malcolm.

"That's quite an admission, Rannoch," Harry said.

"Only sharing information with a friend." Malcolm returned his gaze steadily.

Harry dropped back into his chair and took a sip of whisky. "Quite."

A simple exchange and somehow their friendship had deepened. But then with men like Malcolm and Harry it was what lay beneath the surface of the words that tended to matter. Malcolm leaned back in his own chair and told Harry and Cordelia about Tatiana's birth, his relationship with her through the years, her work as a spy, her death, and the possibility that she'd left a child behind. He spoke concisely, but he held nothing back. Suzanne saw concern and sympathy welling in Cordelia's eyes and even a trace of it in Harry's, but both the Davenports knew better than to put anything of the sort into words.

"You think Princess Tatiana hid information about the child in St. Gilles's painting?" Cordelia asked.

"It seems an elaborate way of going about it," Malcolm said.

"But Tatiana made it a habit to hide dangerous secrets away from her own lodgings," Suzanne said, recalling the box of the princess's papers and possessions that she and Dorothée and Wilhelmine had discovered in Vienna. "Perhaps she kept proof of the father's identity as insurance in case she ever needed it but thought it was too dangerous to have among her own things. If it was concealed in the painting, with or without St. Gilles's knowledge, she'd know she could retrieve it should she ever need it."

Malcolm gave a faint smile. "You know Tatiana well."

"I've begun to understand her."

Harry's gaze moved between them. "You're going to break into the Louvre."

"We have to see what's in that painting," Malcolm said. "I can't tell Wellington and Castlereagh about Tatiana's child. I can't make it a pawn."

"No, of course not," Cordelia said.

Malcolm turned his glass in his hand. "And given the climate about the treasures in the Louvre, I can't see anyone giving us permission to take one of the paintings in any event."

"Including the French," Harry said. "They're angry enough about losing the foreign treasures. They'd never stand for an Englishman taking a French painting. We'll need to get it out and hopefully return it without anyone knowing it's been gone."

" 'We'?" Malcolm asked.

Harry stretched his legs out and crossed them at the ankles. "Didn't think we'd let you have all the fun, did you?"

Malcolm regarded him for a moment. "Thank you, Davenport."

Harry returned his gaze. "Still getting the hang of being a friend, Rannoch, but I think this is what friends are for."

"And there's a child's safety at stake." Cordelia moved to the arm of Harry's chair. "The men who tried to kill Mademoiselle Leroux—was that because someone thought she might lead you to Princess Tatiana's child?"

Malcolm flicked a glance at Suzanne. "I fear so."

"Which rather seems to justify Tatiana's efforts to conceal the child's birth and parentage," Suzanne said. "For reasons we have yet to discover."

"It's obviously more than the scandal," Cordelia said. "Whoever was behind the attack today wouldn't have been worried about Princess Tatiana's reputation."

"Unless the father's concerned for his," Harry murmured. "Or is trying to find the child and wants to make sure no one else finds it first."

"I thought of that," Malcolm said. "Though I'm more afraid someone wants to eliminate the child before we find it."

There was nothing like the prospect of illicit activity later in the evening to add spice to a diplomatic reception. Suzanne took a sip of champagne. Gabrielle and Rupert Caruthers had just come into the salon in the Austrian embassy. Suzanne watched them for a moment. The way Gabrielle's hand rested on Rupert's arm, the smile they exchanged before they moved in separate directions. They seemed both easier together and further apart.

"Having the whole Laclos affair brought up again can't be easy on either of them," Simon said at her elbow.

"Simon." Suzanne turned to look at him, recalling the way he'd spoken—or not spoken—about the Carutherses' marriage at the British embassy ball. The questions about Rupert's and Gabrielle's involvements in the Laclos affair had been answered. As an agent and an investigator, Suzanne no longer needed to focus her attention on them. But she found it harder and harder to ignore the human element. She'd learned that from her husband. "When we spoke about the Carutherses before, you seemed to understand that their marriage was—"

"Perhaps not all one could wish?"

"Yes."

Simon's gaze drifted back to Rupert, now talking to Fitzroy Somerset. "Well, given that Rupert and Bertrand Laclos were obviously madly in love with each other, it's a fair guess Rupert's marriage to Bertrand's cousin is less than idyllic." He turned his gaze back to Suzanne and scanned her face. "You knew."

"Found out. Recently. Was their relationship so obvious?"

"Only to one who knew where to look. I'm not sure even David realized."

"You never talked about it?"

"Not for me to pry into other people's lives."

"No, that's left to investigators."

He touched her arm. "That's different. You had cause."

"Gabrielle knows now. Rupert told her."

"I'm glad. God knows marriage has its challenges. People enter into it for all reasons, and it seems to succeed or fail for all reasons. But I've always thought a marriage built on lies must have the hardest chance of flourishing."

Suzanne's fingers curled round the ebony sticks of her fan. "Quite."

Aline came up to claim Simon for a dance, and Dorothée moved to Suzanne's side. "I never thought to be so grateful for society's short attention span," Doro murmured. "The whispered comments and shocked looks have been quite cut in half since last night." Her gaze turned stricken. "I'm horrid to laugh about it."

"I don't see what you can do but laugh, dearest. How's Karl?"

"Bearing up well. It's my uncle who keeps looking at me as though he's afraid I'll break."

"He had quite a scare. Especially given the way you looked when Malcolm carried you in."

Dorothée fingered the clasp on her diamond bracelet. "He told me this afternoon that he'll understand whatever I choose to do. It was almost as though— Almost as though he was giving me permission to run off with Karl."

"Does that make it easier?"

"It should, shouldn't it? But the look in his eyes when he said it . . ."

"You're afraid of hurting him?"

"No. That is, that's part of it. But I'm more afraid of what I'd be giving up myself." Dorothée stared at the sparkling flower links of the bracelet, then lifted her gaze to Suzanne's face. "When that man struck me and I was falling to the ground—in the moment before my head hit the cobblestones. It wasn't Karl I wanted. It was Talleyrand."

Suzanne watched her friend move off on Clam-Martinitz's arm. Talleyrand was a dangerous man. For many reasons, she should want Doro to find happiness with Clam-Martinitz. And yet—

"Madame Rannoch."

Fouché had materialized at her side. Suzanne forced herself not to stiffen.

"You aren't availing yourself of your influence over your husband," Fouché murmured, voice pitched below the strains of Mozart that filled the room.

Suzanne turned to the minister of police with a bright smile. "Perhaps I prefer to let my husband make his own choices."

"I thought we understood each other three nights ago." His gaze skimmed over her face. "I do hope you haven't been so unwise as to listen to your friend O'Roarke."

"Why on earth should I discuss this with Monsieur O'Roarke?"

"Don't play the innocent, Madame Rannoch. You can't imagine I knew about you and not about your links to O'Roarke. I imagine O'Roarke told you he had me checkmated. And I imagine he didn't add that if he moves against me, I will destroy him."

She couldn't quite control her intake of breath.

Fouché regarded her as though she were a type of unknown insect beneath the microscope. "I always knew O'Roarke was foolishly inclined to idealize causes. I didn't realize that extended to his women as well."

"I think perhaps you're misinterpreting simple loyalty."

"I think not." He tilted his head as though breaking her into parts and toting up her monetary value. "I hadn't realized quite how much you meant to O'Roarke. Even then, I doubt he'd actually be mad enough to move against me. But of course I can't be sure. It's an interesting conundrum. I'm inclined to ignore O'Roarke and do just as I've told you I will if you don't oblige me. Of course, I could be wrong, and O'Roarke could move against me. In which case, make no mistake, I will destroy him. So much risk. And you can prevent it all simply by doing as I asked."

She forced herself not to look away from that incisive gaze. "I've no guarantee you wouldn't expose me in any case."

"My dear Madame Rannoch. Why waste such a valuable bargaining chip? You needn't ever fear I'll use it. So long as you continue to do as I ask."

CHAPTER 28

"It would almost be worth it to see the look on Wellington's face when he learned we'd been hauled in for breaking into the Louvre," Harry murmured.

"Fascinating as the possibilities are, I think that's a scene I can forego," Malcolm said, scanning the street.

Harry cast a glance over the lamplit cobblestones. A seemingly casual glance that held the appraisal of a professional. "Quite like old times. Seems an age since we've had an excuse for breaking and entering. Hope we haven't grown rusty."

"Speak for yourself," Malcolm said, reaching in his pocket for his picklocks.

Harry took them from him. "I'll do it. You two create a diversion to cover me."

He knelt down in front of the door at this side entrance. Suzanne stepped towards Malcolm and into his arms. "Easiest way to create a diversion," she said, raising her lips to his.

Malcolm gave a laugh against her face and met her kiss. He was less prudish about such matters than he'd been when they married. Harry knelt behind them. She could hear the faint scrape of metal, but only because she knew to listen for it.

A carriage rattled by in the nearby street, bringing a flash of torchlight. Suzanne turned in Malcolm's arms so her skirt created a wider shield. She was wearing a dark mulberry spencer and a jaunty plumed black velvet hat over a black sarcenet gown. Dark for camouflage, but also slightly raffish, the ensemble of an actress out for an evening with her lover.

"We're in," Harry said in a lower whisper. "Coast clear?"

Another carriage rattled past, some soldiers strolled by, their voices carried on the evening breeze, and then Harry pushed the door open, and they stepped into the cool, dark quiet of the palace that housed the art treasures Napoleon Bonaparte had gathered up from his conquests across the Continent.

Harry pushed the door to behind them, and Malcolm struck flint to steel and lit a lamp.

Suzanne was too keenly aware of what was being done to France not to sympathize with those from other countries who wanted their treasures returned to them. Yet it was impossible not to feel a thrill at the richness and beauty that surrounded them. Gilt frames; rich, vibrant oils depicting classical scenes, portraits, and still lifes; marble statues; and bronze sculptures flashed past them, taking her back to childhood visits she had made with her father to this very museum. She remembered staring up, listening to her father's stories, asking him to pick her up so she could see better. And later carrying her baby sister. She pushed aside the last memory as it tore at her throat.

Thanks to careful reconnaissance early in the day, they could almost have traversed the corridors to the gallery where *The Daughters of Zeus* hung without illumination. It was a square room near the Grand Salon Carré, featuring works by contemporary painters, mostly French and Italian. Harry stood by the door holding guard. Suzanne held the lamp while Malcolm lifted the painting down and leaned it against a marble bench. They crouched down and studied it in the light of the lamp. Young women in classical garb in a garden. The faces were vivid and arresting, the light luminous as it fell across faces and nestled in the folds of white draperies. But none of the models looked like Tatiana.

"Anything that makes you think of Tatiana?" Suzanne asked.

He shook his head. "Nor anything that seems like a clue to a child." He turned the painting round. Suzanne held it so the paint wouldn't scrape against the bench. Malcolm ran his fingers over the back of the canvas. "The name of the painting and St. Gilles's signature again. No way anything could be hidden."

"A secret compartment in the frame?" Suzanne suggested, looking down over the painting to study it.

Malcolm ran his fingers over the frame, tapped against it, shook his head. Then he touched the inner edge of the frame and frowned when he reached the upper left-hand corner. "The frame's been glued to the canvas." He pulled a knife from inside his coat and carefully pushed the knifepoint between the frame and the canvas. His eyes lit. "Tweezers?"

Holding the painting with one hand, Suzanne opened the steel clasp on her crimson silk reticule and gave them to him. Malcolm reached inside with the care he'd use for picking a lock, tugged, and pulled out a sealed, folded paper. Suzanne drew in her breath. Malcolm lifted the lamp.

Footsteps thudded in the corridor.

Suzanne flung her silk scarf over the lamp and went still. She could feel Malcolm's taut stillness beside her.

"There'll be hell to pay if we're caught." The voice, English and with a north country accent (she was still learning to recognize accents from different parts of Britain), sounded from the corridor.

"That's why we're doing this at night." The second voice was also British and sounded like a Londoner, with undertones of Cornwall.

"We didn't fight at Waterloo so we could skulk about frog palaces in the middle of the night."

"Hookey wouldn't thank you for calling them frogs. And you said it— If they knew—"

"Better to do it by daylight and face them down."

"Speak for yourself. I've had enough of fighting frogs. I've had enough of fighting everyone. Where the devil are we supposed to start?"

"East gallery. Something Italian."

Suzanne drew a breath. Wellington must have decided to pre-emptively remove some of the disputed art treasures. And the soldiers were heading right towards them.

Malcolm looked from her to Harry in the shadows. "Follow my lead."

It was all he could say before the footsteps thudded closer and a tall, broad-shouldered man in the uniform of a British army sergeant appeared in the doorway, lamp raised in one hand.

"What the devil—What the devil are you doing here?"

"I might ask you the same." Malcolm got to his feet. "I doubt Wellington would be best pleased to find you breaking into the Louvre after hours, Sergeant."

"Breaking in—" The sergeant drew a breath. "Wellington sent us."

"Oh, good God." Malcolm exchanged a look with Harry. "You'd think he'd have had the sense not to send us at the same time."

"Probably didn't realize it," Harry said. "You know how orders can get muddled."

"Are you saying Wellington sent you, too?" the sergeant demanded.

"Of course he sent us," Malcolm said, in a tone that would have withered the roses at Malmaison. "You don't imagine we'd have broken into the Louvre in the middle of the night on our own authority, do you?"

The sergeant opened his mouth, then closed it. More footsteps thudded on the floor. A taller, thinner man in an ensign's uniform appeared in the doorway behind the sergeant. "What—"

"They say they're here on Wellington's orders, too," the sergeant said.

The ensign looked from Malcolm to Harry and back at Malcolm. "You're Malcolm Rannoch."

"I'm—"

"And that's Mrs. Rannoch." The ensign's gaze settled on Suzanne with the look of one spotting a favorite actress. He glanced at Harry. "And you must be Colonel Davenport."

Harry rolled his eyes. "So much for anonymity. And you are—"

"Tompkins. This is Sergeant Grey." The ensign moved into the room. The lamplight illuminated his round, well-scrubbed face. "I suppose you're here on"—he coughed—"secret business."

"No, we came here in the middle of the night to do something perfectly commonplace," Harry said.

"You did? Oh, I see." Tompkins coughed again.

Grey's chin jutted out. "Don't see why he sent you and us at the same time."

"Nor do I." Malcolm looked from Suzanne to Harry, then back at the two soldiers. "Our presence here is supposed to be secret."

"So's ours," Tompkins said.

Suzanne touched her fingers to the cameo broach at her throat. "You'll just have to explain it to them, darling."

Malcolm turned back to the two soldiers. "There's secrecy and secrecy. If you ask Wellington he won't even admit he ordered us here."

"He—" Grey shook his head. "What?"

"Deniability," Malcolm said.

Tompkins nodded gravely. "You can count on our discretion, sir. We'll pretend we never saw you. No matter who asks."

"Splendid," Malcolm said.

"I wish I could have been there," Cordelia said.

"I'd never have been able to keep a straight face," her husband replied. "It was hard enough with Malcolm and Suzanne. I couldn't look either one of them in the eye."

"Do you think you can really count on them not to say anything to Wellington?" Cordelia asked, sobering.

Harry exchanged a look with Malcolm. "It's a risk. But so is a lot of what we do."

"At least we'll soon know if the risk was worth it." Malcolm pulled the paper he'd found hidden in the painting from his pocket and spread it on the escritoire in the light of the Argand lamp. The paper was yellowed and crackled as he unfolded it.

Fading print. Suzanne had to lean over Malcolm's shoulder to read it.

This is to affirm that Étienne Laclos is the father of the child
I bore on 21 July 1807.
Tatiana Kirsanova

Below were the signatures of two witnesses. Paul St. Gilles and Juliette Dubretton.

CHAPTER 29

Pale morning sunlight leached between the cramped, narrow buildings. Malcolm rang the bell at the door of the St. Gilles house. He had tossed and turned all night—Suzanne had been keenly aware of it, for she'd scarcely been able to sleep herself—and they had left to call on the St. Gilleses at the earliest possible moment.

Juliette Dubretton opened the door herself. Her hair was slipping free of its pins, with an abandon that suggested she'd been jamming her fingers into her coiffure, and her face was hollowed with strain and fatigue.

"Monsieur Rannoch. Madame Rannoch," she said on a note of surprise.

"Forgive the intrusion," Malcolm said. "But we need a word with you and your husband without delay."

Her mouth tightened. "Paul isn't here."

Malcolm put his hand on the doorjamb before she could close the door. "Where might he be found?"

She drew a harsh breath. "The Conciergerie."

"He's been proscribed?"

"And taken into custody immediately." Juliette swayed on her feet.

Malcolm put a hand on her arm and steered her inside to a

small sitting room overflowing with sketches and stacks of note-paper. Malcolm pressed Juliette into a tapestry chair, while Suzanne poured a glass of wine and put it in her hand.

She gulped down a sip. "Thank you. I don't know what came over me."

"Having one's husband arrested is enough to shake the strongest woman," Suzanne said. "I went through it myself last autumn, and I felt as though the world was crashing to bits round me."

"What's he been charged with?" Malcolm asked.

"Sedition." Juliette took another sip of wine. "They cited his latest pamphlet, though in truth they could have cited almost any of his writings."

"Have you spoken with an advocate?"

She nodded. "An old friend. He says we can attempt to put on a defense, though he has little hope of success."

"I can make the inquiries. My position as a British diplomat may prove advantageous."

Juliette regarded him for a moment over the rim of her glass. "You're very kind, Monsieur Rannoch."

"I don't like to see anyone arrested in this climate. And your husband strikes me as a particularly decent man."

Juliette swallowed, as though the wine had turned bitter in her mouth. "If—"

The door swung open. A boy of about eight and a girl of about six stood there, hair tousled, her white dress and his white shirt catching the sunlight. "Maman?" the boy asked. "Have you heard anything?"

"Pierre. Marguerite." Juliette held out her arm and the children ran to her and nestled against her. "I told you we wouldn't hear anything this morning."

"We heard someone at the door," the girl said. "We were being quiet so we wouldn't wake Rose."

Juliette pulled the girl onto her lap and stroked the boy's hair, a brilliant red-gold in the sunlight. "We need to have our wits about us to help Papa, *mes chers*." She looked at Malcolm and Suzanne. "My son Pierre and my daughter Marguerite. Monsieur and Madame Rannoch."

Pierre studied them with grave blue eyes. "Are you here to help my papa?"

"We came here to speak with your father and mother," Malcolm said. His voice was level and friendly, though Suzanne felt the tension that had shot through him at the first sight of the boy. "But now we know what's befallen your father, we'll do our best to help."

Pierre nodded, as did Marguerite.

Juliette tightened her arms round them. "Go to the kitchen, and tell Solange I said you could each have a macaron. I need to speak with Monsieur and Madame Rannoch, and then I'll come see you."

The children nodded, old enough still to be worried, young enough to be comforted by the promised treat.

The click of the door behind them echoed through the room.

'Your son looks to be about eight," Malcolm said. "I expect he was born in 1807."

Juliette squeezed her eyes shut. "It seemed so easy eight years ago. So clear-cut. He needed us. It wasn't until you came asking questions that I realized what an appalling thing we had perhaps done."

"Hardly appalling," Malcolm said in a level voice. "You gave him a home and family."

"But does that give us the right to keep him from his mother's family? I told Paul after your visit that we should tell you the truth, but he refused."

"He was worried about losing Pierre," Suzanne said. The inchoate fears she lived with, that the truth of her past could lead to her losing Colin, welled up in her throat.

Juliette spread her hands over her lap, smoothing the creased muslin. "It's a fear we've lived with from the moment he was born."

"You were there when he was born?" Malcolm asked.

Juliette met his gaze, hesitated a moment, then nodded. "We both went to the house where Tatiana was confined. She had the midwife put him in Paul's arms immediately."

"I knew your husband was a good friend to Tatiana," Malcolm said. "I didn't realize quite how good." He leaned back in his chair.

"We found the paper hidden in your husband's painting *The Daughters of Zeus*. The document you and your husband witnessed. We know Étienne Laclos was the child's—Pierre's father."

Juliette's eyes widened. Then she inclined her head. "I spoke the truth when I told you she seemed to really love him. But after his execution, Tatiana said it would be ruinous for it to be known she had a child by the man who had plotted the emperor's death. Many would find it hard to believe she hadn't been involved in the plot herself."

"But she wanted to keep proof of the boy's parentage in case she needed it later?" Malcolm asked.

"She thought it might be important if things changed in France. Paul was against it, but in the end he agreed. I didn't know where she'd hidden the paper. I don't think Paul did, either."

"You and your husband agreed to take in her and Laclos's child."

"It was a bit more complicated." Juliette tilted her head against the chairback. Her skin seemed to be stretched taut over the elegant bones of her face. "Paul and I weren't married then. That is, we were when Pierre was born, but not when we agreed to take him. I put Paul through a great deal, as I believe I told you before. We joke about it, but in truth it was difficult for him. I didn't just refuse the legal bonds of marriage, I wasn't sure about trusting myself to a lasting relationship at all. We quarreled, as isn't surprising, and I'm afraid I was more focused on what my choices meant for me than on what our quarrel was doing to Paul. It's not surprising that he sought consolation. Given how close he and Tatiana had always been, it's not surprising he sought it with her. With her grief over Étienne— It's a wonder it didn't happen sooner."

"And given her grief, I don't suppose she was taking precautions with Monsieur St. Gilles, either," Suzanne said. She was amazed how steady her voice was given the echoes of her own life.

"No." Juliette pushed loose strands of hair behind her ear. "At least not reliable precautions. Not that any precautions are entirely reliable."

"And then she learned she was with child." Malcolm's voice was gentle.

Juliette tugged a strand of hair loose from her cameo earring. "She told Paul she couldn't be sure who was the father. Paul believed her. So did I, when he told me."

"That can't have been easy," Suzanne said.

"No." Juliette's mouth twisted. "But it forced me to face some facts about Paul. Such as that my feelings about him were so proprietary I should probably stop denying that I wanted an exclusive relationship. Paul told me he wanted to raise the child. I said that in that case we'd do it together. I hadn't thought I wanted children. Well, to tell the truth I hadn't thought about them much at all, one way or another. When we agreed to take Tatiana's child I felt responsibility. A sort of debt for Paul's sake. But I didn't realize—" She broke off, frowning. "I didn't have the faintest suspicion how I could fall so utterly in love the moment a squirmy human weighing eight pounds was placed in my arms."

Suzanne remembered the moment Malcolm had put the wriggling, bloody newborn Colin on her chest. Exhaustion had fled. "It was much the same for me when our son Colin was born. I still look at him sometimes and can't quite believe I'm a mother. Yet within days of his birth it was difficult to remember a time when he wasn't part of my life."

"I was afraid it would change me," Juliette said. "In some ways it didn't at all—I remember writing with Pierre in his basket beside me, realizing with relief that I was still the same person. But in some ways it changes everything."

Suzanne nodded. "One knows one will never make another decision without the child being part of the equation." Which particularly changed decisions relating to one's husband. "A new loyalty."

Juliette turned to look at her. "That's an interesting way of putting it."

"It's a bond that comes before everything else." And yet the other, older loyalties didn't go away. Which could make for complicated choices. "And it changes the way one thinks about the future. Marriage confers certain legal advantages on children," Suzanne said.

Juliette met her gaze. "Quite. And so I sacrificed my principles and married Paul." Her mouth curved in a smile. "I haven't regretted it once since." Her brows drew together. "I quickly let a few strategic people know I was pregnant. Shortly after Tatiana left Paris, Paul and I left as well. We met Tatiana in the country for the birth. She gave us Pierre." Juliette glanced at a child's framed drawing of a dog that hung beside the fireplace. "It was soon hard to believe he wasn't ours."

"Tania had made him yours," Malcolm said. "There's more than one way to be a parent."

"You're kind, Monsieur Rannoch."

"Only going by observation. Did Tania ever see Pierre?"

"Every few months. She could call on us as a friend of the family. She sent quite extravagant presents. But she always made it clear she considered me his mother." Juliette folded her arms across her chest and gripped her elbows. "I'll always be grateful to her for that."

"Yet she insisted on a document claiming Étienne Laclos was the boy's father," Malcolm said.

Juliette's fingers pressed into her arms. "She said it was in case the tables ever turned and it was dangerous for Pierre to be Paul's son. I suppose you could say she was talking about now."

"Did she ever suggest approaching the Lacloses about the boy?" Malcolm asked.

"Once. Obliquely. After Napoleon fell. She'd been to dine with us. The children had just gone up to bed, and Tatiana, Paul, and I were alone. We'd been talking about the Restoration and the way things were changing. Tatiana was cracking a walnut, and she suddenly said that now it might not be such a bad thing to be connected to a family of émigrés who would soon be flooding back to Paris seeking their forfeited lands. Such as the Lacloses. Paul said Pierre wasn't connected to the Lacloses. He took the walnut from her and snapped it between his fingers. Tatiana just shrugged. But I know Paul worried from then on. It's why he lied to you."

"It's understandable you feared losing your son," Suzanne said.

"Yes, but it's more than that. To own the truth, I think Paul couldn't bear the idea of his son being turned into an aristo."

"I can understand that," Malcolm said.

Suzanne said nothing, a vision of Colin clutching a Royalist cockade sharp in her mind.

Juliette's fingers curled against the bare flesh of her arms. "Tatiana was at great pains to keep Pierre from being branded the son of a traitor. And now that's exactly what's happened."

"We have to see what we can do to get your husband out of prison," Malcolm said.

Juliette's eyes widened. " 'We'?"

Malcolm dropped down in front of her chair. "I hate what's happening in Paris. I'd like to think I'd try to help him in any case. But I owe him a great debt for looking after Tatiana's child. Your son is my nephew. And I can't imagine better people to be his parents."

Suzanne reached across the fiacre and touched her husband's arm. "Darling—"

"I'm all right. More than all right." His fingers curled round her own. "It means a lot to have seen the child and to know he's safe and cared for. I still don't see why Tania was so determined to conceal Pierre's parentage. Possible parentage."

"Étienne had just been executed. That probably affected her sense of the situation."

"Perhaps. It's like Tania to have wanted to hedge her bets and document her son's connection to the Lacloses in case it was ever necessary."

"And if she loved Étienne as much as she seems to have, perhaps she hoped he really was Pierre's father. Perhaps that's why she wanted it in writing."

"Not very logical."

"Even Tatiana may have found logic eluded her with her emotions so strongly engaged."

Malcolm's mouth relaxed into a smile. "Perhaps. In an odd way it's a relief to think so. Though I have to say I much prefer the thought of St. Gilles as the boy's father."

"Yes, but you weren't in love with Étienne Laclos. Do you think you can convince Wellington or Castlereagh to intervene on St. Gilles's behalf?"

His mouth hardened. "No. But I may have more luck with Talleyrand."

Talleyrand stared at Malcolm across his study. "My dear Malcolm, I understand your sympathies. But you can't save every Radical on the proscribed list."

"I'm not talking about every Radical. I'm talking about Paul St. Gilles."

"I wasn't aware you even knew him."

"Tatiana did."

"Ah."

Malcolm slammed his hands down on Talleyrand's desk and leaned forwards. "How much do you know?"

Talleyrand flicked a bit of powder from his sleeve. "She was close to him. She was close to a number of men. Is he the father of her child?"

"Perhaps in biology. Certainly in fact. He and his wife are raising the boy."

"It's a boy?"

"With Tania's hair and eyes."

"A great admission." Talleyrand leaned back in his chair. "I don't know whether to thank you for your trust or chide you for your carelessness."

"You're the one who taught me the value of calculated risks." Malcolm straightened up and leaned against the desk. "We both owe St. Gilles a debt, sir. And I think Dorothée would ask the same of you."

Talleyrand got to his feet. His gaze was direct and less hooded than usual. "I'll do what I can, Malcolm. But my influence is precarious. I don't know that I can get St. Gilles out. But I may be able to get information that will be of help to you."

"Of help?"

Talleyrand moved round the desk and put a hand on Malcolm's shoulder. "When you break St. Gilles out of prison."

CHAPTER 30

"An aristo and a Radical." Wilhelmine looked at Malcolm across the antechamber at Madame de Coigny's to which she, Malcolm, Suzanne, and Dorothée had retired to talk, escaping the press of the political and artistic elite of Paris mingling in her salons. "Even in her fathering her child Princess Tatiana knew how to play both sides."

"Don't be horrid, Willie," Dorothée said.

"No, it's an apt comparison," Malcolm said. "I've thought much the same myself. And I suspect Tania would appreciate it."

Wilhelmine got to her feet. "What can we do?"

"My uncle—," Dorothée said.

"I've talked to him," Malcolm said. "He was not unsympathetic. But he doesn't think he has the power to get St. Gilles released."

Dorothée frowned. "But then—"

"So we have to break him out," Wilhelmine said. "I do hope you aren't going to try to keep us out of it."

"On the contrary," Malcolm said.

Suzanne hesitated outside the door to the card room, weighing risks and consequences, while her heart beat a taut tattoo beneath her corset laces. But sometimes all calculations of risk and reward ceased to matter. Sometimes the stakes were so high one had to roll the dice and take one's chances. She stepped into the room, strolled to the faro bank, and met Raoul's gaze.

Ten minutes later he dropped down beside her in the ballroom on a settee half-hidden by a pillar. "Mrs. Rannoch."

"Mr. O'Roarke. I fear I'm growing old. You find me taking a break from the press of the party."

"I'd say that's more a reflection of the life you lead than your age, Mrs. Rannoch."

"You're very kind."

Raoul turned his head and studied her face. "What is it, *querida?*"

Suzanne swallowed hard, aware of just how much she was muddying her two worlds. But then keeping those worlds apart had always been an impossible challenge. "Paul St. Gilles has been arrested," she said.

"I heard. It's a pity. A brilliant artist and an equally brilliant thinker. We need more men like him to speak out, not be silenced."

"Yes. And he's . . ."

Even now she fumbled for the words, knowing that once they were spoken they could not be taken back. And it wasn't her secret, it was Malcolm's.

Raoul watched her with understanding but did not press her.

"He was Tatiana Kirsanova's lover," she said.

Raoul raised his brows. "I didn't realize. Though I can see how he'd have appealed to her. She liked brilliance and challenge."

"And he may have fathered her child."

Raoul's eyes widened. "I didn't realize—"

"That she had a child? No, she kept it well hidden. Whether or not St. Gilles is the biological father, he's been raising the boy. He and his wife."

"The incomparable Juliette Dubretton. The boy is fortunate in his parents."

"We owe them a great debt."

" 'We'?"

For a moment she felt keenly what Malcolm must have gone

through in Vienna before he told her the truth of his relationship to Princess Tatiana. It wasn't her secret to share. And yet it had to be shared if they were to have a prayer of saving St. Gilles. "Princess Tatiana was Malcolm's half-sister."

She expected the rare surprise to show in Raoul's eyes again. Instead, he inclined his head. "Yes, I know. I presume Malcolm told you in Vienna? I'm glad he did so."

Pieces of seemingly solid information broke apart and swirled in her mind. All these years, and he could still shock her to the core. "How—"

"Arabella confided in me. Malcolm's mother," Raoul said, as though Arabella Rannoch sharing this secret she had guarded so closely was a simple matter. "We were friends, remember. She was young and in distress. I was young myself and a sympathetic listener."

It made sense on the surface and yet did not begin to explain Raoul's ties to the Rannoch family. Suzanne stared into his gray eyes with their unfathomable layers. "So all this time—"

"It wasn't my place to tell you what Malcolm didn't feel he could share. I did try to tell you I was sure Malcolm's relationship to Princess Tatiana wasn't what it appeared on the surface if you'll recall."

"Yes, but—" She shook her head, replaying a dozen conversations. "Damn you, do you have to know everything?"

He gave a low laugh. "Every day I'm more and more convinced of how little I know." He regarded her for a moment with that appraising gaze he'd worn when measuring the extent of her injuries after a mission. "What mattered wasn't so much that you knew the truth of their relationship as that Malcolm was able to confide the truth to you."

She drew a breath, memories of those weeks of uncertainty in Vienna like glass in her brain. "You're right of course. You have a disgusting habit of being right. It's most provoking."

He gave an unexpected smile. "Good to know I still have my moments." His gaze skimmed over her face. "Do you know who Tatiana's father was?"

"Lady Arabella didn't confide that to you?"

"No. It was a secret she guarded closely. I don't think she told her sister, either."

Suzanne hesitated again, but he was going to have to know about Willie's and Doro's involvement. "Peter of Courland."

This time she did see surprise flare in his eyes followed by a flash of understanding. "I begin to understand Arabella's secrecy. Almost like giving birth to a royal bastard. Do the duchess—"

"Wilhelmine and Dorothée know. They've been helping us locate the child."

"An interesting alliance. And they too want to help St. Gilles?"

Suzanne nodded. "We owe him a debt for looking after Tatiana's child. Malcolm will never forgive himself if we don't come to his aid. I don't think I'll forgive myself."

"Quite." Raoul inclined his head. "I'd like to help as well. I'd been wondering if I could do something for St. Gilles as it is. You want me to talk to the Kestrel?"

"If anyone can devise an escape plan—"

"Precisely."

"But I don't see how the devil we're to explain it to Malcolm."

"You aren't going to explain anything. That would be fatal. I shall have to offer my services—and my connections to the Kestrel—to Malcolm on my own."

"How will you explain—"

"I'll need a convenient rumor for how I heard he was looking for aid." Raoul's gaze drifted round the ballroom as though they were engaged in idle conversation. "Believe me, I can contrive something."

She shook her head. "It's—"

"My dear girl, after everything we've been through, don't tell me it's dangerous." Raoul inclined his head to a stout lady with a headdress of purple ostrich feathers who was walking past. "If I cared a scrap for danger, I'd be raising horses in Ireland."

"But this isn't—"

"I'm risking myself for people I care about." He leaned back and watched her for a moment. "Assuming you're all right with the risk. I can keep you out of it, but it does circle closer to Malcolm learning about your past."

She gave an impatient shake of her head. "I'd never let that stand in the way of my obligations."

He smiled. "No, you wouldn't, would you?" He took a sip of wine. "Have you heard anything more from Fouché?"

"No." She drew the silk folds of her shawl about her, chilled despite the warmth of the evening.

"Suzanne."

She shot a look at him. "There's nothing to be gained from dwelling on it."

"Fouché told you he didn't believe my threats, didn't he? That he'd act against you anyway and if he was wrong, and I brought him down, you'd be responsible for my ruin."

Suzanne released a breath of fear and frustration. "This is why you're impossible to defeat at chess."

"Fouché's bluffing. Knowing what I can do to him, he wouldn't dare expose you. Or me."

"You can't be sure."

"No. We can't be sure of anything."

Her fingers tightened on the satin and steel of her reticule. Raoul had always protected his people, but it had been in the service of a larger goal. "You're—"

"Finding a way to go on and make sense of my life. As we all are."

"You aren't immune to danger yourself. And don't you dare say it's different because you're a man."

"I wouldn't dream of it. But I've survived the United Irish Uprising and the Reign of Terror. I think I can navigate the waters in Paris."

"So can I."

"My dear girl, I wasn't claiming anything to the contrary. But indulge me by letting me do what I can."

"I'm—"

"For God's sake, Suzanne." His gaze continued to drift round the room, but his voice cut like glass. "You have a son to think of."

She swallowed hard. "I think of Colin all the time."

"And he deserves to grow up with both his parents. It doesn't mean you can't run risks, but it changes the calculations."

"Juliette Dubretton is terrified of losing her son. I understand how she feels."

"Every parent's fear. But you won't lose Colin."

"If Malcolm learns the truth—"

"Even then I can't see him keeping Colin from you."

"It's difficult to know what anyone will do when they're pushed that far."

"Which is why we're going to do everything we can to ensure he never learns the truth."

"Lying to my husband. Our best hope of happiness. No, it's all right. I'm used to it. Or at least I damn well should be."

"Rannoch."

Malcolm turned at the sound of the voice. "O'Roarke. How do you find Paris?"

"Not as beautiful as I did in my younger years."

Malcolm studied him, remembering the glow in O'Roarke's eyes when he talked about Paris on their rambles in his boyhood. It had been the cradle of liberty then. "I suspect the change is in Paris rather than you."

"Very likely. Victory can take unusual forms."

Malcolm wondered what it had been like for this man, a committed Republican and revolutionary who had been imprisoned during the Reign of Terror but retained his revolutionary ideals and yet nevertheless had fought against Napoleon Bonaparte's forces in driving the French out of his native Spain. Only to see the Spanish liberals turned on by the restored monarchy, the constitution revoked, the Inquisition restored.

"I think I may be able to do you a favor, Rannoch."

"A favor?"

"Perhaps we could step onto the balcony?"

Malcolm inclined his head. They moved through the French windows onto the balcony. O'Roarke turned, his back to the room, and leaned against the balustrade. "I understand you're looking for help getting someone out of France."

Malcolm stiffened. "What gave you—"

"Don't worry, you haven't been betrayed or given yourself away. I have a number of contacts in various parts of Parisian society. I don't know the precise reasons you're eager to help Paul St. Gilles, but I should like to help him myself. Anyone with an interest in freedom would."

"And?" Malcolm said, willing himself to caution.

"I have a contact who I believe can be of use to us."

" 'Us'?"

"You can hardly expect me to stay out of it. It's the sort of adventure one needs to temper the climate in France just now."

"And your contact—"

O'Roarke turned, still leaning against the balustrade, and looked him full in the face. "Have you heard of the Kestrel?"

Suzanne scanned her husband's face as he crossed the room towards her. His features were composed into his public mask, but his eyes held the light of the chase. "I think we have a way to rescue St. Gilles," he murmured, bending his head close to her own as he took a sip from her champagne glass.

"You've found someone who can help?"

"Raoul O'Roarke just approached me. Apparently he has contacts who've helped others get out of France. It's not surprising. He may have fought against the French in Spain, but that was because they were trying to overrun his country. He's a Republican at heart. I'm a bit surprised he sought me out, though."

"He's close to your family," Suzanne said, voice carefully calibrated to show only wifely interest. In truth, she had a keen interest in Raoul's relationship to the Rannoch family.

"Yes, particularly to my mother and grandfather. He was kind to me as a boy. He'd give me books and talk to me about grown-up subjects. I still remember him giving me the Beaumarchais trilogy and encouraging me to analyze the different sides in *Henry IV*. I was sorry when he had to flee Britain after the United Irish Uprising."

"Did he say how he can help?" Suzanne asked in the same carefully calibrated tone.

"He thinks he can put us in touch with someone called the Kestrel. We're to meet him tomorrow at Café Saint-Georges."

Suzanne nodded, prepared for her two worlds to collide.

Wilhelmine came up short at the sight of the figure sprawled in the damask armchair in her dressing room. "I didn't realize you were here."

"Where did you go after you left Madame de Coigny's?" Stewart demanded.

She raised her brows at the peremptory question. "Out. With friends."

"Who?"

She unwound the folds of her shawl from about her shoulders. She'd gone to the Rue du Faubourg Saint-Honoré to discuss further details about Tatiana's child and Paul St. Gilles with the Rannochs, but she had no intention of telling Stewart so. "You're sounding tiresomely like a husband." Which of course was what she had been hoping he would become. It had been so long since she'd had one she'd forgot how they could interfere. Marriage gave a man entirely too many rights.

He pushed himself to his feet. "You've been with the Rannochs, haven't you?"

She dropped the shawl on her dressing table and tugged at the fingertips of one of her gloves. "I told you I'd been with friends."

"Damn it, Wilhelmine. I know what you're up to."

"Do you?" She dropped the glove on the dressing table and started on the next one. "Do pray enlighten me."

"Rannoch's hoodwinked you into helping with his meddling. What's he learned?"

The glove had caught on her emerald ring. She pulled it free. "You'll have to ask him."

"Don't play games, Wilhelmine." Stewart lurched towards her. She caught the fumes of brandy on his breath. "I need the truth."

"Why?"

"Rannoch's poking and prying and asking all manner of questions—"

"What is it to you?"

"Some things are best left well enough alone."

" 'Some things' meaning Antoine Rivère's death? Or Bertrand Laclos's?"

Rage flared in his eyes. She'd seen them lit with passion but never with so much anger. "You don't know what you're meddling in, Wilhelmine. I thought I could trust you."

"What makes you think you can't?"

He seized her wrist. Her pearl bracelet clattered to the floor. "I forbid you to have anything more to do with this."

"Forbid?" She jerked her hand from his grip. "What makes you think you can forbid me to do anything?"

"You know what you are to me, Wilhelmine."

"I know that I'm not your property. Or any man's. First you ask me questions about what Malcolm and Suzanne are doing, then you tell me to have nothing to do with them—"

"I don't want you exposed to lies."

"I think you can trust me to know the difference between lies and the truth."

"You don't know what you're in the midst of."

"No, I don't." She fixed him with a hard stare. "Care to enlighten me?"

"This is no laughing matter."

"No, it isn't. If I hadn't cared to uncover whatever's going on before, I do now. You certainly know how to pique one's curiosity."

He gripped her shoulders. His fingers dug into her skin through the tulle and crêpe of her sleeves. "Don't you dare—"

She wrenched away from him and stared into his hot eyes. "You're terrified."

"Don't be ridiculous."

"For God's sake, Stewart, what have you done?"

"I haven't done anything. You—"

"For heaven's sake. I can tell when you're lying."

"You don't know where this could lead. What you're doing to me."

"Then tell me." She reached for him and took his face between her hands. "Tell me what you're afraid of. Let me help you."

"I didn't say—"

"You're obviously terrified. Charlie, what have you done? What are you afraid of Malcolm learning? What's so important—"

"Don't meddle, Wilhelmine."

"Is it about Bertrand Laclos?"

Rage and fear flared in Stewart's eyes. "Damn it—"

"That's it, isn't it? Charlie, it's dreadful he was framed, but no one can blame you. Even Malcolm believed he was guilty. Yes, you should have told Wellington about that letter from Laclos saying he wanted to give up his mission, but he was already dead when you received it. I can see—"

"Stop it, Willie."

"I'm just telling you not to torture yourself. Unless there's more." She scanned his face. "What? Surely you didn't suspect he was framed when you ordered him killed? Why on earth—"

"I told you to stop it."

"I can't believe you'd have knowingly ordered an innocent man's death."

"I didn't."

"Then what—"

"It's none of your affair."

"Of course it is. I care about you."

"If you cared about me, you'd stop this folly."

"How can I know it is folly? How can you? Unless you know—"

"You have no right to make accusations."

"I have a right to ask what my lover is involved in."

He gave a short laugh. "If you persist in this I won't be your lover anymore."

"For heaven's sake—"

"I mean it, Wilhelmine. Persist in this folly and it's over."

Wilhelmine stared up at the man on whom she had pinned her hopes these past months. Security, position, the power of being a powerful man's wife. The allure hadn't gone. He was being tiresome, but the consequences of being alone hadn't changed. For a moment her future hung before her eyes.

Pleasure. Secure comfort. An assured position. Set against freedom and loyalty. In the end it was no choice really. She lifted her chin. "It's been a pleasant interlude."

"What are you saying?"

She took a step back from him and her hopes for the future. "That it's over."

CHAPTER 31

One of the first things Suzanne had learned as a spy was that sometimes the safest place for a clandestine meeting is in the clear light of day. Sunlight spilled through the thick glass of the café's windows as she and Malcolm stepped through the doors. She wore a light muslin gown and a peach sarcenet spencer and matching bonnet. Nothing overtly flashy, but there was no need to be in disguise for this mission. Or at least for this part of this mission.

She and Malcolm glanced round the linen-covered tables, crowded with a Latin Quarter assortment of students with books spread before them or stacked on the floor; older academics reading, writing, or talking; artists with sketch pads; chess and backgammon players; more than one actor studying a script. Easy enough to appear to be looking for a table. There were indeed few available.

"Rannoch." Raoul looked up from a newspaper. He was at a table in the middle of the room but against the wall and slightly concealed by a sideboard that held bottles of wine and pitchers of water. "Mrs. Rannoch."

Natural enough for Suzanne and Malcolm to thread their way across the room towards him.

"Do join me," Raoul said. "I'd be glad of the company, and tables are in short supply."

Suzanne slid into the chair Raoul was holding out for her, struck by the surreal nature of the scene. She was meeting Raoul to exchange information as she had hundreds of times in the past. But Malcolm was with her and there was no need to keep the meeting secret. At least not from Malcolm. It should have eased the knot of tension inside her. Instead her mouth was dry and her corset laces seemed to be cutting through her chemise and squeezing the breath from her lungs.

"Parisian cafés are a welcome escape from diplomatic crowds. But they present their own chaos." Raoul raised a casual hand to signal a waiter across the room.

"But at least it's less stuffy chaos." Suzanne adjusted the muslin folds of her gown. This was Malcolm's and Raoul's scene. All she had to do was listen and respond, which sometimes was the hardest thing of all to accomplish. Especially when one was trying not to reveal anything to the expert spy at one's side to whom one happened to be married.

The waiter shuffled over to their table, stopping to take two orders along the way. He was gray haired and stoop shouldered, his face dominated by a large nose and heavy jaw and set in the lines of disapproval with which many Parisians these days viewed foreigners.

Malcolm ordered café au lait for both of them. The waiter, seemingly hard of hearing, bent closer to take the order. In the same tones in which he had confirmed the order, he added, "Uniforms would work best. Easiest way to hide a man."

Though Suzanne had been 90 percent sure the waiter was the Kestrel from the moment Raoul signaled him, surprise and admiration shot through her. This close she could tell the nose and jaw had been created with putty and the hair artificially turned gray, but only because she knew where to look. For all her training at looking beneath disguises, she would not have been able to recognize the man beneath the disguise or even to do a reasonable sketch of what he might look like. Nor would she have equated him with the man she had met in Manon Caret's dressing room had she again not known to look.

"How many?" Malcolm asked, in the same tone he'd used to order the coffee.

"Four. I can provide the uniforms. We'll need another two or three to have transport ready outside the city gates."

Malcolm nodded. "We'll be ready. Oh, and you might bring some biscuits with the coffee."

"Biscuits? Oh, you mean gâteaux." The Kestrel-as-waiter shook his head over foreign words and shuffled off.

Raoul shifted his position in his chair, setting his shoulders to the crowd behind them. "Do you know whom you can use?"

"We have Davenport," Malcolm said, also shifting slightly in his chair to face away from the crowd. "And his wife. And Juliette Dubretton. And . . ." He hesitated. Suzanne could see him debating the wisdom of mentioning Wilhelmine and Dorothée. "One or two others."

"And me." Raoul took a sip of coffee.

"You've already risked a great deal, O'Roarke."

"It's my decision what I risk. You're not in a position to turn down help, Rannoch." Raoul's long fingers curled round the handle of his coffee cup. "Unless you don't trust me?"

"Of course not," Malcolm said, with the ease of one who had known Raoul from boyhood and never doubted his loyalties. "But this isn't your fight."

"On the contrary. Opposing what's happening in France now should be everyone's fight."

Suzanne kept her gaze moving between the two men. Malcolm might not know Raoul was a Bonapartist agent, but he had grown up hearing about Raoul's involvement in the French Revolution and the United Irish Uprising. She felt an unexpected wash of comfort at the realization that in many ways the three of them were not so very far apart. At the same time it made keeping track of real and pretend roles that much more difficult.

"Still—," Malcolm said.

Raoul shifted his cup on the worn white linen of the tablecloth.

"I know of St. Gilles's connection to Tatiana Kirsanova. I've heard rumors of your investigation. I can put the pieces together."

Malcolm's expression snapped closed. "I don't—"

"I have no intention of spreading tales. But I have my own sense of obligation when it comes to Tatiana."

Malcolm reached for his coffee cup. "I didn't realize you knew her."

"I rather think everyone knew Tatiana Kirsanova. But I didn't know her well, it's true. My interest in her goes back some years." Raoul held Malcolm's gaze across the table for a moment. "Your mother told me, Malcolm."

Malcolm held every response in check, but Suzanne felt the shock that ran through him like a lightning strike.

"We were young enough to talk more freely than perhaps we should," Raoul said, in a quiet, conversational tone that was somehow directed straight at Malcolm. "I don't know the whole story. But I know enough to know what Tatiana Kirsanova must mean to you."

"And—"

"Your mother was my friend. One of my oldest friends. I miss her. I can't help but feel a certain debt to her children. All of them."

Malcolm's gaze lingered on Raoul. "If—"

The waiter shuffled back to their table and set down the cups of café au lait and a plate of almond cakes. "Do you require anything else, monsieur? Madame?"

"Perhaps some sugar?" Suzanne said with a smile.

The waiter sniffed, as though to indicate a true Parisienne wouldn't sully her coffee with sweetener.

"Papers?" Malcolm asked.

"I'll have them prepared. But they'd be safer if you could get an original seal."

Malcolm inclined his head. "Shouldn't be a problem. How much do you require in funds?"

"I have sufficient to set things in motion. We can settle up when your friend is safe."

The waiter moved off. Raoul regarded Malcolm over the rim of his cup. "You're risking a great deal, Rannoch."

Malcolm blew on the steam rising from his café au lait. "You were just telling me this should be worth the risk to anyone."

"Taking the seal moves the risk a step further."

Malcolm shrugged and took a sip of coffee. "In for a penny."

"You have a career to risk," Raoul said. "In a way I no longer do."

Which was even truer than Malcolm knew.

Malcolm grinned. "You're sounding distinctly paternal, O'Roarke. I'm no longer the boy you introduced to Locke and Paine and had to keep from tumbling into the stream when we went fishing."

"You must forgive the concern of someone who's known you since childhood. But your diplomatic career is not something to risk idly."

"I rarely do anything idly. But when it comes to risks to my career—" Malcolm stared into his coffee for a moment. "I don't know how much longer I can stomach my diplomatic career in any event."

Suzanne froze, her own cup halfway to her lips. She knew Malcolm's increasing frustrations with his diplomatic role, but she had not heard him address it so directly.

Raoul regarded Malcolm steadily. "Carrying out others' policy can be trying. All the more so when one has strong ideas of one's own."

"Quite." Malcolm hesitated a moment, took another quick sip of coffee, spoke in a rush. "In Vienna I still thought I could achieve something arguing on the sidelines. I'm not sure how I deluded myself I could ever have any influence on Castlereagh or Wellington. Talk about arrogance. Perhaps I just needed a way to justify my choices. But now— One can only bang one's head against a wall for so long without starting to feel one's going mad. Or actually going mad." He turned his cup in his hands. "It's hard sometimes, not to wonder what we were fighting for."

Raoul leaned back in his chair and regarded Malcolm for a long moment. For all she knew Raoul, for all the secrets they both kept from Malcolm, in that moment Suzanne felt she was the outsider while what passed between her husband and her former lover stretched back to Malcolm's boyhood and a time before she had known either of them. "I can't say I'm surprised. Or that I don't sympathize. I always thought you were too independent a thinker to be happy for too long doing others' bidding."

"You have to feel it, too, O'Roarke." Malcolm leaned forwards across the table. "You can't tell me a Spain with the Bourbons restored and the liberals' constitution revoked is what you were fighting for."

Suzanne saw Raoul's fingers whiten round his coffee cup. "No. I'd be lying if I didn't admit to feeling distinctly as though I've been banging my head against a wall as well. But if you'll permit a piece of advice from one who was playing this game before you were born, don't let frustration turn into cynicism. It's difficult to take the long view at thirty. But having survived the Revolution and the United Irish Uprising, I can say there'll be a time you'll be glad you didn't throw your career away."

It was remarkably similar to the advice he'd given Suzanne after Waterloo. How odd that in the wake of the upheaval of the past year the same advice should work for both her and Malcolm, for all they'd been on different sides.

"You mean I'll be glad to still have a diplomatic career so I can exert influence when the climate turns more favorable?" Malcolm asked.

Raoul took a sip of coffee. "Perhaps. I was thinking more that you'll be glad you didn't land yourself in prison over a grand gesture."

"I'm too much of a pragmatist for grand gestures, O'Roarke."

"My dear Malcolm. You're one of the most committed idealists I know."

"Then you must move in a world of cynics, O'Roarke."

The waiter returned and plunked down a bowl of sugar.

"How kind of you." Suzanne, who never put sugar in her coffee, reached for her silver spoon.

The waiter sniffed. He bent over the table to adjust the vase of geraniums. "We'll need someone to talk to the subject. Make arrangements. Can you get into the prison?"

"We'll manage," Malcolm said.

The waiter straightened up, ran his gaze over the table, sniffed again, and moved off to frown at the next table.

Suzanne took a sip of her sweetened coffee and managed not to grimace. Part of playing a role was learning to eat and drink things that weren't to one's own taste in the general run of things. "If you go to see St. Gilles, it will be entirely too obvious who's behind his escape, darling."

"I agree," Malcolm said.

Both she and Raoul cast looks at him.

"Did you think I'd throw myself to the wolves?" he asked. "I'm neither so foolish nor so self-sacrificing. We need someone who can get into the Conciergerie in the general run of things."

Suzanne met his gaze. "Rupert."

Malcolm took a sip of coffee. "Rupert's assisting his father, who's interviewing those who've been proscribed. No one could question him going to see St. Gilles."

"But if we ask for his help—"

"Quite." Malcolm set down his cup with a clatter.

"You trust Caruthers?" Raoul asked.

"Trust is always a risk," Malcolm said. "I've judged fairly well in the past, but that doesn't stop me from wondering."

Raoul regarded him for a moment. "The trick is weighing the risks."

"And in Rupert's case I think the risk is a fair one." Malcolm paused as though surprised at the conviction in his own voice. "But these secrets aren't mine to share."

Raoul reached for his coffee cup. "Then I suggest you talk to Juliette Dubretton."

Malcolm inclined his head.

The waiter returned to the table. "We'll have to get the wife and children out of the city. Otherwise they could become hostages. You'll need someone to run that side of things." His gaze moved to Suzanne for a moment. Not by a flicker of an eyelid did he reveal he had met her before, but she was sure he remembered.

"We'll arrange it," she said.

"They should leave before St. Gilles, but ideally only by a matter of hours. Otherwise their disappearance could alert Fouché to an escape attempt."

Malcolm nodded.

"O'Roarke knows how to contact me." The waiter straightened up. "Anything else?"

"Nothing. You've been so kind." Suzanne gave him the demure smile of an expatriate diplomatic wife.

The waiter sniffed at the strange ways of foreigners and shuffled off.

Malcolm tucked Suzanne's arm through his own and glanced up and down the street. "I think it can work."

"If everything goes according to plan."

A smile pulled at his mouth. "Well, that's always the case."

"Or even if it doesn't." She tightened her gloved fingers round his arm. "We're good at improvising." She studied his profile for a moment. "Darling—"

"Don't you start with the cautions as well. O'Roarke was bad enough."

"No. We've never tried to stop each other from running risks. But—" She scanned the face she knew so well for all the secrets between them. "But I've never heard you talk as you did to Mr. O'Roarke."

He looked down at her. "You knew I had doubts. You knew how frustrated I've been these past months."

"I did because I can read you. You haven't talked about it."

"Perhaps not. Perhaps I haven't articulated it, even to myself." His gaze moved over the street ahead. A young man had dropped a sheaf of papers. His two friends were scrambling to help him gather them up before the wind made off with them. "O'Roarke has a way of drawing one out. He always did, even when I was a boy. I've never spoken about my feelings easily, but I'd find myself confiding things to him I'd scarcely even realized I was feeling."

It was a knack Raoul had, though she'd always thought of him as more tactical than emotional. And she hadn't thought of him using that knack on Malcolm.

Malcolm watched one of the young men dart across the narrow

street after an errant paper. "I still can't credit that he knew about Tania. Though he and my mother were friends."

"I imagine your mother must have been desperately in need of confidants." Suzanne could sympathize with a young wife burdened with secrets. And Lady Arabella hadn't had a husband she loved.

They moved past the three students, who had managed to gather up all the papers. "Would you mind?" Malcolm asked.

"Mind what?"

"If I wasn't a diplomat anymore."

"It's your life, dearest."

"Which you've made yours. You're a quite brilliant diplomatic hostess. Don't tell me you don't enjoy it."

"I suppose I do in a way." To her own surprise, she realized she spoke the truth. "At first it was simply a challenge, one I wasn't at all sure I could meet."

"You've never faced a challenge you couldn't meet."

"Oh, darling. How well I've fooled you."

He grinned. "False modesty doesn't become you, Suzette." He glanced up and down the street. "You can't deny you'd miss it."

"I suppose I would, in a way." It might be a role, but for all its artificiality she'd come to enjoy playing it. "But that's what women do. Build their lives round their husbands."

Malcolm grimaced. "Don't let Juliette hear you talk."

"I didn't say I approved the practice. But I could hardly be happy insisting you live a life you don't want simply so I could go on playing a role. And it's not as though I don't share your frustrations."

"So if I did leave the service—"

"You aren't just a diplomat, darling."

"No. But the same qualms apply doubly when it comes to being a spy."

Suzanne tilted her head back so she could look up at him without the brim of her bonnet getting in the way. "I was wondering if you'd miss it."

"The challenge?"

"The adventure."

"That's hardly something one builds one's life round."

"That doesn't mean you wouldn't miss it." For she knew she would.

"For Colin's sake it might be better if we were more settled."

She swallowed. "I don't know that we're settled sorts of people, Malcolm." She looked down at her threadnet glove against the blue superfine of his sleeve. He still had his coats tailored in London. "I suppose we'd live in England."

He stared at a bookseller's sign, swinging on its iron mounting. "I'm not sure—"

"That you want to go back."

She saw the flinch in his eyes, the instinctive recoil from whatever had driven him from his family and the land of his birth.

"Perhaps it's time I faced it," he said. "But I'm not sure I want to put you and Colin through that."

"Part of being married means one doesn't have to go through things alone. Unless of course you'd prefer it."

He shot a look at her.

"Sometimes sharing one's life can be a burden. And I'm not just talking about sharing the dressing table and chest of drawers in cramped lodgings."

His mouth twisted. "I know I don't share myself easily. You put up with a lot."

"Actually, you're a ridiculously undemanding husband, Malcolm." Though it was the last thing she'd have thought when she married him, sometimes she wished his emotional demands were greater.

"And you're a remarkable wife. But you deserve better than the man I fear I'd be in Britain."

It was on their one visit to Britain, a year ago, that she'd realized she loved Malcolm for better or worse. Seeing him in London and in his beloved Scotland, she'd glimpsed sides of him she hadn't seen before. The vulnerable schoolboy. The conflicted son and brother. The loyal, teasing friend. But she'd also realized just how much of himself he kept locked away and how unlikely it was she'd ever discover the key.

"We needn't go to Britain if you'd rather not," she said. "There's the Continent to choose from. And beyond. Though I saw enough last summer to think a part of you would like to go home. And give Colin the chance to grow up where you did." For the world his mother had grown up in was gone.

"Perhaps. Though thank God there's no way he'll have the childhood I had." He put his hand over her own where it curled round his arm. "I won't do anything without consulting with you. I promise."

"I'm good at rebuilding my life, dearest." She drew a breath. "For now we have more immediate concerns. Like how we're going to convince Juliette to confide in Rupert and Gabrielle."

CHAPTER 32

Malcolm turned to Juliette as they stood in the courtyard of Rupert and Gabrielle's house. A gust of wind ruffled the clouds over the moon, illuminating her wide, still eyes. "Are you sure about this?"

"Not in the least." Juliette's voice was level, but she was very pale above the dark blue folds of her cloak. "But we need their help. There's no time to question further."

Suzanne touched Juliette's arm. "Malcolm was imprisoned last autumn. I knew I needed help. I had to decide whom to trust. Whom I could risk trusting. Because the alternative was unthinkable."

Juliette nodded. "So let's just move forwards. No sense postponing the risk once we've decided to run it."

Malcolm nodded and rang the bell.

Juliette cast a glance round the marble-tiled entrance hall. Her gaze moved from the gilt chandelier to the satinwood pier table to the silver filigree basket for calling cards. "Not the sort of place I ever expected to be connected to."

"Even aristocrats can be quite decent," Malcolm said. "Speaking from hearsay of course."

Juliette flashed a smile at him, surprise mixed with gratitude.

Suzanne followed Juliette up the stairs, remembering a time—

not so very long ago—when she had felt as out of place in this sumptuous, alien world. This world she was now a part of. That her own son had been born into.

Gabrielle and Rupert were not alone in the salon. Gui Laclos walked forwards at the opening of the door. "I expect you have matters to discuss," he said after Malcolm had introduced Juliette. "I was just going."

"No." Malcolm exchanged a look with Suzanne. "I'd prefer it if you could stay. This is a family matter."

Gui gave a dry laugh, but at a look from Gabrielle he dropped back into his chair.

"Mademoiselle Dubretton has something to say you should all hear," Malcolm said.

Juliette drew a breath. Suzanne recognized the hesitation before the moment when one voiced a truth that could change one's life as one knew it. The moment she herself couldn't contemplate. Then Juliette told her story with the economy of a master wordsmith.

Gabrielle stared from Juliette to Malcolm and Suzanne, then looked back at Juliette. "You're saying your son is Étienne's son?"

Juliette swallowed but did not look away from Gabrielle's gaze. "I'm saying he might be. Even Princess Tatiana didn't know for sure. My husband and I have no wish for Pierre to be other than what he is."

"I understand that," Gabrielle said. "I have a little boy myself." She leaned towards Juliette. "I think I speak for my husband and brother as well when I say that none of us has any wish to change your relationship to the boy. But we can't help but feel an obligation to him."

Juliette drew a breath. "But—"

"Madame St.—Mademoiselle Dubretton." Rupert got to his feet. "We can discuss this with you and your husband and I'm sure arrive upon an amicable solution. After we get your husband out of prison." He looked from her to Malcolm. "That's why you told us, isn't it? You're going to get him out and you need our help."

"I hope that's why they told us," Gui said.

Malcolm outlined their plan.

"You think it will work?" Rupert asked.

"I think it can work. If we all play our parts."

Rupert nodded. "You have no idea what a relief uncomplicated action is."

"I couldn't agree with you more," Gui said.

Malcolm glanced round the group assembled in their salon in the Rue du Faubourg Saint-Honoré. Wilhelmine and Dorothée seated on the sofa. Cordelia in the damask wingback chair with Harry perched on the arm. David and Simon on a pair of straight-backed gilt chairs. He was used to thinking of himself as living an isolated life, but these six people were friends. More than that. In their own way, they were all family. They listened in admirable silence as he explained the situation. None of them was given to asking unnecessary questions, and by now they'd all been through enough to temper any shocked exclamations or gasps of surprise.

"You want our help," David said when Malcolm finished.

"We're hoping for it."

"Of course. That is, I can only speak for myself—"

"As can I," Simon said.

"I'd be distinctly cross if you left me out," Cordelia said.

"A mission where one can be confident of being on the right side," Harry said. "I didn't think those existed anymore."

Malcolm met his friend's gaze. "If Wellington or Castlereagh finds out—"

"Don't be an idiot, Malcolm. I know what I'm risking. And I know you'd do precisely the same in my situation."

"You're a man after my own heart, Colonel Davenport," Wilhelmine said. She looked from Malcolm to Suzanne. "I don't pretend to your expertise in these matters, but I know the easiest way to get Juliette Dubretton and her children out of Paris. No guards dare to ask questions about the carriage of a Princess of Courland."

"Two Princesses of Courland," Dorothée said.

Wilhelmine smiled at her sister. "And I'm known to often travel with my maids' children."

"I confess I was hoping for as much," Suzanne said.

Malcolm quickly outlined the rest of the plan. Harry nodded

matter-of-factly. Even David, who was a stranger to such adventures, merely looked a bit disappointed that his own role didn't require more.

It was already late, so the company broke up soon after. Wilhelmine moved to Malcolm's side amid the rustle of fabric and murmurs of "good night."

"Malcolm."

Malcolm looked down at his sister's sister. Her direct gaze held unaccustomed trouble. "Stewart?" he asked.

"He knows I'm working with you. Needless to say, he wasn't happy about it."

"I'm sorry."

She shrugged. "He's not the first lover I've quarreled with. Or the last. Were it merely that, I wouldn't have burdened you with our tiresome quarrel. But he actually went as far as to order me to stop assisting you."

"I don't imagine you took that well."

"How well you know me. He was...afraid." Wilhelmine plucked at an embroidered fold of her skirt. "I don't think I've ever seen him so afraid."

"Of?"

"Something he fears you might still discover." She drew a breath. "I think it's to do with Bertrand Laclos. Stewart knows something about him. Something beyond the fact that he subsequently proved to be innocent. Something he's deathly afraid will come to light."

Malcolm scanned her face. "Do you have any idea what?"

She shook her head, brows drawn. "I can't believe he knew Laclos was innocent at the time he ordered his death. But— He refused to confide in me."

"Do you think—"

"That I can draw him out in the future? I fear I won't be in a position to do so. Stewart gave me an ultimatum. I don't take kindly to ultimatums."

Malcolm studied her proud face and steady eyes. "I'm sorry."

"I should have realized it would end sooner or later."

"He meant a great deal to you."

"More than he should have. I don't know how I could have been mad enough to imagine tying myself to him. For weeks I'd put up with knowing all about him and the fair Ninette at the opera, not to mention God knows how many others."

Malcolm touched her arm. "The man clearly has no taste if he couldn't see— What did you say her name was?"

"Ninette. Do you know her?"

"Rivère also had a mistress who was an opera dancer named Ninette. An odd coincidence. Which I suspect is something more."

Wilhelmine gripped his fingers where they lay on her arm. "Stewart is foolish and pigheaded. But he's also dangerous. Perhaps never more so than when he's cornered. And if he finds out what we're doing he'll go straight to his brother and do incalculable damage for you and Colonel Davenport."

Malcolm nodded. "We can but be careful."

"I don't know how I could have come so close to being seduced by a safe existence. Adventure is so much more satisfying."

"That sounds like something Tania would have said."

Wilhelmine smiled. "Well, she was my sister."

Blanca stared at Suzanne across Suzanne and Malcolm's bedchamber. "You're going disguised as a maid."

"Don't say that with such disdain. I've played a maid before."

Blanca snorted. She'd served as Suzanne's ladies' maid since Suzanne's masquerade as Mrs. Malcolm Rannoch had begun, but in truth was more of a companion. "It will probably do you good to be reminded of how most of the world lives."

"Yes, that's just what I was thinking."

Blanca pulled a face at her, then laughed and set down the chemise she'd been folding. "And Mr. Rannoch will be there as well?"

"Not with me, but on the same mission. Yes." Suzanne took a nightdress from the laundry basket beside Blanca and began to fold it.

Blanca reached for another chemise. "And Mr. O'Roarke."

Suzanne smoothed the muslin frill at the neck of the nightdress. "Yes, he'll be part of it as well."

Blanca folded the chemise, her gaze not leaving Suzanne's face. "You're playing with fire."

Suzanne pressed a stubborn crease from the frill. "When have I done anything else?"

CHAPTER 33

In general, civilians were a drawback on a mission. They were liable to get overexcited and take unnecessary risks. One could never be sure which way they'd jump in a crisis, and they often needed rescuing at the awkwardest moments. Yet Suzanne couldn't deny that the excitement of Wilhelmine and Dorothée was infectious. Their bright eyes and high color took her back to the start of her time as a spy, when choices and loyalties had seemed simpler, when the thrill of adventure was as bright and unsullied as new-fallen snow. A thrill of adventure that, if she was honest, was as much a part of her love of her work as were her Republican ideals.

Juliette could hardly be said to share that thrill. Her face was set with determination, but her hands were steady as they held Rose, a baby of about ten months, in her lap. Rose, mercifully, had fallen asleep as they pulled away from Wilhelmine's house. Juliette and Suzanne wore gowns borrowed from Wilhelmine's maids Hanchen and Annina, who had once served Tatiana Kirsanova. Six-year-old Marguerite sat bolt upright on the seat between Juliette and Suzanne, studying the two glamorous women across the carriage from them.

Wilhelmine and Dorothée leaned back against the watered-silk squabs, ruched and flounced skirts spread round them. Pearls showed beneath the satin ribbons on Doro's bonnet and emeralds beneath the tulle scarf that anchored Willie's hat. They had dressed to accentuate their positions as Princesses of Courland. They might not be agents, but both knew the role costume played in creating a persona.

Young Pierre sat between them. He and Marguerite were old enough to understand the seriousness of what was happening but young enough still to be wide-eyed with adventure. And to trust that the adults would make sure everything came out right. Trust could be a frightening burden.

Colin squirmed in Suzanne's lap. Bringing him was perhaps another violation of the rules that should govern an agent's behavior. She had told herself it would be helpful to have an extra child in the mix, so the group with them didn't exactly mirror the St. Gilles brood. But the truth was she hadn't wanted to leave him behind, not knowing how long she might be gone. It wasn't the first time she had taken him with her on a mission.

Wilhelmine glanced out the dark glass of the window. "Not far to the gates now." She must have noted, as Suzanne did, the tension that shot through Juliette, for she added, "Doro and I went out of the city together only last week. The guards just wave us through."

"You don't think they'll notice that your maids look rather different?" Juliette asked.

"I very much doubt it," Wilhelmine said. She seemed about to add more, then checked herself as though realizing it was impolitic.

"People don't look at the servants," Suzanne said, steadying Colin as he turned to the window. "It affords the same anonymity as the uniforms the men are wearing."

Juliette gave a wry smile and nodded.

"Do we need to do anything special?" Pierre asked, looking between the adults.

Wilhelmine flashed a smile at him. "Just pretend we're on an adventure. Which we are."

Rose stirred in Juliette's arms and gave a small but insistent cry. Juliette unfastened the flap on the front of her bodice and put the baby to her breast with the ease of long practice.

The carriage picked up speed as they left behind the crowds at the center of Paris, then slowed as they approached the gates. Wilhelmine's coachman had their papers, but she turned to the window and lowered the glass. "Sergeant Hébert. How lovely to see you again. You scarcely get a day to yourself, do you?"

The sergeant's ruddy face appeared outside the window. A sharp, dark gaze swept the interior of the carriage.

"Don't stare at my maid." Wilhelmine leaned out the window to tap him on the shoulder. "You must be used to the sight of a woman feeding her baby. It isn't a display for men to leer at. You will be a dear and not detain us long, won't you? I fear we're shockingly late for the Duchesse de Lagarde's fête. My sister had the hardest time choosing a shawl."

"Don't listen to her, Sergeant." Dorothée leaned over her sister's shoulder. "It was the duchess herself who had to have her hair dressed three times."

Suzanne kept her gaze demurely lowered, in keeping with her role, but she heard the sergeant's easy laugh. Colin cuddled against her. He had a good instinct for when to be quiet. A stir of movement followed, and a call of "Let this carriage pass."

Reins snapped and wheels rattled. Suzanne smiled across the carriage at Willie and Doro as they pulled forwards. Amateurs or not, the sisters had a knack for this.

"Are we safe?" Marguerite asked in a small voice.

"Very nearly," Wilhelmine said. "The rest of the journey should be easy."

"Do you like backgammon?" Dorothée opened a mahogany compartment in the carriage and took out a traveling set. "We can entertain ourselves until we get to the inn."

Now that they had passed the gates and inspection, they rearranged themselves in the carriage, Marguerite and Pierre sitting with Dorothée and the backgammon board, Wilhelmine moving across the carriage to sit by Suzanne and Juliette and the younger children.

"Thank you," Juliette said, looking into Wilhelmine's eyes.

"Your children are a delight." Wilhelmine's gaze focused on Pierre and Marguerite. An ache of loss flashed into her eyes, then was quickly banished. She looked back at Juliette. "And I'd say that even if nothing else bound me to them."

Open country flashed by outside the window as they picked up speed. Suzanne felt some of the tension ease from her shoulders. Experienced or not, one never lost the wariness. Or one did at one's peril.

Juliette switched Rose to her other breast. Pierre won the first backgammon game, and they began another.

"You look so wonderfully relaxed," Wilhelmine said to Suzanne.

"Never that. One can't risk losing one's edge."

The carriage slowed abruptly. Pierre and Marguerite looked about with anxious faces.

"Probably just something in the road," Dorothée said, steadying the backgammon board.

Juliette smiled at her children, though Suzanne saw her fingers tighten on Rose's lavender blanket.

A muffled voice sounded through the glass of the windows. It sounded like "Papers?"

Wilhelmine shot a glance at Suzanne, drew a breath, and opened the window. "Why the delay?"

Another face appeared at the window. "Your papers, madame?"

"My coachman has them. But we already presented them at the gates. I don't appreciate the delay."

Over Wilhelmine's shoulder, Suzanne could see the uniform of the soldier outside the window and at least four more men beyond him. They would have muskets.

A pause, the rustle of paper as he examined the documents Wilhelmine's coachman had given him. "I fear we must ask you to step from the carriage, madame."

"Step from the carriage? Into the mud? What is this?" Wilhelmine demanded. "Do you know who I am?"

"If you'll forgive me, madame, I know who your papers say you are."

Wilhelmine drew a breath of pure outrage, probably only partly feigned. "The effrontery—"

"These are unsettled times, madame. We must use caution. I'm sure you appreciate that as well as anyone."

"How dare you—"

"We've had reports of an escape from Paris by suspected traitors."

"Surely you can't think that has anything to do with my sister and me."

"We must proceed with all caution, madame."

"Willie, what on earth is the delay?" Dorothée demanded. "I never heard anything so tiresome. We're going to be so late for the fête we might as well have stayed in Paris."

"If you'll step from the carriage, madame. Madame," the soldier said, acknowledging both princesses. "This won't take long."

Wilhelmine flicked a glance at Suzanne under cover of looking at her sister. Suzanne inclined her head a fraction of an inch. Their options were limited. If they made a run for it they'd rouse suspicion with armed men on their tail. An easy target.

They climbed from the carriage, Dorothée holding Marguerite and Pierre by the hand, Suzanne carrying Colin, who clung tightly to her, Juliette soothing Rose, who had begun to cry again, sensing the adults' fear.

There were five soldiers, counting the man in a lieutenant's uniform who had ordered them from the carriage. The men stood respectfully at attention, but they ringed the women. Suzanne was all too aware that they were surrounded with the carriage at their back. And her own son in her arms. She pressed a kiss to Colin's head and handed him to Dorothée. Dorothée accepted him without question. Colin looked at Suzanne but went into Tante Doro's arms willingly. It might look odd to the soldiers for a maid to give her child to her mistress, but it couldn't be helped. Suzanne suspected she would need her hands free.

The lieutenant's gaze swept the small group and settled on Pierre. "What's your name, young man?"

"Michel." Pierre delivered the alias with the easy skill of a trained agent. Perhaps some of it was in the blood.

"Right. If you'll come with me, young Michel, the ladies can be on their way."

"What?" Wilhelmine's arm shot out in an instinctive gesture to protect the child, the way Suzanne would protect Colin when their carriage came to a sudden stop.

"No need to trouble yourself, madame," the lieutenant said. "All we want is the boy."

Tension ran through the women in a palpable wave. Juliette's hand tightened on her son's shoulder.

"That's absurd," Dorothée said. "He's only a child."

"Nevertheless."

"You can't possibly imagine I'd acquiesce," Wilhelmine said at her most imperious.

"I don't believe you have a choice, madame." The lieutenant drew a pistol from inside his coat and leveled it at them. "The boy."

CHAPTER 34

Children changed everything. Suzanne had heard that more than once when she was pregnant with Colin. She'd nodded her head, but she hadn't properly understood it until Malcolm placed the baby on her breast and she felt the joy and terror of what she owed this small, blue-tinged, squirming human. It was never truer than when one faced danger. Any number of options for escape were impossible with the safety of four children at stake. And yet the threat to the eldest of those children made escape imperative.

Suzanne gave a cry and crumpled to the ground, twisting her legs under her to avoid banging her knees in the trick her actress mother had taught her for fainting onstage.

"Maman!" Colin screamed. Heartrending but effective. Fortunately, they'd been speaking French in the carriage. Colin switched back and forth between calling her "Mummy" and "Maman."

"Margot!" Wilhelmine dropped to her knees beside Suzanne and began to chafe her wrists. "I think she's hit her head. Oh, what have you done?"

"She's just pretending," one of the soldiers muttered.

"She isn't," Wilhelmine cried. "Come and see."

Suzanne could hear Doro murmuring to Colin. The lieutenant's boots thudded on the ground as he took a step forwards. Suzanne moaned, half pushed herself up, then gave a cry and reached into her bodice as though gasping for breath. Her fingers closed round her pistol, tucked into her corset. She moaned again and collapsed back, the pistol concealed in her palm.

The lieutenant loomed over her, muddy boots and buff breeches. "Here now, what the devil—"

Suzanne pushed herself up, the pistol pointed between the lieutenant's legs. "I advise you to let us go. If you ever want to produce children of your own. Or even enjoy the attempt."

His gaze shot down. The look of horror that crossed his face would have been comical in other circumstances. "You damned bitch—"

"Watch your tongue." She pressed the pistol into his groin.

"My men are armed."

"Oh yes. They could do incalculable damage. But not before I unmanned you. Not that I think much of the sort of father you'd make, but somehow I don't think you want to lose what I could destroy."

A vein fairly popped in his forehead, yet his mouth was white with fear. "Who are you?"

"I might ask the same question, but I fear we haven't time for pleasantries."

He drew a breath.

She pressed the gun into his flesh. "Tell your men to drop their muskets and withdraw to the tree line."

Gut-churning silence for perhaps the length of half a dozen heartbeats. Then, "Sergeant," he said in a hoarse voice. "Withdraw."

A moment of silence, then the clatter of muskets being dropped to the ground.

"Very good," Suzanne said. "And drop your own pistol."

The lieutenant did so.

"Madame," Suzanne said to Wilhelmine, not taking her eyes off the lieutenant, "get everyone back in the carriage. If we have the least trouble, I fire," she added to the lieutenant.

A rustle of fabric and patter of footsteps followed as the Courland sisters and Juliette got the children into the carriage with admirable economy. Suzanne picked up the pistol the lieutenant had dropped on the ground. Gaze trained on him, she eased herself to her feet.

The lieutenant shot out a hand to grab her arm. Suzanne dealt him a blow to the side of his head with his pistol. She pulled out the string she kept threaded loosely through her corset and bound his wrists in case he had any thoughts of going after the dropped muskets before they were away, then dealt him another blow to the head. Wilhelmine's coachman was already back on the box with the steps raised. Suzanne shot him a look of approval and sprang back up into the carriage. He gave the horses their office as she was slamming the door closed behind her.

She fell back on the seat beside Wilhelmine and Dorothée and took Colin from Doro. Colin's arms closed tight round her neck. "All right?" he asked, tilting his head back to look at her.

"Splendid." She kissed his hair and tightened her own arms round him.

Across the carriage Juliette had Rose pressed to her breast and Marguerite and Pierre snuggled up on either side of her. Suzanne drew a breath. Dorothée turned to look at her. "You're frightened."

"I'll own it was more of a near run thing than I'd have liked." Suzanne smoothed Colin's hair. Her fingers were shaking. Not the worst danger she'd ever been in, but the threat to Pierre had put it in a whole different key.

Marguerite's wide blue gaze swept over the adults. "Why did those men want Pierre?"

Silence washed over the carriage, different from the fear of a few moments before. "I don't know." Juliette reached out to touch her son's cheek.

"Did they want to put me in prison like the soldiers who took Papa?" Pierre asked.

"I don't think they actually were soldiers," Suzanne said. "The uniforms were good, but the insignia on the lieutenant's sleeve was wrong."

"Then who were they?" Dorothée asked.

"I'm not sure." Over Colin's head, Suzanne's gaze locked on Juliette's. Juliette looked back steadily.

"Will you show us how you stopped them?" Marguerite asked. "That was splendid."

" 'Once more unto the breech.' " Simon adjusted his bicorne hat. "Takes me back to our undergraduate days."

"Wrong play." Malcolm smoothed the facings on his coat. He and David had met Simon and their friend Oliver in an Oxford production of *Henry IV Part I*.

"Same characters." Simon twitched his cuffs straight. "This one's more appropriate for adventure. 'Follow your spirit, and upon this charge—' "

" 'Cry God for Harry, England, and St. George.' " Malcolm cast a glance up and down the street. "Pity Davenport isn't here."

Harry had in fact volubly objected to not being part of the party that went into the Conciergerie disguised as soldiers. Malcolm had had to forcefully point out that one of them with legitimate diplomatic connections had to remain on the outside in the event that anything went wrong. Harry had muttered about Malcolm's "annoying logic" but had subsided. David hadn't appeared particularly happy about his role, either, though with typical David restraint he'd refrained from objecting. He couldn't quarrel with the fact that Simon was more skilled at playacting. So Simon and Malcolm were making their way over the Pont Neuf and along the Quai de L'Horlage along with O'Roarke and Rupert, garbed in the uniforms of French soldiers. Malcolm felt the resentful glances cast their way. One or two men actually muttered curses as they passed. Frenchmen who fought for the king were not popular with some of their compatriots.

"St. Gilles knows what to do," Rupert said. "He's a quick study. It should all go smoothly."

"Quite," O'Roarke said.

To their right rose the stone walls of the Palais de Justice, the massive Gothic palace that had once been the home to French kings. Four towers marked the portion of the palace known as the

Conciergerie, which had served as a prison for over five hundred years. Malcolm could hear his voice explaining them to Colin, perched on his shoulders, on a ramble round Paris. He'd told Colin about the Tour d'Argent, which had held the royal treasure, and the Tour de l'Horlage, which bore the first public clock in Paris. But not about the Tour de César, where the public prosecutor had sent hundreds of Royalists to their deaths during the Terror. Or the Tour Bonbec, the babbling tower, where prisoners held for torture learned to speak.

They presented their credentials and made their way down a maze of passages, beneath vaulted ceilings that rose to darkness, past shadowy cells in which movement was dimly visible behind iron bars. Rupert and Malcolm walked ahead, Rupert silently leading the way. Head held high, no need to hide, relying on the cloaking power of the uniform like a magic garment in one of Colin's fairy tales.

Once they were in the door, the jailers didn't trouble them. The prison was full, the jailers were busy, few stopped to ask questions. Everyone assumed they must have legitimate business.

Rupert stopped in front of an iron-bound door. St. Gilles's cell was conveniently located just past a bend in the passage. While O'Roarke and Simon kept watch and Rupert covered him, Malcolm attacked the lock with his picklocks. It gave with surprising ease. Old and heavy but not particularly complicated.

St. Gilles was on his feet when Malcolm pushed the door open.

"I gave even odds on whether or not you'd actually appear," St. Gilles said.

"You should have more faith in our word," Malcolm said, pushing the door to after Rupert followed him into the cell.

"Not that. I thought you might not make it this far."

"Then you should have more faith in our wit."

Rupert was already stripping off his uniform coat. In less than ten minutes, St. Gilles was dressed in Rupert's uniform, Rupert was buttoning the coat that he'd smuggled into St. Gilles's cell on an earlier visit along with breeches, waistcoat, shirt, and boots, and Malcolm was arranging St. Gilles's discarded clothing over the pillows. With the blankets drawn up, it should serve to deceive a guard glancing through the grill in the door. Long enough to let them get away. In theory.

Without speaking they returned to the passage. Malcolm used his picklocks to relock the door. He and St. Gilles fell in step beside O'Roarke and Simon. Rupert moved past them and made his way briskly through the maze of passages to the gate. A breeze from the courtyard carried the guard's surprised accents down the passage.

"Didn't realize you were here, Monsieur Caruthers."

"Didn't you?" Rupert asked with careless unconcern. "I've been in the plaguey place an hour or more. Tiresome errand for my father. I'm inclined to tell him he can ask his own questions."

"Doesn't seem to have been noted down." The guard was different from the one who would have been on duty an hour ago. They had timed that carefully.

"Doesn't it? Well, I'm not entirely surprised." Rupert leaned forwards across the desk in a confiding attitude. "Renard seemed a bit distracted when I arrived. A pretty wife was presenting her papers to see her husband. I'm sure Renard would appreciate it if you amended the record. I won't tell anyone if you don't."

The guard coughed. "Thank you, Monsieur Caruthers. Much obliged."

Rupert strolled out into the courtyard. When Malcolm, St. Gilles, O'Roarke, and Simon reached the desk, the guard was absorbed in scribbling on a piece of paper (no doubt amending the record to show that Lord Caruthers had indeed entered the prison). He hastily pulled a ledger over the paper and waved them through, too concerned with his own indiscretion being discovered to pay them much heed.

Malcolm released his breath as they stepped out of the shadow of the prison walls.

"Don't tell me you were nervous," St. Gilles said.

"Always."

"I thought you were a professional."

"Enough so to be aware of the risks."

St. Gilles gave a low laugh. "You're very like your sister."

Malcolm nearly stumbled on the cobblestones. He forced himself to keep walking and swung his gaze to St. Gilles. "She told you."

St. Gilles looked back at him steadily. "Tania and I were closer than my original account might have led you to believe."

"Yes, so I've discovered."

"And the physical intimacy was the least of it." St. Gilles regarded him for a moment with a steady blue gaze. "There was a note in her voice when she talked about you. Though she moved through throngs of people, she was very much alone. But if she had any family it was you."

"You're a kind man, St. Gilles."

"I didn't say it to be kind."

"I thought I knew her. I thought we were close. Closer in some ways than I am to my brother and sister in Britain. But not close enough apparently for her to confide in me about her child."

"She said much the same about you when you married."

"When I—" Malcolm stared into St. Gilles's steady gaze. "I told Tania I was marrying Suzanne. It was just before she left Spain."

St. Gilles's eyes glinted in the sunlight. "So Tania told me when she returned to Paris. And she said you hadn't begun to explain how you felt about your wife. Or why you were marrying her. But she was sure it was infinitely more complicated than you admitted. She said it with a laugh, but in truth I think she was a bit hurt."

"That wasn't—" Malcolm broke off. "I had other people to think about." Though in fairness, he'd been protecting himself as much as Suzanne and Colin. His feelings about his wife and marriage went too deep to share, even with Tania.

"I think Tania felt the same."

"But I wouldn't—"

"Have revealed her secret? She'd have said the same to you."

Malcolm recalled Tatiana's teasing, faintly mocking voice when he told her about his marriage. Had he missed an undertone of hurt? He'd prided himself on being good at reading his sister. But God knows he'd been preoccupied at the time. "I still don't see why she was so determined to keep it secret," he said.

For a moment something shifted in St. Gilles's eyes. Then he gave a low laugh. "Perhaps she was embarrassed. I was hardly in her usual style. But Laclos—"

"Was dead. Whatever we may think of Napoleon's government, they didn't prosecute the children of traitors. In fact, they were rather more respecting of liberties than my own government."

St. Gilles drew a breath. "You knew Tania. She could be quixotic. Oh, look— Those must be our horses."

From the side one would swear the Kestrel really was an old woman. Cordelia studied the line of his shoulders, curved inwards beneath the frayed paisley shawl. The profile, surely more delicate than that of the seemingly elderly man she had first met before he changed into this disguise. The mouth sunken, as though half her teeth had been pulled.

"You're looking at a master," Harry murmured. His own hair was disordered, his face smeared with dirt. Though he was far less disguised than the Kestrel. As was she. Cordelia studied the Kestrel, head bent over a piece of knitting. She suspected he wasn't in disguise only to hide from the authorities. Was there anyone, she wondered, watching the droop of his eyelids, with whom he was really himself?

A clock struck twelve-fifteen. "Time to be off," the Kestrel murmured without raising his head. He spoke in the Gascon French they were using in their guise of a peddler family.

"How do we know they made it out on time?" Cordelia asked.

"We have to assume they did," the Kestrel said.

Harry flicked the cart reins to set the donkey in motion. Cordelia climbed onto the seat beside him. He cast a surprised glance at her.

"We're supposed to look like a devoted couple," she said. "Don't worry, I've been well coached. I won't give us away." She tucked her arm through his. "I like seeing what your work is like."

"It's generally less agreeable than this." Harry cast a glance back at the Kestrel. "I envy him."

" 'Envy'?"

"Serving no master, choosing whom to help, doing what he thinks is right."

She leaned her head against Harry's arm. "You do what you think is right. It's one of the things I've always admired about you."

"I'm flattered. But if I were that independent I'd have been court-martialed long since."

As they neared the gates, Cordelia caught sight of a quartet of soldiers, pulled up to the side of the road in the shade of a stand of trees.

"Right on schedule," Harry murmured. She felt his gaze on her.

"It's all right," she said. "I know what to do." She let her shawl slither down on her shoulders and tugged her laced bodice lower. Not so different from interrogating Edmond Talleyrand.

Harry pulled the cart up at the guard post. A thickset man in a sergeant's uniform approached the cart. Cordelia felt his gaze linger on her. She shifted her position on the seat, affording him a glimpse of her ankle beneath her calico skirt and linen petticoat.

"Papers?" the sergeant asked Harry, his gaze still on Cordelia's ankle.

Harry pulled out the creased papers the Kestrel had supplied. The sergeant tore his gaze away from Cordelia's ankle long enough to glance through them. "These are water spotted."

"Rosewater," Harry muttered. "My wife knocked it over on them. Can't keep her things from spilling over the dressing table."

"I could if I had one of my own." Cordelia looked at the sergeant from beneath her eyelashes. She hoped the Gascon accent would mask the fact that she wasn't a native French speaker. Her French wasn't as good as Harry's, but thanks to her émigrée governess it was better than that of most Englishwomen.

The sergeant sniffed the papers, which had indeed been soaked in rosewater, in just the right place to blur the forged signature.

"All the same, you'd best get out of the cart. Let me have a look."

"Damnation," Harry said. "We come through here every—"

"*Chéri.*" Cordelia put a hand on his arm. "Don't make things worse. And don't alarm your mother."

"Maman's made of tougher stuff than that. Aren't you?" Harry looked back at the Kestrel.

The Kestrel set down his knitting, cast a baleful glance at the sergeant, and clambered to his feet. "Give me a hand, young man," he said to the sergeant, who was extending a hand to Cordelia. "And stop ogling my daughter-in-law."

The sergeant handed Cordelia down from the cart. Cordelia kicked up her skirt to afford a glimpse of the garters on her white cotton stockings as she slid to the ground. The sergeant managed to brush his hand against the side of her left breast in the process of assisting her and then turned with a grimace to assist the Kestrel. Harry glared at him in character.

"Don't be stupid," Cordelia muttered to him in a stage whisper. "You'll get us taken in."

The sergeant jerked his head at two of his men to go through the cart, while he patted each of them down. His hands lingered on Cordelia. It was no worse than the wandering hands of under-graduates in a Mayfair ballroom, but Cordelia thought Harry's glare was not entirely playacting now.

"What's this?" One of the soldiers held up a bottle from beneath the floorboards.

"Water," Harry said.

The sergeant sniffed the bottle, took a swig, and gave an appreciative grunt. "No, it's all right, I won't confiscate it. If you were selling it you'd have more bottles."

"Nothing else," another of the soldiers said a few minutes later. Which was as it should be, for the cart did indeed contain nothing more than their supposed peddlers' wares.

"Well?" Harry demanded. "Can we go?"

The sergeant glanced in the cart, glanced at them again, then inclined his head. He handed Cordelia back up onto the box and managed to get his hand on her right breast this time.

"Pulled a thread, you have," the Kestrel said, picking up his knitting.

Harry snapped the reins, the cart wheels groaned, and they rattled forwards, through the gates of Paris.

Cordelia leaned against Harry's shoulder. The solid warmth of his flesh felt singularly reassuring. "We made it," she said at last.

"We'd probably have made it without having to get out of the cart if the sergeant hadn't wanted to get a better look at your legs."

"But you have to admit it left him thoroughly befuddled. If he's asked about us, I'm all he'll remember."

"Very true. I'm just sorry you had to go through being mauled."

She shrugged. "It's not the first time. Oh dear, that is—"

He lifted a brow. "I'm difficult to shock."

"I'm glad flirtation has a productive use."

"You're a natural at this." His mouth twisted in a dry smile. "I mean espionage."

She looked up at him. "Did you ever—"

"I'm hardly the sort to whom seduction comes easily."

"But there's very little you can't do when you put your mind to it. In the service of Crown and country." Her voice was playful, but the images that flashed into her mind were distinctly unsettling.

"You've heard me rail against Crown and country often enough."

"But I know just how loyal you are."

Harry fixed his gaze on the donkey's back. "I fear there are few deceptions I've failed to put into practice in the course of my work."

Cordelia swallowed. Hard. "I wouldn't have expected anything less, dearest."

O'Roarke put down his spyglass. "Good. They're safely away. That took a bit longer than anticipated, but I think that might be due to Lady Cordelia's powers of distraction."

He tucked the spyglass back into his coat. They waited another five minutes, then touched their heels to their horses and galloped from beneath the shelter of the stand of trees and down the main road to the gates.

"Have you seen a peddler's cart?" Malcolm demanded of the sergeant who stood guard, pulling up on the reins of his horse and making his breath sound labored.

"Peddler's cart?" the sergeant repeated.

"Yes, man. The peddler would have had his wife with him. And his mother."

The sergeant cast a glance about, as though already fearing he had made a mistake. "Er . . . yes, sir. It passed this way not ten minutes past."

"Damnation." Malcolm cast a glance over his shoulder at his three companions. "We've just missed them." He gathered up the reins.

"Sir," the sergeant said, "what—"

"That old woman is wanted for questioning by Fouché."

The sergeant blinked. "What would Fouché want with—"

"It's a disguise, you fool," O'Roarke said. "Open the gates. Quickly, man. We've already lost precious time."

"You heard the captain." The sergeant jerked his head at his men, perhaps eager to avoid questions about his detailed examination of the fugitives he had allowed to escape. "Open the gates. Be quick about it."

Two soldiers ran to comply. Malcolm, O'Roarke, Simon, and St. Gilles galloped through and out of the environs of Paris.

They had passed the first hurdle.

Gabrielle glanced out the inn window. "This does seem loweringly tame compared to what everyone else is doing."

"Waiting can be the hardest part," David Mallinson said. "And without us to meet them they'd be able to make it no further than this inn."

The two of them and Gui were in a first-floor private parlor of this inn along the road to Calais. The clothing and papers that would take Paul St. Gilles and Juliette Dubretton and their children out of France were stowed in a false compartment beneath the wicker hamper on the back of their barouche, presently in the inn's stable. No one had thought to question the fashionable aristocratic party, all easily recognizable and plainly bent on pleasure.

Gabrielle smiled at David. She'd always thought he had a kind heart, but she hadn't realized quite how much until now. Such a pity she couldn't find a man like him or Rupert who was interested in her. They were both much finer men than Antoine Rivère had been.

Gui paced across the room and poured himself a glass of wine from the bottle on the pier table between the windows. "That doesn't make the waiting easier."

Gabrielle bit her lip. "Don't. I can't help but worry—"

"I'm sorry, Gaby." Gui crossed to her side and gripped her shoulder. "But in his position Rupert would be the safest of any of them if they're discovered. Except perhaps Malcolm."

"I would have said so a few days ago," Gabrielle said, looking up at her brother. Her pretend brother. No, she couldn't stop thinking of him as a brother. "But now I'm not at all sure Lord Dewhurst would come to his rescue."

"He would." Gui held the glass out to her. "He'd want to save the family from the scandal if nothing else."

Gabrielle took a swallow of wine, deeper than she intended, and coughed. "There is that."

Gui squeezed her shoulder. When she made to hand the glass back to him, he shook his head and curled her fingers round the glass. She took another fortifying sip. "You must be worried about Mr. Tanner," she said to David.

"I—" He opened his mouth as though to protest, then said simply, "Yes."

She sensed that single word was an admission of trust. She looked into his eyes and smiled. An answering smile broke across David's reserved face.

Gui wandered back to the windows and picked up a fresh glass. "If— Good God." He froze in the midst of uncorking the bottle of wine, gaze fastened on the view outside the window.

"What?" Gabrielle sprang to her feet and ran to his side, prepared for armed soldiers or her husband in irons. Instead she saw a chaise drawn up in the inn yard. An ostler had hurried forwards to see to the horses. A man in a top hat and blue coat who must have descended from the carriage was speaking with the ostler. Then he turned towards the inn. "Dear God," Gabrielle breathed.

"What?" David hurried to her side.

Gabrielle reached for Gui's hand and squeezed it hard. "My father-in-law."

"What the devil is Dewhurst doing here?" David watched Dewhurst stride towards the inn.

Gabrielle swallowed. "Suppose he's learned that Rupert—"

"There's no proof of that." David touched her arm. "It could just be a coincidence."

"Well, whatever it is, we need a plan of action," Gui said. "We have a fugitive arriving at any moment whom Dewhurst will recognize."

"Do we have any laudanum?" Gabrielle asked. She was only in part joking.

"Whether it's a coincidence or not," David said, "that's the way to play it."

"With laudanum?" Gui asked.

"As a coincidence."

Gabrielle and David hurried out the door onto the landing. In the hall below, Gabrielle could hear her father-in-law's decisive accents and nearly native French. She couldn't quite make out the words, but she caught something about "dark-haired man." Dear God, was he trying to describe St. Gilles? But from her one glimpse of him at an exhibition at the Louvre she wouldn't have called St. Gilles dark haired.

"Lord Dewhurst!" She gathered up the jaconet folds of her skirt and and ran down the newel staircase. "We saw your carriage through the windows. What a surprise!"

"Gabrielle." Relief flashed across Dewhurst's face as he stared up at her. "Thank God."

Gabrielle nearly skidded on the stairs, caught herself on the railing, and ran down to her father-in-law's side. "Were you looking for me?"

"For Gui." Dewhurst caught her hands in a hard grip. "Is he with you?"

"Yes, he's just upstairs." Relief that Dewhurst seemed to know nothing of St. Gilles warred with confusion. "He came with Lord Worsley and me."

Dewhurst squeezed his eyes shut. "God be praised." He released Gabrielle's hands and ran up the stairs, pushing past David without acknowledgment.

Gabrielle exchanged a look of confusion with David and ran back up the stairs after Rupert's father, aware of a confused look from the serving maid and groom in the hall below.

She reached the landing as Dewhurst stepped over the threshold into their private parlor. "Gui. Thank God I've found you. You must come back to Paris immediately."

"Sir." Gui's footsteps sounded on the floorboards, concern sharp in his voice. "Is something the matter? Is it my uncle? Or my aunt?"

Gabrielle reached the open door to see Dewhurst stride across the room and seize Gui by the shoulders.

"Of course it's your uncle and aunt," he said. "Can you imagine they wouldn't be distressed to the breaking point by such a letter?"

Gui jerked away from Dewhurst's hold. "That's my affair, sir. Not yours."

"What letter?" Gabrielle demanded.

Dewhurst whirled towards her. "This is a private matter, Gabrielle."

"Private." Gui gave a harsh laugh. "It's more her affair than yours, sir."

He pulled away from Dewhurst and walked towards Gabrielle. David, who had followed her into the room, made to withdraw. "No, you'd best stay as well, Worsley," Gui said. "There's no point in making it a secret. That was the sum of the letter I left for my uncle and aunt."

"For God's sake—," Dewhurst said.

"I'm not going back to Paris with you," Gui said, ignoring Dewhurst and moving towards Gabrielle. "It's time this farce came to an end. Perhaps I should have said that to Oncle Jacques and Tante Amélie in person, but I fear I was too much of a coward. I left them a letter telling them I am not the son of Georges Laclos and can no longer go on trespassing on their hospitality. Easier for all of us to make a clean break."

"Oh, Gui." Gabrielle put up a hand to brush his hair back from his forehead. "You can't think you can just walk away."

"On the contrary. As I told our uncle and aunt—your uncle and aunt—I don't see what else I can do." He cast a glance over his shoulder. "I didn't realize Oncle Jacques would go to Lord Dewhurst. Why did my uncle send you after me, sir?"

"Because he wants you back, you damn fool."

Gui's mouth twisted. "If he truly wanted me back, surely he'd have come after me himself. My uncle—my supposed uncle—has never been shy about making his wishes known. You were kind to me when I was a boy, sir, but I wish you'd stay out of this."

Dewhurst drew a breath of frustration. The door from the passage burst open, and Rupert strode into the cross fire. "Gaby, I've just realized—"

He pulled up short, taking in the scene before him. "Father." His voice turned as cold as a January wind. "What are you doing here?"

"Your father is delivering a message from my uncle," Gui said. "He's just leaving."

"On the contrary," Dewhurst said. "Rupert—"

"I have nothing to say to you, sir."

"So you've made abundantly clear. I didn't come here to see you as it happens. This is a private matter—"

"Rupert knows," Gui said. "I told him and Gaby." Gui turned to Rupert. "I've told my uncle and aunt the truth. Or rather I left them a letter. I'm making a clean break. It's better for all of us."

"You don't know what's better for them," Dewhurst said.

"Gui." Rupert took a step towards him, back ostentatiously to his father. "You can't know what your family is thinking—"

"No," Gui said, "and neither can you. Nor your father."

"Gui." Dewhurst put a hand on Gui's shoulder. "If I could speak with you for a moment in private—"

Gui jerked away from Dewhurst's hold. "For God's sake, sir. See to your difficulties with your own son and stay the hell out of my life. If you feel guilty because you brought me to England, I absolve you of it. I wasn't a child."

"You were a boy."

"I was old enough to know I was colluding in deception."

"You don't understand—"

"You're right. I don't understand what on earth makes you think this is any affair of yours. Is it that you knew I was Georges Laclos's bastard? Or Oncle Jacques's?"

Dewhurst stared at him. "Is that what you think?"

"It's one explanation for my easy acceptance in the household. It doesn't change things. I'm still not the rightful heir."

Dewhurst drew a harsh breath.

"If you knew—"

"I know enough to know you should stay well out of it."

"You can have no notion—"

"What gives you the right—"

"Because I'm your father, you damn fool."

CHAPTER 35

Gabrielle felt all the blood drain from her face. Beside her, Rupert had gone stone still. So had Gui, his gaze fastened on Dewhurst. First with disbelief, then with dawning comprehension and a burst of anger. "So that was why— You seduced a housemaid on your friends' estate. Did the Lacloses know I was your bastard?"

Dewhurst drew a breath, cast a quick glance at Gabrielle and Rupert.

"Cat's out of the bag, Father," Rupert said. "And your other sins make this one laughable."

Dewhurst's gaze clashed for a moment with Rupert's. Then he turned back to Gui. "Your mother was—" He swallowed. "I was very fond of her. When I learned she was with child, naturally I made provision for both of you."

"You paid another man to marry her."

"That's not—"

"No sense in wrapping plain facts up in clean linen. That, I suppose, you could reconcile with your gentleman's code. But what about passing me off as part of your friend's family?"

"Yes." Rupert took a step forwards, arms folded across his chest. "I should like to hear your explanation for that as well."

Dewhurst's face twisted. "For years I thought you were dead. You have no idea what that was like."

"To lose someone you love?" Rupert said. "We can imagine it."

Dewhurst spared him a brief look, then turned back to Gui. "France was in chaos in those days. Anyone could fall prey to the rabble—"

"Sounds rather like now," Gui murmured.

"It was nothing like now. The rabble were killing without heed."

"And now the Royalists are. Go on."

"At last I managed to track down some of your mother's connections. They were reluctant to talk at first, but I persuaded them."

"Bribed them?"

"Made them see I could offer you a better life."

"But you didn't offer it to me, did you? You got the Comte de Laclos to do so."

"You must see." Dewhurst's voice was pleading. Gabrielle could almost feel sorry for him, had she not known everything else he had done. "I saw the unique chance to give you a life you might only have dreamed of. And to make my old friend happy because he had his brother's child back. What harm did there seem in that? Of course at the time I never dreamed—"

"That I'd become the heir."

"No."

"Which I assume mattered a great deal to a man of your convictions."

"It was an unfortunate series of events."

"Which you contributed to," Rupert said.

"Oh, my God." Gui stared at Dewhurst. "You didn't— That wasn't part of why you acted against Bertrand, was it? So I'd become the heir?"

"Of course not. I was thinking solely of—" Dewhurst bit back the words.

"Your desire for your own heir?" Rupert demanded.

"I had nothing to do with what happened to Bertrand Laclos. Who was a traitor."

Rupert lunged towards his father and smashed his fist into his face. Dewhurst collapsed backwards on the worn carpet, blood streaming from his nose.

"Glad you did that," Gui said. "I've been itching to do it myself. But he is your father."

"And yours." Rupert turned to Gui, as though a fact had only just occurred to him. "It seems we're—"

"Brothers," Gui concluded. His gaze lingered on Rupert's. "Of all the revelations lately about my relations, that's one I'm not sorry to hear."

"Nor am I." Rupert reached out and gripped Gui's hand.

"You see," Gabrielle said to her brother (her husband's brother). "You can't simply walk away, Gui, you are part of this family." She dropped down on the carpet beside Dewhurst.

"Gabrielle," Rupert said in a sharp voice.

"He's hurt, Rupert. We can't just leave him." She tugged her handkerchief from her sleeve and put it to Dewhurst's nose. "Tilt your head forwards, Lord Dewhurst." Gabrielle slid her arm behind his shoulders.

"Thank you, my dear."

"Don't think I'm not sickened as well. But it serves little purpose for you to be bleeding over the carpet."

Dewhurst groaned, then sat bolt upright, spattering blood not only over the carpet but on her skirt as well. "What's that commotion?"

"More arrivals at the inn, I shouldn't wonder." Gui walked to the window.

Dewhurst pushed himself to his feet and strode to the window, holding the handkerchief to his nose. "What the devil is the Duchess of Sagan doing here?"

"Rupert." Gabrielle gripped her husband's arm. "I need you for a moment."

Rupert let her pull him out onto the landing. "I could kill—"

"Not now, Rupert. We have the Courland sisters and Suzanne and Juliette Dubretton below. And St. Gilles and Malcolm and Monsieur O'Roarke and Simon Tanner will be here at any moment.

Along with the Davenports and the Kestrel. What are we going to do with your father?"

"I could hit him again and knock him out."

"That's not funny."

"No, it's an honest suggestion."

"Satisfying as that might be, we can't be sure it would work for long enough."

Steps sounded on the stairs. Gabrielle turned, expecting the Courland sisters, and instead found herself looking at her cousin Christian.

"Good lord," he said. "What are you doing here, Gabrielle? Caruthers?" He swept an extravagant bow, got his legs tangled up, and had to clutch the stair rail to keep from falling.

"We're on our way to the Lagarde fête," Gabrielle said in a voice bright as polished silver.

"So am I as it happens. Suppose it's not surprising we stopped at the same inn. Should have driven out from Paris together."

The door creaked open below. Christian peered over the stair rail. "Good God. It's the Courland sisters. They must be on their way to the fête as well. Quite a coincidence."

Gabrielle flashed a glance at her husband, wondering how far they'd be able to stretch the idea of coincidence.

"A private parlor." Wilhelmine of Sagan's voice carried up the stairwell, ringing with confident assurance. "And a light meal as soon as is convenient."

"Duchess." Gabrielle picked up her skirts and ran down the stairs. "What a coincidence. Are you on your way to the Lagardes' as well?"

Wilhelmine of Sagan stood in the midst of the hall, dominating the scene. Dorothée Talleyrand stood beside her. Behind them, lingering back at the respectful distance appropriate to servants, were Suzanne Rannoch and Juliette Dubretton, Suzanne holding Colin, Juliette with the baby in her arms, a little girl and a little boy hiding behind her skirts.

"Madame Caruthers." It was Dorothée who spoke. "How pleasant to see you."

The plan was for Gabrielle to offer them the use of her private parlor. Instead she said, "We're encountering so many friends today. My brother is upstairs with my father-in-law."

She saw the briefest flicker of recognition in the duchess's eyes, followed by a polite smile. "What a coincidence indeed."

"Madame Rannoch?" Christian took a step forwards, blinking at Suzanne.

"Monsieur Laclos." Suzanne stepped forwards with a winning smile that somehow gave the impression that she wore pearls and silk rather than gray-spotted muslin. "How lovely to see you."

Christian's gaze darted over her gown and simple straw bonnet. "Did—"

Booted feet thudded on the stairs. Gui and Lord Dewhurst came into view. Dewhurst's nose had stopped bleeding, though red stains showed on his shirt collar and cravat. "Dewhurst is feeling a bit unwell," Gui announced. "I'm going to take him back to Paris."

Gabrielle sent her brother—Rupert's brother, poison, she would never sort this out in her head—a look of gratitude.

Christian blinked as the men moved past him. "I say, Dewhurst, is that blood on your neckcloth?"

"I tripped," Dewhurst said in repressive tones. "The carpet was loose."

"Dashed shame. Perhaps we should report it to the inn—"

"I don't think that will be necessary," Gui said. He inclined his head to the Courland princesses and their supposed maids. "Ladies."

Gabrielle released her breath as her brother and uncle stepped out of the inn. Only then did she realize she had been holding it. She smiled across the hall at Wilhelmine and Dorothée. "We've had refreshments sent up. Far more than we can eat ourselves. Do join us."

It was the planned script, save that they had not expected to have to include Christian in the invitation. Only of course she could hardly fail to include her cousin. Christian, deaf to any undercurrents that he might be unwanted—but then Christian was always deaf to undercurrents—bounded cheerfully up the stairs after the ladies.

In their private parlor, she saw David's gaze flicker to Suzanne, so briefly she doubted anyone else noticed. Then he set about pouring out wine and passing out cakes. Pierre and Marguerite knelt on the window seat and peered down into the inn yard.

"Pity your father fell, Rupert," Christian said, accepting a glass of wine. "Should be a splendid party. Good of old Gui to take him back to Paris."

"Gui is the best of brothers," Gabrielle said.

"Oh, quite," Christian said, though Gabrielle caught a note of doubt in his voice.

"A cart just pulled in," Pierre reported from the window seat. "It looks like peddlers."

"Anyone will stop at inns these days," Christian said.

Dorothée took a sip of wine. "Lovely weather we're having."

They made desultory conversation about the weather until footsteps pounded on the stairs. Gabrielle barely had time to be worried before her brother burst into the room. He checked for a moment, taking in Christian with a quick glance.

"What happened?" Rupert demanded. "Did Father—"

"He's unconscious," Gui said.

"What?"

"He tripped in the inn yard."

"I'll take a look at him." Suzanne was already on her feet. Dorothée moved to take Colin.

"Good lord," Christian murmured as Gabrielle sprang to her feet as well. "Dewhurst does seem accident prone today. I hope it isn't his heart."

CHAPTER 36

"What really happened?" Suzanne muttered to Gui as they ran down the stairs with Rupert and Gabrielle behind them.

"Dewhurst appeared to trip over a coil of rope. But I have the strangest suspicion the Kestrel made it happen. We met him coming out of the stables. He'd just arrived. Davenport and Lady Cordelia are with Dewhurst."

Rupert shook his head as they reached the ground floor. "Didn't the Kestrel realize you were getting Father out of here?"

Gui's brows drew together. "I had the oddest feeling he was afraid."

"Of Father? He doesn't even know Father."

"I think perhaps he thought your father would recognize him."

"That doesn't make any sense. They don't know each other."

"How do you know?" Gabrielle said. "We don't know who the Kestrel is behind all that makeup."

Lord Dewhurst lay on the floor in the stable. Cordelia knelt on one side of him, Harry on the other. "His pulse is steady," Cordelia said, looking up at Suzanne.

Suzanne dropped down beside Cordelia and ran her fingers over Dewhurst's head. No blood, and his breathing was steady. "He should come round," she told Rupert and Gabrielle. "We should carry him inside and put him somewhere he can be comfortable and not catch a chill."

Suzanne and Cordelia ran ahead to ask the innkeeper for a room on the ground floor to find that Wilhelmine had already done so. Dorothée came in, carrying Colin, who wriggled to be set down. David went to help the men with Dewhurst. Rupert and Harry laid Dewhurst on the sofa in the parlor. Suzanne knelt beside him to check his pulse. It was still strong.

Footsteps sounded on the stairs. Rose squawked. A moment later, Juliette poked her head into the room, jiggling a fussing baby. "Have you seen Pierre and Marguerite? I went to change Rose and suddenly they were gone."

"Perhaps they ran outside," Dorothée said. "We can—"

A yelp from the inn yard put an end to her words. "Stay with Lord Dewhurst," Suzanne murmured to David. She scooped up Colin, who was clinging to her skirts, and ran outside, followed by the others.

They found Christian Laclos in the center of the yard beside a chaise, clutching his arm. A defiant Pierre and Marguerite faced him.

"What happened?" Suzanne asked, arms tightening instinctively round her own son.

"I bit Monsieur Laclos," Marguerite said.

Juliette ran to her elder daughter. "Why on earth—"

"Because he was trying to make Pierre go into his carriage."

Christian Laclos put his hand up to his cravat. "There's been a misunderstanding—"

"It wasn't a misunderstanding." Pierre ranged himself by his sister.

"You've been very brave," Suzanne said, aware of Colin taking in the scene with wide eyes. "And it occurs to me we've shockingly neglected giving you anything to eat. Cordelia, could you take the children to the kitchen?"

"Of course," Cordelia said.

Marguerite looked at the adults in indignation. "We stopped him—"

"I say—," Christian sputtered.

"—and now you're going to just send us away?"

Juliette knelt down beside her daughter. "We'll tell you later, sweetheart."

"All of it?"

Juliette drew a breath but kept her gaze steady on Marguerite. "As much as we can."

"That's not—"

Pierre touched his sister's arm. "Come on, Marguerite. They can't talk with us here."

Cordelia took Colin from Suzanne's arms and reached for Marguerite's hand. Marguerite cast a lingering glance over her shoulder, but when Pierre took her other hand she permitted herself to be led away.

A gust of wind cut across the cobbled yard. "Terrible misunderstanding," Christian Laclos muttered.

"My children are remarkably unfanciful," Juliette said, pulling Rose tight against her. Rose craned her neck to look around, eyes bright with curiosity. "Or are you calling them liars?"

"Of course not. I was just trying to . . . distract them."

"An interesting euphemism for kidnapping," Suzanne said.

Christian Laclos stared at her. "My dear Madame Rannoch, what on earth would I have wanted with the child?"

Suzanne stared into that affable face and those wide blue eyes. If this was an act, he was a master. And yet— "An inheritance."

Juliette glanced towards the kitchen, where Cordelia had taken her children.

Christian blinked. "Get things a bit confused, but don't see how a painter's son could have anything to do with—"

"Not unless you realized the identity of the woman who had given birth to him. And the man who might have fathered him. You were part of Étienne Laclos's failed plot. It would have been only natural for Étienne to have confided in you about his feelings for Tatiana Kirsanova."

Christian's gaze slid to the side. "Well—er—yes." He coughed. "Ladies present. Don't like to—"

"I assure you we aren't in the least shocked," Wilhelmine said.

Christian's gaze lowered to his boots. "Of course Étienne did mention it. Princess Tatiana. He was mad for her. Are you saying— One of those children is theirs?" He shook his head in a perfect show of confusion.

"The boy may be," Juliette said.

" 'May be'?" Christian shook his head again. "You don't know? Well, that's—that's Princess Tatiana, I suppose. That is—no wish to cast aspersions. But even if you were sure he was Étienne's son, the boy wouldn't inherit anything."

"He would if his parents had been married." Suzanne glanced at Juliette. "There are more papers hidden somewhere, aren't there?"

Juliette drew a harsh breath. Horse hooves pounded, cutting the still air. Malcolm, Raoul, St. Gilles, and Simon rode into the inn yard. Suzanne met her husband's gaze. A gasp sounded. She looked round to see Christian holding a pistol to Dorothée's temple.

"Don't be an idiot, Laclos," Malcolm said in the sudden taut silence. "You can't get past all these people."

"On the contrary," Christian said. He glanced at the chaise, but there was no coachman on the box. "All of you back away. I'm going to the stable. When I've ridden out of here I'll release Madame Talleyrand."

"You bastard," Wilhelmine said.

"Oh no, I assure you, *madame la duchesse,* I'm a Laclos to the core. Unlike Gui over there."

Christian backed into the shadows of the stable, pulling Dorothée with him. Doro was stone still, her face white above the satin ribbons on her bonnet. He'd let her go, Suzanne told herself. Probably. He was a desperate man and so much could go wrong when someone held a pistol. She met Malcolm's gaze and then Raoul's, weighing the pros and cons of action. Too dangerous with the gun to Doro's temple. But if Christian drove off with her—

The inn door swung open. A maidservant ran out and screamed. Christian spun towards her, leveling his gun. Malcolm hurled himself across the yard and knocked the maid to the ground. A report echoed through the yard.

A scream tore from Suzanne's throat, but it was Christian who crumpled to the ground, blood gushing from his temple. Dorothée swayed and would have fallen to the ground as well, but the Kestrel, still garbed as the old peddler woman, stepped out of the shadows of the stable and caught her in his arms. In one hand he held a smoking pistol.

Malcolm helped the maidservant to her feet and ran to Christian. Rupert got there at the same moment. Malcolm put his fingers to Christian's throat, looked at Suzanne, and shook his head. Wilhelmine ran to take Dorothée from the Kestrel. Suzanne came up beside them as the Kestrel dropped down beside Christian. "God help me," he said in English, a low, barely accented voice that Suzanne had never heard from him before. "I hoped I was done with killing."

Rupert sat back on his heels and stared at the Kestrel. He didn't move a muscle or utter a sound, but Suzanne felt his absolute stillness.

The Kestrel lifted his head and the look that passed between them would have smashed glass.

Rupert drew a breath that trembled in the air. "Bertrand?"

CHAPTER 37

The man known as the Kestrel gave a wry smile. "I should have known. You were always damnably good at seeing past appearances."

Rupert stared at the man kneeling across from him with the expression of one who sees but cannot accept reality. "You—" He broke off, hoarse with disbelief.

The Kestrel sat back on his heels. "I'm not a ghost, I assure you. Or perhaps that's not true. Bertrand Laclos died four years ago."

Wonder battled with uncertainty in Rupert's gaze. And something else that might have been anger. "For God's sake, why—"

Bertrand cast a quick glance round the assembled company, but when he spoke it was straight to Rupert. "It's a long story, which I agree must be told. But first—" He looked down at Christian.

It probably took only a quarter hour to move Christian's body inside and reassure and mollify the innkeeper (Raoul did that, few dared question him), but it felt longer. As though, Suzanne thought, they had stumbled late into someone else's story. Which was inextricably bound up with their own. At last they all gathered in a parlor across the hall from the one where David and Simon sat with Dewhurst. Bertrand Laclos was now dressed in a shirt and breeches. He had removed the wig to reveal a shock of auburn hair and the putty from his face to reveal fine-boned features and the sort of flexible face that melds effortlessly into a variety of characters. Rupert's gaze shot to Bertrand at once. Then Rupert crossed the room and stood leaning against the wall, arms folded as though physically holding himself in check.

Bertrand's gaze lingered on Rupert for a moment, then swept the company, settled on Gabrielle for a moment, moved on, carefully neutral. "I took a knife cut to the ribs in the tavern brawl in Spain. I lost a lot of blood and consciousness. I suspect my would-be assassin really did think I was dead or on my way to it. I thought so myself when the world went black. I came to to find Inez bending over me." He turned to Rupert. "You remember Inez? The brewer's daughter with an unfortunate tendency to confuse me with a romantic hero. By that time she'd accepted that we wouldn't be more than friends, but it seemed to make our friendship stronger. In fact, she'd taken to confiding in me about the draper's assistant who was courting her. It turned out her cousin Diniz was in the tavern at the time of the brawl. He got me out. Inez's family couldn't have been kinder." He gave a wry smile. Even that lit his face. "Particularly when they realized there was no question of a marriage between Inez and me."

"Had you lost your memory?" Rupert demanded in a harsh voice. "Because I can't see why else—"

"At first I was too weak to think or do anything," Bertrand said. "Then Diniz and Inez told me the word abroad was that I'd been killed. I knew the brawl must have been set up. I had Diniz summon one of my contacts. He made some inquiries for me. That was when I realized the British thought I was a traitor. At which point it seemed politic to lie low."

Rupert started to speak, then bit the words back. Tension radiated from every line of his body.

"As soon as I was well enough, I began to make inquiries myself," Bertrand continued. "I'd acquired a certain knack for disguise and moving silently. Eventually I traced the accusations of treason against me back to . . ." He hesitated. "Their source."

"My father," Rupert said in an even voice.

Bertrand looked him full in the face with a look that reminded

Suzanne of when she had to admit a harsh truth to Colin. "I was hoping you'd never know."

"Why? To salvage my relationship with a man who is scarcely worthy of being called a man? If you'd come to me then—"

"Rupert . . ." Again, Bertrand hesitated.

Suzanne exchanged a look with Malcolm, but it was Gabrielle who spoke first. "You need to talk alone," she said to her husband and cousin. "We should see how Lord Dewhurst is."

"Gaby—," Bertrand said, his face a study in conflict.

"It's all right, Bertrand." Gabrielle smiled at him. "I know rather more now than I did before you left."

The door clicked shut. Rupert stared across the inn parlor at the features he could trace from memory, still scarcely able to believe he was seeing Bertrand in the flesh. "Do you think Father recognized you?"

"I can't be sure. I doubt he'd have seen past the disguise, but I reacted on instinct. I only wanted to distract him."

"He deserved worse."

Bertrand met Rupert's gaze for a long moment and drew a breath that was rough with despair and shattered illusions. "All those years. I never realized how much your father hated me."

"Not you." Rupert's voice shook with rage. "He wanted me married. I think he'd been hoping I'd conform to convention. He'd come to realize that I wouldn't, so he took drastic action. I only learned what he'd done a few days ago, thanks to Malcolm. I'd never realized how much I hated him."

Bertrand regarded him with the gaze of one whose worst fears had come to pass. "Which is precisely why I didn't tell you I was still alive."

Rupert stared at his former lover. "Damn it, Bertrand—"

"What would you have had me do, Rupert? Bring about a complete breach with your father? Have you accusing him of treason?"

"Damn it, yes."

"And then what?" Bertrand's gaze locked on Rupert. "There was no chance for us. No place we could be happy. If I hadn't seen that before, your father opened my eyes."

"Damn my father to hell." Rupert stared at the man he had loved for as long as he could remember. "I wept at your grave."

Bertrand took a half step forwards, then froze. "Rupert—"

"And you thought it was worth throwing away what we had so I could maintain a relationship with the man who tried to kill you—"

"I knew what it would do to your relationship with your father to know he'd tried to have me killed."

"And so you simply decided—"

"There wasn't anything simple about it." Bertrand's voice echoed from the floorboards to the smoke-blackened beams of the ceiling. He drew a breath that scraped raw. "My God, Rupert, do you think my first instinct wasn't to go right to you? Do you think I didn't wrestle with this, didn't pace the streets, didn't write you a dozen letters only to burn them? But in the end I saw—"

Rupert stared across the room at him, held by his lover's gaze.

Bertrand's gaze held the knowledge of unbearable loss. "Whatever he did, he's your father, Rupert. That doesn't go away. I loved you too much to give you a choice between me and your family."

"I wouldn't have hesitated for a moment."

"And the first time we quarreled?" Bertrand asked in a rough voice. "Or when you became Lord Dewhurst with no heir and no prospect of one, estranged from your family?"

"I married Gabrielle," Rupert said in a low voice.

"I know." Bertrand's face was carefully schooled. "You have a son. I've followed your life rather closely."

"Magnanimous of you. But do you know what it's done to Gaby to be married to a man who can't love her as she deserves?" Rupert drew a breath. His chest ached as though it had been pummeled black-and-blue. "I can't believe you didn't trust me."

"Rupert— I trust you with my life."

"You didn't trust me with my own." Rupert glanced away, then forced his gaze back to Bertrand. "And so you decided to disappear into the streets of Paris?"

"I was tired of the war, tired of both sides, tired of the killing."

"And I should have been the first one you turned to."

"In another world. A world without families and conventions.

Where we could be ourselves." Bertrand's mouth twisted. "A world that doesn't exist."

Dorothée shook her head. Her skirt was damp where she'd attempted to sponge out Christian Laclos's blood. "Why did it never occur to me that Christian's bumbling was just a shade too perfect?"

"Yes," Suzanne said. "You'd think I could recognize a good actor." She, the Courland sisters, Gabrielle and Gui, and the St. Gilleses had returned to the first-floor private parlor. Simon and David were with Dewhurst, and Malcolm, Raoul, and Harry were seeing to the arrangements for the remainder of the St. Gilleses' journey.

Gabrielle had been staring out the window, arms locked over her chest. Now she spun round to look at Suzanne. "You think Christian betrayed Étienne? That he wanted the Laclos title and estates even then?"

"Perhaps. Though he couldn't have known then that Bertrand would die."

"But even then—," Dorothée began.

"I'm not really a Laclos." Gui looked up from contemplation of the carpet. He waved a hand to silence Gabrielle as she protested. "Never mind the details, but obviously Christian knew."

Dorothée looked at Suzanne. "When we talked to Christian. He said Bertrand had written to him asking questions about Gui."

Suzanne nodded. "Perhaps when Bertrand suspected Gui wasn't really a Laclos he wrote to Christian. In any case, Christian knew. I think when he said that to us he was sowing the seeds of suspicion. He must have been planning to reveal the truth or to arrange for others to reveal it. Then the title would have been his. Except for Étienne's son." She looked from Juliette to St. Gilles.

Juliette glanced at her husband, swallowed, and turned to Suzanne. "When did you realize?"

"Not until the fake soldiers tried to abduct Pierre on our way here. I was singularly slow."

St. Gilles reached for his wife's hand. "Étienne was a romantic. I wasn't surprised when he insisted on marriage. But I was when

Tatiana agreed to it. That was when I began to suspect how much he meant to her."

"Insisting on marriage is just the sort of romantic gesture Étienne would have been likely to make," Gabrielle said. "And now I think of it, it fits with the letters he sent me. He was writing about this woman he'd fallen in love with as though he was going to bring her home to the family. Introduce her to all of us. How could he do that unless she was his bride? If she'd been anything else I doubt he'd have even mentioned her to me."

St. Gilles nodded. "After his death she said she'd been a fool. It would be ruinous to have the world know her as the wife of a man who plotted Napoleon's death. Or to have her son the heir of an executed traitor. And we really didn't know who fathered Pierre. That much is true."

"But whoever fathered Pierre, Tatiana was married to Étienne at the time of his conception," Suzanne said. "Or so close to the time as to render it impossible to tell. Legally that makes him Étienne's son. And the rightful heir to the Comte de Laclos."

"Perhaps it's selfish of us," Juliette said, shifting Rose against her shoulder, "but I like to think he wouldn't care."

"Very likely not," Gabrielle said. "But you must see from our perspective we can't deny him what he's entitled to."

St. Gilles shook his head. "Pierre may well not be—"

"You don't believe in inherited privilege," Gui pointed out. "So it shouldn't matter whose son he is."

St. Gilles gave a reluctant smile. "You reason like an advocate, Laclos. By the same token your own birth shouldn't matter."

"My point exactly," Gabrielle said.

Wilhelmine took a sip of wine. "Right now it's Pierre's safety that's important."

Juliette met her gaze across the parlor. "Precisely."

Cordelia looked up from the deal table in the inn kitchen where she sat with Colin on her lap and Pierre and Marguerite beside her. Suzanne met her friend's gaze for a moment, ruffled Colin's hair, and smiled at Pierre and Marguerite. Colin had milk spattered on his chin and biscuit crumbs adorning his face and shirt, but the older children had half-full mugs of milk and plates of barely touched biscuits before them. "Your parents will be with you shortly, and you'll be on your way."

"Is everything all right?" Pierre asked.

"It will be," Suzanne said. She hoped she spoke the truth.

She went out into the inn yard to find Bertrand Laclos standing beside a traveling carriage. She moved to his side. "Cordelia is getting the children ready."

He nodded. "Thank you. We won't be entirely safe until we're out of France, but the rest of our journey should be far less eventful."

The revelations of half an hour ago might never have happened. Suzanne hesitated a moment, then said quickly, "I can't know what it's like for you. But I do know the world isn't easy on many relationships. I'll always be an outsider in my husband's world. Sometimes I wish nothing more than that we could live somewhere else, where people didn't make judgments about foreigners and—" She couldn't say the rest of course. "But this is the world we live in. And I'd rather share an imperfect world with him than be separated."

Bertrand met her gaze. His eyes, which seemed so changeable, now looked very definitely green. For a moment she thought he meant to turn her words aside, but then he gave a smile that was unexpectedly sweet and filled with regret for something out of reach. "You're a kind woman, Madame Rannoch. And obviously a clever one. But I doubt you ever felt association with you could destroy your husband's life."

Suzanne returned the smile. "You'd be surprised," she said, startled by how much she'd admitted.

Before either of them could say more, Malcolm and Raoul came out of the inn. "The St. Gilles family is making ready," Malcolm said. "You can still proceed?"

"Of course," Bertrand said. "The overly dramatic revelations about my own identity don't change anything. I'm not sure how much Lord Dewhurst saw—"

"We'll make sure he doesn't cause you trouble one way or another," Malcolm said.

Bertrand nodded and moved towards the inn.

Suzanne looked between Malcolm and Raoul. "Christian Laclos was obviously much cleverer than he looked. But it's hard for me to believe he set up the attempt to kidnap Pierre today and the attack on Christine Leroux entirely on his own."

"No." Malcolm's gaze flickered to the spot where Christian had died. "And it doesn't make sense that Christian betrayed Étienne all those years ago because he foresaw a way to get rid of Bertrand and Gui and claim the title. After all, at that point the estates had been confiscated. But if Christian wanted to advance in the world and had no qualms about turning on his family—"

"It's far more likely he'd have turned government informant," Raoul said.

"Quite. Christian sold out his cousin Étienne for the promise of who knew what favors. But before he died Étienne had told both Christian and Rivère about his love for Tania. Perhaps even told them he'd married her. Rivère realized Tania had a child just after and put it together that the father was Étienne. Somehow he discovered she'd hidden papers about the child in St. Gilles's painting."

"Do you think the marriage lines were there as well?" Suzanne asked.

"It's possible. Perhaps they were hidden behind different parts of the frame and Rivère only had time to retrieve one or didn't realize there was a second. But his knowledge made him doubly dangerous to Christian. Christian must have already feared Rivère could put it together that he'd betrayed Étienne. And now Rivère had proof of the legitimacy of a child who could stand between Christian and the title that could suddenly be his. Which leaves the question—who was Christian working for and who is helping him now."

A gust of wind cut across the inn yard. Suzanne put up a hand to anchor her bonnet. She didn't risk a glance at Raoul, but Fouché's name hung between them. A chill cut through her that had nothing to do with the wind.

* * *

Gabrielle ran across the hall of the inn and seized Bertrand's arm. "You're not going to leave without talking to me."

Bertrand looked down at her, guilt and regret chasing themselves through his gaze. "Gaby—"

She pulled him into the now-empty parlor in which they had all gathered to hear his story. "I know you have to leave to take the St. Gilleses to the coast. But then you have to come back to Paris. To us."

Bertrand took a step towards her. "Gaby— I'm so sorry. I never meant for you to be caught up in any of this."

She shrugged. "I made my own choices, and I can take care of myself. You must have realized with you gone Rupert was more likely to marry."

"I—" Bertrand glanced away. "I knew it was a possibility."

"And whatever girl he chose would have found herself married to a man who couldn't love her as a wife wants to be loved. Did that not seem so bad because it would be an unknown girl, not your cousin?"

Bertrand drew a breath. "I didn't think—"

"No, you were too busy wallowing in the nobility of your sacrifice. I'm sorry, Bertrand— I know you faced an impossible choice. I can't imagine the hell you've been through, and I know you were trying to spare those you love pain. But you have to realize that the choices you made caused pain as well. And especially now he knows the truth, I'm sure Rupert would rather be miserable with you than without you. Save that I don't think he'd be miserable at all."

The breath Bertrand drew was that of one who dares not hope.

Gabrielle seized his hands. "You have to come back now. You must see that. Rupert knows about his father—the damage is done. In fact, if anyone can help mend matters it's you. And your parents need you. Oh, the devil, I need you."

A smile broke across his face, a smile that took them back to the nursery, when choices had been simpler and they'd been allies against all else. He raised a hand and stroked her hair.

"There are a dozen times a day I'd welcome your advice," she said. "And Stephen needs to meet his uncle."

"I can't come between—"

"You're right. You can't come between Rupert and me. The divide is already there. Or perhaps it's more accurate to say you've always been between us, even when Rupert thought you were dead and I didn't have a glimmering of the truth of his feelings for you. But that doesn't mean we all have to be miserable."

"You're amazing, Gaby."

"I'm a pragmatist. Unlike the recklessly idealistic men in my life." She tightened her grip on his hands. "We found a way to muddle through when we came to England. We can find a way to muddle through this."

He shook his head. "You always had a fondness for fairy tales."

"Meaning you won't come back?"

Though she still held his hands, he stared down at her as though looking at something out of reach. "I have to get the St. Gilles family to England. I can't think beyond that."

Paul St. Gilles turned before climbing into the carriage after his wife and children and regarded Malcolm. "I owe you a debt, Rannoch."

Malcolm's gaze drifted inside the carriage to where Pierre sat within the circle of Juliette's arm, Marguerite cuddled up beside him, Rose in their mother's lap. "It was your wife who set things in motion. She's a remarkable woman."

"That I know well. But Juliette's told me everything you did."

"I'm the one who owes you the debt. For protecting Tania's child."

St. Gilles glanced at his family as well, then looked back at Malcolm. "I never thought of myself as the sort to keep secrets. Pierre changed things."

Malcolm glanced across the courtyard to where Suzanne stood with Cordelia and Dorothée. His wife was holding Colin, his legs wrapped round her waist, his hand fisted round her collar. For a moment Malcolm was pulled back to the moment Geoffrey Blackwell had placed Colin in his arms, squalling, blue-tinged, wobbly head—the most beautiful sight he'd ever seen. "Having children does."

St. Gilles cast a quick look at him. "I know—"

Inside the carriage, Marguerite giggled at something Pierre was saying. "We may never have the answers to some questions," Malcolm said, "but there's no doubt in my mind you'll always be Pierre's father."

St. Gilles's eyes held a gratitude that went beyond simple relief at knowing he wouldn't lose his son. And for an unnerving moment, Malcolm felt the other man glimpsed more of his own life than he'd meant to reveal. "Thank you."

CHAPTER 38

Wellington stared at Malcolm across his study at Headquarters. "I don't suppose you can prove any of this."

"Would you want me to, sir?"

"Absolutely not," Stuart said.

Castlereagh shot a look at him.

"Sorry," Stuart said.

"You're sure Christian Laclos was behind Rivère's death?" Wellington said.

Malcolm surveyed the three men. He and Harry had managed to give them an account of Christian Laclos's actions that excluded mention of Tatiana's son. "Rivère must have worked out that it was Christian who had betrayed Étienne and that Christian was a government informant. With Napoleon in power, Christian had no fear of retribution. But now that the king is restored, that information could have ruined him." Malcolm didn't add that Antoine Rivère had also known about the child who could come between Christian and the Laclos title and lands.

"A blow for the Laclos family," Castlereagh murmured.

"But softened by the fact that they have Bertrand back," Harry said.

A current of unease ran through the room.

"Is he coming back?" Castlereagh asked.

"I don't know," Malcolm said. "But he has to be officially cleared so he has the option."

Wellington and Castlereagh exchanged glances. "His alleged crimes were never made public," Wellington said. "As far as the world knows, he was an émigré who went to fight for Bonaparte and died. If we simply reveal that he was in fact our double agent, he'll be a hero."

"The St. Gilleses are safely in England." Suzanne, balancing Colin in her lap, looked round her salon at Dorothée, Wilhelmine, and Cordelia.

"You heard from them?" Dorothée asked.

"From the Kestrel. Bertrand Laclos. He got a message through to Malcolm."

Dorothée shook her head. "I still can't believe—"

"I can." Wilhelmine reached for her coffee cup. "At times it seems very tempting to be able to start again, with none of the baggage of one's previous life."

Suzanne steadied Colin, who was reaching for the plate of biscuits. "You gave up a lot in the course of this investigation, Willie."

Wilhelmine blew on the steam from her cup. "Loath as I am to admit it, my little sister was right. Stewart would have bored me. In fact, it's amazing how a man could be at once so dull and so reprehensible. I'm all but certain he'd learned Bertrand Laclos was still alive after the tavern brawl in Spain. He kept quiet to protect himself. That's why he was so afraid of what the investigation might uncover. I suspect he babbled about it to the opera dancer Ninette and she told Antoine Rivère." Wilhelmine took a sip of coffee. "There are worse things than being alone."

"Like being married to the wrong person." Dorothée picked up a biscuit, broke it in half, and gave a piece to Colin.

Wilhelmine shot a glance at her. "Vienna might not free you from all your baggage, but it would be a fresh start."

Dorothée spread her hands in her lap, her gaze on Colin. "I know. Which would be both a blessing and a curse." She looked at

Suzanne. "What will happen to Pierre? Will the Lacloses acknowledge him?"

"They want to. They'll have to sort things out with the St. Gilleses." Suzanne looked down at Colin, who was gravely studying the piece of biscuit clutched in his fist. "I think they can reach an accommodation about acknowledging him as the heir as long as Juliette and St. Gilles understand no one is trying to take him away from them." She pressed her lips to the top of Colin's head. Colin took a bite of biscuit.

"And Bertrand?" Cordelia asked. "Will he come back to France?"

"I don't know," Suzanne said. "Though it will be difficult for him to hide now, even if he wants to."

"Poor Gabrielle Caruthers," Dorothée said.

"I don't know." Cordelia cast a glance at Livia, who was at a table by the window, drawing a picture. "At least they have honesty now. That's more than a lot of marriages."

Wilhelmine shot a look at her. "The events of the past days can't have been easy on your own marriage."

"No. But they were something we were going to have to go through sooner or later. I'd like to say we're the stronger for it. But I suppose time is the only real test of that."

Dorothée looked at Suzanne. "You're lucky, Suzanne. Married to the man you love without the baggage of the past."

Suzanne tightened her arms round Colin and managed a smile.

Before she was compelled to answer, the door opened and Valentin announced Prince Talleyrand.

Dorothée set down her coffee cup. "I didn't realize it was so late. Are we due at the Austrian embassy already?"

"No, I came early." Talleyrand waved her back to her chair. "I was hoping for a word with Madame Rannoch."

"Of course." Suzanne set down Colin, who ran over to Livia, and got to her feet. Given Prince Talleyrand's knowledge of Malcolm's family, it wasn't entirely surprising he would wish to speak with her. Or so she told herself as she took Talleyrand into Malcolm's study. In truth, her mouth was dry and the tension that had lain coiled within her ever since Fouché's threats pulled tighter.

"My thanks again for all you've done for Dorothée," Talleyrand said as she closed the door behind them.

"Doro's a good friend." Suzanne sank into one of the two crimson damask chairs in front of the desk.

Talleyrand sank into the opposite chair. Every motion was controlled, but he moved as though his bones ached. "I know Clam-Martinitz wants her to go to Vienna with him." He tilted his head back against the damask. "I expect she'll agree."

"I think she may," Suzanne said. "Though as her friend, I'm not sure that's the option that will make her happiest in the end."

His thin mouth curved in a smile. "You've very kind, Suzanne."

"I didn't say it to be kind."

"No, you wouldn't." He regarded her for a moment. "I asked to speak with you to tell you that you needn't fear any longer that Fouché will trouble you."

Suzanne's fingers closed on the muslin folds of her skirt. Even with Talleyrand, where she should have known to be prepared for anything, she hadn't been prepared for this. "I beg your pardon?"

"Did you imagine Fouché could know about your work while I did not? I'm hurt. Oh, I'll grant you O'Roarke was good at keeping your identity secret. He went to rather extreme lengths and few have his talents as a spymaster. But it's difficult for an agent of your caliber to remain undetected."

Suzanne swallowed, a host of scenarios racing through her mind.

"Yes, I know," Talleyrand said. "The board has shifted and it's difficult to tell now if we're allies or enemies. I'll confess I have enough affection for Malcolm to have been not best pleased when I learned he'd been saddled with an enemy agent for a wife."

She jerked her hand free of her skirt. Her nail snagged on the muslin.

"But then in Vienna I had the leisure to observe the two of you together. Malcolm is not a man to heed my advice on the dangers of personal relationships. Losing you would spell disaster for him."

"Surely you of all people wouldn't make a decision based on such considerations." Suzanne was amazed she managed to keep her voice steady.

"Not entirely. There's also what you've done for Dorothée. And what I've observed of you myself."

Suzanne looked into his hooded blue eyes. "Those still don't sound like considerations that would weigh with you."

"No? Well, I must be permitted my idiosyncrasies. Suffice it to say, Fouché will not trouble you further."

"How—"

"My dear Suzanne, it must have occurred to you and Malcolm that Christian Laclos betrayed his cousin Étienne to the authorities."

"You're saying Christian went to Fouché with the information?" It was what she had suspected.

Talleyrand's mouth curved. "I always thought it surprising the Laclos cousins and Rivère got as far as they did without Fouché knowing about it. It was only recently that I realized Fouché had known all along."

Suzanne stared into Talleyrand's cool gaze. "Are you saying that Christian Laclos was Fouché's agent from the first? That Fouché instigated the plot?"

"Nothing like a plot that threatened his family to make Bonaparte frightened. And a frightened Bonaparte made him easier for Fouché to control. You must have wondered what happened to the gold Dewhurst and Carfax sent with Étienne."

"Fouché pocketed it?"

"How else would it have disappeared without trace?"

Suzanne spread her fingers in her lap, rearranging the pieces of information. "So Christian Laclos was Fouché's agent provocateur. And Fouché knew Rivère was giving information to the British."

"And like me found him a useful way to pass along misinformation. But with the Restoration Rivère could connect Fouché and Christian Laclos to entrapping Étienne Laclos, whose father is a friend of the Comte d'Artois. Even Fouché treads on dangerous ground these days. He can't afford to give d'Artois an excuse to try to get rid of him."

"You're saying Fouché ordered Christian Laclos to get rid of Rivère?"

"I think Christian had his own reasons for wanting to get rid of Rivère. But at the very least, I think Fouché protected him."

"Which is why Fouché wanted Malcolm to stop the investigation. Ironic that Christian's death will end it in any case." Fouché's voice echoed in her head, threatening to use his hold over her indefinitely. Her fingers closed on her elbows.

Talleyrand eased his clubfoot straight and regarded the diamond buckle on his shoe. "I know Fouché is known for his wealth of information on people, but I would hardly have survived this long did I not have information of my own. As I said, you need not fear Fouché will trouble you in the future."

She held him with her gaze, wondering what on earth he had had to threaten Fouché with. "You also wouldn't have survived this long if you hadn't learned not to waste bargaining chips."

A smile curved Talleyrand's thin mouth. "My dear girl. I don't consider it wasted."

Cordelia pushed open the door of Harry's study. The late summer sun cast a golden wash over the room and burnished her husband's brown hair. Livia ran to give her father a hug and show him the picture she'd drawn at Suzanne's. Cordelia perched on the edge of Harry's desk and waited until Livia had darted off to show the picture to her nurse. "The St. Gilleses are safely in England."

"Yes, Malcolm sent word." Harry leaned back in his chair. "It happens so rarely, I'd almost forgot what a satisfying feeling it is when things work out."

"They'll have challenges to face." Cordelia stared at the rays of sunlight slanting through the window to dapple the desktop, then looked at her husband. "As will we all."

"We've faced a number already."

Cordelia studied his face. The sardonic curve of his mouth, the familiar creases round his eyes when he smiled, the way the smile lit the eyes themselves. So impossible to think now that he'd once been almost a stranger, that they'd been apart for five years. She picked up a pen from the desktop and twisted it between her fingers. "We'd be fools to think this is the end of it."

"No. We've both lived much too complicated pasts for them

not to intrude. And we may not come through it as easily next time."

She set down the pen. "You don't sugarcoat things, do you, Harry?"

"There are no guarantees." He reached for her hand. "Only the will to make it work."

She leaned forwards and twined her fingers round his own.

Suzanne set Colin in his cradle. He'd fallen asleep in her lap after the Courland sisters, Talleyrand, and Cordelia and Livia left. She'd sat holding him in her arms for a long time, savoring the solid warmth of his body, the even rise and fall of his breathing, the soft brush of his hair beneath her fingers. The most genuine thing in her life, her anchor in this web of lies. She drew the yellow-flowered quilt, a gift from Malcolm's aunt, over Colin and stared for a moment at her son's initials, worked in one corner. She could scarcely believe the gift Talleyrand had given her. Yet she knew how precarious her life remained.

"I never get tired of watching him sleep." Malcolm's voice came from the doorway.

Suzanne turned to smile at her husband. "I told Doro and Willie and Cordy that Paul and Juliette and the children are safely in England."

Malcolm moved to her side and slid his arm round her. "Since that night Rivère told me Tania had a child, this is the first time I've known the child was safe." His lips brushed her hair. "I'll never forgive myself for failing Tania. Knowing Pierre is safe doesn't change that, but— It's a long time since I've done anything I could be unquestioningly proud of."

Suzanne pressed a kiss against his throat. She knew all too well that guilt couldn't be banished, but there were shadows gone from his eyes that had been there since Vienna. "Tatiana would be grateful to you. And I think she'd have done the same for Colin."

Malcolm's gaze went to the cradle. Colin was flopped on his back, one arm curled round his stuffed bear, the other flung up over his head. "I owe O'Roarke an incalculable debt."

Her throat closed. "I think he was glad to do it." That much, she thought, was the truth.

"When I was a child he was one of the few people I could depend on. I hadn't realized how much that was still the case." He rested his chin on her head. "I found myself envying him, acting on his principles, not serving a particular master."

Suzanne turned her face into her husband's cravat to stifle a laugh or a sob. "When are we leaving for England?"

"I didn't say I'd decided."

She tilted her head back and studied her husband's face. The changeable gray eyes, the flexible mouth, the determined lines of nose and cheekbones. "I don't always need words to read you, Malcolm. I don't think you'll be able to put up with Castlereagh and Wellington much longer."

He gave a bleak smile. "They've at least agreed to clear Bertrand Laclos."

"Do you think Bertrand will come back?"

Concern flickered in his gaze. "I hope so." He pressed his lips to her forehead. "I hope he's learned that you can't run away from the past."

She swallowed. Hard. Then she touched his face, her fingers not quite steady. "No. All one can do is focus on the future. Wherever it may lead."

Rupert closed the door of his study and dropped down at the desk. Gabrielle was out with Stephen and the house felt quiet. Oddly, he felt easier with Gaby now he was no longer trying to make himself think of her as his wife. Instead he could see the friend of his childhood. It was something to be grateful for.

The afternoon heat had leached into the room. He unbuttoned his coat and tugged at his cravat in a way that would horrify his valet. He'd had no word from Bertrand since Bertrand had driven out of the inn yard with the St. Gilles family. And it was Malcolm to whom Bertrand had sent word of their safe arrival in England, not him. Which made sense, Malcolm was the one who had engaged Bertrand's services. But that didn't take away the sting.

A month ago Rupert would have said he could simply be happy knowing Bertrand was alive and safe. But now he knew that was laughable. He felt torn in two.

He looked round at the stir of the door against the carpet, expecting the footman. His breath stopped. Bertrand stood in the doorway, the shadows from the passage at his back, the light from the windows falling over his face. It was still hard to believe he was real and not a ghost.

For a long moment, they simply stared at each other.

"It won't be easy," Bertrand said. "And we can't go back."

"No," Rupert said. It hurt to breathe. As though the wrong step could shatter his every hope for the future. "But we can find a way to move forwards."

Bertrand met his gaze and stepped towards him.

HISTORICAL NOTES

Unlike *Vienna Waltz* and *Imperial Scandal,* in which I was specific about dates, with *The Paris Affair* I have used a more open time line so I could weave in a number of events in the late summer of 1815. For instance, Edmond Talleyrand's duel with Karl Clam-Martinitz and the Duke of Wellington's ball took place on 30 July. Harriet Granville and her husband were present, but Caroline and William Lamb had not yet arrived in Paris. Wellington's difficulties with Frances Webster's husband came to a head later in the month, and Wilhelmine's affair with Stewart also came to an end later than it does in the book. Fitzroy Somerset was in England recovering from his wounds at the time, but I have put him and his wife in Paris.

The Royalist plot in which Étienne and Christian Laclos and Antoine Rivère were involved is fictional, but the British are known to have financed a number of Royalist plots. Fouché is also suspected of having employed agents provocateur.

Clam-Martinitz did wound Edmond Talleyrand in the face in their duel, but Edmond did not attempt to strike Clam-Martinitz in the back (my apologies to Edmond for this bit of authorial license). Dorothée attended Wellington's ball the night of the duel (Harriet Granville remarks on how she danced as though nothing had occurred), but she did not attempt to stop the duel and she did not get caught up in an anti-Bonapartist attack afterwards.

SELECTED BIBLIOGRAPHY

Boigne, Adèle d'Osmond, Comtesse de. *Memoirs of the Comtesse de Boigne,* vol. 1. New York: Helen Marx Books, 2003.

Cooper, Duff. *Talleyrand.* New York: Grove Press, 2001.

Creevey, Thomas. *The Creevey Papers: A Selection from the Correspondence & Diaries of Thomas Creevey, M.P.* Edited by Sir Herbert Maxwell. London: Murray, 1904.

Frazer, Augustus. *The Letters of Colonel Sir Augustus Simon Frazer, K.C.B.* London: Longman, Brown, Green, Longmans, & Roberts, 1859.

Granville, Harriet. *Letters of Harriet Countess Granville 1810–1845,* vol. 1. London: Longmans, Green and Co., 1894.

Gronow, Rees Howell. *Reminiscences and Recollections of Captain Gronow,* vol. 1. London: John C. Nimmo.

Jones, Proctor Patterson (editor). *Napoleon: An Intimate Account of the Years of Supremacy.* San Francisco: Proctor Jones Publishing Company, 1972.

Kincaid, John. *Adventures in the Rifle Brigade.* London: T. and W. Boone, Strand, 1830.

Longford, Elizabeth. *Wellington: Pillar of State.* New York: Harper & Row Publishers, 1972.

McGuigan, Dorothy Gies. *Metternich and the Duchess.* New York: Doubleday & Company, 1946.

Mercer, Cavalié. *Journal of the Waterloo Campaign.* London: Greenhill Books, 1989.

THE PARIS AFFAIR

Teresa Grant

About This Guide

The suggested questions are included
to enhance your group's reading of
Teresa Grant's *The Paris Affair.*

DISCUSSION QUESTIONS

1. Compare and contrast the marriages of Suzanne and Malcolm, Cordelia and Harry, Rupert and Gabrielle, Paul and Juliette. How do secrets affect each marriage?

2. How does the solution to the mystery of Tatiana's child parallel the issues in post-Waterloo France?

3. Discuss the different ways in which issues of inheritance drive various characters in the book.

4. Did you guess who was behind Antoine Rivère's death? Why or why not?

5. How are Malcolm and Suzanne similar to a modern couple struggling to balance family and the demands of careers?

6. Which new characters in this book do you think might play roles later on in the series?

7. How do you think Malcolm and Suzanne's relationship will change if they move to Britain?

8. What did Suzanne gain in giving up her work as a French spy? What did she lose? Without that work, is she more or less herself?

9. How do you think Paul and Juliette and the Lacloses will resolve the question of Pierre's inheritance?

10. What do you think lies ahead for Rupert, Bertrand, and Gabrielle?

11. How do the events of the book change Malcolm, Suzanne, Harry, Cordelia, Wilhelmine, and Dorothée? How do the relationships among them change?

12. What do you think Gui will do after the close of the story?

13. How has the outcome of the battle of Waterloo shaped the choices faced by the various characters?

14. Discuss how both Talleyrand and Raoul O'Roarke have influenced Malcolm in the absence of a strong relationship with his own father.

15. Suzanne says, "Sometimes honesty can make things worse." Malcolm replies, "Than living a lie? Difficult to imagine." Would their situation improve if Suzanne told Malcolm the truth? Or would it make it impossible for them to go on living together?